Embrace the Boogeyman
from The Scrolls of Dust

Georgia Temple

Sweet Mischief's Press

Sweet Mischief's Press
P.O. Box 11392
Midland, Texas 79702

This is a work of fiction. Names, characters, places and incidents are either the product of the author's imagination or are used fictitiously and any resemblance to actual persons, living or dead, business establishments, events or locales is entirely coincidential.

Where Have All The Flowers Gone words and music by Pete Seeger (1955) (c.) 1961 (renewed) by Sanga Music Inc.

First Copyright © March 1996 by Georgia Temple
Second Copyright © April 1997 by Georgia Temple

First U.S. Printing 2002
10 9 8 7 6 5 4 3 2 1

Cover illustration, Viking ships, and Glossary images by Charlotte Seay
Inside illustrations by Georgia Temple

ISBN 0-9703717-4-8
Library of Congress Number 2001098927

Printed in the United States of America
on Acid-Free Paper

This book is dedicated to my mother, Leslie Lorraine Lowery
Todd Johnson, considered by those who knew her to be one of the
great beauties of her day. Known by her family as Raine, by my
father as Lady and by my step-father as Lorraine, she persevered
in the face of disaster, cooked meals Heaven envied, revived dying
plants with a caress and complained not about the time taken from
our relationship for the writing of this book and those that follow.
A valiant soul, she escaped death on four occasions I know of that
the doctors had written her off as gone, and chose her own exit
time, leaving this world behind in November of 1997.

The
Scrolls
of
Dust

Prologue

In the days of light, a dragon came to Earth. Before the dark beckonings held the planet in thrall and the march of humanity cast time upon the world, this ethereal creature contained in a single breath the sum of all colors and none. The glory of the dragon could be seen in the hushed pink rising and the golden-red setting of the sun, in the silvery radiance of the moon sailing a clear midnight-blue sky amidst the twinkling of stars, and in the translucent aquamarine waters of the deep.

This dragon had a singular purpose: guarding Earth, protecting not the gold that later spurred man's greed but the life that sustained all. The breath of the dragon whispered through all the dimensions existing upon Earth, lending aid and support to all in harmony with the grand purpose: the survival of the planet.

Mankind has since masked dragons in many disguises. They have been viewed as celestial symbols of the life force and as instruments of diabolical tendencies, guardians who must be defeated to claim the treasures they protect. These are not the dragon I have known, the one who is here still for those who can hear the almost silent song.

I am among them; I am in the rose, the dove, the oak, the sea, the stone. I saw night turn into the first day and welcomed the dragon to our domain.

I am the chronicler. I need no pen or paper, no place to store my work, for Earth houses my words. The tale that unfolds in the pages that follow is of the horror endured by another of my kind, one who came later than I. The account does not speak of the beginning and has little to do with the dragon or with me.

Before any stories inspired by me passed into human hands, I felt duty bound to clarify the meaning of dragon.

Inscribed on The Scrolls of Dust in the Time of All Reckoning

Contents

List of Illustrations by the Author

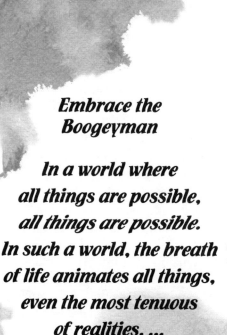

Embrace the Boogeyman

In a world where all things are possible, all things are possible. In such a world, the breath of life animates all things, even the most tenuous of realities. ...

The Author

Twentieth Century A.D.

*N*ight closed around Sylvian DuClair as she stole from the solitary car parked on the deserted parish road. Ghostly shadows floated overhead. A breeze whispered through the pines, rippling the dark, indistinct foliage of the live oaks and cypress giants surrounding her, then stilled, chilling her with its absence.

Her nails scratched and jabbed the size-five jeans she'd wiggled into hours ago on the floor of her apartment. Her forehead furrowed, pressing her finely arched charcoal brows into a straight line. She stepped tentatively away from the automobile and paused, hesitant to close the door. Every caution she'd learned in her almost twenty-five years begged her to jump back inside, lock the doors, and remain secure until first light.

Shaking off the tremor threatening to overwhelm her, she chided herself sharply, yet silently, for the stillness felt unwelcoming to the spoken word. There are *no* boogeymen. No ghosts. No ghouls. No anyone for that matter. You're afraid. You're standing on a lonely, dark country road, way past midnight, with no idea where to go from here. You're overreacting simply because you're lost.

How had she used so much fuel in such a short time? The tank registered full in the economy-class rental when she checked the gauge before pulling out of New Orleans's Moisant International Airport and onto the expressway.

She kicked the tire. The gray bomb had no real get-up-and-go. Driving on the rain-swept, darkened freeways left her feeling vulnerable to the larger cars and trucks speeding past her.

Straining to read the signs, staying in the right lane, avoiding being run over — too much — the stress had all been too much. She kicked the black rubber again, harder, and succeeded in ramming her toes against the hard surface of the tire. Great. Just great, she thought. Leaning against the hood, she removed the soft leather loafer and rubbed her foot to ease the pain.

The car shook from her weight pressing against the frame. Tin can, she thought, disgusted. She barely weighed a hundred and twenty pounds. She frowned. First the missed turnoff, then the exit to nowhere, and now this ... this stupidity.

Her eyes surveyed the darkness; the breathing shadows pressed in on her. She slid her shoe back on and stepped into the small area of light cast by the open door, ready to leap back inside if ... what? You're the only chicken here, she scolded. This place is deserted. No homes, no farms, no businesses, no lights, no road markers showing the way back to the city. Empty like the fuel needle now quivering ominously close to dry.

She perched sideways on the edge of the driver's seat, weighing her options while she twisted her throbbing foot in circles in front of her. The hint of jade green rimming her golden brown irises widened and diffused in the faint glow cast by the overhead light. Still the fear, she cajoled silently. This area has more than two million people. Surely you can find one of them to give you directions.

"Hey, people, where are you?" she whispered in an attempt to lighten her spirits. A long-forgotten song slipped, somewhat altered, into her conscious mind — Where have all the people gone, gone to graveyards every one"— Stop!" Sylvian exclaimed, startling herself.

Morbid thoughts serve no useful purpose, she coaxed. Your co-workers would laugh themselves silly if they could see you: The fearless news writer cowering in her tracks. And your psychology professors would insist that you quit acting like the children you want to help and face your fear. So, find out what lies ahead. Now.

And be grateful for small blessings, she urged, noticing for the first time the absence of rain. She breathed in slowly. No musty scent. No odor of decay. No hint of gasoline or diesel fumes. The air smelled clear, clean, somehow virginal as if the waft came from a cooler climate with no foul breath of pollution.

Sylvian shook her head, her long, black hair rustling gently. She stood and brushed off her jeans. Nothing made sense. Humidity didn't suffocate New Orleans after a rain? Impossible. Although a stranger to this city, she well knew Texas towns along the Gulf of Mexico. In Galveston, the summer humidity, particularly after a rain, could make breathing labored. Even Houstonians, whose city wasn't on the Gulf but lay almost due west of where she was standing, suffered. New Orleans could hardly be different.

Again, she took a deep breath. This time, she caught the faint hint of salt water from the Gulf of Mexico. Ah, that's better, she thought. Perhaps an ocean breeze cleansed the air of all other scents.

The solution had little time to settle her nerves before the idea began nagging at her. Lake Pontchartrain bordered the city on the north and the Mississippi River on the south. The city might be surrounded by water, but miles and refineries separated New Orleans from the Gulf. She would not be smelling a Gulf breeze.

Even as she puzzled over the confusing smells, she became aware of another problem. Her mind recorded a total absence of sound around her. Deafening silence.

No owls. No dogs. No crickets. No frogs. A tremor ran through her body. A storm approached. She must hurry. Quietly, she closed the door, and walked stealthily down the unfamiliar road.

Just as she'd given up hope that the route ahead led to civilization, she glimpsed what appeared to be a break in the trees on her right. Another road? Heartened, she quickened her pace.

She reached the opening, turned, and stopped. Tiny, twinkling beacons from hundreds of fireflies filled the woods. The silvery light of the full moon sparkled like diamonds off a lake not one-hundred yards from where she stood.

The stars shone brilliantly overhead, seeming at once near

enough to touch yet light years away. Awed by the vision, she wondered briefly how a storm could be nearby in a night sky whose pristine glory reflected so brightly off the dark water.

The forest bespoke the rapture of another time, another place, another world — one which called to her. Without another thought, she walked into the woods. Laughter and music greeted her. Cautiously, she peered ahead.

Five radiantly illuminated, youthful women with spring garlands in their hair danced barefoot in the moonlight close to the water's edge. Their lithe forms moved with pagan abandon; their feet painted circles in the pearly sand while their hands drew patterns in the air, reaching in unison for the heavens and the earth. She found the dance unlike any she'd ever witnessed; the movements sensuous, alluring, and somehow innocent.

The beguiling scene had a twilight feel, and Sylvian feared if she spoke or moved down to the sandy beach, the dancers would vanish. She dismissed the notion as silly. Still, she remained silent. Motionless.

The quintet moved in adagio tempo to the lyrical strains of a haunting song. She could not find a source; the rhapsody seemed to be borne on the air. The rhythm intensified, growing faster, deeper, harder until the ground beneath her reverberated.

Abruptly, the music ceased.

The dancers fell to their knees on the sand, folded inward on themselves, then arched their backs and stretched their arms upward. Rising as one, they turned to the water.

A sailing vessel similar to the ancient ones she'd seen in the Hall of the Viking Ships in Oslo, Norway, gleamed on the surface. Sylvian blinked her eyes, once, twice, three times. The mirage did not go away. She repeated the process to no avail.

This is the twentieth century. The ship is a replica. Reassured, she quietly stepped forward, using the trees as camouflage.

At the helm stood a tall, muscular man clad in a sleeveless, short byrnie[1] fitted over a lavender tunic, which extended almost to his knees. A skull-fitting golden helmet covered his head. Although his ship and his appearance should have been obscured

[1]armor. See word usage.

by the distance and the night, they weren't.

A fierce dragon's head formed the prow. The rectangular red sail, full-billowing despite the utter stillness, proudly carried three golden dragons emblazoned across the fabric, separated by a V-shaped swatch of lavender inset with gold crests. The dominant dragon in the triangular formation bore silver-tipped wings and a spiraling tail. The smaller, non-winged dragons clenched their tails in their teeth.

The warrior drew her attention. She could see him as clearly as if she stood openly on the ship with him instead of hidden behind the trees.

He stood battle ready. A sheathed sword hung at his waist. Blond locks flowed from beneath his helmet and floated above the long, red cape fluttering behind him as though the ship were at full sail.

The helmet's faceguard concealed most of his features, while heightening the sensual fullness of his mouth. His eyes pierced the distance.

They were deep violet.

Unreal. Arresting. Commanding. Sylvian fought the desire to walk toward him.

He did not sail alone. Four warriors stood behind him. When the Viking ship landed, the five men alighted. The dancers sprint-ed through the shallow water toward them.

They embraced. Tenderly.

Suddenly, savagely, the men slaughtered the women. The water ran red with blood.

Sylvian screamed. She turned and ran. Rain beat against her as she struggled to reach the security of her car, crashing into its metal body before she could see the vehicle.

Shaking, she jumped in, locked the doors, started the engine, turned the compact around, and took off. She sped down the black-top parish road faster than safety allowed on the slick surface, wondering what she'd just witnessed. Nothing made any sense. Who were those people in the woods? Five of them were surely dead.

Glancing at the dashboard, her eyes widened in surprise. Her gas tank registered three-fourths full. Had the dial been stuck before? Did she have gas or not? She prayed she did.

Her breath came in short pants.

Calm down, she cautioned. Breathe deeply. Pay attention to the signs. Otherwise, you'll never be able to direct anyone to the location.

What would she say? She couldn't mention the Viking ship. They'd discount her words if she did. Besides, how could a sailing vessel sail with no wind — not even a breeze? And the rain. It rained — poured — then it didn't, then it rained again. How could she explain that? She began piecing her story together in words the police would find acceptable.

The lights of an all-night diner appeared ahead. Odd, she thought. She'd driven all over the area trying to find her way back to the freeway. Surely, she hadn't missed seeing something so brightly lighted. Somehow, she'd not come this way before.

She stopped. Once inside, she felt safer. This world she understood. The air conditioning chilled her drenched body; her jeans and emerald green, short-sleeved shirt clung to her. She ordered coffee, as much for the reassurance of warmth as for the taste, and cradled the steaming cup in her hands, her slender fingers wrapping themselves around the heat.

Studying the double stem of white lilies leaning stiffly in a Mason jar on the counter, she wondered who'd set the flowers in this dreary place. Her eyes held an appraising look as they passed over the chrome-trimmed, gray Formica table tops and black vinyl booths, before coming to rest on the pay phone hanging on the wall. Sighing, she decided. No time like now. Make the call.

The police dispatcher's words further unsettled Sylvian. He insisted she dialed him from Laplace in St. John the Baptist Parish, northwest of New Orleans. She'd turned the wrong way onto the freeway when she left the airport, he snapped, then ordered her to stay there and hung up. She vowed never to arrive in a strange city at the witching hour again and sat down to wait.

When night and day have had their way, and all that is known has been said and done, what is there left in life but love?

*Inscribed on
The Scrolls of Dust*

2

Fourteenth Century B.C.
Diary: Astraea, Nightstar of the Nyx,
Guardian of the Shrine of the Nightstar

*T*he air is still; the wind, silent. And I am restless. The urge to write of my world is strong. I am uncertain why, except perhaps my desire is fueled by the despair and cruelty I have witnessed in mortals during the centuries I have spent in their realm. As long as they do no lasting harm to the Earth, I have no cause to care about their tragedies. And yet, since my eyes fell upon him, I do. My affection for him and my concern for his kind distract my concentration. Unfamiliar emotions rule my thinking.

I must control my senses, for I am Astraea, avowed protector of the shrine celebrating the wondrous universe through the Nightstar. Everything else pales in importance when weighed against my duty to the Nightstar, to Earth, and to my people.

Our world is ancient. We are Nyx and Dag and Seers who walked the Earth eons before mankind called upon Geb and Ra, Enlil, Ishtar or Marduk. We are the fortunate ones: War and hunger are unknown in our golden domain.

We are not oblivious to the pain of mortals. Duty requires we remain uninvolved. We guard the boundaries between worlds and protect the Earth, not the inhabitants who walk the soil.

Unlike mortals, we measure our years in hundred-year increments based on the cycles of the moon. Throughout my childhood and as a young maiden, I, like the others of my kind, remain little touched by the passage of time.

17

Our race, ten thousand strong, is bound by numbers and colors and images. A complete understanding of these comes with millennia of continual study. Only the Seers, who guide us through the Council, have such an awareness. In the mortal world, no such comparable knowledge exists. Mankind obscures truth through the destruction of old records and the alterations of existing ones.

Twenty-five, the sum total of the five odd numbers one, three, five, seven and nine or the four even numbers two, four, six, eight and the odd number five, is the square of the number five and as such symbolizes the perfection of the five senses. More I am not free to mention, except that, for us, the number twenty-five represents the shrine and is sacred to the Nightstar, marking my approaching twenty-fifth anniversary as the guardian an auspicious occasion.

Our world has no spoken or written name. Only those privy to the Council know the word or words by which our land exists. To breathe the name in any form is to court danger. Thus, the secret lies locked within the Council members who are born with the knowledge.

Long ago, we learned the difficulty of speaking about a nameless land; thus, we call our world Fayre. Others have called us Enchanters, but we avoid the misnomer for the number and vibration of the spoken word do not bode well for us.

Harmony permeates Fayre. The seven colors of the rainbow — red, yellow, orange, green, blue, indigo and violet — are bright and fresh and born anew with each rising sun. Subtlety exists only in the shadows that appear not so much as gray but rather as lighter hues of these colors. The primary colors of yellow and red and blue abound in our realm with black and white serving as a contrast and, at times, softening the most brilliant of tones.

The moon, long important to our vitality, has inspired through its phases the shapes of our musical instruments. Even without such objects, music fills all creation; the rock and the oak have their own song. Like threads of a tapestry, each is different yet related to its specific family and to the larger creation as well.

Embrace the Boogeyman

Our people can hear the individual notes emanating from all, particularly my sister Arva, who has a gift for such things.

As my eldest sister, she is the one most removed from me. I have always been awed by her and a little unnerved in her presence, for I have never known her as a child, a companion of my youth, but only as an adult. More swift in flight than a diving falcon, Arva hears all the night wind knows.

The second born in my family is Rana. She has been an adult as long as I can remember, but she is very different from Arva, and we are close despite our distance in age. The oceans respond to her as a child to its mother. The age and habitat of all manner of life are known to her through her legendary sense of smell, a gift of love from the one who bore her charge before her. I have ridden the waves on her enchanted barge, and we have on many occasions fished mercurial waters together.

The next are Niniane and Nata, who are closer to my own age. I remember them as young maidens constantly at odds even when I was a child. Their predictable bickering exasperates Arva and amuses Rana. Only their actions betray their affection for each other, and I find them tenacious in their own right. Niniane is a great healer, who is at home in the forest. Nata, the most skilled of all our dancers, is a firebrand in more ways than one with a sense of taste unequaled among our kind. A single intake of air across her tongue warns her of danger, releasing her reflexes with a speed even Arva holds in awe.

My sisters wear the traditional white-lined, gold-and-silver Nyx attire as opposed to the green-lined, blue-and-gold costume worn by the Dag. I have been told by the Dag that the green in the lining shifts to white by the light of the noon sun, thereby briefly revealing to others of their kind snowflakes and beehives outlined within an intricate geometric design. This information I take on faith for I am Nyx, not Dag.

As for us, a silver design of five-petaled blossoms, stars and starfish enclosed in geometric forms is outlined within the white lining of Nyx clothing. This pattern is only visible by twelfth hour moonlight and only to other Nyx. Although the shades of gold

19

and silver fluctuate across the outer fabric, both colors are evident most of the time. Gold stands for the life-giving sun and the conquest of the impossible; silver, through the changing moon, for universal cycles and knowledge of the unseen. My sisters wear this uniform but not I. Not yet. Instead, I wear a white garment, the sign of purity, laced with a silver cord.

I am the last, the chosen one, responsible for the Nightstar, for I can see the dark matter of the universe as clearly as mortals see the world by the light of day. We are as one. The lyre of the Nightstar binds in harmony our dear Earth with all that lies beyond. The silver stand the ancient instrument rests upon bears witness to the singular ray of light glowing from the dark moon the night of my birth: the sign that I was to be whom I have become.

We are the children of Seleme and Aster of the second-born, Council elect, clearly marking us before our births as members of the Nyx. Only the eldest, Arva, who is privy to Council edicts, is bound to the Fayre oath of silence outside our realm. I am free to write what I have written and more. I just never have felt moved to do so before.

Instead, I have always saved my diary for more personal comments. But today, as the sun sets golden and I await the time for my walk, my words have served to remind me of the long tradition that binds me. Although time has little relevance to us, loneliness does seep into the hours spent away from all that is familiar and dear. And yet, I would have my life no other way.

However, I would have him whom I have seen in the moonlight. I know we are meant to be together not for a day that the ocean erases when the tide moves over the sand but forever. How can that be? He is mortal. And I am not. Nor am I free. Even now my sisters plead for my cause, and time, which before I met him meant so little, hangs heavy on my hands.

I cannot escape my duty nor do I want to. The universal meanings inherent in the shrine define who I am. The intricate patterns dictate my duty. I alone am free to write about my charge, my life. Not even a Seer may do so, but that would not stop one from laughing at my words if I were unfortunate enough to have a Seer find my diary. Only Seers with their seven-fold wisdom can offer concise and complete definitions. And I am not a Seer, not even close to one. Nor do I want to be near even one of the long-winded, beak-nosed bores.

I have little patience for any of them. I have always been relieved that I am not the eldest and thus stuck with the duty of listening to their all too-often dire pronouncements. The frightful shrieks they make leaping about, howling and striking one another with their lightning bolts unnerve even the most tenacious Nyx and Dag. Often, I have wondered, as have others, what would happen if the geometric forms and colors on their ever-changing garments ran amuck, unable to fix on a specific coordinated design. Would they just go on forever and ever in that ridiculous fashion? Would such an occurrence make prognostication impossible? No one knows.

But, without fail, if any among them found this diary, they would descend en masse, howling and shrieking, twisting my words with jabbing retorts. I will not let possible ridicule rule my life. I will write what I choose, remembering my words are as safe as I am from the hackling of Seers. I sound far braver than I am. No Seer can enter the shrine without my permission. Before I would allow any of their kind entry, I would destroy what I have written.

I do not write for them or for those of my kind. I write for him who has captured my heart. The desire to explain who I am and what my guardianship means fuels my energy.

For millennia past my memory, the shrine of the Nightstar has made its home in the twilight world of mortals offering refuge for those who have lost their way. However, finding the sacred temple requires a certain sense of direction and timing, and more often than not, the intercession of destiny.

This work of the Heavens stands on the highest mountaintop on the island and can only be seen by mortal eyes by moonlight. The seven steps leading into and thus out of the temple are the phases of the universe and must be passed with caution.

All geometric forms are interlaced within the dome of the shrine, but those found individually include:

The circle, an emblem of the sun, relates to the number ten and stands for eternity, perfection, and spirit. The circle inherent in the circumference of the dome represents a return to unity from multiplicity.

The square, as a source of the order and stability of the world, encompasses the four phases of the moon, the four cardinal points, the four directions and the four winds, the correct shape for the pit housing the sacred fire.

The octagon is the intermediary form between the square and the circle that symbolizes the path of earthly divisions toward eternity. The water in the gold-and-silver font is limitless and immortal, representing the beginning and the end of all things on Earth.

Above the flames, in the center of the dome, the five-pointed star, or emblem of immortality, is a symbol of the spirit, particularly in its struggle against evil. Unlike mortals, we do not believe evil ones hide within the protection of darkness and the night waiting to ensnare their next victims. We find them basking in broad daylight as often as we find them slipping through shadows. They are, as we are, part of All That Is and present the threefold challenge: to watch without condemning, to study without succumbing, and to learn without judging. We endeavor, by this path, to dispel their influence.

The sacred fire burning below represents transformation and regeneration. Seven pedestals surround the flames.

Caution must now guide my hand. I am tempted to write all I know, even though in this particular instance I am not free to do so. Long have I abided by the orders of others, particularly the Seers whose hearts beat in stone chests. Here duty must come before desire. Thus, the definitions that follow are all I may explain about certain aspects of the shrine:

The caduceus, a wand with two winged serpents twined around it, alludes to the integration of the four elements — earth, air, fire and water.

The chalice represents containment.

The cycles of the Moon signify our ordering system.

The dove denotes life.

The white dragon stands guard.

The forest speaks of that which lies hidden or unknown on a conscious level, particularly in the conflict with evil.

The lake of diamonds is a mirror that presents an image of consciousness, meditation, and revelation. Diamonds represent light and brilliance as well as moral and intellectual knowledge.

The laurel shows victory achieved through struggle.

The lamb indicates innocence, meekness, and sacrifice.

The sceptre radiates light as is reaches toward the stars.

The sword holds spiritual evolution.

The trefoil set upon a mountain signifies a portal to knowledge of the divine that is not crossed lightly.

No crack or imperfection mars the unity and strength of the stones forming the floor of the shrine. Were even one to shatter, then dismemberment, psychic disintegration, and eventual annihilation could follow.

The likelihood of that happening is nil. The stones were forged in the Heavens. No earthly force, not even the fearsome earthquake, has the power to cause even a minuscule fracture across their perfection. I alone, as the Nyx protector of the Nightstar, have the power with my thunderbolt to cause damage to the shrine. Nothing could force me to harm the living temple, forged of the dark blood of the universe and made visible through starlight and moonlight, the latter conveying the softened and healing reflected rays of the sun.

Words are hollow and inadequate in describing the glory of the shrine, but they offer me solace and renewed energy to focus my attention on my duty. The Seers speak of the island as a symbol of isolation, of solitude, and of spiritual death. This is not that island, but it is after all, an island.

I have been here too long without the company of my own kind. With this anniversary I come of age as the guardian and acquire the freedom to move the shrine wherever I choose. I shall not remain here. Of that I am certain. All else remains in question.

Enough words. Surely by now he waits in the valley to catch a glimpse of me, and I do not want to disappoint a mortal as glorious as he. Not at all. In all my long centuries here, he is the only one whose mind I cannot read. This time we may even meet. Then I will know his name.

3

*S*inewy arms seized Astraea from behind. The stench of decomposing flesh filled her nostrils. She gagged. Her captor jackknifed her body, contorting the hour-glass shape, and, in one quick stroke, broke through the silken folds of her dress and undergarment, plunged deeply into her, and began draining her virginal power.

She convulsed. Simultaneously, the golden vases on the pedestals surrounding the shrine's sacred flames shattered. White lilies quivered delicately on their erect, rigid stems, then fell to the stone floor, and disintegrated into blackened ashes. Shrieks rent the air as the lyre shivered on its silver stand, then toppled over, its strings broken.

"Isn't love a glorious disaster?" The intruder expelled poison into her chaste body. "Already our liquid seeds prepare your exquisite form for a new host."

The sacred flames sparked, then flickered low over the coals. The fire cast an eerie, phosphorescent glimmer over the broken lyre, the ashes, and the pedestals. A gust of arctic air whipped through the shrine, extinguishing the torches burning throughout the temple.

Fingers adeptly twisted themselves around the sable strands of Astraea's long, ebony hair, tightened their grip, and whipped her body upright. The despoiler licked her ear. Hot, rancid breath seared her neck, scorching the flawless, honey-complexioned skin a dark purplish gray. "Love made you ripe for our plucking. We've watched you and that boy of yours for five days now, letting him prime you with stolen kisses, knowing his touch would weaken your defenses."

Astraea cursed her foolishness. Thoughts of her beloved had canceled her caution, allowing her to be caught unawares at her duties as guardian of the shrine. Her sisters had warned her. The Seers prophesied doom for a member of the Nyx. She must maintain her guard at all times, they said. How could she have come to this? She had listened, had she not?

"Lucky us! Obviously not." Coarse laughter exploded the unnatural silence that had blanketed the mountaintop and its temple in the moments since the attack began. "Your boy has certainly missed a tasty treat. Your fruit is so sweet. Your power so pure. Soon, we will have all your immortality." Her tormenter bit deeply into her neck.

Blood gushed from the wound. Even as Astraea struggled to free herself, to shake the trespasser off her back, the words stung her — Lucky us, obviously not. She had not spoken her doubts aloud. How had the one binding her known?

The debaucher licked the blood, murmuring, "So succulent. The nectar of the goddesses. Unblemished by mortal touch," then suckled the wound.

Astraea flung her arms backward to rip the leech away. Her hands yanked out chunks of rotting hair. Maggots squirmed over her fingers, casting chalk-white blotches against the golden sheen of her skin. What kind of abomination held her? she wondered as she squirmed to free herself from the loathsome embrace.

Thirsting lips slipped from the bleeding wound. "Ah, you're eager to embrace us. And we you. Particularly now at the dawning of your twenty-fifth anniversary when your virginal power is" — the defiler snorted — "*was* at the zenith, leaving you the most vulnerable for attack of all your kind."

Astraea kicked her assailant. How *did* the ghoul know?

"Your thoughts are ours for the picking, our sweet. And we do so appreciate the compliment. Ghoul has such a delicious ring, don't you think?" The invader's tongue buried deep into the wound, suckling noisily and greedily. Unspoken words formed clearly in her mind. *For eons, we've watched your kind from afar. Listening to your thoughts. Learning your ways. Planning for this moment. All your power and energy must be ours. Only then can we claim the secrets you Nyx Enchanters guard. And with you, our lovely pet, we gain the Nightstar.*

"Never," Astraea whispered. She frowned. This enemy had eavesdropped on her people. Somehow. Sometime. Some place. Her lips, neither thin nor overly full, compressed in a determined line. Hobbled, she could not fly. She wanted to disappear and leave the molester clutching emptiness, but she dared not. Wherever she materialized, she risked melding herself with her ravisher — forever. Nay! She had to break free to enter the sanctum sanctorum[2] and the protection of the sacred flames. She must exert all her energy toward that goal and none other.

The blood-sucker quit drinking and spit into the wound.

Wrenching cramps seized Astraea; waves of nausea swept through her ravished body.

Her adversary snorted. "Oh, our pretty one, are you nauseated? Our seeds do our bidding. Not yours. Struggle all you will. You have no hope for escape. We are more powerful than you and your kind."

Who is this — pest? Astraea wondered, endeavoring to remain calm.

"Pest? Oh, our sweet one, we're more. So much more. Already, we have challenged a fearless Nyx Enchanter and won. But, pardon our manners, in our eagerness to embrace you, our lovely pet, we didn't introduce ourselves. Now that we have been intimate lovers" — the corruptor's forked-tongue licked Astraea's ear, thrusting partly inside the canal before withdrawing — "we're appalled at our oversight. We are a desire, a dream, a shadow passing over the land. We are pleasure. We are pain. We are The Hunter. We are The Beast. We are the one and only Hunting Beast. We are Drakus, and we are your nemesis. We are the one the Seers speak of only in whispers. We are the horror haunting their visions. We are us, and soon we will be you. No Nyx will be safe then. Not your sisters, not your world, not even the Nightstar can evade our net." The hunter's hungry mouth

[2]the holy of holies. See word usage.

closed over the open wound.

Empty threats, Astraea decided, designed to terrorize her, to convince her this depravity was privy to the Nyx mysteries.

The slick, narrow tongue slid inside the gaping wound, severing muscles, tendons, and veins as it snaked toward her heart. *You think no one knows how you're undone.* The beast gurgled with pleasure. *First, your virginity's creative power, then your blood's life-sustaining purity, next your tears' healing waters, and, finally, your brain and the knowledge sealed within. Then we control all your secrets. Fire, wind, and water will do our bidding. Earth will be ours to command.*

Narrowing her thoughts, Astraea forced aside the panic building within her and channeled her mind into a single, repetitive plea, a distress call to others of her kind.

Scaly hands tore through her dress, scratching her flesh. *"Too late, our tasty morsel. No Nyx can help you now."* Jagged nails punctured her breasts.

She screamed, her shrill cry piercing the temple like a lost child's lament. As the agonized shriek echoed across the mountaintop, the petals dropped from the wild roses growing in profusion around the shrine.

The ravisher's tongue slid from inside the wound. "Isn't pain exquisite, our pretty pet?" Drakus cooed. "We do so enjoy watching others suffer. The experience is most refreshing. Soon, our sweet, your regenerative form will be ours. No longer will we be forced to wear the shells of those we've absorbed. We shall have your living, breathing flesh forever. Midnight hair shimmering in the moonlight; golden-kissed, dusty eyes hinting of pleasures to come. Such beauty will ensnare many followers. We shall savor them all." The tongue retraced its course toward her heart.

Despite closing her mind to Drakus's threats, the unsettling words gained control of her thoughts. Fear. Terror. Illness. Death. Unknowns until now. She saw her world broken, corrupted and dying. She wanted to weep and knew she could not.

Why fight what will be?

28

The question yanked Astraea out of her stupor. Her reflexes rose to the fore. In seconds, the verdant specks in her hazel irises deepened; the pupils glowed golden red. She gauged her adversary's position behind her, narrowed her vision, and shot two bolts of fiery energy toward the stone floor. Two of the white stones exploded; dust and shards of shattered rock flew into the air, striking them both. A sliver pierced her attacker's foot.

Drakus howled and collapsed, taking her down with the fall. The beast's sinuous tongue slipped from the wound, but the grip holding her tightened. The creature cackled.

Her foe's nails cut even deeper into her tender flesh. She felt their rapacious touch draining the fluids from her body and bit her lip to hush the cries of pain begging for escape.

"Astraea! Astraea!"

The call came from outside the shrine. Tilting her head up slightly, she saw with her Nyx vision across the outer chamber, through the pedestals forming the boundary to the sanctum sanctorum, and beyond the entrance. Six men, grown strong through their labors in the fields, ran across the clearing toward the temple. Sorrow flowed through her. Her beloved had brought his father and brothers to meet her.

They came unarmed. No mortal carried weapons of death to this shrine and survived. Their double axes lay fifty paces down the steep path as custom dictated. Unarmed or armed little mattered now. No human could match the one imprisoning her. Some force unknown to her sustained the beast's destructive power. Her thoughts warned them to turn away, to flee and not look back.

"Too late," Drakus hissed. "Had they arrived a few minutes later, we could have greeted them as you. But don't you fret, our pet. They won't hinder our pleasure. Our creations will take care of them." Snarling wolf-like gray hounds with red-glowing eyes appeared around them. "Ah. Our pets are stronger than flesh and blood. So beautiful. So deadly. See them do our bidding." Drakus's voice rose in a single command, "Kill."

Astraea focused her thoughts on the men and called forth the

power of fire to their aid. Flames engulfed the hounds, inciner-
ating them.

Drakus screeched, "More!"

Twice as many slavering hounds materialized around the
men, destroying each one-by-one until only her love remained.
The pack surrounded him. Astraea ignited them all, but as quickly as she destroyed the abominable hounds, more sprang up in
their place. Her beloved ran toward the shrine. Sprinting to the
outer steps, he fought his way to the sacred fire smoldering in the
center of the shrine before the predators brought him down.
Falling upon him, they ripped open his chest, and then evaporated as quickly as they had formed.

The battle momentarily diverted Drakus's attention. The
hold on Astraea loosened fractionally. She wrenched free, rose,
and saw her opponent for the first time.

Cloaked in a human body, the accursed hunter appeared to
be a lithe and muscular, dark-tanned, handsome young man with
a smooth countenance, gray eyes set under sharply arched, bushy
black brows, a slender, straight nose, and pouting lips open in a
seductive smile.

Deceiver, Astraea thought. In the past days, a human hand
caressed her skin, human lips kissed her lips. Her assailant was not
mortal flesh and bones but a decaying, maggot-infested ghoul.
Refocusing her vision, Astraea's acute Nyx sight cut through the
disguise to the truth lying underneath, to the enemy she had
touched when she tried to wrest free of the creature's embrace.

Drakus stood bared before her: male and female, human
while still part animal, part reptile, and part inorganic matter. A
bewitcher and an incubus, the monstrosity wore the skins of
those its unrelenting appetite had destroyed. Their mortal flesh
and blood, their essence — their Breath[3] that animates all life —
helped fuel an insatiable energy. Maggots teemed under the skins,
feeding on the refuse.

A shadowy image of her shape swirled around the entity. She
knew not what dark spell had forged this evil, but soon the thief
would have enough of her form to merge their bodies as one.

[3]spirit. See word usage.

Nay. She must not let that happen. Her preternatural flesh would permanently heal Drakus's decaying mass; her innate abilities combined with the fiend's existing sorcery would make the transgressor indestructible; her birthright as the Nightstar of the Nyx would give the destroyer the key to the portal guarding her world and countless others. Already, the usurper's sinister powers held more potency than before.

The bodies of her beloved and his family bore silent testimony to her condition: Her energy had been halved; her might, weakened. Had she seen the attack coming, she could have protected herself from the monster and its poison — perhaps even destroyed the abomination. Now, that time had passed. Venom coursed like molten lava through her body, replacing her purity with disease. Too crippled to fight, she could not reclaim what the thief had stolen. She had erred in judgment, failing to guard her responsibilities wisely. She could afford no more mistakes.

Regardless of the toll the universe exacted from her, she *must* escape, releasing the Nightstar as she fled. But how? With her diminished powers, sustained flight became impossible. And she could not maintain the cloak of invisibility long enough. Perhaps she could slip to safety through the sacred fire? Nay. Escaping in the consecrated flames would be too dangerous. The demon would follow her and might succeed in bridging the dimensions. Her vision fell on her love's crumpled body, lying where he had fallen by the pit of hallowed flames. Ah. Uniting with his mortal form would block the trail of her energy and thwart Drakus's pursuit.

Mustering her remaining resources, she crossed the shrine faster than sight registers movement and stood at his side. In a single, fluid motion, she freed the silver cord that laced the white gown to her body. The blood-soaked cord no longer shimmered in the light, but its threads remained unbroken. She picked up his remains, looped the cord around the two of them, knotted it, and stepped backward.

The instant she touched the live coals, they exploded into a cylinder of fire, igniting the red embers into a blue-tipped, golden blaze that shot upward through the star-shaped opening in the domed roof. The framework encircling the five-pointed star cast a fleeting, iridescent glow. Blood-red teardrops formed in the interlacing geometric designs carved in the ceiling around the aperture.

The tears fell on the floor below and soaked into the stone. The ground shook, then roared. Cracks formed in the steps leading to the shrine; their tentacles spread across the floor toward the sacred flames and up the pedestals now bereft of their vessels.

Etchings hidden within the seven marble bases appeared: the cycles of the moon, a forest outlined against a starry night, a trefoil set upon a mountain, a lamb asleep under a laurel tree, a dove in flight over a lake of diamonds, a caduceus guarded by a winged, white dragon, and, finally, a chalice floating between a silver sword and a golden sceptre. The concealed drawings materialized, fractured, and disappeared.

Fissures split the stone floor around the pit housing the sacred flames, then stretched past the pedestals toward the columns supporting the roof. Water evaporated from the gold-and-silver font enclosed in an octagonal marble basin standing at the entrance. The vessel vanished, rupturing the basin. The dome began crumbling as the fire lifted out of the pit.

Drakus sprang to the hallowed flames. Spying two luminous forms floating skyward, the Hunter leapt into the blaze shrieking, "You Nyx witch! You will not rob us of our victory! You will *not!*" The heat scorched the beast. Howling, the interloper jumped from the inferno.

"I already have." Her words were a sigh on the breeze rising even as the flames rose toward the stars and faded into darkness, leaving behind no trace of their existence. Not even the ashes remained.

The simplest and most necessary truths are always the last believed.

Modern Painters (1856)
John Ruskin, 1819-1900

Twentieth Century A.D.

Sylvian's voice barely concealed from Harold the frustration she felt over her encounter last night outside New Orleans. "The story sounds crazy, but I know what I saw." Even as she said the words, she thought, The story is crazy. She didn't blame the police for being exasperated with her. They'd searched the edge of what turned out to be a bayou, not a lake, for hours in the pouring rain but found nothing.

No bodies. No evidence of violence. No ship.

Nothing.

Only Harold's insistence to the police, when she'd called him from the station in the early morning hours, that she rarely drank, and never too much, did not use drugs or advocate sensationalism, had kept them from accusing her of filing a false report about a violent crime. He was a good boss, and she heard the concern now in his voice over the telephone.

"Take time off," Harold barked. "Forget the concert tonight. Scratch the interview. We'll pick up the review from the wire."

"Thanks for the offer but no." Sylvian toyed with a strand of hair that had fallen loose from the oversized barrette holding the thick locks away from her face. Harold Lann had been more than fair to her, encouraging, actually insisting she finish her master's degree course work. She wouldn't disappoint him. "No. You wanted an interview and review before they play the Astrodome. This is their last show until then."

"I'll send Ed?" Harold's tone questioned. "He can catch a

flight and be there before the concert."

The contour of Sylvian's high cheekbones softened as she smiled. "Absolutely not. He hates rock music. We both know what he'd say. He'd question what happened to real music — Glenn Miller, the Dorsey brothers, Dick Haymes, Jo Stafford. He wouldn't want the assignment."

"You'd never heard of these guys, either," Harold reminded her. "Rock isn't exactly your style."

"Agreed." Sitting cross-legged in the king-sized bed, still wearing the oversized, pink-and-white striped T-shirt she'd collapsed in when she'd finally reached her room, Sylvian looked at the books and papers covering the bedspread. Staying abreast of her education beat and working on the master's degree in psychology, kept her too busy to fret over up-and-coming stars. "But I appreciate all forms of music regardless of the vintage. If the sound's not classical or pre-nineteen sixties, Ed finds the music suspect."

Shuffling through the stack of notes and newspapers on the pillow next to her, Sylvian pulled out *The Wall Street Journal*. "I didn't forget the article that piqued your interest. I have the newspaper in my hands. Right now. Come on, Harold, you know Ed. Will he ask about their investment savvy? Their work with youth? Or will he be so incensed by their loud music and the money they make playing 'noise' that he blurts out something like, 'How often have you been arrested for sound pollution?'"

Harold chuckled. "Ed's sitting right here. He said he'd cover the concert and be on his best behavior for the interview afterwards. He promised he'd be fair."

"I know he would." Ed's offer to cover for her didn't come as a surprise. He had a generous nature toward young staffers. Besides, they understood their boss. Harold Lann was a bull terrier; once he decided on a story angle, he wouldn't let go. He wanted to beat the larger Houston-area newspapers on a spread about the financial wizards who were currently the talk of Wall Street. "He'd be miserable. Worried about his hearing.

35

Convinced his ears were ruined forever. We can't do that to Ed."

"You're sure?"

"I'm sure." Sylvian felt better already. She had no more answers for what happened last night than she had before Harold called, but the idea of conservative Ed Todd covering a rock group struck her as too droll. She stifled a laugh. "You'll have the story and review before tomorrow's deadline."

"OK. But, I don't want to see any part of your exhausted, wrung-thin, five-foot-seven-workaholic a —" he paused "— person in this office until next week. Enjoy New Orleans. One more thing. When you're poking around, watch your back."

"The police convinced me," Sylvian said a bit too quickly. "I'm not snooping around."

"Right." Harold laughed. "Just remember. You're walking unknown turf."

"Thanks. I will. I mean I'll enjoy the free time." Sylvian hung up before her boss offered more advice. Fortunately, she'd skipped summer school. When Harold suggested she take a break for the summer, she'd balked. Now, she relished the freedom.

Excited, she sprang off the bed. The pages of her thesis, previously resting in her lap, fell to the floor. "Klutz!" Sighing, she knelt down, pressed the pages together in a stack and dropped the bundle on the bed. The cover page slipped through her fingers and floated toward the floor. Grabbing the paper in mid-air, she set the sheet on top.

Mockingly, she commanded, "Stay there you slippery rascal!" Her smile froze, as the words came into focus. "What the … ?"

Embrace the Boogeyman. She'd never written that. She grabbed the page off the stack. "*Embrace the Boogeyman.* What the hell does that mean?"

Sylvian spun around. "Who's here! What's going on?"

The small room, empty save for Sylvian and the shadows cast by the light, seemed to accuse her with its repose. Quiet moments passed until she could bear the silence no longer. "This is not my cover page. I've never seen these words before."

She felt foolish complaining, actually whining to inanimate

objects. Or did she? Yes. No. Maybe. Maybe. No. Definitely not! Some trickster had tampered with her work. She held the evidence in her hands.

Unnerved, she checked the bathroom, the closet, and the balcony doors. Locked. Bolted from the inside. She walked to the hallway door. The night lock secured the room. She released the latch, opened the door, and peered into the hall. Vacant. No signs of life. Turning away from the door, she stepped toward the bed and bent over until she could see underneath. Nothing. She felt silly. What had she thought she'd find hiding under the bed — a boogeyman?

She locked the door, crumpled the paper, and threw the wad in the trash. Immediately, she regretted the action and retrieved the vexing page. Spreading the paper out, she gasped. *Family Life Through the Ages Molds Today's Youth.* Her cover page. Her premise. How?

Dropping the rumpled page as if it were cursed, she kicked the offender aside and walked to the sink and mirror. Her hand shook as she poured a glass of water.

In the mirror, the room's elusive shadows seemed menacing as if they had their own life. The words — *Go the Distance* — embossed in black across the T-shirt's inch-wide stripes taunted her. "I'm not leaving New Orleans until I have some answers. I'm not crazy. Someone may be but not me!"

At the concert hours later, a calmer Sylvian — dressed for work in her red silk suit and black patent-leather heels — settled into the seat on the Louisiana Superdome's plaza. Instantly, she regretted Harold's nixing the front-row ticket on the arena floor the promoter had offered. Her boss said she might get claustrophobic with the audience behind her. She'd agreed. She usually shunned enclosed places.

This seat courted confinement. The plaza jutted out almost eye-level with the stage. Bobbing fans periodically obstructed her view. She'd wanted to see both shows: the spectacle on stage as well as the multitude of young people who paid money for their concert tickets. Instead, she found herself buried in the midst of thousands of expectant fans.

When the lights dimmed for the headliner, the crowd's anticipation built to a frenzy. The fans, as if propelled by one mind, stood and began chanting the name. "Dragon! Dragon! Dragon!" Darkness, followed by silence, descended over the hall.

The lights came up slowly to reveal a panoramic view of stars and waters and a sandy shore watched over by a full moon. Five young women sang and danced around the microphones close to the audience. Their dresses twinkled with the brilliance of diamonds caught in the sunlight.

A frisson[4] of apprehension coursed through her body. But the temperature in the room didn't cause the unnatural chill. The air felt warm, almost muggy, inside the arena. She had watched this scene unfold before. She also recognized the music immediately. She'd heard this song last night.

The music stopped. The dancers fell, rose, and turned away from the audience. *This is too familiar.* Sylvian stood on tiptoes, the tips of her fingers pressed on the back of the seat in front for balance, intent upon not missing what would happen next. A rainbow flash of brilliant light shot from the stage.

The Viking ship she'd seen last night glistened on shimmering water. She couldn't tell whether the sailing vessel contained solid material or only a projectionist's magic, but she immediately knew the warrior standing at the helm, his body bathed in golden light.

Sylvian's heart raced. As the dancers moved toward the ship, she strained to see through the illusion to the reality behind the setting.

The lights went out, throwing the hall into total darkness. Music blasted from the stage. The lights came up again to reveal no ship, no dancers. Instead four agile, virile males cavorted across the stage, singing and playing their instruments, while the fifth member of Dragon, already ensconced behind his drums, pounded out a driving beat.

[4]shudder or thrill. See word usage.

An enormous, lifelike dragon, his markings and color identical to the one that had been featured dominantly on the ship's sail, reared his head behind them, his tail whipping the air some thirty feet above the musicians.

The audience went wild. Sylvian admitted the show dazzled, but the resemblance the stage setting and the musicians' attire bore to what she'd seen last night filled her with dread — and curiosity.

She wanted to move closer, but she didn't have a ticket allowing her access to the arena floor. Sighing, she resigned herself to staying in her seat, angry that despite having a clear memory of packing the binoculars she'd borrowed, she hadn't found them in her bag. Only one plausible explanation existed. She'd left the field glasses on her bed at home.

The music vibrated the arena with hard-hitting intensity. The sound rose around her; the energy generated by the amplified instruments charged the air. The words and the beat touched something in Sylvian. They sounded almost familiar, yet not, as if she had heard a fragment of the lyrics before. A phrase here, another one there. But as quickly as she seemed to recall the words, the memory of them, if one existed at all, slipped out of her grasp.

She watched the lead singer, Kirth Naran, who, along with the others, removed his helmet at the close of the third number. Next came the ring mail,[5] then the shirt underneath, until they twisted and danced and jumped across the stage half-naked, their muscular torsos gleaming with sweat.

The show was primeval. Barbaric. Electrifying.

Yet, some of the lyrics enchanted her. She'd not felt the magic of words since she'd been a child, sitting in the overstuffed armchair with her father.

As distinctly as if the scene had happened only moments ago, she saw her dad — his hair tossed back from his wide forehead where his skin was often burned from the harsh Texas sun, his long, tapering fingers turning the pages unnoticed while his melodic voice spun pictures of distant worlds.

39

[5]flexible armor. See word usage.

Even as she tried to hold the vision close, the image blurred, then refocused to a later time. She hid crouched in the corner of the utility closet praying they wouldn't find her and punish her again. She worked to make herself as small as possible, but her effort failed. As usual. She dangled from her foster mother's hand, promising she'd do her chores and never, ever read in secret again as the belt strap popped her flesh. The vignette of her torment faded as quickly as the picture had formed, leaving her eyes wet with the sorrow of unspent tears.

She would *not* lose control. Her grandmother's words at her parents' funeral rang in her head — DuClairs don't show emotion in public. It isn't done. A sob choked in her throat. She blinked rapidly to dispel the unwelcome weeping.

Get a grip. This is not the time or place. Struggling to still her heart's lament, she repeated over and over again — stop it — while she gradually forced her breathing to move deeper and lower in her chest. Her sobs eased. With her fingertips, she dabbed away the unwanted tears. That's better.

Sylvian turned her thoughts to the exuberant fans singing, stomping, clapping, and screaming. Unbidden, faded images of children and their keepers flickered across the dark recesses of her mind like an aged and too-often viewed, low-budget, silent black-and-white film. The mask of the clown. Laughing. Crying. Folly. Life is folly, she thought, pained by the memories of the foster homes and the orphanage she'd been confined to after her parents' deaths and her grandmother's rejection of her. As she struggled to focus her attention on the stage show, the pictures on the frames faded to gray then vanished.

The pounding, driving force of the music rushed over Sylvian, and her sorrow washed away in the positive energy that charged the arena. After nearly two strenuous, pounding hours, which included three encores, the performance ended. She felt no exhaustion; her ears didn't ring from listening to the amplified sound.

Oddly enough, she felt renewed. Her doubts about life, the choices she made, the purpose and meaning of daily existence, had been erased. In their place, she felt at rest. Comforted, even though she'd not known she needed comfort.

But she had, and she'd had none since childhood. Six? No. Seven. No. Almost seven. Her father's death had cloaked her spirit like a shroud. Gray. Dank. Stifling. She'd allowed nothing and no one to penetrate the protective shell.

Sometimes in her dreams, she saw her father's face in the water underneath her. A last look. A glance. He pushed her up toward the surface then turned back to the wreckage and his wife. But Sylvian had seen her mama's vacant stare, the blood swirling around her twisted body, and knew death had already claimed her. Too late, Sylvian reached for her father. He had slipped away.

You let him drown. His blood stains your hands. Her grandmother's harsh words at the funeral rang false now. Before tonight, she'd avoided thinking about her parents' deaths. When she did, her grandmother's parting words to her seemed true. She had been the last to see him alive. She hadn't stopped him. She let him drown. During the concert, she saw herself as a seven year old. A child. Not responsible for the actions of an adult, not even her father. The music stripped the shroud away and, with the cloak removed, the guilt vanished.

Now, standing in the midst of the fans, she felt safe for the first time in almost eighteen years. Yet, she knew no one. Could find no familiar face in the crowd.

Stranger still, at some time during the show, she'd become a part of, instead of standing apart from, the people around her. Individual, yet connected. When the music ceased, the hall basked in an afterglow, leaving her more curious than ever about these daring performers and the mystical power they exerted over their audience.

The arena fell quiet except for the fans who stood in line speaking quietly among themselves and the workers breaking down the stage and storing away a prodigious amount of equipment. Sylvian watched the band members, minus their elusive leader, sign autographs and speak with the youth gathered around the stage.

She'd been told up-front that the interview wouldn't include Kirth Naran, the man with the "golden voice." That's what he'd been called in the interview she'd read — *the golden voice of rock*. Then, she'd laughed at the writer's choice of words and called the expression an oxymoron. After hearing Kirth Naran sing, she knew the wordsmith had properly pegged his voice.

Weeks ago, when his agent confirmed what *The Wall Street Journal* said, that Kirth Naran never spoke with the press and allowed no one to photograph him, she hadn't been disappointed. Then, she had no reason to meet him. Now, she felt an urgency to stand near the man, to hear his natural voice rather than the amplified sound, to get a feel for the person, to know his scent, his subtle mannerisms — him.

One by one, the band members vanished. After hearing their music and observing them, she dismissed her earlier sense of dread as the product of an overactive imagination. Could the similarities between tonight and last night be written off to coincidence — the Viking attire, the ship, the music, the dancers? Surely not; yet she felt no uneasiness. If anything, the resemblances piqued her interest.

A slender man with unruly auburn hair and a slightly distracted manner signaled to her. Standing, she waved and walked across the arena floor toward him. He introduced himself as their manager, Mike Gallante, and she followed him backstage. He ushered her into the Star Suite and introduced her to the other players — Rogert Greene, Hale Knight, Eric York, and Gaylor Witt.

Forty-five minutes into the interview, they had switched roles on her, asking her personal questions, the kind she should be asking them. She maneuvered her comments to regain control of the interview. Hale unexpectedly stood, nodded at the others, and left. Stunned, she watched him go. The interview wasn't working out, she thought regretfully.

"He'll be back." Gaylor poured himself another glass of iced water and offered her one silently.

"No, thank you." Sylvian had noticed the lack of alcoholic beverages backstage. Was that for her benefit?

"He's gone to see if Kirth's still here," Rogert explained. "He'd want to meet you. Not to do an interview. He doesn't, you know, do interviews."

Rogert's green eyes questioned her, waiting for her response.

"Yes," she replied. Before she could say more, he continued.

"Just to visit. Get to know one another. You're into psychology. Studying youth and the motivations behind their actions. He's involved with kids, too. We all are."

"I'd love to meet him, but I have everything I need for the story." Sylvian rose. *What did they think she was*? *A groupie*? "I understand Mr. Naran values his privacy. I wouldn't think of disturbing him."

As she gathered her recorder and notebook she almost laughed aloud at the notion that a rock idol would want to chat with her about their common interest. Even if he did, he still wouldn't do an interview. Rogert had made that clear. Did she look that naive? she wondered. Kirth Naran refused all interviews, and she could think of only one reason why he'd want to meet her. Sylvian didn't much like the thought. She wasn't a one-night stand.

Common sense dictated caution, she reminded herself silently. She'd seen the helmets and mail they'd removed during the show packed in open boxes by the stage. The quick but hard look she'd given the medieval costumes on the way to the dressing room renewed her suspicions. The short byrnies had the same construction of small, overlapping metal rings as the mail worn by the men she'd seen the previous night. The helmets looked identical.

During the interview, she'd asked the band members what they'd done since they'd been in town. They said they hadn't arrived until today. *Questions without answers.*

Now, she sensed their unwillingness to let her leave. Her fear of enclosed places surged to the fore. The room's white walls closed in on her, and she felt as if she might suffocate. She definitely needed out of here — this dressing room, this building. *This instant*. She wanted to be back in her hotel room away from distractions. Alone, she could sort out the contradictions.

They walked with her to the barricade backstage. If there hadn't been so many fans still waiting outside, she had the distinct feeling they would have provided an escort to her car instead of handing the job to Mike.

"No problem," Mike told Gaylor. He turned to Sylvian. "The guys are right. Better safe than sorry. Wait here with Eric and Rogert for just a few minutes."

"Thanks. I'll be OK," Sylvian protested. "I really must go." "Not long," Mike pleaded, holding his hands together as if in prayer. "Promise. Gaylor's wanted in the office. I'll take him and be right back. Please. Please wait."

Unwillingly, Sylvian consented. To do otherwise would be rude. Still, every nerve in her body screamed for her to run. What had she seen last night? Logic urged that a connection existed even though the musicians didn't seem capable of the brutality she'd witnessed at the bayou.

Dark-eyed, dark-haired Eric appeared to be a Teddy bear under his gruff manner, and Rogert had the outward manner of a priest. Well, her idea of a priest. Serious. Intense. Studious. Even the tall, lean, blond Gaylor of the refined manners and winsome brown eyes and the charmer, Hale, whose reputation as a heart-breaker preceded him, didn't seem likely murder suspects.

If she believed them innocent, why had she become so ill at ease? So jittery? Her discomfort must have been triggered by the unsettling interview. Kirth Naran never talked to the press, and Hale went to get him. Just to talk? Not in this lifetime. And their curiosity about her life. What inspired their questions? Why did they care? She didn't like their prying. Not one bit. She was the writer. She asked the questions. They answered. Not the other way around.

As they waited for Mike to return, Eric and Rogert stole glances in her direction. Their attention alarmed her. She felt unexpectedly shy, awkward, and trapped and lost in the same breath. She struggled for words to dissipate the tension.

Before she spoke, a member of the road crew solved her problem by tripping over a cable and falling off the stage. Part of the equipment toppled to the arena floor with him.

Eric and Rogert rushed to help him. Sylvian heard them insist he remain still. Rogert waved to her and walked off, passing Mike on his way. The two exchanged a few words, then Mike came toward Sylvian.

"Ready?" he inquired.

Sylvian eyed the worker, who still hadn't stood. "Will he be OK?"

"May have a twisted ankle. Rogert's gone to get Doc Wade."

"Is this Doc Wade a doctor?"

"Definitely."

"And the equipment?"

"What equipment?" Mike looked toward the stage. "Oh. That." Mike whistled and motioned to another crew member. "Check the amplifiers before you load 'em." He turned to Sylvian. "Now, where are you parked?"

Sylvian dropped her stenographer's notebook, tape recorder, and black purse on the bed in her hotel room, chiding herself as each item landed on the coverlet. "Dumb. Dumb. Double dumb. You blew it. *Fool.* You wanted to meet Kirth Naran all night. The opportunity presents itself. You go ballistic. Think you're on display. Meat on the hoof. And you run. Not smart. Triple Dumb."

She unpacked and set up her notebook computer. The mundane task calmed her. Later, she could find out when they had arrived in New Orleans. The answer would substantiate or disallow what the players told her.

For now, she must set aside her questions and work. Instead of composing two stories, she opted to write a combination review and interview, starting with the review and ending with their comments backstage.

45

Flipping through her notes, she stopped at the band members' statements about Dragon. They'd all had something to say about the group's name and purpose.

Gaylor insisted the word dragon did not derive from the Greek word *drakon* for serpent but from the Greek word *derkein*, which means *seeing* or *to see clearly*. Eric claimed the dragon to be strong and vigilant with exceptionally keen eyesight and the duty of guarding temples and treasures. Rogert called the gift of life the greatest treasure, while Hale explained their purpose — filling others' hearts with the joy they felt in creating their music.

Alternately pressing the fast-forward and reverse buttons on the tape recorder, she quickly found the spot she sought.

Rogert's voice filled the room. "The world has too many doomsayers."

Hale exclaimed, "Negative energy drains people. Makes 'em hostile, distrustful, fearful. We're charged with positive energy. We pass that on to our fans."

She stopped the tape, kicking off her black patent-leather heels as she did so. Before tonight, she would have argued with Hale, with all of them. And now? She didn't know. She experienced a catharsis during the show. The repressed painful memories had disappeared. She popped open one of the soft drinks she'd bought from the vending machine in the hallway, sat down, turned on her notebook computer, and began typing.

The words poured forth: "The golden voice of rock 'n' roll mesmerized a capacity crowd of Dragon fans Sunday at the New Orleans Superdome. The veteran rockers hit hard licks for close to two grueling hours. After three encores, the tightly synchronized five-member band called it a night. The concert marked the last chance for fans to catch the act until the Houston Astrodome on the tenth. Disappointed the show was over, fans, nonetheless, left the arena in high spirits. Dragon dreamer Chase Thibodaux, eighteen, of Baton Rouge said of the popular bandsmen: "I listen to them constantly. Their music is therapeutic — magic. The sound carries positive vibes. Energy. Soul. Makes me feel good about life. Houston, here I come."

The soft tap, tap, tap of her long, polished nails striking the keyboard stopped. Silence filled the room. *Houston.* She could see them in Houston. Ten days from now. She sighed. She hoped she had answers before then.

She stood and stretched. Hours of writing lay ahead. She stepped to the sink, slipped off her jacket, hung the bolero in the nearby closet, and freed the pearl-colored shell from the skirt's waistband. When she did, the solitary, eight-petalled red rose, hand-painted in bold strokes across the bosom of the blouse, shimmered in the artificial light.

By habit, her hand reached for the facial cream she used to remove her makeup. Rubbing some on absentmindedly, she recalled Mike's parting words in the parking lot: "Call me later at the Hyatt. I'll get you together with Kirth."

She patted her face with the washcloth before realizing she hadn't rinsed off the cream. "Give me a break!"

Yanking on the faucet, she washed off the cream and make-up in warm then cold water. She shook her head knowingly at the mirror while she dried her face. The whole damn thing was strange.

5

*S*ylvian spiraled into nightfall as dark as a tomb. She opened her mouth, but no sound came out. Down and down she fell, the scream silent on her lips. Abruptly, the free fall stopped. A cold blast of wind whipped around her. The swirling mist cleared, and she stood on a beach.

Alone.

A fierce wind forced her down until she knelt like a child in the sand. Looking up, she saw Viking ships anchored at the water's edge.

A tremor shook the ground.

She turned her head away from the water and toward the land. Gold-tipped flames leapt in the distance. Instantly, and without any awareness of moving, she stood in the middle of a village set aflame. Tumultuous voices pounded in her ears. Men, women, and children lay dead around her. She knew them but couldn't call their names.

A man's body pressed against her. When she pushed him away, she discovered she held the sword that had slain him. Horrified, she looked around for other assailants.

Five helmeted warriors, clad in mail, formed a semi-circle around her. She brandished the sword to keep them at bay. Her heart pounded. She was overmatched.

The tallest one stood across from her. His eyes penetrated the distance between them, capturing her, commanding her, calling her to him. Violet. His eyes were violet just before the flames turned them red.

Blood red.

Murder lay in their depths. She tensed, grasped the sword firmly in both hands, and waited for the assault, knowing she would die.

A sardonic smile teased his lips. "This one's mine." He raised his sword to her.

His crackling volcanic laughter pierced her body and unsettled the ground beneath her. Fear overwhelmed her, blinding her. Pain, greater than any she'd ever known, filled her. She screamed soundlessly and fell into a black abyss.

"No!" Sylvian rasped, sitting up in bed. Covered in sweat, her pearlescent silk nightgown stuck to her skin. Flinging back the covers, she started to rise. *Smoke? Did she smell smoke?*

Instinctively, she reached for the bedside lamp and turned on the light. Nothing appeared amiss in the room. She slid out of the king-sized bed and moved to the door, checking the wood for heat. The painted cypress felt cool to the touch.

What a nightmare. She walked back to the bed and stopped. She smelled smoke again and the disgusting odor of rotting, putrefying flesh.

"Ugh." Her dreams about her father's death and her grandmother's accusations felt mild compared to the intensity of this nightmare. Never had her dreams emitted foul odors. Yet, the horrid stench of burning flesh and rancid smoke clung to her. And the smell grew stronger, not weaker.

She stepped away from the bed, and the foulness grew fainter. She stood in the middle of the room, undecided. Again she stole closer to the bed. The horrid odor invaded her nostrils. She gagged.

Rushing to the balcony doors, she unlocked them and flung them open wide. The sultry heat of a New Orleans night hit her full blast. She didn't care. The air didn't smell of death.

She turned and studied the bed.

Violet eyes.

Again.

She'd never met anyone with violet eyes and had heard only

one person described as having that remarkable color of eyes — Elizabeth Taylor.

Viking ships.

Again.

Sylvian tapped the tips of her manicured nails together. Maybe she had too many unanswered questions to sleep peacefully. She began mentally counting them off. The butchery at the bayou. The dancers. The warriors. Not an illusion. Flesh and bones. She grimaced. The blood had been real, too. Then, the Dragon show. The similarity between the two.

Now the nightmare. A warning? She needed to be wary of anyone with violet eyes. None of the band members had violet eyes. She didn't know the color of Kirth Naran's eyes.

Sylvian checked her wrist watch. Almost five-thirty. Surely, rock musicians slept at this hour. Thank Heavens she'd sent her story to the office last night. She had other things on her mind now — retracing, as best she could, her drive the first night and seeing the site in the daylight. Maybe she'd find something the police missed in the dark.

First, she'd camp out at the Hyatt. If Kirth Naran didn't surface by ten o'clock, she'd call Mr. Gallante's room. She didn't like the idea any more this morning than she had last night, but she did have the option. She preferred to watch unobserved. Besides, Kirth Naran would be easy to spot. That mane of dark, golden locks would give him away.

Tingling nerves flashed up Sylvian's spine, across her shoulders and down her arms. Warmth bathed her body. And something else. Tears. Sorrow. No. Longing. An overwhelming aching for ... *her*?

"Who's there?" She spun around as she spoke, sensing another living presence in the room. The long shadows reached out for her, calling her into their folds. She quick stepped to the door and switched on the overhead light. The simple action illuminated the room and erased the offending darkness. That's better.

Jitters. Nerves. That's all. Shrugging off her uneasiness, she walked into the bathroom and turned on the shower. While the water heated, she rummaged through her suitcase, unrolling from the plastic she'd wrapped them in her washable silk, emerald shorts, shirt and matching jacket. Cool, comfortable, yet professional looking. Just in case she had to call Mike Gallante. She stepped to the closet. Fortunately, someone had left coat hangers. The few wrinkles would drop out in the steam from the shower.

She hung the clothes in the bathroom and closed the door. Dialing room service, she ordered the works — bacon, eggs over easy, grits, biscuits, orange juice, milk, coffee. Her favorite breakfast and why not? If she didn't eat now, she might not have the chance.

Her mouth felt chalky. No wonder. In all the excitement, she'd forgotten to brush. She could barely think much less talk until she did. Stepping to the vanity, she grabbed the tube, the trusty red-and-white label reassuring her some things never change. She'd used this toothpaste since childhood, flatly refusing to try another brand. Not only was she addicted to the taste, she had perfect teeth — pearly white and even. Two good reasons to hang onto the familiar.

Not until steamy water washed her body did the words of an interview she'd conducted last fall come back to her. The man had said inconspicuous. You need a strong presence, yet still be inconspicuous, able to melt into the background, the walls, the furniture, unseen, if you want to be a successful bodyguard or an undercover agent. He'd been both before becoming a teacher. She'd found the interview alive with incongruent ideas that made sense when she thought about them. A persona when needed, invisible when necessary. Watchful for details while appearing to not pay attention. Helpful.

She mentally surveyed her clothes again. What looked the most like everyone else? Jeans, of course. And a white shirt. Nondescript. Perfect. She didn't want to wear anything that would cause her to stand out in a crowd. She planned on getting answers, and she could best do that unnoticed.

After dressing, she ate every bite of her breakfast, savoring the texture of freshly squeezed orange juice and the taste of the yolk sopped up into the biscuit. Her energy recharged, Sylvian headed for the parking lot armed with her pen, note pad and tape recorder. A smile teased her lips as she opened the car door. She had a hunch this was going to be a day to remember.

She turned the key in the ignition. Nothing. No response at all. Again, she turned the key. Again the silence. No grinding sound as if the starter tried to kick in but couldn't get the engine powered up. No click, click, click. Nothing. Over and over she wiggled the key and pumped the gas pedal. Even as she went through the motions, praying to get a different response, she realized the futility of her efforts. The damned thing wouldn't start.

Typical. The best laid plans go south, Sylvian thought. She popped the hood, wiggled out of the bucket seat, and stepped to the front of the car. Reaching for the latch, she spied a muddy fingerprint in the precise spot she was about to touch. The mud was only slightly darker than the gunmetal finish, and she almost missed seeing the splotch at all.

She froze. Had someone tampered with the car? She stepped back, leaned over and looked underneath. Nothing. Scratching her nails against her jeans, she stood staring at the fingerprint and debating whether to open the hood or not. Whose fingerprint was it? A policeman's? From last night? But why? She'd been in a patrol car. They hadn't been in her car.

Probably the muddy print belonged to someone at the car-rental agency or the last person who had serviced the car. Determined that this was the answer, Sylvian sprang the latch and raised the hood. Her eyes widened.

No battery.

Of course, Sylvian thought, berating herself for overlooking the obvious — the car had been vandalized. The fingerprint most likely belonged to a thief. Besides, if anyone else left the fingerprint, the impression had survived the rain.

Closing the hood, she studied the mud closer. The pattern stood out too clearly to have been washed by rain, she decided. She locked the car and headed for the lobby. Robbery meant police. She'd talk with them only if she couldn't avoid doing so.

In less than fifteen minutes, Sylvian settled back in the taxi the clerk at the front desk had called for her. The agency employee said he'd take care of reporting the theft — there'd been a rash of them in the area the desk clerk said — and promised to deliver her another car in an hour.

Leave the keys at the front desk, she told the agent. She didn't want to talk with the police any more while she was in New Orleans unless she could prove the truth of her bayou experience. And she didn't want to miss the elusive Kirth Naran.

Even though she didn't believe in such things, she'd about decided a curse plagued her trip to New Orleans. She'd never had two days so filled with confusing experiences.

Had she seen five young women slaughtered by men dressed as Viking warriors? The police didn't think she'd seen anyone murdered. They thought she'd lost her mind, and she hadn't even mentioned the Viking ship or the strange attire. What would they have thought if she had?

Could the officers be right? She'd gone over the deep end. Sleep deprivation could do many things to a person's mind. Sylvian knew that. In the last six months, she'd slept little. Work and her master's thesis had taken their toll.

Had the weeks she'd spent in Scandinavia last summer colored what she saw last night? Her passion for learning about early cultures made the opportunity to study the Norse on a grant too good to refuse, and then the two weeks had exhausted her. The sites had left her disappointed, almost as if she'd expected to find *something* that wasn't there — but what? The moment of revelation she had yearned for never came, and she had no more answers now than then.

Even before she'd arrived in New Orleans, discontent populated her thoughts like a cynical jury. She examined, looked, searched, questioned. Everything. Why couldn't she accept the positive things that came to her without wondering what price life demanded back in return? The study grant led to her job. She needed to be grateful. Period.

Her thoughts swung back to the strange episode, her mind probing all possibilities. The police had good reasons to doubt her story. No evidence of foul play existed. She'd wondered initially if getting lost had unnerved her enough to put her into shock. Her mind had drawn on the sites and relics she'd seen a year ago to create the ensuing experience.

The concert squelched that theory. She'd been relieved, yet even more baffled. Musicians capable of playing soul-touching music seemed unlikely murder suspects, she decided.

Perhaps she'd chanced upon a *son et lumiere*,[6] walking unknowingly into the dramatic spectacle. The fireflies represented nothing more than modern-day magic created through special effects. If so, the production crew hid well the equipment and their vehicles. She'd seen no audience. Dress rehearsal? Maybe. Maybe not. When she returned with the police, no trace of anyone having been there remained.

She found another explanation more feasible. Dragon had a sick, rich fan who used the group's motif to play out his macabre games. The dragon ships had the same markings and identical colors. The helmets and mail and capes looked alike. Absent from the stage were the swords and the battle-axes and the blood.

So much blood — even in her nightmare, which had served to unsettle her more. Every detail of the horror lay etched in her mind, including the stench. In the dream, she was as isolated as in life. Couples and families filled her world, but even with her friends, she felt out of focus somehow as if she didn't quite fit.

Never. Never did she speak of those feelings. Now, her carefully controlled world seemed to be splintering. Last night, the music brushed her soul. She felt safe, a part of, instead of apart from humanity. The feeling wouldn't last. Logic said destroying one's own demons couldn't be that simple. Soon, she feared, she might not know the difference between fantasy and reality. Maybe she was already there.

Unbidden, disquietude slipped through her lips like a prayer. "I refuse to accept that. I'm not insane." Alarmed, Sylvian glanced at the taxi driver to make sure he hadn't heard her. She

[6]dramatic spectacle. See word usage.

was relieved to see him preoccupied with his own knitting.

The briefest of smiles shadowed her lips. Her mother's words not hers. *Tend to your own knitting, little one. Let others tend to theirs.* Sylvian loved the endearment — little one. The cherished words had made her feel safe, and she didn't know why. Nervously, she tapped her fingers on her purse. At least in this business she followed her mother's advice. Tending to her own knitting. After all, she had seen the slaughter.

She must find the source of those compelling, violet eyes. The intensity might be fake — colored lenses. First, she had to see Kirth Naran. If she'd been willing to stay at the arena last night, she might now know the color of his eyes. She also could have given them the name of her hotel. They'd certainly wanted to know. But no, she'd been determined not to leave the impression that she was an easy mark and available for something more than an interview.

Sylvian leaned forward, then tapped the driver on his shoulder. "How much farther?" The words were barely uttered when she saw a moving van swerve wildly across the intersection ahead and turn wide onto the one-way street. The truck careened toward them, brushing aside the cars parked in its way.

Metal crushing metal was the last sound Sylvian heard before the pain hit her, and she plummeted into darkness.

**The first principles
of the universe are
atoms and empty space;
everything else is merely
thought to exist.**

*Democritus
circa 460 B.C.-370 B.C.*

6

Seventh Century A.D.

*I*cy wind whipped Sylvian's face while the salty bite of sea air invaded her senses. Her eyes opened on a twilight world inhabited by brawny men rowing long oars. Dismayed by the sight, a single thought screamed at her — *run*. Her reflexes sprang, but her body didn't bolt. She felt the rope binding her, securing her hands behind her and her legs at the ankles.

Her mind scrambled for an explanation. The moving van. The taxi. The sound of crushing metal. Her body twisting. She bit her tongue. Then nothing. No. Wait. Something. A whirling gray mist all around her. She fell and fell and fell into the darkness. Now this — what? A continuation of her nightmare? The idea chilled her even more than the cold wind.

She closed her eyes, hoping that when she opened them again the ship and its rowers would have vanished. This is a dream, she coaxed silently. A disturbing dream but a dream and not reality. Your body's in shock. Your mind's presenting you with an illusionary world. These people aren't real. The wind isn't real. Nothing you see is real.

The ship's forward motion drifted to a stop. Sylvian still tasted the salt in the air and heard voices shouting around her. She opened her eyes in time to see a ruddy-looking man clad in mail, a tunic, laced leggings, brown cloak and gilded bronze helmet, reach down, yank her to her feet and throw her over his shoulder. The wool cloth brushed against her face as her body bounced unceremoniously against his back. The rough texture scratched her skin.

The man slipped her off his shoulder and into another's arms. The second man, whose cloak also rubbed her skin harshly, carried her ashore. He stopped where a tent had been pitched and a fire started, dumped her in the sand next to the blaze, and walked away.

She struggled to sit. The sand ground beneath her fingernails, the unpleasant sensation triggering an alarming thought. What if this world is real? And the men? Norsemen? Ridiculous. She discarded the idea as soon as the notion struck her. Actors dressed as Norsemen for some outdoor drama made more sense. But that didn't explain how she got here. Surely, she'd been injured in the accident. A moving van. A taxi. She had to have been hurt. She must be in a hospital.

Of course, she thought. Drug-induced hallucinations. Her drug-addled mind conjured the Norse motif. She'd only seen the sail down, but she suspected the fabric had the same pattern she had seen her first night in New Orleans and at the concert.

That rectangular sail dated the ships to at least the seventh century and the vessels most likely to eighty-foot-long keeled dragon ships with a lateral-steering oar fixed to the starboard quarter. In the daylight, she'd be able to tell how well her mind served up history.

She almost laughed. In the daylight, she'd be out of here. Back in the real world, she hoped.

Again, she closed her eyes. She tried to make the feel of sand under her hands, the heat of the fire, the taste of salt air, and the smell of burning wood go away. She could hear a voice calling her across a deep void. She focused her thoughts toward the soft-spoken words, felt herself being pulled in their direction, when, unexpectedly, a hand yanked her upright.

Furious, she kicked the intruder, missed, and tumbled back in the sand. As the man leaned over her, she kicked at him again. This time she didn't miss. He yelled and Sylvian heard another man laugh. Twisting her head, she saw there were two of them.

"She has spirit," said the heavy-set man she'd kicked.

"You better leave her alone," the lean, laughing one replied. "Kith's claimed her as his. He won't favor your meddling."

"I'm not going to harm her. I just want a closer look at a woman who can go sword-to-sword with our chief, scratch him, and live."

"There'll be plenty of time for that. Kith said to stay away from her. You don't want to cross him."

The two walked off, leaving Sylvian more confused than ever. Kith, their chief? She'd fought him with a sword? Her nightmare came back to her. The burning village. The five warriors. The one with the violet eyes and the sardonic smile. Kith?

Listen to yourself, Sylvian chided. You're wondering what two characters from your imagination are talking about as if they were real people. And this Kith. A name fraught with Freudian meaning. Kith and kin. She had few friends and no kin. At least none she claimed.

She struggled to sit again, and the long dress maddened her. The heavy fabric clung to the sand and made sitting upright difficult. She wished she could rip off the skirt. Where had her white blouse and jeans gone? Had someone undressed and then redressed her? The thought chilled her even as she realized her mind must have created the confining attire.

By now, the sun had set completely, and the moon rose in the eastern sky. Sylvian paused in her struggles and raised her face toward the incandescent saucer. She felt strengthened. She always did with a full moon. She looked toward the ocean and saw a fleet of ships pulled ashore. Fires burned along the beach. Men sat around each bonfire except the one warming her.

The red-and-gold tent behind her held no people, no pets, no anyone. Alone here. Isolated. How many times had she felt that way? Too many. The concert came to her mind. The music erased that distant feeling she'd carried throughout her life.

Her drugged mind wove a rich tapestry, Sylvian decided. Down to the details — her infuriating dress, the coarseness of the men's wool clothing against her skin, the feel of the sand, the smell of salt water and burning wood. She'd embarked on a mystical journey where some great truth would be revealed to her, changing her life forever.

Sylvian laughed at the fancy, noticing with alarm that her laughter carried no sound. A side-effect of the drugs, she decided. Mysticism belonged in fairy tales along with the Brothers Grimm. The thought reassured her. She prided herself on being a realist. An empiricist. No truth existed in what she saw around her, only a fictitious world created through a drug-fueled, elaborately conjured sleight of mind.

This nightmare must end — *now*. Closing her eyes again, she shut out the sounds around her and focused her thoughts on escaping the hallucination. A distant voice still called to her. She could almost catch the words when a voice nearby said, "No one harmed her. We kept watch from the next fire."

A flash of heat burst through her body. Silver streams of light juxtaposed against dark, brooding images flashed before her. The voice in her mind faded. She sighed and opened her eyes. Five warriors stood over her. The tallest she recognized immediately.

He knelt in front of her, his violet eyes commanding hers to look at him. "We'll cut your bonds and let you eat if you promise not to fight or run. We harbor north of the Rhine. You are far away from your village — on a strange shore." His soft tone caressed. "Do I have your word?"

She questioned him with her eyes, then nodded yes. This wasn't how she planned on locating the man with the violet eyes, but the message seemed clear, obvious. She'd been obsessing about finding those damn violet eyes when the wreck occurred.

"Good." He reached up and one of the warriors handed him a knife. He cut the rope binding her feet, then rubbed her ankles. "These were too tight. They've cut into her skin."

"I was lucky to bind them at all, Kith," came the reply from the one who provided the knife. "She kept kicking and biting. One of the men offered his quietener.[7] The sandbag would have lessened the task, but your orders forbid its use. Don't hit her. Don't knock her out. It took two of us to tie her up."

"I wouldn't repeat that to the others." Kith smiled at her.

[7]sack used to muffle or silence slaves. See word usage.

"They'll think you weak."

"She stabbed you, but you didn't hurt her," the voice growled, clearly incensed at the implication. "The men are all talking about your leniency."

"Let them talk, Ragnar." Kith looked intently at Sylvian while he continued to massage her ankles. "I could not harm her. She has too much fire. I shall take her to wife instead."

"No!" She gasped, her eyes widening at the suggestion.

Kith laughed. "Steady, fierce maid. You will have time to think on my proposal before we return home. For now, we have a truce. Agreed?"

She nodded again. *Marry you — never.* Who does he think he is? Then again, why respond to an illusion, a figment of her imagination?

Rising, he pulled her to her feet. In one swift movement, he cut the rope binding her wrists. "I'm Kith the Bold, son of Njall, descendant of Arnfinn the Rune Master. These are my brothers — Tyr, the eldest, Baldur, and you met the twins, Ansgar and Ragnar."

Sylvian acknowledged each and sized up the two who had bound her. Armed and dressed in mail, the ruddy-complexioned, fair-haired twins appeared quite capable of securing a woman by themselves. Actually, all had strong physiques and were attractive in an unkempt, barbaric way. She found Kith the most striking.

"These are Kith's men." Tyr pointed to the others strewn down the beach. "He's the chief here even though the youngest among us."

Sylvian watched the studied look in Tyr's pale-blue eyes when he spoke. She wondered briefly about the scar running across his right cheek parallel with his square jaw. A battle wound. Lower and he wouldn't be here talking, she thought. His words drew her attention to Kith again.

Kith's laughter filled the air. "You are too kind, brother. They all have their own men. They came to guard me because our father asked them. He had a vision. Great harm would befall me if I set out alone, but I must go. The treasure I would bring back would be worth the trip. The voice in his vision warned not to leave our homes undefended. Their men remained behind."

Visions. Warnings. Some hallucination, Sylvian thought. Her stomach growled. Now, hunger pains.

Kith cocked his head. "You understand everything we say, don't you?"

She nodded. Her eyes fixed on the ring-shaped, silver fibula holding his cloak together at the neck. The head of a winged serpent formed the end on both sides of the ring. Runes covered the silver bar securing the cape. She'd seen a similar clasp — where? Ah. Stockholm. The museum. A trick of the mind only. Besides, she didn't speak Norse, yet she understood their words. In the real world, she wouldn't.

"What's your name?"

Sylvian looked at them silently. They were her subconscious creations; they should know her name. She shook her head no. She didn't plan on doing so but she did. Strange.

"Let's call her Svanhild," Ansgar suggested. "She's a beautiful battle maid."

"No," Kith replied. "Horses tore Svanhild apart. This one would bite and kick the horses to death."

"Aye! And quickly," Ragnar said knowingly.

Robust laughter broke out among them.

Turning his attention again to Sylvian, Kith said, "Aasta." He turned to his brothers. "She is of the night. Look at her raven hair reflect the moonlight. The full moon is not often with us. Our friends who guide us, the stars, are. They are loved by seafarers." To Sylvian, he added, "Aasta has two meanings. 'Stars' and 'the loved.' The name shall be yours."

Kith's comments confirmed Sylvian's conviction he came from her imagination. The men of the North were known for their warlike abilities and seafaring ways, not their romantic prowess, unless having more than one wife said something for their staying power. The idea didn't appeal to her, not one iota. Then again, nothing about this delusion did.

Ansgar pointed at Kith and said, "It's time you settle down, but she's a slave. Yours by right. No need to wed."

"I shall, though." Kith's tone invited no disagreement.

"Have it your way." To Sylvian, Ansgar growled, "I wish he had found a woman among his own to wed." He shrugged. "You may as well accept the idea. Kith wants you. No man will stand in his way. The women are — different. All the single ones would change places with you."

"Some of the others, too." Ragnar snickered. "Given a chance."

"Aye," Tyr said.

Baldur scowled, his bushy brows nearly meeting themselves above his aquiline nose. "Your people attacked an undefended settlement. They left no one alive. Some they sold. We've done the same. You would already be dead had you not fought so valiantly. To be here with us is your fate. Agree to our brother's offer or suffer."

"My people are lost to me." The voice came from Sylvian, but the words were strangers. Yet, the simple statement fueled Sylvian's mind with horror: green vines and olive trees surrounding white stone buildings belching fire and smoke; ear-splitting death screams, the stench of burning flesh, and clear water flushed with blood.

"My parents died many moons ago," the voice whispered. The world around Sylvian faded; savage images flashed uninvited before her. A stout man fell, cleaved in two. Laughing men encircled a young beauty, taunting her, taking turns making sport of her, all the time questioning her. She refused to answer. They fell upon her, pushing and pressing, their rough hands tore her tender flesh. After they had their way with her, they yanked her to her feet. She made no sound, no whimpers, no screams, no cries of pain or for mercy. Dark bruises marred her flawless skin, her right eye had swollen shut, her long, raven hair hung matted with her blood. She fell forward in the dirt, her eyes open, looking at Sylvian. The images faded. Sickened, Sylvian wondered about their meaning — who was this woman that died so proud?

"The ones you killed murdered the children under my care and took me," the voice continued. "The night skies tell me we marched northwest. You've been honest with me. I will do the same. Although I've been a slave to more than one conqueror, no one who has tried to put his mark on me has lived."

"There must have been many, and you killed them all and lived?" Tyr asked, his tone doubting her words.

"I did not kill them. They died. No one in the village you destroyed would touch me. They feared harming me. Kith fought me, and he lives. Ansgar and Ragnar tied me up, and they live. One of you carried me from the ship. I can't speak for the man who approached me by the fire —"

"What man?" Kith commanded, looking at Ragnar.

"I watched," came the quick reply. "The men are curious. One tried to get a better look at her. She kicked him hard enough he yelled. That's all."

Turning back to Sylvian, Kith smiled.

The expression yanked her out of her reverie. Her heart quickened. His smile, which bore no resemblance to the scornful one in her dream, beckoned her to move nearer to him. Stop reacting like a school-girl, she thought, irritated. Of course, you find him appealing. He's your creation.

"Good. His disobedience did not go unpunished." Kith's expression darkened. "He did no harm, but he could have. I'll not ignore disobedience. Tell the men, Ragnar. Anyone who wants to challenge me comes down here *now*. Otherwise, they leave this prisoner alone. Completely. She's not a prize to be shared. I've claimed her. She is no spoil."

Kith's words surprised Sylvian. Whose disobedience? The conversation had gone on with her attention elsewhere. How could that be, if this is a dream? An hallucination? And would she even be aware of herself in the midst of an hallucination? She dismissed the last concern as irrelevant. She knew herself. Everything else was suspect.

"No one's going to challenge you," Ansgar said, jumping in to defend his brother who'd been left in charge of keeping the men away from the woman while he secured the ship.

Ragnar put his hand on Ansgar's shoulder. "I'll go. Kith's right. I'm responsible. They approached the fire because I'd gone to get more wood. I saw them but had walked too far away to protect her."

"That's not the point," Tyr growled. "The men knew to stay away. If some are uninformed, let them hear the orders now. If they knew and approached her anyway, they must be challenged. Ansgar's correct. None will come down here. Kith's strategy is on the mark. All will realize he knows and does not view any breach of orders as harmless. This move will stop any loose talk."

Sylvian watched Ragnar nod and walk off toward the other fires. The laughing man said Kith would be displeased, she thought, relieved she understood the subject of their conversation. She knew dreams, but she had no experience with hallucinations. She wondered if she could stop this one without having to wait for the drug to wear off and felt the intensity of four men's attention directed at her. She decided to tell them they were part of her dream and not real and to ask them what they wanted. Maybe the question alone would break the hold on her mind.

She looked into Kith's eyes and heard her voice say instead, "I believe Baldur is right. This is my destiny. Being here with you." Sylvian wanted to scream, but couldn't. What the hell is going on? she wondered as the voice continued, "As for your offer? I don't know. I must think longer on the proposal. I accept the name. Your eyes are as kind as your voice. And I am drawn to you as you are to me. But the decision must be mine and made not as a slave but as a free woman."

Kith's eyes bored into hers. "Done."

"Kith!" Tyr exclaimed. "You've won her fair. She's yours by right."

Kith raised his hand to silence his brother. "I know. I want our children to be free. Not slaves."

"She hasn't said yes," Tyr argued.

Kith smiled. "She will. You are free, Aasta, to make your decision. No reprisals."

"I will answer soon," the voice promised. "Little time remains. Five nights from now, I turn twenty-five. The night sky will be dark. I see only blood and death. I fear none of you will be safe. Your father's vision may hold more truth than you know. But, for now, we are safe, and I am hungry."

Kith nodded at Ansgar who walked away from the group. "He will bring you food."

Sylvian couldn't explain the origin of her words. They came from her mouth, but the thoughts were alien to her. As the words poured forth, she saw the events lying behind them as if she had lived them herself. Could she be trapped within universal archetypes, cornered in the collective unconscious Carl Jung espoused? Warriors and blood. Savagery and slavery. Marriage and rape. Visions of disaster. What did the symbols mean?

Where are we? When? What year is this? Who are you? What do you want from me? She wanted to ask those questions, but no matter how hard she tried to speak her thoughts, she failed. She couldn't even scream and be heard.

She prayed her speechlessness didn't indicate her personality had split, and she no longer controlled herself. The chilling idea made her feel as lost as a child who's just realized she's alone for the first time, that somehow she's overstepped the faces and objects in her familiar world.

Nothing made sense; yet, the pieces all seemed to fit into some kind of master puzzle. Somehow. She looked at the sea, the sky, the sand, the fire, and finally the three men who faced her. Something about this place, this time, and the men felt all too real.

The feeling is false. This is fantasy, not reality. Perhaps she could determine what time period the hallucinosis had conjured up. Her mind searched for the answer. They are Norse, but are they Vikings? The Viking Age lasted roughly three-hundred years, beginning in the late eighth century. Raiders. Slavers. Plunderers. The ships are no earlier than seventh century. Hum. Seventh century. Vague. Mostly unknown to historians.

She studied Kith. A warrior? Definitely. A butcher? A man

who sells human flesh in the marketplace? A participant in religious blood sacrifices of humans and animals? If he is a Viking, surely he has to be. The words of the English prayer slipped into her mind — *Save us, O Lord, from the fury of the Northmen.* Savagery is commonplace in his time, and yet his kindness toward her makes believing him capable of such actions difficult. Then again, he isn't real so he can be whatever her mind elects him to be.

"You'll sleep there." Kith pointed to the tent. "We will be outside." He glanced at his brothers. "We have much to discuss." They nodded their agreement.

Kith looked across the campfires. "Much can happen in four days. Our father's vision disturbed him. Now I am concerned by your words. Perhaps I did not weigh his words heavily enough. Tyr, pass the word. We leave for home at first light."

"What reason shall I give?" Tyr inquired. "The men will ask. Returning home now means less income for them."

"We have no secrets, but there's no reason to repeat all that's been said. They know of the vision. Tell them I've had my own. I saw the water in our cove run red with blood, heard the cries of the women, and smelled green-wood burning. We go home. If all is well, we leave again. If not, we need to be prepared for battle."

As Kith spoke, Sylvian saw a cold, still, deep, blue-green lake, mountains cresting to the sky, water cascading from snow-covered peaks, patches of green and dense forests of oak and pine and aspen, naked rock gleaming in the light. Even as she marveled at the beauty, blood stained the lake, women ran, clutching their babies. A tremor coursed through her. She looked at the others whose faces registered an angry alarm, one which showed no fear.

"I saw the destruction when you spoke," Kith said, looking at Sylvian. "You see the vision, too, don't you?"

Her eyes met his. "With your words," the voice whispered. Sylvian was frightened as she had never been before, not just for herself, for them all. She didn't know why. She barely knew these men; she had never been to their homeland. They were, after all, fictions.

Turning to Tyr, Kith said, "I'll speak with everyone before we leave in the morning."

"I'll pass the word." Tyr walked away, pausing when his path crossed Ansgar's and Ragnar's.

Sylvian watched them comply as dutiful and loyal soldiers. The sway Kith had over them amazed her. Tyr said Kith was in charge. The stories she'd read of the Norse ran red with the blood spilled among brothers. These seemed to be an exception, further proof that she did not stand on a foreign beach in some distant time. Instead, she was trapped in a drug-fueled dream without a clue as to how to escape, to make the imaginary world disappear, and her world come back to her.

Kith entered his tent and returned with a red, woven-wool blanket he spread on the sand. "You will find eating easier sitting than standing."

"That's kind of you." She walked to the blanket and sat down. Ansgar returned and handed her a soapstone bowl containing cod, dried herring, mushrooms and curds. While he set a bronze cup filled with beer beside her, Sylvian studied the food.

Fish. She should have known. Fish is more than a staple food in Scandinavia; it's a way of life. During the two weeks of the study grant, she'd eaten her weight in cod, salmon, eel, trout, and herring. Especially herring. The Scandinavians served herring for breakfast, for dinner, for any occasion. She'd sickened of fish, especially herring.

"You must eat," Kith said. "We have a hard journey in front of us. I don't think you're accustomed to sailing," Kith cautioned, sitting across from her.

"I'm not," the voice replied. She took a bite. The herring tasted better than Sylvian's Texas taste buds remembered. As she lifted another morsel to her mouth, her eyes fell on her nails. Shocked, she stared at them. Short, stubby, unpainted — what had happened to her nails? Her manicure? The Candied Apples polish? She sipped from the cup, barely noticing the warm and bitter taste. She struggled to make sense out of what she saw and heard herself say, "I am pleased with your kindness."

Kith nodded at Ansgar. Instead of joining them, the twin motioned to the others, and together they moved to the other side of the fire and began talking among themselves.

"Your brothers follow you as they would the eldest." Sylvian's thoughts brooded over her nails while her body and voice paid no attention, seeming instead to have a mind of their own. "Isn't that unusual?"

"They are not always this cooperative. The situation is as Tyr said. These are my men. I am in command. My brothers are with me at our father's request. If I were with one of them, I would do the same. There can be only one leader. One in command. If our father were here, he would give the orders; he did before we left." He shrugged. "It is our way."

"I had four sisters once. I was the youngest. But the time was so long ago, I remember them only in a dream." *Remember them in a dream*? Where did that fantasy come from? The mystery of her nails slipped from her thoughts as Sylvian toyed with the voice's latest fabrication. She had no brothers or sisters. Yet, the words left her unexpectedly sorrowful. Why?

"It would be hard on me to never see my family or home again," Kith said.

"How far are we from your home?" the voice asked.

"Four days with good winds," Kith replied.

Yesterday

7

*K*ith fell silent and studied her while she ate. He found her beauty greater in life than in his dreams. He could not remember when he'd not known her face. He'd seen her graceful form, her long black hair, her hazel eyes and charcoal brows countless times in his sleep and even during his waking hours. The instant he spied her, he knew her presence in the village drew him there.

Captivated by seeing her in the flesh and discovering she really did exist, he'd been slow to react when she attacked him. That's how she'd been able to cut his arm with her sword. His surprise momentarily blinded him. Fortunately he'd suffered only a superficial wound, but she'd been prepared to kill him. Despite her fierce nature, he knew she was as much his as he was hers.

All he had to do was convince her. "Tell me about this feeling you have about what will happen five nights from now."

Sylvian looked at him and wanted to say: I didn't know any of that story until the words poured out of me.

Instead, when her mouth opened, she heard the voice say, "The feeling comes from a dream I often have. I feel a shade pass through me, then darkness descends. Someone — some foul thing — grabs me; his touch is repugnant. I fight him. He is strong, powerful. He steals my breath and prepares to kill me."

Her body shuddered. "But he is stopped. Diverted somehow. While his back is turned, I step into the fire, taking someone

71

with me. Not the one who attacked me. Someone else. My attacker is outraged. He yells curses at me. The world turns black. I spin into a dark void. Coldness chills me. Then nothing."

Kith placed his hand over hers. "I won't let anything happen to you, Aasta. I, too, have had my dreams. They've all had you in them, even in my waking hours. I don't know what perils lie ahead, but I will protect you with my dying breath. Beyond, if the gods allow. We are meant to be together. That much I do know."

What a romantic notion! He'd dreamed of her all his life. She had no idea her imagination could be so creative. Was she that lonely for a man? Her body's next move surprised her as much as her earlier words. She reached out and brushed his cheek with her fingertips.

Kith found her touch against his skin so gentle, yet each slight movement struck him with the power of lightning. The caress stripped his defenses. He closed his eyes and remained perfectly still. If he moved, she might stop.

"I've made my decision," she said. What decision? Sylvian wondered.

Kith's eyes opened, and he fixed his steady gaze upon her.

"I will marry you." Her words shocked Sylvian. Even *the voice* barely knew this man. He swore his undying love and protection for her, and she agreed to marry him. She struggled to understand. In her nightmares, she didn't know to call the experiences dreams until she awakened. Then, their impact lessened. Here, she had to be dreaming. Yet, the dream not only persevered, its power grew stronger, drawing her, against her own volition, into this world.

She felt as if she had stepped into another's form whence she could feel the sensations of the night air and the sand and the fire burning close. She tasted the food and found she was famished. His hand electrified her body with only its weight on hers, as his touch did earlier when he'd rubbed her ankles after removing the bonds binding her.

She'd not spoken the words she uttered. Not knowingly. Not

consciously. They sprang forth guided by some other will.

As she looked deep into his eyes, she sensed that she'd been waiting her entire life for this moment. Whether he was real or not, she wanted desperately to be in his embrace. Had she lost her mind?

Kith's arms moved around her, enclosing her in their strength. He pulled her toward him, lifting her until she lay beside him. His eyes closed just before his mouth branded hers with its intensity and passion. She moaned. Her lips parted and allowed the tip of his tongue to caress them before moving inside.

The taste of him filled her as no other enticement had before. She drank heartily of his essence as if she had been drained and broken and now sought to be full and whole. The touch of his hand moving down her dress set her on fire. Pulling the gown loose from the bronze clasp, his fingers stroked her breasts until they ached with pleasure.

Her mouth released his, freeing his lips to kiss her neck and then her chest. Heat more consuming than fire erupted in its wake. Her fingers clasped his hair; she pressed his head down on her silken skin. His lips brushed her hardening nipples, engulfing her body with want. She floated through translucent veils, each finer, thinner, more revealing than the last. Some truth, hidden until now, waited for his touch to give it life; its pulsating presence called to her even as its diamond brilliance began shattering the separating shades.

"Take me now before it's too late," the voice urged. "Quickly." Her body spiraled into the approaching white hot stars.

His free hand pulled her gown up around her thighs.

Kith's body trembled with desire. As he rose to move over her, the ground shook violently, throwing him off balance. Howling sounds filled his ears. His eyes lifted to see fiery eyes and dark forms racing toward them. He jumped to his feet, grabbed his battle axe and sword.

She gasped and sprang to her feet, her fingers busy fastening the clasps that held her dress at the shoulders. "Give me your sword." She *had* lost her mind, Sylvian decided.

"Stand behind me. Close to the fire," he ordered. Raising his voice, he shouted for his brothers.

"They will not hurt me, but they will kill any of you they can," the voice insisted, as all the brothers joined them, including Tyr, who had just returned. "Give me your sword. Now! I will strike as many as I'm able."

Kith's eyes pierced hers. Silently, he handed her his sword.

"They fear the flames," Sylvian heard herself yell at the others. "Stay close by the fire."

"What are they?" Baldur shouted, seeing the red eyes approaching across the dark and desolate stretch of sand.

"Demon wolves. Darkling creatures. We may have to battle them until dawn. Protect your brother. He's the one they want. But they will take any of you. Their bite carries deadly venom."

"You've seen them before?" Kith asked, his tone incredulous.

"Yes. The night I was taken as a slave. The creatures descended upon the one who claimed me as a prize. Tore him and the men who tried to fight them to shreds. Once he died, they vanished as quickly as they came."

"They protect you then, Aasta?"

"Nay. If that were true, they would have saved the children slaughtered by those savages. They did not appear until my owner tried to take me. I've never been with a man. I didn't want his advances. Tonight, I wanted yours. I hoped the results would be different."

Predatory eyes glowing in dark gray fur now surrounded the fire. They stood half a man's height and circled, looking for an entry. Finding none, they drew closer and closer. Five separated from the pack and moved forward with fangs exposed, blood dripped from their lips.

"Stay next to the fire! Whatever I do, whatever happens, *don't* leave the fire." Holding the sword in both hands, Sylvian stepped toward them. Not only was she not in charge of what she said, she had no control over her actions. Please let this be a

dream and not reality, Sylvian begged silently. Her pleading evaporated as a singular frightening question filled her thoughts.
Could a person die in a drug-induced dream?

Fear flooded her mind; yet her body remained calm. She balanced the long sword back and forth in her hands, and despite the
weight of the double-edged steel, the blade felt light. Her eyes
watched the hounds, which stepped back as she moved toward
them.

She stopped and stood ready. They would try to charge past
her. She had to strike as many as she could. Who was she kidding? Herself? She'd never used a sword. She was going to die,
now, in the next moments. And her life had meant ... what?
Nothing. Absolutely nothing. But she didn't care. She wanted to
live.

As if moved by one mind, the hounds jumped. She severed
the heads of two of them and rammed her sword into a third. She
heard the other two yelp and knew they were dying quickly.
They had survived the first attack. Surprised by her expertise,
Sylvian prayed for the dawn and steadied herself for the next
onslaught.

Wave after wave, the wild animals attacked until, hours later,
blood-drenched, charcoal carcasses covered the beach around the
fire. From the number of eyes still glaring at them, Kith found
the task of counting how many remained too difficult.

He'd watched them circle, then break away from the main
pack in groups of five and ten and at times, fifteen, and hurl
themselves at them. Aasta was right. They'd avoided her and
focused their attention on the men.

When the remaining creatures withdrew, running away in
the same direction from where they had come, he knew the
dawn approached. He cautioned the others.

"Don't move from the fire until the light is upon us," he said,
marveling at Aasta's strength. She killed as many as had he and his
brothers. The actions of the wolves puzzled him. He'd never seen
animals fling themselves at people the way these had and suspected their powers were fueled by some unseen force.

Relief flooded over Kith when the first rays of light flushed the night sky, but he stood vigilant. The others followed his lead.

None moved from their watch until the sun had broken over the horizon.

Sylvian welcomed the sunlight, but her body did not respond by relaxing. Instead, the voice cautioned, "Don't touch the dead. We must burn them where they lie."

"The weapons must be purified as well," Kith said. "Tyr, tell the others to stay away from the carcasses. Baldur, take care of the weapons. The animals' behavior was strange. Burn the blood off, cleanse the blades in the ocean, fire them again, then dry them. And clean the mail. We will burn the carcasses and what's left of my tent."

Sylvian looked at the torn tent. Dark splotches of blood stained the gold-trimmed red fabric; several dead animals lay by the front flap.

"I'll get your things," Ansgar said.

"Leave them," Kith said brusquely. "Most are still on the ship. The creatures whisked in and out of the tent. I'll not carry anything they touched away from here with us. 'Tis odd, don't you think, that our clothes don't seem to have blood splattered on them?"

Ansgar, Ragnar, and Sylvian looked at one another.

"Aye, 'tis strange," she said at last. For once, Sylvian concurred with the voice.

"I know this area well. We all do. I've not seen wolf packs here before. Certainly not creatures weighing more than half my weight. Demon wolves. Released by someone or something."

The other brothers agreed.

Pointing inland from where they stood, Kith continued, "The stream just over the rise there, we'll bathe, then change. I want the outer clothes burned as well. Ansgar, pass the word to Tyr and Baldur. After you've changed, find clothes to fit Aasta. And bring me something to wear as well."

Sylvian heard herself say, "You're wise to leave nothing to chance." Had she been able to do so, she would have complimented him herself. She admired his common sense, leadership, and flexibility. He'd followed the voice's counsel about the hellhounds without question.

Although Sylvian still had no answers for her questions about how and why she was here, she was becoming caught up in the drama happening around her. She'd never felt so alive. Kith and this world seemed too three dimensional to be created solely by her mind.

Ansgar walked off, and Kith turned to her, "We have many things to speak of, but now is neither the time nor the place."

"Agreed. You'll not need oil to fire the carcasses. Most will burn in the sun's heat. Others, when touched by fire, burn faster than dry kindling. I have no explanation. They just do."

Kith watched the bodies he ignited burn like dry leaves in winter. "Not flesh as we know it. These creatures are merely shells, touched by a dark spell, but real enough to kill."

Once they disposed of the carcasses, they cleaned up. The water felt cool and refreshing. Sylvian wondered how much time would pass before she bathed again — hours or a lifetime. She didn't know. No longer did she feel a desperation to wake up. Worse, she was beginning to enjoy the hallucinosis.

Before they cast off, Kith spoke to his men. "All know where we're going and why. You've been told of last night's attack. We've lost sailing time we must recover. If any among you question the decision I've made, let him speak now or remain silent." He looked over the men.

No one spoke, not even among themselves. Despite the distance between their bonfires and their leader's, the howls should have awakened someone. Yet everyone rested in the hudfats[8], the skin sacks sheltering their bodies and keeping them warm through the attack. Even the sentries saw and heard nothing untoward until morning when the dawning light revealed a beach strewn with carcasses. They needed no more proof to blame some unseen mischief.

Silence settled over the beach. Finally satisfied, Kith ordered, "Set sail! May the wind be with us."

[8]skin sacks used as sleeping bags. See word usage.

8

Sylvian's eyes scanned the horizon, searching for the pale blue-gray etchings against the sky that signaled land. Distant whitecaps broke the illusion of a motionless sea. Nearby, the crests swirled with foam, illuminating the North Sea's variegated shades. Her vision shifted to the other ships slicing the relentless waves. Fueled by the dogged determination of sailors going home, the ships had made good time in the four days and three nights they'd been at sea. They would make home by midday.

The voyage so far had passed without incident; Sylvian now understood that to be the exception and not the rule. On the evening of the second day at sea, Kith claimed Aasta brought fortune to the fleet, and his men had agreed. Sylvian had thought the idea amusing in its naivete, but she didn't say so. She couldn't. The voice that belonged to Aasta still controlled the spoken word.

During the first day of the voyage, Aasta spoke to Kith about her dreams, recalling for him fragments of a golden land that had once been her home. There, the subtle hues of every color were vividly etched in all things. Sylvian listened for place names. Aasta gave none. The tale touched a familiar chord in Sylvian, reminding her of Wordsworth's line about birth being a sleep and a forgetting.

The conversation then turned to Aasta's life, and Sylvian experienced the memories in the retelling as if she had participated in the events. She felt the child's emotions: her rage watching the men slaughter her father and brutalize her mother; her sorrow in seeing her brave mother fall, her unbruised eye staring vacantly at her in her hiding place, warning her with its deadly silence to remain still, unseen; her pain at discovering the men had sacked the Cretan village searching for her; and her terror when the barbarians found her where her mother had hidden her.

Someone offered a big price for her, Aasta said. Who would go to such extremes for one child? Kith had asked. Aasta didn't know. The ship sank in the Mediterranean Sea; the answer died with the men.

Salty water gagged Sylvian when Aasta told of being lost at sea. She panicked at being alone in the pitching waves, saw the shoreline as Aasta did and knew the urgency of reaching its haven before the sea claimed her life. Resting on the beach for time out of mind after the strenuous swim, fearful when she awoke that others had survived and would find her, she stumbled into the dubious safety of the trees. Carefully, quietly, she slipped from the protection of one evergreen to another until she spied an open altar in a clearing. White pillars supported a stone roof. She collapsed under the shelter, her energy spent.

Sylvian sensed the passage of years as Aasta spoke of her time at the shrine. She saw the children at play — orphans of the plagues sweeping the countryside — and knew each one by name. She felt Aasta's ease of learning languages and recognized the two shipwrecked men Aasta nursed back to life as Northmen.

Aasta called the country Septimania. She'd passed years there: happy, joyous, and free until savages desecrated the shrine, killed the children, and enslaved her. Sylvian remembered reading about a narrow strip of land along the Mediterranean coast called Septimania in Dark-Ages Europe. The land, whose people remained an enigma, now lay in southwestern France.

Both tales — especially with drugs in the equation — could have been drawn from her imagination, Sylvian had decided. At first, she'd wondered time and again when the drug would wear off and she'd awaken in her world and pick up the pieces of her life.

Other questions had nagged at her as well. What if there were no drugs? No hospital in New Orleans? She had stepped into the past, and the world she knew no longer existed. Was such an occurrence even possible? She reassured herself with the scientific answer prevalent in her world: No. She saw nothing that disproved this rationale. She had no control over her words and actions, and she understood a language she'd never learned. If she were actually walking and talking and breathing in a different century on a foreign shore, neither would be true. Anything was possible in a drug-induced hallucination; thus, drugs were the only answer that made sense.

As the days at sea progressed, she had pondered these questions less and less. Yesterday, she awoke exhausted from her internal conflict and surrendered to the illusion. This simpler world burst with the immediacy of living and embraced no deadlines, no CNN, no clocks, no computerized marvels to separate her unknowingly from the feel and touch and texture of a life lived intimately with nature. Here, the hallowed gods stood exposed as hollow and deathly thieves of time.

Yawning, Sylvian stretched and sat down. Half a day or better stretched ahead before they reached land. She cradled her head in her hands and closed her eyes to block the morning light breaking across the deck.

Here, she had time to think, a luxury she hadn't allowed herself before. Her life and her world moved so quickly that she realized she'd been standing still. She'd settled for an existence, living on automatic pilot, doing the next thing and the next thing until what? she graduated, became a psychologist, got married, had a family. Always she had worked toward some event powerful enough to strip away her doubts about her worthiness. She'd spent her life searching for something or someone to jolt her alive.

Like an understudy, she memorized a role she didn't enact. Sylvian winced. She didn't know exactly how to do so, but she vowed to change her life. Her attitude. Whether she remained here or found her way home, she would savor the sheer joy of being alive. She'd find a way, she thought, as the waves lapping against the ship lulled her asleep.

In her sleep, she dreamed that she floated over vast stretches of empty space containing vague images of her life. Gradually, the fuzzy impressions gave way to one clear, perfectly formed picture: her white Thunderbird parked at the curb outside the newspaper office.

Sylvian locked the car door and walked up the steps. A shiny, chrome-and-glass revolving door stood at the entrance. Odd, she thought, what happened to the dual set of tinted, double doors? She stepped back and studied the revolving door. New. But why? She'd ask the staff. Someone might know. Then again, they might not. The public used this door, not the staff.

So what was she doing here? Why had she parked at the curb and not in the lot? She turned back toward the street. Fog lay so deep she couldn't see past her hand. Strange. She hadn't noticed the fog before.

Quickly, she spun around to see if the office had vanished in the fog as well. The door with its shiny chrome and sparkling glass stood within her grasp. Relieved, she slipped between two of the glass leaves and reached for a handrail. There was none. The door began revolving without any encouragement from her. Automated, she decided, like the faucets that turn on and off by themselves.

Halfway around, she found the area that should have opened into the building but didn't. Nor could she escape the revolving door by stepping back outside. The fog had miraculously lifted, and she could see out: the trees, the grass, her car with the dented passenger door, the street, and the buildings on the other side. But, she couldn't get out. Glass walls blocked both exits.

The door picked up momentum. She looked for an escape as her feet tried to keep up with the increased speed. She saw none. A glass cylinder seemed to encase the turnstile, which moved faster with each revolution. Shortly, she was exhausted and slowed her steps.

The glass-and-chrome leaf behind her pushed her along. She

increased her pace until she stood in the middle of the compartment and stopped, hoping the door would do the same. Instead, she was thrown against the glass leaf in front of her. Fearful she would fall and be crushed by the doors, she quick stepped to stay between the two leaves, her eyes frantically searching for an escape.

The door revolved faster and faster. Sylvian ran to stay in place. She screamed for help and saw herself standing outside in the grass. Wildly, she leapt toward the figure, hoping to shatter the glass and escape.

The revolving door vanished. Her world — the office, the car, the grass, the trees, even the other buildings — narrowed into a line on the horizon and disappeared, leaving her alone in the darkness. Terrified and enraged, she cried out: Give me my life. Now!

A figure appeared. Bathed in a halo of light, the form's features lay hidden in the shadows. Arms extended toward her.

No hands. Sylvian could see no hands protruding from the arms. Tentatively, she reached for the outstretched arms.

An ear-splitting scream behind her broke the silence: No!

Sylvian turned toward the cry. A young woman, who looked much like her, stood behind Sylvian, her hands covering her eyes. The outline of a perfect circle surrounded her form. Even as Sylvian watched, the young woman stretched her left hand and then her right hand toward her. Aasta? Sylvian wondered.

Sensing a movement behind her, Sylvian glanced over her shoulder. The haloed form had moved closer; the arms still stretched toward her. She paused, tempted to see if the figure had substance or not. She leaned closer. Reflected in the soft glow from the silent figure were swirling gray shapes reaching to touch her.

The sight chilled her. Quickly, Sylvian turned and clasped the outstretched hands of the one who looked like her. The instant their hands linked, light flooded the darkness. Aasta's life poured into hers as their personalities merged. Where there had been two separate identities, now there was one.

Sylvian awoke. She opened her eyes; daylight temporarily blinded her. The sun had climbed high in the sky while she slept. The brightness and warmth of the sun's rays made the dream seem faraway. Her eyes refocused. The ship and the sea and the sky filled her vision. The view was the same, yet different.

Life flowed through her with a harmony she'd never before known. Even though an uncertain future peopled with strangers and unknown hazards lay before her, contentment enveloped her in its protective cocoon. Despite being adrift somewhere in time, a sense of wonderment filled her.

She felt at peace resting in the oak timbers of Kith's ship. Days ago, his touch had awakened feelings she'd never experienced. No longer would she deny how she felt. She longed to be in his arms, to feel his hands stroking her breasts, to taste the fire of his kiss.

As she thought of him, her eyes unconsciously sought him out. He moved through the men toward her.

"We are within sight of land." He pointed north.

Her eyes followed his hand. Sticking up through vaporous mists, she saw hazy, blue-gray mountain peaks faintly outlined against the sky. "The mountains," she said, rising. "I see them."

"Home is there." Looking at her, Kith added, "We wed tonight."

Her body tingled with anticipation. She wanted this man as she'd wanted no other.

Kith smiled. The days they'd spent in sail had not lessened his desire for her. He could still feel the softness of her skin under his hands and ached from his passion to fill her body with his.

He stood ready to battle a thousand wild animals if that's what he must do to claim her as his. Even now, he wanted to take her in his arms but dared not. He didn't know if touching her could trigger an attack. From their talks, he knew she didn't have the answer either.

The beasts descending upon them did not operate solely

under their own power. Something or someone controlled them. Forces were at work that he did not understand.

He'd searched for the woman in his dreams in the face of every female he'd met. Now that he'd found her, he would not let her slip away from him. Logic dictated another attack could be imminent. He refused to imperil Aasta, himself, or his men. At sea, they could all be lost. When he fought, as surely he would, the battle would be on land.

"The waters we've sailed are treacherous, but we've been fortunate this trip," Kith said. "We're returning with the same number of ships that left." Silently, he hoped they would find the same luck held true at home.

"Your helmsman's skilled." Sylvian wished he would take her in his arms, and knew he wouldn't.

"He's among the best, as was his father before him." Kith replied, finding it difficult to stand this close to her without putting his arm around her, or at the least, running his fingers through her night-kissed hair. "You're observant. Most who have not sailed know little of the dangers sailors know all too well."

She smiled. "I love sailing — the wind, the smell of salt in the air, the feel of life moving under my feet."

"You have better balance than many men who've sailed all their lives." Admiration sounded in his voice. "I'm glad you like being at sea. I'm gone frequently. It's our way. Some wives travel with their husbands when they can. I'd like for you to be one of them."

"I'd like that, too."

"Some trips are too hazardous, and women aren't allowed along," Kith said.

"I wouldn't be afraid," she replied.

"I know that," Kith said. "I might be distracted, worrying about you. My preoccupation wouldn't be good for the men."

"I can wield a sword."

"Of that I have no doubt. Remember, I carry the proof. Besides, I've seen you in action."

"Safety is an illusion. A dream. You told me yourself that you raided because of the destruction of one of your villages. I'd rather die at your side, than die at home, alone."

A shadow passed across Sylvian's face. Kith looked up and was relieved to see a cloud overhead. "Let's not talk of death on our wedding day." A sense of foreboding moved through him.

"You felt the searing cold, too. A shadow moving across the world."

"The cloud above temporarily blocked the sunlight."

"A cloud passing overhead didn't cause the dread that chilled my heart," she insisted. "Whatever caused the feeling contained great harm."

Their silent look at one another spoke more eloquently than words. He wanted to reach for her, feel her against him, stroke her hair, kiss her lips. "I felt the shadow," he said at last. The effort not to sweep her up in his arms required more strength than facing a man with his battle axe. "I do not know what evoked the dread, but fear won't rule my life."

"Nor mine," she vowed. Her want of him burned fire hot inside her body, wetting her with desire.

"If I were all that mattered here, I would take you as mine now," Kith promised. "But, I'm not."

"I would welcome your advances if I were the only one who could be harmed by such a move," she replied. "But, I'm not."

Kith looked fondly over his men. "Even touching for the briefest of moments is too great a risk."

"Agreed." Her eyes followed his. She could feel the warmth of his love for his men, and she knew from their days at sea that they returned the devotion. The depth of their commitment to one another had been a revelation for her just as Kith's relationship with his brothers had been the first night.

"We're home," Kith said. His words were simple, yet they carried all the emotion that single word implied. Home. "I have things I must do."

He walked away, leaving Sylvian alone. She saw only sheer cliffs and a narrow beach. No signs of life. No village. The thought that they had been destroyed pierced her. She chided herself. The beach held no space for dwellings.

The ships fell into position one behind the other. Although they appeared to be heading for a wall of cliffs, no one around her seemed alarmed. The jagged coastline looked uninviting. Certainly, the rocks ahead claimed any ships daring to attempt a beach landing.

The nearer they came to land, the more ominous the terrain appeared. There must be an opening in the cliffs, one she could not see. Why else would they be bearing down on what appeared to be a solid wall?

Just as she despaired, the cliffs opened to reveal a fjord. She watched the waters dash against the rocks, yet the ships slipped through as though they floated on the open seas. Only a seasoned sailor and, most likely, one who knew the way would hazard the opening if he ever came close enough to see the narrow slip in the first place.

The passageway between the lofty cliffs finally parted to reveal an immense lake. On the far shore, Sylvian saw ships, a sandy beach, a waterfall, and a village perched uphill from the water. Stunned, she realized she looked upon the land Kith saw in his vision.

She imagined that when they arrived at the camp, she would have some idea of its location. After all, she'd visited most of the ancient sites. No place she'd seen had a hidden harbor. Nothing she'd read in any of her research helped either. She felt as lost as before.

"What do you call this place?" she asked Kith as he rejoined her. Maybe she would recognize the name.

"This is Eimund, the place of Eldrid, where our father, Njall, lives. His village guards the entrance to the communities and farms that lie upriver." Kith pointed past the town to the mountains rising into the clouds. "They border Arnfinnland and insulate our people from land invasions. At the far end of the waterway, sheer cliffs alone separate the village of Boden from the sea. There Tyr governs."

"Where does the sacked village lie?"

"Miles up the coast. The community did not have the same protection as these. Our family has lived along this waterway longer than memory. The leader of our people always lives here, in Eimund, as Arnfinn and the Eldrid — the old council — decreed."

Stately pines and massive oaks surrounded the perimeter of the village, seeming to shelter the living in protective arms. The settlement was larger than Sylvian anticipated. Rectangular timbered houses dotted the far landscape. In the foreground were rows of shops.

Sylvian had never heard of Eimund or Arnfinnland. Surely, this soil would, in the centuries ahead, become Norway. Perhaps the specific location didn't matter. The world she knew would not exist for more than a thousand years.

"I don't live in the long house of my father as many unmarried sons do," Kith said. "I have my own lodging. My brothers will join us there. They are finding clothes for you. All of us, together, will go and see Njall."

An uneasy feeling filled Sylvian at the mention of Kith's father, yet later, when she met him, she couldn't explain her earlier discomfort. Slightly shorter than Kith, he had a robust physique and a quick mind.

"You were prudent, Kith, to return," Njall told them. "I've had another vision since I received word your ships had been spotted coming through the straits. With your return, safety nets us. Tyr, Baldur, Ragnar, and Ansgar will begin the journey home with their men today. They will return with their wives for the wedding, which will be at the next full moon. That will give us time to prepare for such an event."

Despite their initial protests, Njall's will prevailed. Sylvian remembered Kith's words on the beach that first night. There could be only one leader. Here, that is Njall.

Not more than an hour later, they watched the brothers' ships depart. Sylvian knew a disaster she was powerless to stop lay ahead. "At least your brothers will be safe," she told Kith, who stood next to her.

"Did you not hear our father? As long as they are gone before the sun sets on the water, we will be safe," Kith replied, also uncertain of the wisdom of his father's words. He knew of no reason why their leaving before the sun set would make Eimund safe from harm.

"What does their being gone have to do with our safety? Their absence lessens the chances of success simply by decreasing the number fighting on our side."

"I do not disagree with you," Kith said. "The others feel the same. But, we must do as we're told. Our father would not place us in jeopardy. Surely, you cannot think he would?"

She sighed. "No. I don't. But, his vision is wrong. From the time of this sunset until the next, I will be in danger. I know that to be true. We will not be wed at the next full moon. I will not survive that long."

Kith longed to reach out for Aasta and comfort her. He also had his doubts. Aasta had been correct about the demon wolves. Their father's vision that Kith would have been killed if his brothers had not been with him had also been true. He and Aasta would not have been able to fight off the attack alone. He'd already expressed his concern before everyone. "Our father said you are safe here, with us, in this village."

"If that is true, why must we wait?"

"He wants the families present for the wedding."

Exasperated, she said, "I understand that. But, if I'm safe here, why must we wait to consummate our love?"

"What are you suggesting?" He knew the answer to the question before he asked. He'd had the same thoughts, but he'd not dared express them to her.

"We go to your home, now, lock the door, and finish what we began four nights ago on the beach."

"We won't be married."

"We wouldn't have been married the other night either," she pointed out.

"Yes, and we know what happened," Kith replied.

"Your father said I am safe here. Sheltered — his word — against this unusual power. He insisted that is why we can wait and have a proper ceremony. If he is right and I am wrong, then no harm will come to us if we spend time together now."

She looked across the water, then she turned her attention back to Kith. "I want you, and you want me. Neither of us is being forced against our will. We can say our own vows."

"Our own vows." He liked the idea.

"If your father is wrong and I am right, I will be dead before sunrise. And you may be dead as well. The only hope we have, that I see, is to finish what we began before it's too late, if it isn't already so."

A mischievous glint appeared in Kith's eyes. "Why are we standing here?" He wanted to embrace her. Instead, he began walking up the beach toward the village.

Before they reached his house, a guard Njall sent to find Kith stopped them. One of the men had spotted dead animals lying in a heap about a half mile inside the forest. Njall wanted Kith to see what could have caused the carnage and report back to him. Kith turned to Sylvian. He saw her doubtful look and hoped his words would reassure her. "I'll return as soon as I can."

She feared for them both. "May I not go with you?" Her eyes implored him to say yes. "I've not seen the forest except from a distance. To walk under the trees would help me feel at home."

"Stay close by me," Kith said, sensing her alarm. "We won't have long. The woods get dark early."

The deep, dark, primeval forest felt alien to Sylvian despite the familiar pines, spruce and oaks. They searched for the better part of two hours but did not find any mound of dead animals.

The young soldier, anguished by his failure to lead them to the carcasses, swore again and again he didn't make up the story. Sylvian believed him. The longer they searched, the stronger she sensed an ominous presence lurking nearby.

They passed through a particularly thick grouping of trees. In the dense underbrush, she temporarily lost sight of the others. She walked forward cautiously. Instead of firm ground beneath her, she stepped off into a ravine and tumbled forward. Her hands frantically grabbed for something to hold on to but found nothing. She rolled over herself.

Seconds later, Sylvian lay flat on her back. The ground felt colder than death. Before she could scramble to her feet, an icy blade pierced her heart, pinning her to the ground. She screamed and reached for the sword. Nothing was there. Chills shook her body.

"Aasta! Aasta! Where are you?"

"Here! Over here!" She struggled to her feet. The phantom blade frightened her more than the demonic wolves. They, at least, had form — bodies they had burned in the morning sunlight.

"Aasta!"

Kith's voice came from above her. Not until then did she realize the depth of the ravine.

"Take my hand." Kith reached down for her.

Shaken by her experience, she resolved not to make matters worse. "I can climb out." As much as she wanted to let him pull her out, she feared touching him, especially in this unprotected place. She felt as if she were standing in a grave. "Stand back and let me try." After a few false starts, she managed to get a strong enough hold to hoist herself out.

"Are you hurt?" Kith asked, his tone gentle.

"No, just a little dirty and shaken." She dusted herself off.

"I know these woods well." His thoughtful tone brooded. "When I last passed this way, there wasn't a drop off this steep by the path. We're going back. The lengthening shadows mock our search. And the woods feel treacherous to me."

They made their way back to the town without another mishap and still with no sight of what they had been seeking. The men grumbled among themselves about their failure.

"We'll return in the morning when the light's better," Kith told the guards as they neared his home. "I do not doubt you saw what you saw. So, for tonight, keep a sharp lookout and double the sentries. Tell Njall we will look again tomorrow."

The men looked slightly more optimistic when they parted.

Kith bolted the door of his house as soon as they stepped inside. Despite the lack of fire, Sylvian found the room to be not uncomfortably cold. The turf walls, which looked to be at least six feet thick, well insulated the interior.

Soon, he had the fire blazing.

Sylvian wondered as she watched the smoke rise through the vent in the roof how she could feel safe and in danger at the same time.

"We're finally alone." Kith sat on a pallet of furs he had placed not far from the fire. "Will you join me? We've been through much to steal these moments."

"I don't know your forest, but I felt an unhealthy presence lurking in its midst." She sat down next to him.

"Do you still believe your life is at risk tonight?"

"Yes." Her voice trembled.

"Do you think if we finish what we began four nights ago on the beach that your life will be safe?"

"I don't know." She looked into his eyes, then shook her head. "I'm not sure. Such a bold act may cause your death and do little to save me."

"What if we don't?"

"I'm lost. Of that, I'm sure."

His arms enclosed her so quickly she had no time to object or speak before his lips closed over hers. Again, she felt as if his breath gave her life. She drank in his kiss, matching his passion with her own. For stolen moments they remained locked in the kiss, their bodies flaming with an intensity that paled the glow of the fire blazing nearby.

"Take me now," she gasped.

Before Kith could respond, someone began pounding on the door.

"Hurry," she urged.

The bolt splintered apart and the door flew open. Njall burst

91

into the room. "We're being attacked from the woods. Come with me," he ordered.

"I'm right behind you," Kith replied, standing up.

"Now," Njall demanded. He turned and pointed to the men who had followed him inside. "They'll guard Aasta."

"Leave me a sword," she requested, also standing.

"You'll find weapons in the other room." Kith grabbed his sword and battle axe. "A sword is among them. I must go."

"You'll be safe here." Njall turned and followed his son outside.

Despite the warmth of the room, Sylvian shivered. Would she ever see Kith again? Desperately she hoped so, but she feared the worst. Her earlier apprehension about Njall returned. He terrified her. And she didn't know why.

Walking into the other room, she found a sword and battle axe. She picked them up and stood staring at the weapons. Had she come this far to die just when she'd learned how to live? She prayed not. She returned to the fire. A small voice within urged her to keep the flames white hot.

She sat on a bench close by the fire where she could see the door — the only way in except for the vent in the roof. She then did the only thing she could. She waited, alert and vigilant.

Ambush

9

*T*he carnage of Kith's men drenched the meadow with blood. In the forest where he lay dying, their still forms served as silent, accusing reminders of his foolish trust. His pierced chest pounded with excruciating pain.

The warrior leaned close and hissed, "Your woman is ours."

Kith wheezed and struggled to rise.

"Your efforts do you no good," the butcher bellowed arrogantly. "You are frozen to the ground. Your voice, a gasp. We've seen to that. We have such delectable plans for your precious Aasta. So, pretty prince, close your eyes and see the future."

Kith's eyes closed. He heard the malicious delight in his adversary's voice when he spoke again.

"While you lie dying, dream of our fingers running through her midnight hair. Stroking her satiny skin. Caressing her rose-peaked breasts. See our conquest of her ripened maidenhood. Such exquisite torture for you, isn't it?"

Rage boiled white hot in Kith. Laboring as hard as he could, he couldn't move. His eyes remained shut; his mouth, voiceless.

"There is more. So much more. You and your family kept us from victory once. You won't again. Now is our time to howl on your graves. And we will." The usurper's fingers pressed Kith's wounded chest. "Open your eyes, Norseman!"

Kith's skin burned where his opponent touched him. He watched helplessly as his foe licked his blood-drenched fingers. "Ah, revenge is sweeter than the taste of blood on our lips." His enemy dipped his fingers again and sucked them dry.

Kith struggled fruitlessly as the fiend leaned over, slid his tongue down the flat side of the blade that pinned Kith to the ground, and lapped at the gushing wound. His form began changing as he drank, altering into that of the fallen Norseman.

His attacker rose, jammed the blade deeper into the ground and smacked the remaining blood off his lips. "Once we've had our fill of your woman, we will drain all her energies. She will die. We will take her form and possess her power. Her scrumptious body will be ours forever. You will hear every word, every moan, every cry, every scream until we have absorbed her. Our victory shout will be the last cry your mortal ears will ever hear, vexing you until you draw your last breath."

Low, guttural laughter exploded from the body thief. "Isn't that delightful? Close your eyes, now. Die slowly, Norseman, and dream of your love in our arms."

His adversary vanished.

Kith lay helpless, his body racked with pain, his heart flooded with agony while he dreamed of his fair beauty ravished by his slayer. He cried to the gods he'd never believed in to save him. In desperate prayer, he sought to stop the monster.

Aasta screamed, and Kith felt the heat of a thousand fires burn around him. Silence as deep as the death that filled the forest shrouded him; the gully that earlier trapped Aasta had become his grave. The enemy had been of their own kin, Njall's men, lurking shadows hiding invisibly in the night's protective darkness. Their slaughter had been merciless.

He cursed his foolishness. He'd blindly followed his father into the woods. And yet, why would he do otherwise? He had no reason to fear his own father.

When Njall turned on him, he'd been ill prepared to fight him. He tried; he ran his sword through him. Njall threw his head back and laughed, the sound rising deep from within him and resonating throughout the woods.

Then Kith knew — the being standing before him was not his father. The body looked like Njall's, but the mannerisms and the voice changed. The words rasped, hissed, bellowed; the sound echoed inside Kith's head. We and us replaced I and me as if a collective presence spoke to him through his father's body.

The pain in Kith's chest exploded. He choked on his own blood and gasped. His hold on consciousness slipped. He felt something brush against his chest, ripping away his byrnie, which had protected him in so many battles until this one. The sword was lifted out.

A cool and refreshing liquid fell on his chest and face. Fingers gently moved his lips apart, and the elixir trickled into his mouth. The fluid tasted of earth and herbs and spring water. He could not drink enough.

"Awake." The voice was as gentle as a spring breeze.

Kith opened his eyes. A comely, green-eyed beauty knelt over him, her tears fell freely on his body. The pain in his chest vanished. "Is this death?"

Her responding laughter carried the heat of sunshine, the shimmer of moonlight, the rage of storms, and the gentleness of a spring shower. When the laughter ceased, sorrow wrenched his heart.

"Do not speak," she whispered. She put her fingers to his mouth. Her touch was as fleet as a hummingbird's flutter. "Arise."

He rose. She motioned for him to follow her. They walked out of the woods to the water's edge. He turned to look at the village.

"Do not look back," she commanded, her voice firm yet soft. His eyes were drawn back to hers. "Only look ahead. At the lake."

He did as she wished. She turned, waved her arm over the water, and an ornately carved, silver-and-golden hued barge appeared in front of them. The vessel's sails shimmered with starlight. "Take my hand."

Kith's hand closed over hers, and instantly he was aboard. He sensed they no longer navigated on the lake, but instead sailed in the open sea. Before he confirmed his instinct, she placed her fingers on his forehead, and smoothing them over his eyes, said,

"Sleep now and rest."

How long they sailed, he didn't know. When he awoke, his eyes beheld the clearest night sky his memory recalled. The stars appeared close enough to reach out and touch, while the moon bathed the world around him with a brilliance that breathed with life. He lay on a mound of dew-dampened grass beside a sandy beach. He sat up and looked around. The barge rested on the sand not ten feet away. He was alone.

Kith wondered what land he stood upon. *Where had his savior gone?* He carried no weapon, yet he felt unafraid. He stood and turned around. The light from a fire some distance inland caught his eye. He walked toward the flames.

10

Drakus glowered at the dark, still waters of the lake. Thoughts murkier than the coal-black irises of The Beast's eyes ignited the fiery pupils with rage. The night held secret the creature's shaking body, the form alternately shape shifting[9] between the burly Njall and a sinewy-limbed being.

The Norseman could not be found. Kith the Bold, Drakus snorted. Bold. Ha! Stupid. We rammed him through with the blade. Left him dying, dying. He should be dead, dead, his body rotting, *rotting*. But no. Gone. The body — gone!

Dead bodies don't get up, brush themselves off and walk away. Nor does Valhalla claim these puny creatures. The vain Kith the Stupid does not sit in Odin's palace. Nor does he feast on the wild boar, Saehrimnir.

We are Valhalla for these petty beings, Drakus grumbled silently. We are Drakus, The Beast, The Hunter, the one and only Hunting Beast. We drank his blood. Our power traces his body. Drakus spit. Smoke rose from the soil the saliva touched. Nothing. We find nothing.

An answer stole from the outer reaches of Drakus's memory and burst full blown into The Hunting Beast's cavernous mind, wiping out all other possibilities. No. Yes. No. Yes. Had to be. Had to be. An unspeakable deed had been done.

They saved him.

The Nyx witches spirited the weakling away.

The Beast sniffed the air, feeling, waiting, evaluating. Did the

[9]changing the appearance of the body. See word usage.

Nyx walk this shore? Drakus sniffed again. Nothing. Too subtle a scent.

Pacing the ground, The Beast tried to feel the Nyx with each step. No trail. Many came, The Beast decided. One would not risk coming alone.

The Nyx have Kith. The thought enraged Drakus almost as much as the missed opportunity with Astraea. How could the careful hunt fail? The might, the right to take her is ours. Ours. Timing. Everything hinges on timing.

Long moments passed as the sorcerer's mind traced and retraced the events prior to Kith's disappearance. The Norseman bleeding to death in his own blood. Drinking only enough to take the weakling's appearance. No more. Just enough to turn the spell and leave Kith alive to hear his love's lament.

Aasta. Drakus snickered. The fool Norseman didn't even know her name. We did. The beauty would have been under proper supervision years ago if the ship hadn't wrecked at sea. The foolhardy captain chanced dangerous waters and lost. Had we but been on board, we would have followed her.

No time for regrets. We could not go near her until now without risking losing everything. We found her lackey lover. No small task. We designed the perfect plan. Nothing could go wrong. The Nyx witch is to blame. She didn't fight.

The moment her twenty-fifth birthday lay upon her, the witch stood by the fire, a sword in one hand, a battle axe in the other. Her thoughts lay obscure. But we felt her determination. We did. We did. The moment we walked into the house, she resolved to fight. We felt her heart beating fast. She prepared to strike. The Beast ripped off Njall's byrnie, crushed the interlocking metal rings between its hands, and threw the balled remains toward the lake. The fire. The fire. Our nemesis. Again the fire.

Astraea breathed with mortal breath. Not the timing, the disguise. How could she see through the illusion? With mortal eyes she couldn't distinguish us from Kith. But, she did. Somehow — she did. Our minds linked through her blood, her virginal power, but her thoughts lay dark. Why did she not fight? Had she fought, she would be ours now. And the door would be open to the Nightstar. We could slip through. How did she know?

Drakus paced back and forth. How? How? She held the weapons. She meant to fight. She didn't. She didn't. She stepped into the blazing fire. Even then instinct said follow, follow, fast, now. Too quick she moved. Too fleet of foot. The fire exploded. Now nothing remains of the house. Nothing. Not even ashes.

How! The Beast smashed fists against hands. Again and again. Over and over. Witch. Such a slight slip of a being. Sideways she could barely be seen at all. No more than a morsel. A treat. Yet, she eluded her hunter. The Nightstar warned her. Must have. Must have. No other way.

The Beast's viperous eyes narrowed. We must have the rest of her. All of her. Everything. Only when our hunting beast form lies clothed in her supranatural body can we walk unharmed into the flames; drink the salt water and have no energy drain from our glorious selves; need no longer replenish our body with the disgusting and inadequate shells of humans.

Then, only then can we alter the face of the Earth; control the weather, the mountains, the accursed seas, and bring our legions to life. Twenty-one-hundred years we waited for the moment. And victory slipped away again. Twenty-one-hundred years. Surely, the Nyx witch will return sooner next time!

The Beast threw back its head, opened its mouth and screeched. The high pitched shriek shook the ground. Rocks secured by solitary pines and oaks broke loose from the cliffs surrounding the lake. Avalanches of wood and leaves and stone and soil rumbled down the mountainsides. *If we had your power you Nyx witch, we could destroy this land and everything in it.*

Howling, Drakus called the hellhounds and turned to Eimund. The Hunter's acute night vision passed over the destruction. The eyes glowed. Fire shot from the pupils, scorching the ground nearby. Disgusting. We can make fire, yet the flames burn our flesh. They might destroy our magnificent body. Don't know. Don't know. Maybe. Maybe not. The pain from flames say run.

Sever Eimund's history. Yes. Yes. Sever Eimund's history. Drakus smirked. The idea pleases us. Kith's followers turn to dust. We have no claim on them. Njall's are ours. All ours. Even now they wait to satiate our hunger. Petty creatures. Their lust for power caused our failure. They warned the witch. Not the Nightstar. They will pay. We will take their history, absorb them until no one remains. Without a past, Njall's people have no future. We shall leave no trace behind.

Drakus roared with delight. The rats. When we're done, we call the rats, their sharp teeth will erase the words of these spawn of Arnfinn from the earth.

Five villages. Drakus sniggered. Much to do. The Beast slithered toward Eimund, the hellhounds lapping at its heels.

The fiend's shadow swelled in the torch light as Drakus walked up the broad, dirt avenue separating the shops from the houses. The Beast's feet crushed the already broken bodies lying in its path. Ah! The feel of bones breaking under our weight. So refreshing. So right. So perfectly delicious. A baby cried ahead. Hunting eyes glowed as they searched the body-strewn road for even the slightest movement among the dead.

In two quick steps Drakus stood over the baby. The Beast's lips curled up in a sneer. The Hunter picked up the infant — a maiden would have been, an offspring of Njall's. Ours to claim. A treat. Biting the baby on the neck, Drakus drained the blood, dropped the body, and, stepping on the rag-doll remains, walked toward the center of the community.

Licking wet lips with its forked tongue, The Beast smiled. They caused us to miss our chance. They will pay with their Breath. Tomorrow another life, another time, another chance. Kith still lives. He will be ours. We will capture him, torture him, own him. We will. We will. The Nyx make the Norseman strong. No matter. Kith cannot endure against our might. We will have the Nyx witch as well. Astraea will be ours. Then our little surprise for the powerful Nightstar. We know the way. The control to the power. The Hunting Beast rubbed its hands together with glee. Next time we will have them both. Forever.

Now, fuel. Fuel. We need fuel. Controlling minds costs too much energy. Our human army may provide enough energy to avoid the long sleep. Drakus fondly eyed the hounds waiting for orders. Our creations can take the other villages, but these humans belong to us. Our treat. Ah, such pleasurable moments lie ahead.

Casting its eyes upon the bodies covering the ground, The Beast levitated several into a pile, sat on top and growled. The hounds stood at attention behind their creator. Concentrating, Drakus drew Njall's men. Quietly, they left their posts and lined up in five single files in front of The Beast. When they'd all responded, Drakus froze them in place and released their thoughts to roam freely, then called their women and children.

We must have enough light so the humans can see, Drakus thought, but not too much. Not too much. Light with shadows. Humans fear the shadows. The darkness. Hands circled above the shape shifter's head. Still, enough to see by. The torches blazed with the intensity of late afternoon when the shadows of night begin stealing across the world.

Stepping off the human seat, Drakus walked up to the auburn-haired youth standing closest. Young flesh. Barely eighteen. Tasty. The Beast ripped the man's byrnie open, bit into his neck, purposefully avoiding the jugular vein, and chewed the morsel, watching expressions of rage form on the villagers' faces.

The Beast bit again, this time taking a larger chunk of flesh. The young Norseman screamed. Such sweet music. The sound of suffering. Rage gave way to horror as the others struggled to move and found their feet frozen to the ground.

Drakus's hands roved across the youth's broad chest. Jagged nails punctured the skin; dexterous fingers dug deep until they closed around the heart. The Beast yanked the beating organ out into the open, savoring the shocked look on the man's face in the instant before death overtook him. In the same frozen moment in time, the incubus opened its mouth, and breathing deeply, absorbed the escaping spirit.

The Beast sucked the heart dry, crushed the organ in its

palms and threw the remains on the ground. Licking wet fingers, Drakus commanded, "Feed," and knocked the dead body over. The hounds fell upon the corpse, ripping flesh from bones.

Drakus smiled at the Norseman next in line. "Come." The Beast motioned with its fingers.

"Nay." The strapping blond, strong from battle and rowing the long oars, struggled to refuse without success.

Drakus howled. "We are your Valkyries. Your Valhalla. You are ours. All of you. For all time. When we are through, no part of you will be left for the carrion seekers to eat. We will —" Drakus pointed to his creations "absorb every morsel of your being. Fight. Struggle. Scream. Cry. Curse us and whatever vain gods you believe in. Your cries of torment are sweeter than the plucking of a harp to our ears."

Drakus's hands ripped the seasoned warrior's woolen garment from his shoulders and tore his leather-padded breastplate from his chest. The Beast's fingers slunk across the flesh, its index finger resting on the throbbing jugular vein. Drakus knew the man's thoughts even before touching his flesh. "You know your fate. In moments we will contain your Breath. First pleasure so the pain will be all the more intense when it comes."

Drakus planted the sensations in the Norseman's mind that his young, favorite wife, Ingrid, stood before him, caressing his body. The Norseman's flesh hardened; he moaned with pleasure.

Drakus cackled. Humans are so easy; they are almost no fun at all. Almost. They are the abomination, the scourge of Earth, an accident, and ours to harvest. That truth had always been and always will be. The Beast basked in the fear.

But would their terror be enough to totally recharge? Drakus frowned. We don't know. The Beast sighed. If not, we must seal ourselves off until we are strong again. Not such a bad trade, The Beast thought, looking over the human suffering that would provide entertainment, amusement during the long sleep.

Next time we'll have Astraea and the infernal Nightstar. Then we never have to hide again. The thought made the Hunting Beast's body tingle all over.

The Beast turned its attention back to the tow-headed Norseman and imagined scorpions stinging his body.

The warrior screamed in agony.

Drakus chuckled. Ah! Such a glorious sound. But the fun could be so much greater. The Beast called the young Ingrid from her place with the other women. She struggled against moving without success. The Beast yanked her lithe body over the corpses covering the ground between them.

When she lay at its feet, The Beast looked upon her with pleasure. Her body quivered like a cornered doe's. Her eyes, the color of a clear, morning sky, darted about desperately seeking escape. Reaching for the thick, blonde hair plaited in a braid that fell to her waist, Drakus pulled her upright until she stood facing her husband. She wept as The Beast's fingers ripped the wool dress off her shoulders; its hands reached for her fulsome breasts and squeezed them, not too hard at first. She screamed.

"Lovely, isn't she?" Drakus smiled at her husband, whose once virile body swelled from the poisonous stings. The Beast's jagged nails pierced the husband's neck; its tongue darted forth and licked the wound. One jagged nail skillfully pierced the right nipple of Ingrid's breast. The Beast lapped Ingrid's blood, then adroitly buried its tongue in her husband's wound.

"Our parting gift to you," Drakus hissed, taking strength from the man's agonized moans. "You lovers are together forever in us. Her blood runs with yours. You feel her terror, her pain even now, just as she feels yours. The pain is delicious, is it not?"

The Norseman sobbed.

Drakus chuckled. "As we thought. Delectable. Even after we've inhaled your Breath and our creations have cleaned your bones and they've been ground into a fine powder for our bed, we can play this sport again and again. Forever. Whenever we choose."

Drakus turned to Ingrid. "We shall save you 'til last." The Beast's hand rubbed across the open wound. Her loss of blood slowed to a drip, then stopped. Her heart beat faster than a bird's. The Beast's touch lingered, savoring the glorious trembling of her terror. "We shall have such fun, our pretty one. We promise."

"No, please, please don't," Ingrid whimpered.

"Oh, but we must, our sweet pet." The Beast licked her blood from its palm. "It is as ordained. We are Drakus, The Beast, The Hunter, The Hunting Beast. We are health. Humans are disease. Born to die. We are salvation. You are lost, dust only without us. We are your power, your greed, your reward for readily betraying your kinsmen. You are our harvest. We shall never let you go."

The Beast sneered, its teeth gleaming like tiny daggers as the creature's shape shifted back and forth between Njall and its multi-limb form.

Ingrid screamed. Tears flowed down her flushed cheeks. Her body shook uncontrollably. Her breath came in short pants.

"We please you." The Beast relished her fright, finding her suffering and horror more refreshing than cool water wetting parched lips. Drakus converted her pain into fuel for the hunting beast body, then leaned toward the tormented Ingrid, seared her skin by licking her teary cheek, and whispered coarsely, "You will lie with us in the long sleep, our little treat. We may even take your form. Such an honor for you. Centuries have passed since we walked in a woman's body."

Drakus could wait for the Nightstar, especially when the rapture of such bounty lay ahead. The ghoul bit the Norseman's stout neck, its sharp teeth ripping the man's jugular vein. In moments, The Beast drained the blood and inhaled the Breath, then knocked the body over for the hounds to finish.

Ingrid wailed, her cry rising unattended into the night.

"We mustn't let our pretty pet sob alone. The Norse feign bravery, but we know what to do." The Beast twisted its arms over its head.

Scorpions scurried across the ground, crawled up the men, women and children the bewitcher held in its spell, and began stinging the Norse until their tearful cries washed the night with a cacophony of suffering.

"Ah, the music of ecstasy." Not too much, Drakus thought.

We mustn't let any die before we've attended to them personally. The Beast cocked its head and listened. Satisfied, the creature snapped its fingers. The scorpions vanished; the tortured cries built to a crescendo.

Drakus stepped to the next man in line. "Shall we dance?"

Tremors shook the man's body.

Drakus chortled with delight. Duty called. Hours of darkness and pleasure lay ahead.

Timeless

11

*D*awn colored the night sky as Kith drew nearer the fire. He saw four women sitting by the flames. One was the green-eyed beauty who had brought him to this place. Despite their loveliness, for they were wondrous fair to look upon, and their appearance of being human, he knew instinctively they were not. He drew closer until he could hear their words, then he stopped.

"Our sister is dead again," said one. Her silvery blonde hair sparkled in the moonlight. "Gone far away from our influence. We could not save her. Even though she rode the mortal breath to life, she is still one of us. To bring her back would call The Beast to our world. She knew what she had to do. We have no choice but to continue to watch and wait until she returns again. For return she will. We know this for certain now."

Did she speak of Aasta? Kith's heart pounded. He knew the answer. Dead. Lost to him. The revelation devastated him. He wanted to scream but forced his silence.

The one whose words had laid waste to his dreams looked in his direction. Standing, she motioned for him to join them. "You are a different matter." Her attention focused on him.

As if she issued some silent command, he stepped closer. She was almost as tall as he. "Our sister, Rana, brought you here. You forfeited your life before when you rushed in to save the one you call Aasta. Had we not intervened, you would have died again."

They were all standing now. Kith's eyes moved from one to the next. "My wounds were mortal. How did you call me from the dead?"

108

"We have not the power to raise the dead." The willowy blonde looked at him as she spoke. Her brown-and-gold cat eyes mesmerized. "Your life slipped from you, but you still lived. We have the power to intercept death, but are only allowed to do so when the mortal we heal has been touched by one of us. Your Aasta is our sister. Although as you knew her she was human flesh and blood, she originally came from our world."

"Is this your ... country?" Kith asked, looking around at the wild terrain. He felt certain he stood on an island, but the trees were unfamiliar to him and taller than any he'd ever seen. The lush vegetation had an uninhabited look. Yet, something about the landscape seemed vaguely familiar.

"No. We are between our worlds," came the reply. "Many of your generations ago you were here briefly when your body sealed this entrance. There then existed a doorway between this fire and the flame at the shrine." She pointed to the smoldering blaze. "You do not remember the portal. Life had slipped from your body, but your Breath lingered nearby and glimpsed this land and the sea and the fire before passing on."

The green-eyed Rana spoke. "Your thoughts are correct, Kith the Bold, son of Njall, descendent of Arnfinn the Rune Master. We are not human as you know flesh and blood. Nor are we from your world."

Amazed, Kith questioned, "You read my thoughts?"

"The task is not hard. Particularly with someone I have touched. You will find the ability easy to master."

"Are you gods then?" Kith asked, more confused than ever.

"Nay, although humans who glimpse someone from our world, sometimes mistake us for gods," Rana replied. "When our sister tended the mountain shrine, we walked freely in your world. Now we pass unseen."

She looked at the others. Silence followed. Kith sensed the sisters were speaking even though their lips were still.

"We live in a world that runs parallel to yours," Rana continued. "We have the same sun and moon. Walk the same ground. Breathe the same air. Yet, our dimension is different from yours. So, although our worlds border one another, they do not merge."

"What do I call you?" Kith asked.

"We are of the Nyx; members of the watch who nightly guard the flames lying at the north and south portals separating worlds," said the statuesque blonde. "Our counterparts, the Dag, stand guard in the light. All of our kind, Dag or Nyx, share similar abilities, but each has an expertise. I am as the silent bird in flight, the wings of the night, the night wind. I am Arva. I hear sounds no mortal has ever heard." She shrugged. "And those other immortals seldom hear."

She turned to the one who had brought him there. "You met Rana, whose sail floats over the ebb and flow of the waves at her bidding. She is most at home on water, particularly the oceans. Her sense of smell is legendary even among our own people. The dangers that ride the night breeze are hers to be read with a single, focused breath." Rana wiggled her nose and smiled at Kith.

"The magic of the night fills Niniane." Arva pointed to the sister with hair the color of dark earth after a storm. "The forest responds to her intimate touch as do all living creatures. Her greatest strength lies in her ability to heal." Niniane bowed her head to him.

Kith acknowledged the introduction then watched the redhead, whose energy he could feel across the twenty or so feet separating them.

"This is Nata, the dancer whose rhythm is unmatched among the Nyx. Agile and fearless, she bears the sacred flame. Her sense of taste is acute. In an instant, she knows the night's pleasure and pain."

"You named our sister well, Kith the Bold," Nata said. "She is Astraea, bearer of the Nightstar. Her vision is as clear by moonlight as it is in the daylight and almost as penetrating in the dark."

Kith mistrusted Arva's words. He felt certain they had greater powers than her words allowed.

"Your perception is correct," Arva said, acknowledging his unspoken doubts. "But what I have said must suffice for introductions. Only by having these abilities can you know what they mean."

Not until then did Kith realize the sun had not risen. Instead, the night sky had remained the same, with just the trace of dawn. The moon still hung heavy overhead. Those singular differences let him know more than their words had that he did not stand in the world he'd always known.

"We float in the midst of dimensions between worlds and outside of time," said Rana. "The sun will not rise here nor will the moon set, but one always takes precedence over the other. Now it is night. The moon is bright. At dawn, the silvery light of the moon gives way to the golden glow of the sun. Yet, the moon is still with us. Here." She waved her arms to encompass the land and the sea and finally the sky. "At this portal."

The ease with which she read his mind unnerved him, but he didn't know how to stop her.

"You will learn." She smiled.

Kith understood action. He'd never been one to dwell on what he couldn't do but rather on what he could accomplish. He decided to try another approach. "What do you want of me?"

"You love our sister, and she loves you," said Arva. "You knew each other before. Then you gave your life trying to save her. She carried you with her into the fire. Both your lives passed away in the flames."

Kith frowned, trying to remember. Arva's words made no sense. He had died before? He and Aasta. Together. How could he die, yet live? The words of his attacker raced through his thoughts: *You and your family kept us from victory once. You won't again. Now it's our turn to howl on your graves. And we will.*

Arva continued. "The memory will come if you become one of us. We offer you that choice. You may become as we are and live without death or return to your world as you are. If you choose the latter, you will age and die."

Kith shook his head. "Your words confuse me." A tremor shook him. "You said your sister died many years ago? Yet, you say you are immortal."

"All life is immortal," Niniane said softly. "Even in death there is life. For us, death does not come in the same way it does for mortals."

"Niniane, enough explanation," Nata said, curtly. Niniane opened her mouth to object, but Nata cut her off again, saying, "Our friend needs an example."

Scowling at Nata, Niniane snapped her fingers. The sisters lowered their heads like rams squaring off for a fight. Silent moments passed, as the air stirred restlessly between them. Finally, Niniane sighed and looked away. "Go ahead."

Nata turned to him, the smoldering intensity of her stare passed through him. "Watch." She stepped slightly away from the fire.

Her hand formed a fist, then opened as she threw her arm forward slightly to the right of him. Blue-white bolts of lightning shot from her fingers, singeing the ground next to him. The energy crackled in the air; tiny flames flared in the dirt. Kith watched in amazement as she controlled the individual blazes with her eyes. Some grew larger, others smaller. She waved her hand as if dismissing them, and they vanished.

Kith turned his view from the charred ground and back on her. She stepped into the fire, then vanished. Before he could speak, she reappeared and walked out of the flames unharmed.

"We pass unharmed through the flames," Nata said. "Most humans do not. The Nightstar's life force had been halved. The creature who had just corrupted her body and stolen most of her blood had acquired enough of her power to follow her through the flames. She did what her duty required. She blocked her assailant's entrance with your body and remained in the fire. You were consumed together."

Kith shuddered. He sensed the experience lying just outside his memory. "Is this the one who has destroyed my father? And now me?"

"Yes," replied Arva.

"Who is he? What is he?"

"Drakus — The Beast Drakus," Rana said. "The creature's

origin is unknown to us. We know what the fiend is not. The incubus is neither male nor female, but rather an androgynous being with the characteristics of both. Yet the parasite prefers a masculine host. Neither is The Beast human nor one of us, but rather a mixture of all I have named and more. Part of its original power the creature acquired through murder and theft." She glanced questioningly at Arva.

"The alchemist to whom the creature apprenticed had much knowledge," Arva said. "A powerful wizard, the greatest of his kind, he could read the secrets of the Earth and knew of our existence. But he fell blind to his pupil's dark nature. His failure to see the truth cost him his life."

Anger overwhelmed Kith. "I will return to my world and kill this creature. With my brothers' help, we can succeed."

Niniane's voice was as soft as a gentle shower. "Nay. You will go to your death. And your brothers will die as well. The Beast Drakus cannot be stopped by human power alone."

"You can help me stop this beast!" Kith exclaimed.

"Nay. If we lift a hand against our foe, the creature might gain admittance to our world," Niniane explained. "Our elders say nay."

"You would allow our world to be destroyed as long as yours is protected!" Kith roared, enraged.

"Our enemy can rule neither world unless it gains access to ours," Arva replied. "That is why we must not act overtly against it. As it exists now, The Beast works evil by influencing humans' minds, twisting them to its will, manipulating them through the subterfuge of illusions, while feeding on their fears."

"The Beast's negative energy is powerful but unstable," Rana added. "Direct confrontation lessens its control. The power required for an all-out war on mortals could cause the creature to build enough energy internally to destroy itself. It will not run that risk."

More disturbed than before, Kith demanded, "What about my father! This thief took over his mind and body."

"Aye, the bewitcher holds that power," Niniane said, confirming Kith's words.

Nata spoke up. "The bloodsucker would have taken your life as it took your form, but, fortunately, the creature wanted you to suffer during its victory. The Beast hoped to fool our sister and failed. When you remember your first encounter with our enemy, you will understand about your family. About you. Until then —" she shrugged " — the knowledge will elude you."

"What about my father's men? They attacked their own kin!"

"The Beast is a master of lies," Rana said. "Often the entity appears as an illumination in the dark recesses of the mortal mind. An insight. An answer. Subtly, the interloper begins altering the human conscience. Once the creature has its victim's attention, the fiend passes as a shadow into the person."

"Does this not take time?" Kith asked. "There were only hours between our arrival at Eimund and the attack."

"The transformation can be gradual over days or months, even years, or the change can happen in minutes," Arva replied. "The time required depends on the mortal and the creature's desire."

Not convinced by Arva's words, Kith questioned, "A whole clan in hours?"

"'Tis easier, faster when the victims have a collective mind," Rana said. "We have seen the creature sway a nation overnight."

"Such control has a price," Niniane said. "Domination drains energy. To replenish, The Beast has to rest for long periods of time."

"Only if our enemy succeeds in possessing and then destroying our sister will the creature gain all her power," Rana added. "Locked inside her is enough knowledge of our world to allow the thief entrance. The Beast would be able to harness nature for its own purposes."

The force of the words, though spoken gently, staggered Kith. *Harness nature? What kind of power did these women have?*

"Our race has walked Earth since the dawn of time, protecting nature and its secrets," explained Arva. "We are of Fayre.

Nature responds to us as we do to her. We ride the wind with the same ease with which we walk on the ocean floors and the mountain peaks. Weather does not affect our bodies nor does time. We have the gifts of healing and lightning and fire. All of this knowledge hangs in the balance."

"What if I choose to go back now? Do what I can to stop this thief and its plague?"

"As a mortal you will fail," Nata said. "The Beast is too powerful. You will die as will your brothers."

The mention of his brothers drove a wedge in Kith.

"They are beyond your help," Rana said. "If you return, they will surely die. If you stay, they might die anyway."

"You speak of this beast Drakus as if it is one being, but that's not how the creature speaks of itself." Kith watched their reaction. "The bloodsucker uses we and us. Is it not more than one entity?"

The sisters looked at each other. Kith felt the air stir between them and knew they were communicating silently again. Finally, Arva spoke aloud. "The Beast absorbs humans and other life. Perhaps that is why it uses we."

"Nay," Kith replied, sensing they had never stood as close to the monster as he had. "The tone is too arrogant. The Beast feels superior. It would not include inferiors in its speech as part of itself."

"Imperial we," Arva said. "Like a ruler. Or a god."

The others nodded their agreement.

"And you are correct," Nata said. "We have had no conversations with Drakus. To do so is too dangerous for both our worlds for any Nyx or Dag. Only Astraea has been in the physical presence of The Beast."

And she didn't survive, Kith thought.

"She did and she did not," Niniane said. "As we have said, The Beast did not steal all her power or this would have been resolved twenty-one hundred years ago. She has now returned once. She will be back again."

"How long ago?" Twenty-one hundred years? Had he heard

her correctly? Kith wondered.

"Yes," Niniane replied. "You heard true."

"So, we must wait another twenty-one hundred years?"

"We think not," said Nata.

Kith shook his head, questioning her words. "Why?"

"Centuries of remembering and forgetting have passed since the attack," Arva said. "The old ways are passing into a dream. Earth guards its secrets but the power of the dragon remains."

"The power of the dragon," Kith said, slowly repeating her phrase while his thoughts focused on the tales around Fenrir. None had referred to the giant wolf as a dragon.

"Not Fenrir," Niniane said, responding to his thoughts.

"What is the name of this dragon?" Kith asked.

"Unspoken," Niniane replied. "The name remains sealed. But we speak of the guardian of Earth."

"Enough!" Arva snapped. "Think no more on it, Norseman, ask no more about it. You understand, or you do not. We are forbidden to say more to an outsider."

"Focus on what touches you," Rana suggested. "Our sister, who will return again. This time sooner than the last because mankind now slumbers in the growing twilight. Light follows night and brings the hope that time will be merciful."

Arva raised her hand, and Rana fell silent along with the others. "Concern yourself with your decision. Do you choose to become one of us or not?"

Kith looked from one sister to the other; his glance lingered on each. "What if I accept your offer?"

"You will not age; nor will you die," said Nata. "There is much to master. You will learn here." She waved her arm. The gesture encompassed the island, the beach, and the ocean lapping against the shore. "You will know when to return to your former world. This place is a sanctuary. Here your wounds will heal."

Kith turned away from them toward the sea. When he spoke, his tone was thoughtful. "You said your sister died — both our lives passed away in the flames and that we were consumed together. Why did she not come here?"

"She had been drained," Niniane said. "Her power lessened. Your spirits dissipated together. She could not return here to heal. Part of her lies there." Niniane pointed to the stars. "Since much of her power lies in your world, she will continue to return to reclaim what is hers by right until she succeeds or is totally absorbed by the interloper."

As Kith turned back to face the sisters, he saw Nata run her fingers through the fire. Despite her earlier demonstration, he found the movement shocking.

Amused at his expression, Nata smiled.

"This is not a game, Sister," Niniane scolded softly.

"I never suggested it was," Nata snapped.

"The smile?" Niniane inquired.

"Read my mind if you are so curious," Nata retorted.

"Your thoughts are closed," Niniane replied.

"Wonder then." Nata put her hands on her hips and stared at Niniane, daring her to speak.

Rana stepped between them. "Our guest awaits an answer." She turned to Kith and said, "Astraea's memories of us will fade with each lifetime. She will not know who she is. She will not know you. She will be drawn to you once you meet. If you are mortal, and born again as you were this time, you also will not remember."

"If I become as you are, will I see Aasta again?" Kith asked, watching Nata pace back and forth in front of the fire.

"The Seers say yes," Niniane replied. "And that you must be ready to claim her as yours. Only by consummating your love, can her spirit be reunited with her birthright, the Nightstar."

"Is this the star we see in the North, the one that guides us?" Kith asked.

"Nay, but the Nightstar serves a similar function," Niniane replied. "We see the stars shining in the sky on a clear night, but we do not see the Nightstar, for its essence is dark and casts no reflection. Only in the form of its protector does it take shape. And only when called."

"None among the Nyx are so bold," Nata snapped. "Or so

crazy."

Niniane smiled smugly at her sister. "For once, Nata is correct. To call the Nightstar is dangerous past knowing. The Nightstar is a harness for the lightning bolt, created by All That Is at the inception of time to balance worlds." Niniane paused and looked at Arva.

"We are vowed to protect this trust," Arva said. "One alone has the obligation. Our sister is not the first to bear the Nightstar. Others have gone before her. But she was born for this honor. And only she can pass the power of the Nightstar to her successor. Until she does so or reclaims her right, the Nightstar is vulnerable. Among the Nyx, Astraea is not the strongest or bravest or oldest or even the wisest. She has the greatest light. Drakus wants to shatter that light, fold its goodness to the bewitcher's own dark purpose."

"Light?" Kith asked. What did that mean?

"Innocence." Arva's voice caressed the word. "Our sister is — was — an innocent. The light of wonder, faith, belief, hope — all those and more — shone through her. She is a protector, not a fighter. She kept The Beast from achieving victory, but she did not escape unharmed. The entity's poison filled her, tainting her essence."

"Creatures touched by some magic attacked us on the beach," Kith said. "They are The Beast in disguise?"

"Nay!" Nata flipped her arm in the air. A bolt of fire shot forth, burning the ground next to Niniane. "They are its creations. Quite deadly to humans."

"Then the creature is the one who has kept us apart?"

Niniane replied tersely, "Aye." She stared disbelievingly at her sister.

The tension between them amused Kith, but their answers did not satisfy him. Something was missing from their explanation. Something vital.

"The origin of the attack and the manner of her death indicate that unity for Astraea lies in sexual bonding," Niniane said. "At first, this unity will weaken her by draining her energies and leaving her disoriented. Thus, our enemy's advantage lies in assaulting her again. Only in that way can the creature be guaranteed of being present at her weakest moments."

"The Beast was there," Kith said. "Why interfere before and not after?"

"The Beast has limitations." Nata studied her fingernails. "The savage initially attacked Astraea at her most vulnerable time, in the first seconds of her twenty-fifth anniversary as a guardian. To recreate the incident, The Beast must attack Astraea with the same timing on her twenty-fifth birthday. If the creature strikes sooner, the power the usurper has drained from our sister and used these many centuries will be lost to it. Later, the thief loses its advantage." She looked at Kith.

Aasta's dream, her urgency in marriage, suddenly made sense. Excited, Kith said, "We have no such limitation."

Nata nodded. "Correct. If you become one of us, you will have to honor the rules we are forced to obey. But you will still remain free to consummate your love."

"The creature who is after the Nightstar will never rest until it succeeds or is destroyed," Arva said. "If the fiend succeeds, it will have immeasurable power in both our worlds."

"That must not happen," Rana insisted. "With our gifts, you will have the power to contain The Beast. Our sister is the only one who can stop the abomination. You are tied to her through love. Love is what blocked the doorway through the fire. This battle is yours whether you fight the war as a human or as one of us. You cannot escape your destiny."

Kith looked away from them. *Life without death. Is such an existence even possible? If so, is immortality a blessing or a curse?* "When must I decide?"

"Now. If the answer is nay, you must return immediately," said Nata.

"A few minutes at least?" Kith asked. "I'd like to walk along the beach."

"Do not tarry long," Arva warned. "To do so seals your choice."

"I'm here whether I want to be or not?" Kith asked.

"Not necessarily," Arva replied.

"Home?"

Arva ran her fingers through her silvery blonde hair. "Not necessarily."

"Another fate? One we've not discussed?"

"Possibly." Arva's eyebrow arched. "To make no decision is a choice of its own. So, do not tarry long."

Change

12

*T*he sisters watched Kith walk down to the shore, his face turned to the ocean. The redhead spoke first. "Our sister has chosen well. He is strong enough to survive the transformation."

"And loyal," said Arva. "His loyalty tears at him now."

"You did not tell him everything," Niniane scolded. "Not a word about the sleeping death."

"Nay," Arva replied. "His heart will decide the matter. His love is strong enough to survive the isolation, the loneliness. Only the centuries can teach him what forever means."

"And you failed to mention what could happen to his spirit if The Beast absorbs him," Niniane taunted. "There are fates beyond agony."

"Enough!" Nata insisted. "None of this would have mattered to him. He is Norse. He scoffs at fear. Dying in battle earns him Valhalla."

"Valhalla he knows; our way he knows not," Rana said, the cadence of her words signaling an approaching storm. "I am responsible for his being here. I brought him, and I will be the one to return him as a mortal or as one of us to the world he has left behind. His bravery could cause him to be an immortal prisoner, forever shackled to Drakus's tether. By our silence, are we not giving our enemy a tool to use against us?"

Arva's eyebrow arched. Her gaze fixed steadily on Rana, she suggested, "We must be of one mind on this if the transformation is to succeed. We must give him all we can. We cannot do so divided. Agreed?" She looked from one to the other.

"I do not like it; it is not fair," Niniane said tersely.

"What does fair have to do with it?" Nata spat. "Fair! What is fair? Life is not."

Niniane scowled. "You know what I mean."

"No, I do *not*," Nata replied. "Your talk of fair is to cover your fear. You are afraid of the elders."

"Am *not!*" Niniane exclaimed.

"What they will say if we fail," Nata snapped.

"Stop bickering!" Arva commanded. "He is strong, brave, quick, and smart. He will not fail."

"Niniane is right," Rana said. "We must be fair. We owe him — and ourselves — the truth."

"He is in love," Nata hissed. "He will still make the same choice."

"So why not tell him?" Niniane glared at her sister.

"We are divided equally." Arva sighed. "Our sister would cast the deciding vote but —"

"She would tell him," Rana said. "She has no guile in her. Astraea may be the youngest, the most vulnerable, but in some ways she is the wisest. She has faith in the natural order of things. She would tell him everything. Let him decide."

"That is it then, we tell him," Arva conceded.

They looked at Nata. She threw up her hands. "Agreed. Just in time, too. He comes back."

They watched Kith turn away from the sea and walk back up the beach to them.

"What do I do to stay?" he asked.

"First, there is more we must tell you," Arva said. "The transformation is dangerous. If the procedure works, and you become one of the Nyx, you will spend much of your life celibate until you succeed in marrying our sister. To mate with a mortal is often lethal for them. Some are able to stand the exchange. Others are not. You will have to be careful. Your healing abilities will not always be able to revive those you have bedded. Regardless, you cannot have children with a mortal."

"Our sister tells you this because you will be one of us. Not in our world. In yours," Rana said. "Our enemy is linked to you through our sister. Once you become as we are, Drakus could follow your energy through the flame."

"The Beast has powers it has acquired through others," Niniane said.

"Stolen!" Nata exclaimed.

Niniane gave Nata a hard stare. "Stolen from others. With an immortal, there is no death as mortals know it. If Drakus were to overcome you and successfully drain all your power, your spirit might not escape. It might be imprisoned. Forever."

"I voted against telling you these things, but perhaps doing so is best," Nata said grudgingly. "So there is more good news. Not that anything we say matters. When you love someone as you do our sister, that is first." She fell silent and paced back and forth.

Casting a wilting look at Nata, Niniane continued, "Since your energies will be tested in your world, they will have to be replenished. You will spend time, buried here, recovering from your wounds, while life goes on without you. But you will not sleep. Not really. You will be a part of Earth. Know its pain. Sense the passing of time and what is happening in your world. You will not be able to take action. No matter how much you desire doing so. Only when your energy is at its maximum will you be able to break through." She shrugged and looked at the others. "I think that is everything."

"Is that all that can go wrong?" Kith asked.

Stunned by his matter-of-fact tone, Niniane asked, "Is it not enough? You do not seem surprised."

"I didn't think immortality would be free," Kith replied. "At least not the kind you offered."

"You suspected we had not told you everything?" Arva asked.

"I knew you hadn't. Why would you? You want your sister returned. I want her, too. Your plight and mine are akin. But you've not explained the elders." Kith watched the sisters exchange hurried glances and knew they were silently talking among themselves.

"You heard us speaking," Arva said at last.

"I'd be a poor warrior if I hadn't — not capable to lead others. Certainly not someone your sister would love or trust."

Arva's eyebrow arched, and the golden flecks in her eyes flashed as she studied him. Moments passed before she replied. "The original guardians, the wise ones, inscrutable holders of secrets, mysteries unexplained."

"Who are the Seers?"

"The foretellers of the future who live in our world," Niniane said. "You will not have to deal with them."

"A blessing," Nata quipped.

"Nata!" Arva exclaimed.

"The Seers are disturbed creatures," Nata said, staring at Arva. "Better not to deal with them at all."

"Enough," Arva snapped.

Nata shrugged and looked toward the fire.

"And birth?" Kith asked, knowing he would learn no more about the Seers. "If there is no death in your world, is there birth?"

"There is birth accompanied by great joy and celebration," Niniane said. "Your world and ours are two of many dimensions. We are free to travel in some and not others. Your world holds too many hazards. Passage to your dimension is guarded."

"No death? Ever?" Kith asked, his tone doubtful. "Does that mean no change?"

"Nay," Rana said. "When our tasks are completed, we move on. The process is similar to human death because we leave our world behind. Our bodies do not die. They evolve."

Nata spoke up. "Will you see those humans you have loved again? This is the question you have and have not asked, is it not?"

"It is," Kith said.

"We can offer you no peace there," Nata said. "The answer lies outside our understanding."

Kith surveyed the sisters again. He felt the answers were honest and as close to the truth as they were willing to reveal. He'd learn no more from them now. "Nata is right. Love is every-thing. I have dreamed of Aasta all my life. She's haunted my wak-ing and sleeping. Why would another life be different? I'd be no better prepared to keep her once we found each other — if we did. She'd know less each time. I would as well. Yes is the only choice that makes sense. So what must I do?"

"Do as you are told without question," Arva replied. "Do I have your word that you will?"

"Yes."

Nata reached into the flames and retrieved a fiery object. She passed her hand down over the blaze, and it vanished. When she raised her arm, the fire burst forth from her palm.

A gust of wind howled across the land and then died down. In the ensuing stillness, Kith could hear his heart beating. The world began changing, altering, breaking apart in front of him. Thunder rolled across the sky. Lightning struck the spot where he stood, and the brush-covered hillside vanished. Kith fell feet first down an embankment and plunged into icy water.

He pushed upward toward the surface. An undercurrent wrapped around him and forced him deeper and deeper into the murky water. Struggling free, he began his upward climb again. Before his head cleared the water, he hit an invisible shield. He pressed hard against the barrier, but it held. Swimming at a par-allel angle, he tried to get out from under the obstruction with-out success. He beat on the barrier. Harder and harder he struck.

Just when he thought he would drown, the obstacle van-ished. Water propelled him upward. Twisting his body faster and faster, the water burped him onto dry ground. He rolled several feet. Breathless, he lay gasping for air.

"Stand up, *now!*"

Gulping air, he jumped to his feet. Sheer walls stretched sky-ward around him on all four sides. Aasta's sisters sat on the ground across from him. A spitting fire burned in front of them, heating a cauldron.

Arva spoke. "Sit there, Norseman." She pointed to the one lone, gnarled tree growing in the pit. "Up against the tree trunk.

Remain silent."

The instant he lay against the tree, the branches grabbed him; the roots rose out of the dirt and entwined themselves around his legs and lower torso. He couldn't move.

The sisters stood and placed their hands over the cauldron, their fingers touching one another's. Blood dripped from each into the fiery brew, while a long, wooden spoon stirred the mixture guided by an unseen hand. In perfect rhythm, as if responding to a beat they alone heard, they moved their hands away from one another and leaned forward until their heads were touching. Their tears, as their blood had earlier, fell into the container.

Silently they rose and linked their hands together, then began circling the fire, moving clockwise faster and faster until Kith couldn't distinguish one from the other. They became a whirlwind, touching then not touching the ground.

The beating of wings accompanied by a high-pitched scream assaulted his ears. The ground rumbled and vibrated his body until he felt certain he would shake apart. As the pressure built he struggled to keep from screaming out in pain.

The whirlwind dissolved. The sisters again circled the cauldron, this time in a counter-clockwise direction. He had no idea when they changed direction nor when the billowy, white cloud that now floated above the cauldron had formed.

Each sister pulled a hair from her head, threw the strand into the brew, and turned around three times. Slowly, gracefully, they began dancing, their hands alternately reaching to the sky and the earth. Kith watched their long, slender fingers gather up dirt as they dipped toward the ground. This they also pitched in the boiling mixture.

On their fifth turn around the cauldron, their hands stretched toward the sky and stopped. Raindrops fell from the cloud, hissing as they hit the heated liquid. Mist rose from the drops. As the sisters lowered their hands, the cloud swirled downward and was consumed by the bubbling brew. Steam shot upward toward the Heavens, releasing a pungent odor of decay into the air. Although Kith's eyes watered, he refused to close them. To do so might indicate weakness. The steam dissipated, leaving behind another scent, one Kith found more pleasing, that of roses abloom.

Nata stepped away from the others. Above her head, she held the flame she'd taken from the fire. With a quick twist of her wrist, she threw the fire into the cauldron. Flames shot skyward as far as Kith could see. The blaze died out.

Niniane opened a vial, poured the contents into the brew, and stirred. Rana dipped a luminous cup into the bubbling potion. The vessel floated across the space separating Kith from them.

"Drink it all," Arva commanded.

His mouth opened involuntarily. The steaming drink burned his tongue and throat, then spread like wildfire through him. The brew attacked his body as if it were a living organism intent upon altering every cell. Pain, more intense than that he had known when he lay dying, exploded inside him. He screamed but no sound came out. Instead flames poured forth.

Internal rigors shook him, spreading outward until even his toes and fingers quivered. His muscles cramped. He strained to curl inward, but the tree held him securely in place. His breathing became more and more labored. He gasped for air; piercing pain filled his chest.

His head began throbbing. The world around him faded away. His mortal life overran him, and he could see clearly those who had lost to him in battle. He heard every scream. Felt every wound he'd inflicted on another. The tormented pictures that filled his mind gave way to darkness; silence surrounded him. He stood isolated, alone, and in agony. How long he suffered, he didn't know. Time and meaning ceased. Blind and deaf, pain became his sole reality.

His bones and his blood chilled as inertia began freezing him forever in its grasp. He concentrated his energy on breaking the bonds that held him. The wood ripped apart. He hurdled himself forward away from the imprisoning branches. The ground collapsed under him, and he fell. With incredible force, he again plunged into icy waters.

His vision returned. This time the liquid didn't sting his eyes. Breathing came naturally despite the lack of air. He tasted the water. Salt. The sea. He propelled himself upward. His body broke free, and he found himself riding the air. He looked down and began falling. The ground rushed up to embrace him. He landed with a thud. Surprisingly, the fall didn't hurt.

He stood up quickly and found himself airborne again. He heard laughter, looked down, saw Aasta's sisters beneath him, and began falling again. This time when he hit the ground, back first, he didn't jump up.

"Welcome to our form," Arva said, looking down at him. "It is best if you remain still. For now. Relax. Do not put forth any effort. Remain silent. Clear your mind. I will help you sit up."

Kith found his body moving without any effort on his part.

"Did we give him too much?" Rana asked anxiously.

"Nay," Nata replied. "Had we done less he might not have broken free."

"The transformation is complete," Niniane said. "Aye, we had to make the elixir strong. Otherwise, we might have had to repeat the process. Twice could have destroyed him. He is tough, resilient. He will survive."

Nata sat next to Kith. "You are a newborn. All your involuntary movements must be learned again. Otherwise, you will bounce around like a ball — as you just did. Your body is less dense and your energy greater. The natural world responds to your slightest touch. When you have mastered your new form, you will leave no footprint in the sand, create no ripple in the waters, stir no breeze in the air —"

"I'm relieved." He laughed. "I... ." His body sailed backward across the sand and into the shallow waters.

Peals of laughter filled the air around him. "Follow instructions." Arva chuckled. "Do not speak. Do not move."

The sisters floated toward him. They hovered around him like clucking hens. "This is going to take a long time." Nata said knowingly. "And much work."

Courage leads to the stars, fear toward death.

Hercules oetaeus
Lucius Annaeus Seneca
(the Younger)
circa 4 B.C.-A.D. 65

13

Twentieth Century A.D.

Kirth Naran walked along the bayou, his loafers leaving no impression in the soft and fertile black delta soil despite his solid two-hundred-pound, six-foot-four frame. The freshness of his starched long-sleeved shirt labeled him invulnerable to the sweltering southern Louisiana heat. Protruding from the buttoned cuffs, his deeply tanned hands spoke of strength gained from a life lived out-of-doors.

His long, tapered fingers touched the cypress trees and the Spanish moss hanging from the live oaks. His keen ears had picked up the pitiful cry hours ago when he arrived in New Orleans; his senses now guided him miles northeast of the city to this lonely, uninhabited spot outside Laplace. His old enemy had been here. Recently.

He felt the lingering presence, tasted the death and decay that always followed The Beast Drakus. The faintly acidic smell twisted him inside.

Lifting his head slightly, he sniffed the air. West. Drakus withdrew west. His eyebrow twitched. The hint of a smile played across his decisive lips. The Beast had great difficulty sensing his presence when he stood in the creature's wake. Still, a spell harbored risk. If he held the vision of the Nightstar too long, his adversary would zero in on his position.

Moonlight reflected off the corn-silk sheen of his shoulder-length hair as he paced back and forth, studying the surrounding terrain, weighing the consequences. If his energy drew The Beast, they'd fight. So be it. If he didn't call the Nightstar, he wouldn't be able to later. Now or never.

Kirth turned toward the bayou and narrowed his thoughts. Lifetimes whisked by in his mind's race backward to a world lost in antiquity. Seconds stretched into minutes while the night stilled silent around him. The gentle lapping of the water against the shore ceased as Nature held her breath. He closed his eyes to pinpoint the image. When he opened them again, the black centers glowed. He raised his right arm, palm upward, until his hand lay within his vision. Golden flames kissed his fingertips.

"Nightstar," he commanded, pointing toward the dark and soundless water. The fire burst forth from his hand, scorching the soil it touched on its course to the bayou. Vaporous steam rose off the water. Mists heavy with the smell of salt drew close around the man and the fire. With a quick twist of his hand, a stream of fire raced across the still waters, forming a perfect circle. The flames burned brightly. "Reveal yourself to the guardian of the flame."

A blue-white bolt of lightning struck the water, cutting the outline of a star inside the circle. Golden flames leapt skyward off the five points of the star. As they died down into the dark, still waters, the ethereal form of a young woman appeared. Her midnight hair fell free over and down her silky, smooth skin. Her dusty eyes held him in their embrace.

"The wind whispers that the battle draws nigh," Kirth told the floating figure, careful to keep his arm stretched forward to maintain the energy between himself and the Nightstar. "Already The Beast prepares. The interloper wove a spell here within the last twenty-four hours. The implication is clear. The fiend has found your guardian's split spirit." Silently, he expressed the names and endearments he dared not say aloud: my lovely, Astraea, my darling, Aasta. "Her identity remains obscure to me even now. But The Beast knows."

He frowned. "I suspect the creature knows what guise I wear. Only now may I speak to you. I am wiser. No matter what trap the hunter sets or disguise the interloper employs, I'll not disregard the rules now that I understand the price."

Anguish passed over Kirth's face. He willed himself to remain steady. Regardless of the consequences, what his conscience called upon him to do must be done. "I beg forgiveness for my arrogance so that this battle bears no mark of my transgression."

Silvery light suffused the image. She raised her right arm, palm upward. The light flowed into her hand. Her mouth opened; her lips formed a circle. Gently, she blew on the incandescent sphere that now danced on her fingertips.

A single moonbeam pierced the distance between them, striking Kirth in the chest. The air in his lungs chilled, leaving him breathless. The ray separated into two beams which enfolded his body, encapsulating him in their radiance. The temperature around him dropped to zero.

Kirth felt his own death close in on him. He'd not been mortal in more than a thousand years, but now, wrapped in the mantle of the Nightstar, his immortal flesh became vulnerable. In her grasp, he was defenseless. A firstborn of creation, her dominion encompassed all worlds. Her powers predated the Nyx and the preternatural abilities he'd acquired from them. He silenced his mind. If she intended to evaporate his momentarily mortal breath, he'd not die a coward.

As the light passed into his body, the arctic blast thawed and altered the world around him. He bathed in moonlight under a starry sky on a primeval ocean shore and breathed the brisk yet refreshing air. Lightning rose out of the deep, charging the undulating waves with light. A gold-and-silver font appeared. Blood dripped from the basin into the waters below.

The sea, still and silent before, churned. A whirlpool, rising beneath the receptacle, poured into its deep basin. The waters leapt toward the sky. As they fell back into the sea, they kissed the shore, purifying Kirth in salt, washing away the dark center of guilt he had carried since his last battle with Drakus.

Be at peace with yourself. The words softly slipped into his thoughts. The scene before him faded, and he again stood facing the apparition of the Nightstar.

Forgiven. His eyes met hers. *Thank the Heavens*. "Our vow is unbroken. We will reunite you with the rightful bearer of your mantle and end this curse forever. Faith, trust, and love will reforge the two of you as one. Now, awaken! Hear the cries of those who fight for you. Be watchful of the trickster and guide our way."

As he lowered his arm to release the moment he had held in his sway, the earth trembled violently. Kirth collapsed on the soft soil, his body jerking, his arms and legs tingling. He struggled to control his coordination and spied erectile tails tipped with venomous stingers bobbing within his view. Scorpions. Where did they come from? He felt the vibration of tiny feet scurrying toward him. He tried to stand and failed.

The scorpions scrambled over his body, stinging him until his skin swelled from the poison. He reassured himself. The venom wouldn't kill him, but healing that many stings took energy he hesitated to expend.

Trapped. Some other source now controlled his spell. He closed his eyes, focused his mind, and willed his body to rise from the unsteady ground. His ears began ringing. The weak sound became stronger and easily recognized. Insects swarming a hive. The faint fluttering of dainty wings breathed on his skin. He sighed and opened his eyes. Bees. Thousands and thousands of bees.

The scorpions vanished when the bees alighted on him. They couldn't be actual scorpions, Kirth thought. Nor did they carry the dark touch of The Beast's creations.

The tremors ceased and the throbbing pain stopped. His body rose from the soil as if lifted by the bees. The instant he knelt in the dirt, the insects disappeared.

Bees and scorpions and earth tremors, Kirth mused. Scorpions signaled death and the hangman. Bees had many meanings — industry, work, obedience, souls swarming. Earthquakes foreboded calamity and change.

He rested on his heels and chided himself. He'd been warned by Astraea's sisters to never call the Nightstar. Whoever did, they said, risked annihilation. Her ability to reach the conjurer through time and space had more potency than any spell he'd conjured. What did the signs mean? The bees healed the scorpions' stings. He stared at the flames burning on the dark waters. A warning. Scorpions signaled danger; bees sanctuary. Some disaster lay ahead. And *soon*. Had Drakus felt the surge of energy? Kirth wondered. He hoped not. He had done what his heart begged him to do. Perhaps his action had been unwise.

Kirth raised his right arm in front of him as he stood. The night again stilled silent around him. He lowered his arm and the flames extinguished. The mist vanished, taking with it the clean, ocean scent of fresh salt and leaving in its wake brackish water and the musty odor of moss and rotting wood. He focused his vision on the singed path leading to the bayou. The scarring vanished. Crickets beat the air as he walked briskly to the rental car and drove away.

Kirth eyed the flashing red light on the telephone when he walked into his hotel room. He didn't want to speak with anyone, but he must remain alert. Especially now when he suspected the reunion drew near.

"You have a message for me?" Kirth tapped a pen impatiently on the nightstand while he waited for the desk clerk's response.

"Yes. Hale said call him when you get in regardless of the time."

The tapping stopped.

"He said it's urgent."

Kirth's right eyebrow arched. "Thanks." He hung up and immediately dialed his drummer's room. "Hale. This is Kirth. What's up?"

Drowsily, Hale replied, "What time is it?"

"Two. You said it's urgent?" Kirth frowned. Hale slept like a rock. No matter how long he dozed, he had to be dragged out of bed and remained incoherent for hours. "Tell me in the morning." He'd get nothing out of Hale now. He hung up.

Before he had time to unbutton his khaki slacks, he heard a knock at the door. "Now, I'm really curious." Kirth smiled, shocked rather than surprised to find Hale standing on the other side, his blue eyes, barely open, no more than slits, lopsidedly clad in a hastily put-on T-shirt and shorts. The drummer's disheveled, shaggy brown hair gleamed golden in the hallway light. Whatever pressing errand pulled him out of bed in the middle of the night, Kirth thought, had the power to rouse the dead.

"It's her. Sylvian DuClair. We know it is." Hale looked quite proud of himself as he plopped on the bed.

"The reporter? What about her?"

Impatiently, Hale repeated himself. "It's her."

"Her who?"

"Your her. You know. Tall. Sleek. Black hair. Hypnotizing, wide-set, fawn eyes. Finely chiseled features. Straight nose. Rosy cheeks. Her." With that, Hale fell back on the bed, asleep.

Astraea? Kirth shook his drummer. Hard. Harder. No response. Hoisting Hale off the bed and over his shoulder, Kirth carried him into the shower, leaned him against the tile wall, took off the antique pocket watch Hale had on a chain around his neck, and turned on the cold water.

"What the hell!" Hale gasped as the icy water hit him.

"I'm waking you up the only way I know." Kirth laughed. They could jam in the room with Hale sleeping, and he'd never budge. "When your eyes close, you're history."

"Let me out," Hale sputtered. "I'm awake. What are you doing in my room?"

"You're in my room, you dunce." Kirth blocked Hale's escape from the shower. "You're not awake yet. You walked down here. Remember?"

"Oh, yeah. Sort of." Hale leaned against the shower wall. "Something important." He shook his head, trying to remember. Water flew everywhere.

"You mumbled something about 'It's her' before you collapsed on my bed."

"Yeah. Yeah. Yeah. It's coming back." Silence again. "The lady reporter. Sylvian DuClair. We tried to find you, but you'd already left. Turn the water off, man. It's freezing in here. Let me out."

Kirth turned off the cold spray but blocked Hale's path out of the shower. "Not until you finish. I may have to hit you again."

"Yeah. It's a bummer. My mind's mush. Hey, maybe that's a line. Something like — my mind's mush waiting for the rush of your love."

Exasperated, Kirth exclaimed, "Hale!"

"So it's not great. What time is it anyway?"

"After two. Where are the others?" Kirth hoped maybe one of them could speak with him, and he could let Hale go back to sleep. He hesitated to use his telepathic powers to read Hale's mind. His enemy hovered too close and would feel the ripple. Besides, Hale's scattered thoughts couldn't be read successfully.

"On the town. Celebrating. They heard of a jazz place open all night. Rogert's third cousin is playing there. Wait. That's not right. Rogert's third cousin knows ... ." Hale frowned. "Wrong. Someone's relative knows someone playing there. The name's in my room. I think. I hope. Gotta be. I fell asleep while they decided so I won by default."

"Won what?" Kirth asked impatiently.

"Playing messenger. Sylvian DuClair looks like the woman you're forever looking for. That's it. That's the message."

"What woman?"

"Come on Kirth. A raven-haired, brown-eyed beauty named Astraea. Actually, you called her, Astraea, my Aasta. This is her except her name is Sylvian. Sylvian DuClair. She's twenty-four and a real looker."

Kirth's shocked expression brought the shadow of a smile to Hale's face. "We've suspected for years you searched for someone. Especially since last summer."

"You're still asleep," Kirth said, buying time. *How did they know?*

"You wish. Remember the fishing trip? We stayed on the boat? You dreamed about her. Talked in your sleep. Said things would be different. Called her Astraea, my Aasta. Then —"

Fearful the spoken names would draw The Beast's attention, Kirth interrupted Hale, demanding, "Don't say those names!" Immediately, he regretted his harshness, and the confused look his impatience brought to Hale's face. "They're jinxed."

"I bet." Hale laughed.

"Former loves. Nothing current."

"Unhuh."

"Please. Humor me."

"OK. The names are history." Hale zipped his lips. "But you did dream. Each night. And you said those names. We suspected you called to the woman you seek."

"Wrong. Available women are plentiful. You know that."

"Yeah. I know that. We all do. That's the point. You're never with anyone. You shy away from groupies. And anyone who comes to the show. Always. Without fail you watch tall, slim, women with raven hair and light-brown eyes."

He paused and gave Kirth a long, hard look, his penetrating eyes now the hue of the turquoise ceramic tile he leaned against. "Of all the love songs we've composed and recorded — and we've done a ton — you've never written one —"

"I've composed my share of Dragon songs."

Hale raised his arm to silence Kirth. "Hear me out. Love songs? Get real. Nah. Absolutely none. Nada. Zip. Zero. No time. No way. No place. Never have you penned a love song. Not seldom. Never. Certainly, not one we've performed. So get that out of your head. But the kicker —" Hale chortled "— Gaylor's long-legged, raven-haired, brown-eyed beauty."

"I like Gaylor's song," Kirth insisted.

"You balked at the title. Remember? Gaylor wanted *Lady of the Night.*"

"He got it," Kirth said.

Hale's eyes narrowed. "After the debate. *Night Plays. S. Trumpet Rock. Tart Treat.* And, we mustn't forget Eric's immortal off the street and on the beach with *Sandy Slam.*"

Kirth groaned.

"The list goes on and so could I." Hale's right eyebrow arched knowingly. "You hated every suggestion."

"*Lady of the Night* has a ring. A rhythm. Class. The others didn't. They were ... ." Kirth searched for the right word.

Hale folded his arms against himself as if he'd made his point. "You nixed the title until Gaylor changed the would-be streetwalker's entire appearance."

Kirth sighed. "The song charted Number One. With a blonde."

"Give it up, Kirth. That tune won't play. We've been together too long. On the road too many years. We know each other." He shrugged his shoulders. "Can I get out now? I am awake."

Kirth moved aside while Hale stepped out of the shower. He handed him his watch.

"Thanks." Hale pulled the chain over his head. "You'd been jacking with your heartbeat if this had gotten ruined."

"I know," Kirth said, solemnly. The damn thing didn't run. Never had. He pitched Hale a towel.

Hale grabbed the towel and began drying his hair. "We told her the Hyatt. Gave her Mike's number. We'd like to see you get laid, ol' buddy. It's about time. But the guys said she didn't take the bait. She left almost immediately when they told her I'd gone to find you."

"Are you crazy?" *Was this the calamity the earth tremor forewarned?* "I don't talk to the press."

"Not for an interview," Hale replied, annoyed. "We wouldn't set you up, and you know it. She didn't bring a photographer. She didn't have a camera. Not one we saw. Even if she did and she got off a quick shot without your knowing, she'd have nothing." He shrugged. "Don't know how you do it."

"Do what?" Kirth knew exactly what Hale meant. Cameras couldn't capture his features clearly, but he wouldn't tell Hale or anyone else that. He had to feign ignorance.

Hale looked out from under the towel. "Didn't ask. Don't

want to know. You're not photogenic. Camera shy. That's all."
He reached for the towel rack and grabbed a second towel. "We
just wanted you to meet her. But she left and wouldn't tell the
others the name of her hotel, so Gaylor followed her. I fell asleep
before he got back. I don't know what he found out. Now
they're at this club. I'm sure the name's in my room."

"I don't like it." Kirth feared his friends' help might have put
them in peril. Only one certainty existed. The Beast had left its
mark by the bayou near Laplace. And if, as he now suspected,
Drakus knew his identity, the Hyatt's proximity to the Superdome
made the hotel an easy target. They had to move. Quickly.

Hale's loafers squished as he stepped past Kirth. He eyed his
friend. "I prefer showering in my Reeboks."

"Sorry," Kirth replied. "I remembered the watch. Forgot
the shoes. You need a new pair. Those were antiques."

Hale looked down at his feet. "That's why I liked them. Old
and comfortable. Perfectly molded to my feet. At least they
were." He ambled toward the bed, dropped the towels on the
bedspread, sat down, and collapsed on top of them.

"Don't go to sleep." Kirth cleared the space between them
and pulled Hale upright. "This reporter, Miss DuClair, might
tell someone where we're staying. You know how thirsty the
press is. We need to get our stuff and get out. Find the others.
Check in somewhere else."

Hale leaned on his elbows and studied Kirth. "Whatever
you say." He yawned, stood up, and gave Kirth a mock salute.
"You're the chief." He grimaced. "Gotta admit, you've saved us
more than once from making fools of ourselves. Your intuition's
usually right on. But, she's straight ahead. A reporter from a
newspaper in the Houston area. No hidden agenda. If we're
wrong, sorry. We thought we'd found your elusive lady."

"I don't have an elusive lady." Kirth reached for the canary-
yellow, button-down shirt he'd taken off before Hale arrived.
He hadn't lied to Hale. He didn't have Astraea. He only wished
he did.

"Ask Gaylor," Hale said, ignoring Kirth's words. "He's a

good detective. He'll know where she's staying."

Kirth put the shirt back on. "Did Mike say whether our rooms were blocked off in the Quarter tonight?"

"Yeah. They are. Are we history here?"

"The Hyatt's billing us." Kirth began stuffing his clothes into his travel bag. "We won't check out. We'll just move. Our office can handle the details tomorrow.

Hale shook himself off like a dog and smoothed his hair out of his eyes. "Ready. Fresh shower. Clean clothes." Tapping his fingers on the bedside table, he sang, off key, "Who could ask for anything more." He laughed. "I ask you. Who could ask for anything more. Ask for anything more. Anything more. More. More."

Kirth grimaced. "You have time to change clothes as long as you quit caterwauling."

"Why would I want to do that?" Hale snickered. "This is so much more fun. Oh, I ask you, who could ask for anything more. Better hurry, Kirth. I'm just getting warmed up."

"You're squawking to keep from dozing." Kirth took one last look around the room and opened the door. "Let's get the rest of the stuff now. I hope the door's open between your rooms."

"I think it is." Hale's expression was quizzical as he followed Kirth down the hall.

Hours later, Kirth slipped from the Warehouse District's Hotel Chantre where Miss DuClair stayed, strolled silently down the street, then fitted his form inside the darkened doorway of a vacant building and settled in to wait until dawn. By then, he'd have a plan to meet her. Ominous thoughts haunted him while he studied the second-floor balcony he'd identified as hers.

For years, he'd scanned faces in the crowd, his eyes following every gesture that reminded him of her. He searched without success. Tonight, his friends stumbled upon Astraea by chance? Not likely.

Somehow, Drakus had schemed the meeting. His friends

meant well, but they had no business in this ordeal. He knew the danger. They didn't. A false move on his part could lead to their deaths. Or worse. For now, they slept in their favorite hotel, secured by a staff educated in disarming erratic fans. But nothing and no one could protect them from the fiend stalking him.

He frowned. He'd been careful, changing his name and staying on the move. The music offered different towns. New faces. He'd stayed anonymous, and Drakus hadn't closed in on him.

Until now. He feared the culprit to be the band's latest hit single. A rhythm designed to attract Astraea underscored the melody. Instead, the song called Drakus.

Foolhardy, Kirth chided silently. He well knew the scent and sound of New Orleans. Not even the smells of stale liquor and discarded trash that haunted areas of the Vieux Carre could color the heart of The Big Easy for Kirth. He'd watched the city age over the years, while the soul that lay underneath the dirt and crime and noise retained its youthful vitality. That soul had its own beat, its own rhythm, its own beauty. When he heard the wail, the plaintive cry that rode the night breeze, he'd known. The anguished moan reflected the aftershock of The Beast. The deceiver lay nearby, waiting, watching, spreading its evil tentacles outward searching for him.

A sudden drop in temperature alerted Kirth. His nostrils flared. He looked up toward the balcony and saw the dark mist shrouding the windows and the doorway.

Speak of the devil.

Patience.

His foe exerted its power from afar. The target obviously Miss DuClair. If she were Astraea, Drakus couldn't physically harm her or directly confront her until her twenty-fifth birthday. Whatever did The Beast have in mind?

Scare tactics, Kirth decided. Drakus relished others' fear and played with Miss DuClair to frighten her. A definite possibility.

Then, again, maybe The Beast had set a trap. Miss DuClair could be an imitation of Astraea, a fraud created by Drakus to lure Kirth into the open. She would have to be a twin, a double.

Otherwise, Kirth would feel the drain on the fiend's sorcerous power as its energy maintained the illusion.

Whether a counterfeit or Astraea reborn, if The Beast knew he stood below, the creature counted on him to defend her. In that way, Drakus could weaken him through battle before their real war began. Kirth shook his head. He'd jumped into that trap before.

"Nay. I'll not be caught this time." Kirth's words were as soft as a mist falling on the pavement. He'd have to ride out The Beast's energy. When he threw up his defenses, Drakus felt the surge. That would never do. He steeled himself for the whirlwind, knowing the bewitcher created illusions so powerful they replaced reality.

The New Orleans street vanished in a swirling gray mist. Darkness wrapped around Kirth. The ground beneath him disappeared, and he fell, tumbling through emptiness until his body landed, prone, on the ground. He groaned as he recognized the twilight world where his body lay dying; the carnage of his men spread across the meadow and into the forest. Damn. A spell of yesterday, he thought, before the illusion overtook him, erasing more than a thousand years in a single breath.

Vortex

14

*K*irth choked on his own blood; his last breath whispered through his lips as the darkness receded. Gasping, he awakened in the present and quickly looked up at the balcony in time to see the mist withdraw from there as well.

He resisted the impulse to hit the vapor with a bolt of his own energy. If Drakus didn't know he stood below, he wasn't sending his calling card. Not yet.

He shook himself and took a deep breath. The near-death experience held no more pleasure this time around. Had the horror been for his benefit alone?

If not, what vicious imprint had Drakus stamped in Miss DuClair's mind? He had again felt his pain when he lay dying, had she as well? Doubtful. The demonic wolves? Maybe. The carnage in the village they sacked? Possibly. He didn't know. He found the purpose of the illusion clear — alienating her from him.

The ploy wouldn't work. She'd be drawn to him. Drakus didn't have the power to change that. Still, he'd have to be cautious approaching Miss DuClair, or she'd bolt like a skittish Thoroughbred, and he'd have to catch her.

The doors of the balcony swung open. Kirth saw Sylvian DuClair walk to the painted-iron railing and take a deep breath. Hope swelled inside him. He fixed his thoughts on the balcony, not on her lest she feel his presence. Part of his energy followed, leaving his body behind. Her beauty washed him as a summer shower nourishes the earth. He felt rejuvenated, refreshed, renewed. No other but Astraea could do that.

He fought the urge to materialize. *I shall not — cannot — fail again. We must succeed.*

The room smelled of smoke and death. He moved within and opened his mind to her thoughts. She planned to search for him at the hotel. She had time off from work.

Perfect.

She'd not go anywhere without him, he vowed, deciding to follow her to the hotel where she could find him. Every fiber of his being wanted to move closer, allow his mind to brush her skin. He could, but he didn't dare. Although her power slept, her extraordinary senses existed nonetheless. She might feel his embrace. He couldn't chance it.

Soon. Delight filled him. *Soon, my love.*

"Who's there?" Sylvian spun around as she spoke. Her eyes scanned the room.

Kirth's mind quickly withdrew. Back on the street, he silently cursed himself.

Astraea — light and dark, day and night. Moonlight played in her midnight hair, as moonbeams reflected off the waters on a starry night. The light of the sun's rays glowed in her fathomless eyes. Her skin was as pure as the dew in early morning, and, when she spoke, her breath was as fresh as the kiss of springtime.

He'd been overwhelmed; his emotions careened into a free fall of such depths that she felt them. He had to get hold of himself for both their sakes. This was no time to be off balance.

A chill ran through him; the vision of his last failure passed before him. Helpless, he watched her die, writhing in pain, her body in flames. His tears were as dry as the desert sands because he'd acted hastily, ignoring the Nyx warning not to speak to her of their lives together, the ongoing battle, or her identity.

Time and again he'd been told the past would be revealed to her through their union and in no other way. He listened. He believed. At least, he thought he had. Then, he panicked. Fear claimed him, and he broke the rules.

Never again. This time, he would be patient. Not impatient.

Gentle. Not rough. Loving. Not frightening. He understood, as he hadn't before, how being otherwise trapped him and his beloved in the clutches of The Beast.

He paced back and forth for more than an hour, debating whether to move around the corner to the hotel's parking or remain in the shadows.

To get to his hotel, she had to drive past where he now stood. Of course, as a stranger to the city she might take a wrong turn. Nay, most likely she would take a couple of wrong turns. Getting lost on unfamiliar roads, even in the compact, grid-pattern rectangle of streets that formed the French Quarter, was easy. Kirth groaned as the truth hit him. She'd be headed toward the wrong hotel — the Hyatt. He must find her car.

He moved out of the shadows. The air around him chilled noticeably, then quivered. His instinct had been correct; his enemy knew he stood in the shadows. Kirth hadn't fallen for the trap so The Beast now planned to engage him or make him flee. Why bother to withdraw? Drakus would just follow him. Best to get rid of the creature now before he searched for Miss DuClair's car. Besides, he was as ready as he'd ever be to face the Evil One.

Kirth stepped back to his original position, crossed his arms in front of him, cocked his head to the right, and leaned against the doorway. His outward manner appeared calm and gave no sign he wasn't relaxed. Yet, he stood ready to fight or take flight in an instant.

The air in front of him became agitated; then a sound, not unlike a sonic boom, pierced Kirth's ears. A gray mist formed and took shape. Drakus stood in front of him. The hunter's black eyes glowed red in their pupils, revealing the fierceness of their evil.

"We meet again, Norseman," the malevolent Drakus whispered. "Such a pity you won't be staying long. We, on the other hand, will be here forever."

"Why waste what little time you have in idle threats?" Kirth appeared bored.

Drakus's hollow laugh rang in Kirth's ears. "Think what you

will, Norseman. We knew you'd be glad to see us."

"At this hour? In the approaching light of dawn? Has your memory lapsed since last we met, old aging one? With little effort, I can see you as you are. Frankly, it's not a pretty picture. You look worse than you smell." Kirth snapped his fingers. "Ah. I see. This is a new tactic. You hope to nauseate me to death."

Drakus feigned an appalled look. "Is that any way to talk to your dear father?"

"You're not my father." Anger raged in Kirth's eyes. "My father died centuries ago when you destroyed him and stole his body. Now that corpse rots on you along with the others you've inhabited."

"Your father's spirit, his essence, is here with us. You know that, Norseman. That's why you have such difficulty fighting us."

"My father is dead; his Breath is free," Kirth retorted. *Calm down.* The Beast is stirring your fears, trying to get you to attack, to expend your energy. "You're a thief. A liar. A cheat."

"Such flattery," Drakus cooed. "Your words are pearls. But, compliments will gain you no pardon. No quarter. We can, however, guarantee you a painful and arduous death."

A smile brushed insolently across Kirth's face. "Promises. Promises. You thought you could drain the Nightstar's power, claim her life for your own and become immortal. You didn't succeed then nor any time since. And you won't now."

"Ah, but we will. This is our time. Mark our words well. You've never been able to best us. We've killed you once, almost twice. We will again."

Kirth shrugged. "What's really on your mind, Drakus?"

"How's the rest of the family?"

"None of your business."

"The faithful Enchanters? Meddling as much as always?"

"You know the answer to that." Kirth sighed. "Get to the point."

"Norseman, you haven't changed. You never were good at small talk."

"All your talk is small — like you, Drakus." Kirth yawned.

Fire shot from Drakus's eyes.

The flames engulfed Kirth, who laughed. "Is that the best you can do? The heat died away. "We have nothing to say to each other."

"Oh, we do. We do. We have Miss Sylvian DuClair, who even now is getting into that taxi out front. It's a pity her car didn't start this morning. That cabby's about to make a fatal mistake."

Kirth's lightning-quick senses scanned the streets of the Warehouse District then read the driver's future. "Damn you. You know the rules. You can't harm her."

"We're both bound by those rules, the ones you forgot last time." Drakus chuckled. "Your stupidity cost us the Nightstar. But we found the price worth seeing the pain on your face. And so delightful watching you suffer while she burned to death."

Drakus pointed to the cab cruising away from the hotel. "We didn't select the taxi nor the driver that happened to be at the hotel. His fate isn't in our hands, nor in yours."

Kirth knew the driver faced doom. Perhaps he could save Sylvian from harm. In his haste to leave, he failed to conceal his thoughts from Drakus.

"Try," Drakus hissed after him. "Her injuries will be too great for modern medicine. Alas, her fate's in your hands. We suspect you're going to be busy healing our Astraea. Drain your energies, Kith the Bold." The Beast's laughter exploded toward Kirth's receding form in waves of discordant sounds. "Until we meet again, happy tears."

Moments later, when his mind projected its energy into the truck's path, Kirth felt the impact of the head-on blow. He arrived too late to avert the disaster, but his energy did offset the momentum and kept the moving van from compressing the taxi like an accordion.

Drakus lied. No sane driver drove this fast in this area of the city. Kirth felt the touch of The Beast, who'd done something to precipitate the injuries and knew Kirth would save her regardless of how much the effort drained his power. While he channeled his mind to seek her in the twisted mass of metal, he swore they would destroy Drakus this time.

The taxi driver's thoughts had been on a fight he'd had with his wife the night before. With his attention elsewhere, as Kirth had suspected, his reflexes hadn't been quick enough to protect himself and his passenger. He was dead. She still breathed but was unconscious. He sensed her spirit being drawn from her body. Drakus's touch. The interloper was taking her back in time, moving her away from his influence.

As Kirth swept toward the wreck, his mind called forth a whirlwind around the taxi to keep rescuers at bay. He stepped into the wreckage and lifted the pieces of crumbled metal away from his love until he knelt over her limp body.

He disciplined his emotions, reminding himself not to push her rejuvenation too far, too fast. Then, he braced himself for the maelstrom which would surely come with her spirit being moved through time. Leaning over her, his hands began floating in circles across the length of her body, and he started to hum softly until his tears showered down on her, their healing power easing the wounds he sensed deep inside her, while his mind held them solidly in the present moment.

A dark, fathomless void began to rip the ground beneath Kirth asunder, but his energy held firm against it. The warning of the Nyx pounded in his mind. He could not heal in the past. His power to heal existed only in the present. To try to do otherwise would trap him between worlds.

He couldn't rescue her mind from its backward spiral in time, but he could heal her body. Intense heat ignited into flames around him, and fire hot winds beat against him while the void continued to spread below him. He refused to be sucked into the vortex by keeping his mind planted in the muggy warmth of the early New Orleans morning hour.

He saw the one-way street, the lamppost, and the wrought-iron lattice work on the balconies above the twisted moving van and taxi. People watched the rescue team work unsuccessfully to break through the whirlwind encasing the taxi.

Her skin lost its shallow look and her breathing eased. Kirth forced himself to pull away. The humming stopped and so did the tears.

Quicker than the human eye can register moving images, Kirth stood in the crowd. The whirlwind vanished as mysteriously as it appeared. He slipped by the police holding the curious back from the wreck and approached the medics as they loaded her into the ambulance.

"I'm a friend of hers — Sylvian DuClair." His words soothed while his mind erased their questions. "I'll ride back here. Take her to La Crosse General and notify Dr. Wade Tremain. Tell him Kirth said he has a patient arriving."

A tremor ran through him as he sat beside her. He fought the urge to hold her hand. Instead, he whispered in her ear, careful to call her by the name which had the greatest power to call her back to New Orleans.

"Sylvian. Sylvian DuClair. You are wandering in a dream from which only you can awaken yourself. Please come back to your time. You have been afraid. Alone. I'm here now, and I love you. I won't let you be harmed. You are the evening star cast upon moon-washed shores, the light of the night, the glow of moonlight captured in love's vision, the dance that will not end, the music that breathes life into the air. You are mine, and I am yours. Every moment you tarry in the olden world steals our life. I cannot be with you there. Break the bonds of your dream-walk and come home to me."

Memories

15

Kirth studied the moonlight from the hospital room window. He'd moved Sylvian's bed so the light fell on her sleeping form, knowing that even in her twilight state, the rays comforted her as they did him.

He could not awaken her. Twice, she seemed close, almost on the verge of regaining consciousness. Something called her back, and she moved away from him again. Discouraged at first, fearful of whatever evil plan Drakus had concocted, Kirth felt the bewitcher's hold on Sylvian sever when she spiraled away the second time. The thief's energy recoiled violently and withdrew.

Kirth chuckled softly. Drakus committed the ultimate error — underestimating an opponent. Aasta. It had to have been Aasta. Kirth felt the surge of energy when the two souls collided and the explosion that forced Drakus to flee.

His love rested safe for now. He'd healed her body. She now witnessed experiences he could not speak of to her. Drakus had unwittingly helped rather than harmed them. The Beast might make another error in its enraged state. If so, Kirth stood ready to strike.

He fretted over the time remaining before her twenty-fifth birthday. Five days the Texas driver's license said. In all their lifetimes, he'd not found her sooner than five days from her twenty-fifth birthday — not at Eimund when she recognized The Beast through the guise the thief wore and fled into the fire, or at the abbey where he found her scrubbing floors, or when she lived as a slave in the dark king's castle, and certainly not —

"Damn," he exclaimed. The memory pained him still. The roar of The Beast's laughter. The white stallion's blood feeding the sands. The fire enveloping Astraea, her hands reaching, pleading for him. Too late. Too late. His tears were as dry as the desert dust.

"You OK?" The whisper came from the doorway.

"Yeah." Kirth turned around, berating himself as he did so. His attention had been focused in the past to the exclusion of the present. This time, no harm had been done, but next time could be different. He had to be vigilant.

"The others are outside, in the hall," Hale said, slipping inside the room and moving toward Kirth. "We brought dinner. New York strip from the hotel. And iced coffee loaded with sugar from Cafe du Monde. You can't refuse."

"Thanks." Kirth smiled at the drummer. Thoughtful guys. He'd told them not to worry about him, that he'd take care of himself. He wasn't surprised they ignored him. He would have done the same with them.

"Doc Wade said they didn't find any internal injuries." Hale's tone begged confirmation.

Kirth agreed.

"That she's a lucky girl to have come out virtually unscratched. He sounded optimistic she'd come out of the coma."

Kirth again confirmed Hale's comments. "That's why she's in this private room. Otherwise, she'd be in intensive care. Those monitors keep them informed of her brain's activity and her vital signs. But the X-rays and blood work gave her a clean bill of health."

The door opened slightly again. Rogert stuck his head through the crack. Kirth waved him inside, and they all spilled into the semi-darkened room.

Eric, who carried the food, spied the low table in front of the sofa and deposited his load. "Hey, this isn't bad for a hospital. Sofa and all."

"The hospital has a few rooms like this for senior citizens —

like us," Kirth quipped. "A family member can stay in a little more comfort than in the usual room. This one had no patient, and I persuaded Admittance to let me have the room."

"Was she cute and unattached and you used the old Kirth charm on her?" Hale asked.

Kirth shook his head. "Married with four children. Attractive? Yes. But that had nothing to do with my securing the room."

"Right," Hale snickered. "You convinced her that Miss DuClair is your grandmother."

"She had a kind streak and took pity on me."

"Of course," Hale laughed. "Your velvety touch had nothing to do with it."

"Absolutely not," Kirth replied. He hadn't touched the Admittance lady at all. He just planted the idea in her mind to give him this room. Hale liked to kid him about the way he managed to get what he wanted. "I'm famished. And I didn't know it until I smelled the food. Thanks." He crossed his legs as he sat down on the floor. "Who do I owe?"

"Forget it," Eric said. "Gaylor's with Jeanne. She flew in earlier this evening. She's never been to New Orleans. He thought an evening together here would be romantic."

"He's right," Hale declared. "This is a great place to get laid."

"They're married." Rogert shook his head. "You're impossible. Your mind works on two tracks. Women and drums."

"Just because they're married doesn't mean he doesn't want to get laid." Hale made a face at Rogert. "It's even more romantic with your wife away from the kids and the in-laws. Especially somewhere like New Orleans."

"They don't have kids," Rogert retorted.

"Well, knock me down, Einstein, " Hale said. "You think I don't know that? But if they did, it would be even more romantic to get away."

"How would you know? You've never been married," Rogert retaliated. "You'd be an impossible husband. You and your two-track mind would drive any woman mad."

"Stop it," Eric growled. "This is no place to get something going. We're all nervous. Why not just say so and be done with it." He turned to Kirth. "Is she going to be OK? We know what Doc Wade said. We want to know what you think."

Kirth held up his hand as he finished chewing the bite he'd put in his mouth. "I believe she's going to pull through. None of us knows how long she'll be unconscious. But I agree with Doc Wade. She'll come out of it."

"Has anyone been called?" Rogert frowned. "I mean do we know if she's got relatives. What about her boss?"

"One question at a time," Hale advised. "Can't you see he's eating. Or trying to."

"She has a week off, and she doesn't have any relatives," Kirth replied. He didn't explain how he knew the answer to both questions. Instead, he let them assume he called Houston. He started to, but instinct warned him against doing so. At best, he considered such a call chancy. Drakus had found her first, and calling her place of employment or trying to reach anyone who knew her was unwise.

"Finish your dinner, then tell us what the hell's going on," snapped Eric, his square shoulders tense and stiff as he plopped down across from Kirth. The others followed his lead.

Kirth looked at them questioningly. Dark-haired, dark-eyed Eric the Grump would be the easiest to fool, if he wanted to, and he didn't. Kirth's eyes glanced affectionately over Rogert's clean-swept face and haunting green eyes. The serious, thoughtful Monk wouldn't be difficult either. Hale was different. His pretty-boy looks and bantering manner hid an astute mind. He watched them watch him silently while he ate. Their unspoken questions ran deeper than curiosity. They had a right to know why he cancelled his plans for Miss DuClair. He had stood them and everyone else up today for a stranger.

"Go ahead and tell us," Hale said. "Talk with your mouth full. We don't care."

"Patience," Kirth said, swallowing. "At your insistence, I

went to check out Miss DuClair. Before I had an opportunity to meet her, she left in a taxi. I followed, hoping to catch up with her. I saw the wreck. It didn't look as if anyone survived. And the taxi driver didn't."

"We heard," Rogert interjected.

Kirth swigged some coffee before continuing. "The driver of the moving van got pretty banged up himself. He swears the power steering went out, the accelerator stuck, and the brakes failed. I asked the ambulance to bring Miss DuClair here. That's about all there is to tell. Except, I regret missing the picnic. And the kids. We planned our concert schedule around the outing, among other things." He grimaced. "Then this happens."

"No one expected you to come once you'd called and said what happened," Rogert said. "We knew you wouldn't leave anyone unconscious alone in any hospital, even this one. That's not what we're curious about."

Impatiently, Eric spoke up. "Who is she? Is this the woman you called to in your sleep or not?"

"Ah. I see." Kirth paused. This was the difficult question he suspected they would ask. If he said no, they'd wonder when he married a stranger. "Yes and no. When I saw her get into the taxi, I realized she resembled someone I knew years ago. The woman in my dream. I'd rather not say more right now, because we don't know when she'll wake up, or what will happen then. But, if you're asking me if I'm interested in Miss DuClair, then the answer is yes. I am. And I'm not leaving until she's better. We play Houston in ten days. Surely, we'll know something by then."

"I knew it!" Hale exclaimed. "The minute I saw her, I knew she was the one. I told you that."

Kirth smiled. "Yes, you did."

Rogert leaned toward Kirth. "I bet you met her when you took that trip three years ago. Somehow, you lost track of her." His eyes widened. "She doesn't know who you are, does she?"

"No, Monk, she doesn't." Kirth stabbed the last bite of steak and ate the meat absently. An understatement among understatements. He ought to know. He'd made many.

Eric frowned. "I wouldn't call her a fan of our kind of music."

Hale interjected, "She liked the show. She said so."

"So what. Liking a show is vastly different from digging a certain kind of music," Eric grumbled. "She doesn't dig ours."

"What about kids?" Rogert asked. "She digs kids — teenagers, I think. Maybe all kids. Anyway, she's getting a master's in psychology so she can work with kids. They're the key."

"Yeah," Eric agreed. "Kirth needs to focus on kids and stay away from music when he talks to her."

"He can sing to her," Hale suggested. "Women love to have men sing to them. They say it's romantic."

"I like that idea," Rogert squinted his eyes as if he were trying to remember something vital. "I can lend him my guitar. Did I bring it with me?"

"It's on the bus," Eric replied. "I saw it there."

"Oh, yes," Rogert said, relieved. "I'll get it in the morning and bring it up here."

"Aren't you three forgetting something?" Kirth asked. He'd been watching the guys plotting how he would ensnare Sylvian. He wished wooing her could be that simple.

They all looked at him as if he'd just walked into the room and hadn't been there all along.

"What?" Eric growled.

"Miss DuClair is unconscious."

"That's why you need to sing to her," Hale insisted with his usual optimism. "Rogert needs to bring his guitar up here. That way you can play softly and sing to her. Love songs. The kind of things women want to hear. Maybe music will call her back from wherever she's gone."

"That's not a bad idea," Kirth admitted.

"It's a great idea." Looking at the others, Hale implored, "Right guys?"

"Yeah," Rogert agreed.

Eric sighed and stood up. "It might work." He walked over

to the bed and gazed down at Sylvian. "She doesn't appear injured. Just sleeping peacefully."

Leaning over the bed, he whispered, "Miss DuClair, it's safe to wake up now. You've not been harmed. You're well. In good health. Your body's in no pain." He glanced over at Kirth as if to confirm what he'd just said.

Kirth agreed. He stood up and walked toward him.

"No one's going to harm you, Miss DuClair, " Eric continued. "There's no reason to keep sleeping. There's nothing to fear. Wake up, Miss DuClair."

Hale and Rogert joined them. Kirth spoke first. "I've been calling her name. Frequently. Doc Wade said it might help."

"That's what he told us earlier, when we called," Rogert whispered. "Do you think she can hear what's going on around her? That on some level she's aware, but just can't speak?"

"I don't know, but I hope so." Motioning for them to follow, Kirth moved to the door. Outside in the hall, he studied them, weighing his words before he spoke. "I'm going to stay the night. If she's still comatose in the morning, I'd appreciate it if you'd bring me Rogert's guitar before you leave for Veracruz."

"That's no problem." Eric glanced at the others. "We're not going. We're staying here."

Dismayed, Kirth said, "We've planned this trip for months. Just because I can't go is no reason for the rest of you to cancel."

"We already have," Eric stated flatly. "We decided earlier this evening after we'd talked to Doc Wade. The publicity office in California hadn't closed. We let them handle the details. It's done."

"How did Leigh take it?" Kirth thought of Eric's hard-working wife who'd spent months planning the perfect week in Veracruz for all of them. "She wanted to go on this trip before she talked us into it."

"Ask her yourself," Eric said. "She'll be here in the morning."

Each piece of news upset Kirth more than the last. Now, they'd all be here. He cared too much about his friends to want anything to happen to them. Somehow, he had to persuade them to go and leave him behind.

Planting his hands on his hips, Hale proclaimed, "It's no use, Kirth. We've agreed. Both Leigh and Jeanne found the idea of your staying here while we go run and play unthinkable. They wouldn't hear of leaving you with someone you barely know —" he snorted "— but are obviously interested in. Particularly when said someone is injured and hangs between this world and the next. Now you won't get anywhere with those gals once they've made up their minds. You know that."

"We're not budging," Rogert threw in. "You've never left us in a crisis. How could you imagine we would leave you?"

"We'll talk again tomorrow," Kirth said, resigned.

"That's fine," Hale replied. "But, we're staying. If you need us, we'll at least be in the same town."

"When Miss DuClair does come around, she doesn't know you, but we've met her," Eric said. "She's not keen on rock music. She won't look favorably on the world she imagines we live in. It won't hurt to meet Leigh and Jeanne."

"I don't mean to sound ungrateful," Kirth said. If things were different, Eric would be right. Sylvian would find disliking Leigh and Jeanne difficult. They were easy to know, accessible — actually lovely girls, with careers that kept them as busy as their husbands. "I just want you to enjoy the vacation and not let this unusual situation interfere with your plans."

Playfully punching Kirth on the shoulder, Hale grinned. "Get real. This is New Orleans. Who could be bored here? Besides, you knew we wouldn't run off and leave you."

"Get some rest," Rogert added. "You're not thinking clearly if you even imagined we'd go."

Eric scowled at him. "They're right. And you know it. Veracruz will still be there when we can all make the trip. We'll see you in the morning."

Kirth watched them walk away. He felt fortunate. Through lean and fat times they remained friends. He wanted to keep them alive. Shaking his head, he turned and went into the room.

Pulling the chair back beside Sylvian, Kirth longed to take her hand in his, but dared not. Once he touched her, he could not control his desire. He'd learned that well.

Instead, he sang softly to her. She stirred. He continued singing, but she didn't wake up. Leaning forward, he whispered, "Sylvian, we have little time. You are the light of my life as I am yours. Please come back to me."

Although he'd not planned on sleeping, Kirth yawned. Once he started, he couldn't stop yawning. Maybe just a few winks, he decided, leaning his head back on the chair.

Interlude

16

*T*he Nyx summoned Kirth as he slept, tumbling the human world out from under him and floating him in a fluxing kaleidoscope of brilliant color. The hues shimmered, then stilled. A dark path spread in front of him, stretching into a purple sky. Foreshadowed by a golden glow, he walked into the twilight. The call of his name became stronger and louder: "Kithnaran. Kithnaran. Kithnaran."

Slowly the shadows washed away. The pathway became suffused in light. He stopped, blinked, and refocused his vision.

Although he'd never walked this land in person, he'd been here often in his dreams. His initial reaction was always the same. He felt as if he stood in the first morning of time when the world, freshly born, lay pregnant with expectation. The greens and blues and browns of nature glistened under a young sun, whose diffuse light bathed all in a gentle glow.

As he breathed the air damp with dew, he felt the weariness of his forced vigilance hang heavy over him then slip away. He stilled himself and allowed the tranquil setting to fill him anew, then walked on.

In the distance, he saw Astraea's sisters sitting under their favorite weeping willow trees by the banks of the Clearborn River. They wore their changeless Nyx clothes. The incandescent sheen of the gold-streaked, silver fabric sparkled with starlight.

A tranquil scene. The brave-hearted at rest. His eyebrow arched. Ha! These slim, wild beauties were at odds in this pastoral setting.

Nata tapped her fingers impatiently, her fiery energy smoldering, itching to be released. Thirteen centuries ago, she'd passed the sacred flame to him without the slightest hesitation. In all that time, he'd not come close to matching her skill with fire, nor could he taste the night with her ease. He still saw her as the more worthy.

He had the same feeling about Niniane who made him guardian of the forest. A greater healer, she blended more readily with nature than he did. She walked unnoticed across deserts, plains, and forests, adapting her coloring to the earth with the ease of a chameleon.

Beginning with Rana, they'd all been more than generous with him. She had saved him and brought him across the uncharted waters to the others. He eyed her fondly. Even here, away from the sea, the color of her hair and eyes reflected a fluctuating mix of dark shells and smoky-green ocean depths.

His glance fell on the eldest, Arva. Sometimes he wondered how much older, but knowing the women in his world — and why would these be different? — he never asked. The tallest — almost his height — and thus the most formidable presence among them, she looked no older than the rest.

Arva had saved him this last time, when he'd ignored their advice. Her silent movements echoed the beating of wings for those with acute hearing. The Beast quivered at the sound and had faltered when she'd drawn near their battle.She'd not interfered. She couldn't. The rules — the ones he had broken — wouldn't permit her to do so, but the distraction allowed him to escape being imprisoned by The Beast.

His thoughts turned gloomy. His fault. His arrogance. They had all paid bitterly. Especially Astraea. His beloved had not walked this land, either in the flesh or in a dream, in more than three thousand years. She would be lost to her world forever if Drakus won.

"Kithnaran!" Arva commanded. "Here. Now!"

In a flash, he stood at their side.

"We applaud your stout heart, yet quaver at your reckless

action," Arva said, her now soft voice accusing. "Only a brave and foolhardy warrior would ask the Nightstar for forgiveness. Do you know how fortunate you are to be in our presence in one identifiable piece?"

Kirth defended himself. "I had to." He'd stand until he had a better sense of the game afoot. Only standing did he feel equal to sparring with four Nyx, particularly these.

Dismayed, Arva fixed her hypnotic, catlike, golden-brown eyes on him. "In that instant of absolution, the Nightstar could have as easily scorched your Breath"

Nata snapped her fingers. "Faster than snow melts in the hot sun."

"Quicker than a prey's heart beats on the run," Rana offered.

"You would have been fried well done," Niniane concluded.

The others stared at Niniane in disbelief. Nata grimaced. "Well done?"

"Thank you." Niniane smiled smugly. "I thought so, too."

"That is not what I meant!" Nata exclaimed.

"I know what you meant," Niniane snapped. "But someone had to stop the foolish rhyme." To Kirth she added, "Indeed, you are charmed. Only the chosen one contacts the Nightstar. Yet, you called her from the long sleep and not only asked forgiveness but also her watchful blessing over the battle to come. Real —"

Bemused, Kirth suggested, "Daring?"

"Aye," Niniane replied. "And shocking."

"Never been done before," Nata retorted.

"Then it was about time," Kirth said.

"What bag of tea leaves gave you that idea?" Rana asked.

"No tea leaves," Kirth countered. "I read it in the stars."

"Enough!" Arva commanded. "The score is settled. What is done is done. You must accept the gift and let go the guilt. Now, do not be foolish again. Sit down. It is safe."

Kirth sighed. "Just when I'd warmed up to the game." He sat beside them on the grass, which formed a lush, living carpet beneath him.

Arva handed him a tall, slender silver cup filled with clear liquid. "Join us for some refreshment. You will need it. The days ahead are hazardous. Now may be our only opportunity to speak of new developments."

Kirth sipped from the chalice. The liquid spread as a balm through him.

"Our patience has been rewarded," declared Rana, her stormy-green eyes riveting. "The Beast Drakus lies wounded."

"The creature tried to break through time and send its power backward to alter the past, didn't it?" Kirth asked.

"Yes," she replied. "You felt the jolt?"

"When I healed Sylvian, the world broke apart underneath me. I remembered your words and held fast to the present."

Nata's laughter echoed through the air. "Its cunning has been overshadowed by the strength the bewitcher has acquired in this century. Regardless of its other abilities, The Beast's body is partially fueled by our energies. The past is a barrier we seldom attempt to cross. Our foe barely avoided being caught between disparate worlds. By expending almost all of its energy, the brute managed to escape back to its lair."

"Aasta attacked the invader, speeding its withdrawal," Kirth speculated, then observed their response.

"Aye," Niniane said.

Kirth watched as the others agreed, then asked, "How long before Drakus heals?"

"We do not know, but healed or not, The Beast comes for our sister at the hour of her twenty-fifth birthday," Arva said.

"Not healed?" Kirth leaned back on his elbows. "Sounds promising. Astraea battling the ghoul in a weakened state suits me."

"Do not count on such good fortune." The hint of a smile formed at the corners of Arva's mouth. "We do predict the thief will be unable to directly drain your energies as in the past."

"That's encouraging," Kirth said. "The Beast tried to draw me into its web. When that didn't work, the interloper instigated the wreck. I could feel the evil touch even though the creature feigned ignorance."

"Denials mean nothing!" Nata exclaimed, her red hair gleamed with golden highlights. "The Beast's world is lies!"

Rana raised her hand to silence Nata, then spoke. "Some followers tinkered with the car. Another drove the moving van. The Beast had others act for it as it is wont to do. And they are human. We could not interfere without endangering our world." She twirled her glass as she studied him. "The followers are the concern for the next days. As much as you want your friends to be safe, they are not."

Springing from the grass, Kirth blurted out, "They have to get out of New Orleans. I must persuade them to leave."

"Nay. They must stay." Arva reached for the cup he'd tossed in the grass when he moved. She filled the vessel again and offered it to him.

"I must warn them *now*," he insisted and turned to go.

"Impetuousness will not save your friends," Arva chided. "Distance will not keep them unharmed. The enemy hides from active battle in its weakened state. But its followers can hurt those you love. That is how The Beast will harm you now."

Kirth stopped and turned toward her. Arva offered him the drink again. This time he took the cup, fingering the gold filigree design as he drank.

Patting the ground in front of her, she continued, "All those you love are at risk. We of Fayre are with each one, but you are the one who has to take action. You do not like reading the minds of your friends and influencing them in that way, but you must. Plant caution in each — even the wives. No one is safe. The enemy is ruthless. It cares not for anyone but itself. But you know this."

Sighing, Kirth sat back down. The Nyx, male and female, were prickly, tough and nervy, but never ungracious as he had just been. "Please excuse my ill manners, ladies. I forget myself at times."

"'Tis nothing." Arva dismissed his rudeness with the wave of her hand, then ran her fingers through her silvery blonde hair. "The battle has been tiring. You have done well, Kithnaran. You have earned our respect and that of all others in our world who know of this threat. They are many."

Kirth felt strong hands gently begin to rub the back of his neck. "Thank you, Niniane. I am tense."

"Soon, you will not be," came Niniane's reply. "Tension is counterproductive."

"Being alert and ready are vital to his success," Nata interjected.

Niniane gave her a long, wilting look but said nothing.

"Tension which binds your muscles is negative." Nata compromised. "A balance is difficult to find."

"You worry for your friends," Arva said. "We will do all in our power to ensure their safety. If any are mortally wounded, we will intercede as we did with you. Bring them over, if we must. Most would survive the transformation."

"I pray that won't be necessary." Kirth's voice cracked. *Most?* "What would be better for them? To die or be damned to perpetual life, watching those you love age and die while you remain young. I can't bear the thought of either."

Arva reached out and took his hand. "You are distraught. And rightfully so. The decisions you have been forced to make have been particularly trying. You would feel differently if our sister had been by your side these many centuries. Instead, you have spent too long in your own company, recovering, while life here and in your world has moved on without you."

"I sound ungrateful, and I'm not." He had chosen this life. Living as a Nyx trapped in the mortal dimension had meant being condemned to walk forever in the twilight, always remembering his duty while seldom becoming involved directly with humans who would age and die before he returned.

Surviving had required going to ground in the soil between worlds for decades, sometimes centuries, to recover from the wounds he'd suffered in battling Drakus. Although he would make the same decision again, he didn't want his friends to be forced to choose.

"You are deeply loved here," Rana said. "By us and the others of Fayre. You are our dragon. The guardian of the forest while the Nightstar sleeps. The seal against the darkness who keeps the flame burning. Never forget that you have saved others from suffering and the price your world and ours would have paid had the enemy won."

"The Beast's presence has already darkened yours." Niniane spoke softly in his ear, her hands still busy restoring his aching muscles. "If the interloper were free to move at will between the two worlds, both would eventually be destroyed. You kept the fiend contained."

"Your music has been a brilliant stroke," Nata said.

"Yes." Rana agreed. "The songs carry your adventuresome spirit to others, are infectious with joy and hope and have worked, as you imagined, to combat the insidious negative drain our foe exerts over humans."

"We commend you." Arva smiled. "We did not think you could succeed and remain anonymous. Yet, for many years, you did just that. The music has been the single most effective weapon you have wielded against our enemy."

"It's also put those I love in jeopardy," Kirth grumbled.

"Living is hazardous, Kithnaran, whether it be in your world or ours," Rana reminded him. "You, of all people, know the truth of that. Too many spend their time in the half-life of forgetting, neither alive nor dead, but merely existing. Your music has the power to awaken them to the wondrous world in which they live, to set them free. The songs are popular here as well."

The amazement evident in his voice, he asked, "Here? Our songs are played in your world?"

"Oh, yes," Arva replied.

"On what instruments?"

"The instruments are similar to your own," Nata said. "You could play any of them and show our musicians a trick or two." She laughed.

"During the last, long years when you slept and recovered from your wounds, both worlds changed," Rana said. "Ours, like yours, is in a constant state of flux. The appearance that our world is not is deceptive."

Arva shook her head. "Have you forgotten your first lesson? Reality often serves as a veil covering the truth. You must use all your senses to perceive the truth and not count solely on what you see."

Kirth closed his eyes to mute the colors which dazzled his vision. He opened himself to the life around him. Shortly, tainted vibrations came back to him. Shocked, he whispered, "No. I feel The Beast's presence. It's only faintly discernible, but it's here."

"Did you expect our domain to be otherwise?" Arva asked. "The injuries of The Beast healed while you slept. This century during the first great war in your world, the creature awoke to a smorgasbord of strife, hatred, genocide, and fear. Since then, its insatiable appetite has been gorging. Part of its life force belongs to our sister. That energy cannot be used without its discharge touching our world. Now, even victory cannot erase the darkness The Beast has brought to both worlds, but it will save them from total enslavement."

Sorrow washed over him as his senses swept across the web of dissolution The Beast had woven in both spheres while he slept. He breathed deeply and let the horror flow out of him. He let the burden pass. Even though his consciousness existed in a semi-alert state when he buried himself in the soil, he lay helpless until his wounds healed. Only then could he break free.

When he rested, to absorb the pain and pleasure of those walking on Earth slowed his recovery. He learned that lesson centuries ago when the Black Death devastated Europe. He heard every agonizing cry, felt every loss, sensed every second of pain. Reviving, becoming strong enough to break free, had taken him decades longer than usual. Since then, he'd mastered allowing the sensations to pass through him without clinging to them.

A sense of peace filled him. His energy balanced, centered within itself, and no longer felt pulled by those around him. He opened his eyes.

Rana smiled at him. "Your expended energies are refilled.

You are ready." She stood, signaling the end of their talk.

"The hours move no faster in the past than they do in the present." Arva also stood. "But, since the mind of our sister shot into her previous life through the void, the calendar days pass at a speed perhaps comparable to fast forward on one of your tape recorders. When the hold on her loosens, you must propel her forward so that she does not lose the time she has gained nor her way home to you."

"How?" Kirth asked.

The others rose to their feet.

"Stay alert," Nata retorted. "Ready to act."

"Follow your instinct," replied Niniane.

"Only you know what to do," Rana offered, cryptically.

"But I don't know!" Kirth exclaimed.

"You will," Arva assured. "Our sleeping sister awakens soon. She will know more than she has in previous encounters, but this does not free you to speak with her about the past."

"I understand that better than I'd like to," Kirth replied, standing.

"Nor does it alter the contract." Arva's eyebrow arched. "The Seers are adamant."

"I didn't think it did," Kirth replied aloud, while in his mind he cursed the damnable Seers. "Profess her choice in front of witnesses and sign her name on the dotted line."

"They said nothing of the dotted line," Niniane said.

"He knows that!" snapped Nata. "It is a joke, dear sister."

"I know that!" Niniane exclaimed. "You did not let me finish —"

"And I will not now," Nata said. "You did not know it was a joke. Humor is a sign of a quick mind."

Niniane hit Nata with a fireball, knocking her obviously surprised sister into the grass. "Did, too."

"Ladies, please," Kirth begged. He laughed. They were a kick. Always had been. At least as long as he'd known them. "Both of you are right. A joke and not a joke. A figure of speech — sign on the dotted line. May we not part in peace? Please?"

Nata smiled demurely. "Of course." She extended her hand to Niniane.

Kirth grimaced. "Let me —" He moved too late.

Niniane touched Nata's hand; sparks electrified the air around them, and Niniane vanished in a puff of smoke.

"Enough," Arva said. "We have business at hand."

Niniane reappeared beside Rana. She smiled at Kirth. "Go in peace." She scowled at Nata, who fired a bolt in her direction. Too late. Niniane had disappeared again.

Arva breathed a martyred sigh, reached for the empty cup Kirth held, and said, "Hear my words at our parting. You are not alone. Undue fear for your friends colors your judgment. Their character builds their futures. Not you. Love — the greatest power of all in your world and ours — will serve you as long as you honor it well." Her hand touched his face, then gently closed his eyes.

He yawned and fell into a deep sleep.

A movement in the hospital room awakened Kirth. His eyes opened fractionally, and once they adjusted to the semi-darkness, he saw the figure of a man standing on the other side of the bed. The form came into focus. Dark brown hair with a touch of gray at the temples. Dr. Wade Tremain in the flesh.

"She's sleeping peacefully," Kirth said.

Dr. Tremain flinched. "You startled me, Kirth. I thought you were asleep."

"I was." Kirth rose and went to stand beside him.

"I tried not to disturb you, but I make rounds early. I wanted to see how our patient passed the night. All her vital signs are good. And, you're right. She appears peaceful. A sleeping beauty."

"For all our sakes, I hope she awakens much sooner than the fairy tale princess," Kirth teased.

"She's exhibited some signs of waking up?"

"The guys recommended I sing to her. They suggested a love

song, so late last night I tried. She responded but didn't wake up. What did you see that made you suspect she'd tried to awaken?"

"You. Your joking manner. Yesterday, you were not in nearly so good a mood. Something had to account for it. And the only thing you've had on your mind is waking our patient. Singing to her is an excellent suggestion, especially with your voice. Mine, on the other hand, would not encourage anyone to wake up unless to escape the frightful sound."

"You play a mean sax," Kirth said. "Audiences love it when we can get you on stage with us."

Dr. Tremain smiled and motioned to the door. "They just can't believe an old codger and a doctor to boot can rock 'n' roll." They stepped into the hallway. "I bet Hale suggested the love songs. He's really got a poet's soul, even though he hides his sensitivity behind his drums and his talk of sex."

"He won't be pleased to know he's so transparent."

"But you'll be sure to tell him." Dr. Tremain's blue eyes twinkled merrily.

"As soon as I see him. One of the guys will be here early with Rogert's acoustical guitar. I doubt it's Hale."

They both laughed.

Kirth's tone became serious. "So, how is Miss DuClair this morning?"

"You needn't address her in such a formal manner with me, Kirth. I know she's special to you. Unfortunately, I don't know how she is. I wish I could be more encouraging. But frankly, I don't know why she's in this coma. She's in remarkable shape. She seems to have suffered no injuries in the wreck, which killed the driver. Now, I've seen these freak occurrences in accidents. One person is killed. Another is almost unharmed. But, she's more than unharmed. She's in top physical condition, if the tests can be believed. And I've had most of them repeated just to be sure."

Dr. Tremain shook his head. "I'm just guessing now. Perhaps she saw the impending accident and recoiled from the potential pain. If she's suffered some great trauma in her life, her mind may be protecting her from suffering again. When she decides she's safe or heals the trauma, she'll wake up. For all our research, we know almost nothing about how the mind actually works. She's suffered no physical damage. That much I can tell you. The rest is speculation."

"I believe she'll wake up soon," Kirth said. "Today or tomorrow."

"I hope you're right." Dr. Tremain's frustration was obvious. "Take Hale's advice. Sing love songs to her. It's as good a suggestion as I've heard so far. I'll check back when I've finished my rounds."

Kirth watched his friend walk toward the nurses station. Before he stepped into the room, he saw Eric and Rogert walk toward him. They paused to speak with the doctor, and Kirth watched the three with fondness.

He hoped they wouldn't be harmed. His experience had been a hard taskmaster. He'd not protected those he loved. No matter how much he wanted to and tried to save them, he'd not been successful in doing so.

Handing Kirth the guitar, Rogert said, "Doc Wade likes the idea."

"I know," Kirth replied. "Thanks for bringing it. Surely, Leigh doesn't arrive this early?"

"Pretty early," grumbled Eric. "You know how she is. Disgustingly cheerful at the most ridiculous hours in the morning. I didn't want to be my usual glum self when she got here so I decided to get up early enough to be fully awake."

Kirth looked at Rogert. "So what's your excuse to be up before dawn?"

Rogert shrugged. "Lyrics to a new song. I'd been writing for an hour when Eric knocked. Here we are." He held up a sack and a Thermos. "Coffee? Doughnuts?"

"Both." Kirth took the sack and Thermos. "Thanks."

"And a change of clothes, a razor and a toothbrush? Eric held up dark slacks and a long-sleeved shirt. "Hale insisted last night. The lilac." He shrugged. "Said women love it on you. Deepens the color of your eyes or some such nonsense."

Rogert nodded earnestly. "True story. You've never noticed the stares. But you get them, especially in this shirt."

"Won't hurt to look your best," Eric grumbled.

"No, it won't." Kirth opened the door to the room. They stepped inside quietly and walked to the bed.

After a few moments of silence, Eric spoke first. "She looks the same. Doc Wade said you sang to her, and she moved some in her sleep."

"Yes. She seemed to respond." Kirth put the Thermos and sack on the table. He poured himself some coffee and reached in the sack. "Is the song for the new album?" He grabbed a glazed doughnut and bit into it.

"I think so," Rogert replied, his tone tentative. "When it's finished, I'll know. Well. Yeah. It fits in with the others we've worked on so far."

"Good." Kirth sat down. "We're close to having enough material. Our studio date's still a month off."

"Mike said they want to move the date up." Rogert plopped on the sofa. "He told them no."

Eric sat down as well. "It won't be changed. Mike's leaving today. You know how he thrives on haggling face-to-face."

"Yeah." Kirth chuckled. "He'll steamroller them, and they won't even know they've been pressed."

Rogert laughed. "He's a negotiating wizard. No doubt about it."

Business occupied their talk for the better part of an hour. After Eric and Rogert left, Kirth stood with his arms resting on the hospital bed's side rail and studied Sylvian's face.

He wondered if there'd be any signs here if she were harmed there? Was she with him? On the ship? At Eimund? He believed the bewitcher had taken her to that life even though there were three later choices. And her sisters had agreed she walked that tragic time.

When he'd first seen her in the burning village, standing with her feet apart, passing her sword back and forth in her hands, her earthy eyes stealthily watching him, ready to attack, he'd known their destinies were entwined. Yet, he'd not foreseen the horrendous price they, as well as his kin, would pay in the days ahead. In that respect, she'd been more intuitive.

He'd still been mortal then, ruthless in war and cocksure of himself, ready to take on an enemy whose power he only began to comprehend when he lay dying. Had the years made him wiser? He certainly hoped so.

For now, she rested peacefully. He leaned over the bed, stopping himself just before his lips touched her forehead.

Too risky. She always stirred the fire in him. No other woman had ever moved him as she had with just the touch of her fingers on his face or the feel of her breasts under his hands, much less the flames of her lips against his.

Patience. Patience. Patience. He had to be patient.

Picking up the clothes and overnight kit, he stepped into the bathroom. As he lathered his face his thoughts turned to the sisters' cryptic advice. *Stay alert. Ready to act. Follow your instinct. Only you know what to do.*

An idea took form in his mind. *Follow your instinct.* A smile flickered across his lips.

Maybe. Just maybe it would work.

He hummed as he shaved, showered, and dressed. Moving the straight-backed chair five feet away from the hospital bed, he picked up the guitar, sat down, and began strumming softly.

17

*K*irth's haunting voice purred softly in the hospital room, its timbre wrapping the sleeping form in front of him in a cocoon of sensations. He'd called her for hours, caressing her skin with the silken magic of his words and the gentle touch of the guitar.

Moments ago, she'd stirred. The movement pleased him. Time now to intensify the spell.

His eyes altered to a deep, glowing purple flecked with the red of burning coals, their black centers streaked with yellow.

His mind saw them bound together intimately, her mouth one with his before his lips released hers to burn a path across her body, his hands gently touching her skin and leaving tiny goose bumps in their wake.

Sylvian moaned, then moved restlessly in the bed. He focused his considerable mental energy on her hardened nipples, then allowed his touch to move down to the soft mound now damp with desire. Her skin flushed.

Shutting away the physical ache growing within him, he pictured his lips kissing the soft skin inside her thighs, his fingers gently parting her hidden lips thus allowing his tongue to plunge inside.

The sleeping body shuddered. Sylvian's mouth opened. Her breath came in short pants. The heart monitor raced.

Splitting off a portion of his energy, Kirth projected it toward the door, successfully sealing the room from any outside intrusion. He'd spent too many hours building to this moment. He would allow nothing to stop him now.

He continued singing, calling to her with his words of love, while his mind's-eye saw his tongue plunge deeper and deeper inside her and his hands close over her breasts, his fingers gently pinching her nipples.

Sylvian's pulse quickened. The glass shield on the heart monitor machine cracked. Kirth's mind replaced his tongue with his throbbing erection, driving himself inside Sylvian in one quick stroke. The window shattered as the room instantaneously burst into flames.

Sylvian's eyes opened.

The music stopped and with it the spell Kirth had been weaving since his friends had left. The room existed as it had before he began his songs. He quieted the sounds of those trying to get in the door but didn't release the hold he had on keeping it shut.

"Hello, Miss DuClair." He smiled.

Her eyes widened. *Violet eyes.* "Have we met?"

"No," Kirth replied, his collected composure completely covering his former passion and his delight at having her awake. "I'm Kirth Naran of Dragon. You met the other members of the band when you interviewed them. Yesterday, you were in an accident I witnessed. You have no physical injuries but have been sleeping since the wreck. This is La Crosse General, a New Orleans hospital I know well. I have faith in the medical staff practicing here. The chief surgeon is Dr. Wade Tremain. I'm sure you will be meeting him shortly. He will be thrilled to see you are awake."

Kirth smiled to himself. Doc Wade headed this way, alarmed by the nurse's insistence that the door wouldn't open.

"Oh." Sylvian kept her gaze steady while secretly admiring the way the lilac shirt intensified his eyes. "You look familiar." She'd had the most amazing dreams. Right now she couldn't remember what they were. She just knew they were there, somewhere in her mind. She couldn't even recall the accident. Everything seemed foggy. Nothing felt real. She pinched herself.

"I can assure you, Miss DuClair, that I am quite real," Kirth said, noticing her disquietude. "You are quite real as well. You're here. Awake. In New Orleans. It will just take time to get your world in focus."

She gave him a wan smile. "Thank you for the reassurance. I've had the strangest dreams. I can't quite remember them. Yet, somehow I think they were important."

"Give it time," Kirth said, disappointed, yet hopeful that his words would come true. And quickly. He wanted her to remember. He needed her to remember. His task would be so much easier if she did. But, regardless, he knew what he had to do. "Shall I get Dr. Tremain?"

"Yes, please," Sylvian replied.

"I'll be right back," Kirth said, standing. He could simply release his hold, but he thought better of doing so. By the time he opened the door, Doc Wade should be steps away.

When he touched the handle, he felt the shadow hovering on the other side. They'd been found. One of Drakus's followers stood outside the door. Not a staff nurse. He would have known before. No. This is… . What? Ah. A delivery person. Flowers? Yes.

He changed his appearance to that of the hospital's chief administrator as he opened the door, then quickly pulled the handle until it shut behind him. "Would you take those flowers, nurse," he asked, looking at the youth who held them.

Without a question, she did. The youth turned and walked away. Not until he had left on the elevator did Kirth speak again.

"Would you check the card and see who they're from?"

"There's no card," she replied, searching the flowers for one and coming up empty handed. "It must have been misplaced."

Kirth dared not touch the flowers nor allow them in the room. They weren't harmless. "I'd appreciate your carrying them outside to the hospital's incinerator."

The nurse left, her earlier questions forgotten.

Kirth didn't like using mind control, but he had to admit there were moments he called the ability a blessing. Turning to Dr. Tremain, he returned his appearance to normal, released his hold on his friend's thoughts, and said, "Your patient is awake." Dr. Tremain's eyes widened. He smiled. "I'm delighted. How does she seem?"

"A little confused but otherwise OK," Kirth replied.

"You didn't tell her anyone died in the wreck?"

"I remembered what you said. Keep it simple. I told her she'd been in a wreck. She had no injuries, but she'd been asleep since yesterday. That she is in New Orleans. In this hospital. And I gave her your name."

"Excellent." Dr. Tremain nodded his head in approval. "Anything else?"

"No." Kirth replied.

"Shall we go in then?" Dr. Tremain looked at Kirth expectantly. Finally, he shook his head. "Do you want me to meet my patient or not?"

"Of course I do," Kirth replied, clearly surprised by the question.

"Is there something you want to tell me?"

"No."

"Perhaps there's something you don't want me to tell Miss DuClair?"

"No. Of course not. Why do you ask?"

Dr. Tremain frowned. "I've never seen you like this."

"What do you mean?" Kirth feared somehow, in some way, Doc Wade had seen through him.

"Preoccupied. You're blocking the doorway. In fact, you've been guarding that door as if it were made of gold, and you feared someone would nab the prize."

"Oh." Kirth forgot he planted himself where no one could get by him.

"Miss DuClair certainly has an effect on you I've never seen before." Doc Wade grinned. "Shall I tell her so?"

"No. I mean. That's not it. Uh. I mean, uh, I'm glad she's awake. That's all."

"It's OK. Your secret is safe with me." Dr. Tremain punched Kirth's arm. "Shall we go in now?"

"What secret?" Kirth paused before he pushed the door open behind him.

"It's written all over you." Dr. Tremain shook his head despairingly. "You have all the symptoms of the lovesickness. I'm afraid I don't have a cure in my little black bag. But I may be able to dispel any fears or misgivings Miss DuClair has about her condition. That is, if I'm allowed to see her."

Abashed, Kirth pushed the door open and followed Doc Wade into the room. Sylvian had propped up on the bed.

"Miss DuClair, I'm Dr. Wade Tremain. How are you feeling?"

"Confused," Sylvian replied.

"That's common." He took her hand. "Let me reassure you the confusion will clear. We can find no physical damage. In fact, you're in peak condition. Just don't be making any sudden moves. Remember you've been asleep for more than twenty-four hours. It takes time to re-acclimate."

"Did I receive a head blow? I checked but I didn't feel any bandages."

"No. Your head is fine. We didn't find any signs of internal injuries. Or external ones, for that matter."

"Why was I unconscious?"

"Medicine has come a long way since I began practicing, but we still don't completely understand why some people fall into an unconscious state. Perhaps, the trauma of seeing the wreck and being powerless to stop it." Dr. Tremain paused. "You did see the accident, didn't you?"

Sylvian nodded that she had.

"Your unconscious state may have been your mind's way of protecting you."

"But, I had the most unusual dreams. I awoke far off on a distant land long ago. With five brothers. I mean … I didn't awake with five brothers. The dream contained five brothers. I think they were Vikings. But I'm not sure." She frowned. "They were Norse. And these wild dogs. With glowing, reddish-orange eyes and dark gray, almost black fur. They attacked us on the beach." She grimaced. "And their father was an evil man. Actually, it's jumbled. He was their father, yet he wasn't." She frowned. "I think."

"Don't force the memory. It will come. With time. I'd say you have a creative imagination. Ah ...." Dr. Tremain paused as if some insight had just occurred to him. "I understand you were at the concert?"

"Yes."

"And that you interviewed Dragon members afterwards?"

Again, she agreed.

"Well, they dress like Vikings. And Kirth did sing to you while you were unconscious. Perhaps your mind blended the two?"

"Maybe," Sylvian said, not convinced. Feeling more intrigued by the news that the golden voice of rock 'n' roll serenaded her than by her condition, she gave Kirth a curious look. "You sang to me?"

"Yes." Kirth felt the heat of two pair of eyes focused on him. "Hale Knight's idea. You met him. He's the drummer. And Doc Wade agreed. That's what Rogert's acoustic guitar is doing here. The guys brought it to me early this morning. Before dawn."

"Were you here all night?" Sylvian asked, her tone incredulous.

"Kirth's been here since the ambulance brought you in," Dr. Tremain said.

"We didn't know whether you had friends in New Orleans or not," Kirth explained. "It seemed, uh, only right that someone be in the room with you when you woke up, Miss DuClair."

"Call me, Sylvian," she replied, then impulsively quipped, "After all, we have spent the night together." Sylvian couldn't believe she said that. She was flirting with the guy. She chided herself, recalling she'd felt differently about him before the accident.

He smiled at her.

The simple gesture stole her breath. His personal magnetism and virility were as strong up close as they were from the stage. She felt drawn to him, seduced by his hypnotic violet eyes and compelling smile.

The air hung expectantly between them. The doctor looked from one to the other, smiled and said, "I'll be back later."

Before Kirth or Sylvian could respond, he left, closing the door silently behind him.

"That was sudden," Sylvian said.

"Doc Wade's that way," Kirth replied. "He must have remembered something he needed to do. I, uh, took the liberty of having our office locate your hotel. Paying for a room you weren't using seemed pointless."

Sylvian cast a cursory look around the room.

"You won't find them here," Kirth said aloud to her unspoken question. He wondered how to persuade her to come with him. "Except for some toilet articles and a change of clothes, the rest of your things are locked up at our hotel. We wanted to ensure they were safe."

"That was kind of you." Sylvian wondered why Kirth Naran, the idol of millions, would drop his life to care for her.

"I'm afraid I've been a real bother."

Kirth shook his head. "Not at all. I'm glad to see you're unharmed. The guys will be pleased as well. They should be here shortly. With their wives. The two who are married." He felt like a schoolboy with his first crush. Worse, he sounded like one — inane. Almost dumbstruck.

Was the driver of the other vehicle associated with Dragon or Kirth Naran? That would explain their interest, Sylvian reasoned. A truck hit the cab. Perhaps carrying their equipment? Instead of asking the question directly, she chose a subtler route. "Tell me about the accident. Please. You did say you saw it?"

"Yes," Kirth replied. "A moving van veered into the path of the taxi you were in. The driver received minor injuries. He was talking to a policeman when the ambulance left with you, so I didn't hear all of what he said. I did hear him claim mechanical failure caused him to lose control."

"And the cab driver? How is he doing?"

"I'm afraid he wasn't as fortunate." Doc Wade told him to tell her the truth if she asked but not to upset her. He gave her a long, appraising look.

Sylvian read the concern in his eyes. *He is drop-dead good-looking. No wonder he'd become such an idol. He must have* women hanging on him wherever he goes.

"He didn't make it, but he didn't suffer. He died instantly."

A shiver passed through Sylvian. His words brought back the last thing she'd seen and heard before the world turned dark. "I'm not surprised. I can't imagine how I came through unscratched. I thought it was over."

"Doc Wade's seen numerous cases where one person's injured and another's not. Oh. He didn't tell you before he left, but I'm sure he will when he returns. He doesn't want you left alone."

Sylvian's startled look urged Kirth on.

"At least not for several days. Not until he's satisfied that you're fully recovered. I believe he will discharge you later on today if you will allow us — myself and my friends — to keep an eye on you. We're spending the week here. In the French Quarter. The hotel has a decidedly Old World atmosphere, and the food's good. We have a room no one's using. Mike Gallante — you met him?" Kirth looked at her questioningly.

Sylvian nodded that she had.

"He left today."

Sylvian studied Kirth before she replied. Life had a funny way of turning on itself. She'd wanted to get a closer look at Kirth Naran. Had prayed he wouldn't be gone before she got to the hotel. She'd never made it, but here they were. He'd found her.

Now, he offered her the opportunity to be inside his circle of friends. She could refuse, but did she want to? She still had questions without answers. The riddle of what she saw her first night in this strange town remained unanswered.

Even before she spoke, she knew her answer. He'd been in her dreams if dreams they were. She'd known that since shortly after she awoke, and her vision had passed over her brightly painted fingernails. Odd how such a small thing as Candied Apples fingernail polish on manicured nails could speak volumes more than words. She just couldn't quite remember the role he'd played. Friend? Or foe? "Your offer's intriguing and so kind," Sylvian said. "If you're sure I won't be in your way?" She paused.

"I'm sure." Relief flowed over him like the ocean at high tide reclaiming the shore. "Absolutely."

"I'm used to being on my own, but I do still feel a little shaky." Looking around the room, she shrugged. "As pleasant as Dr. Tremain is, I really don't like hospitals. Not as a patient. And not much as a visitor. It's too sterile for my tastes. And a little like being imprisoned. So, I'd like to accept."

"Good," Kirth replied. "That's settled then."

"I think I have a rental car parked at the hotel. I'm not sure because the one I drove wouldn't start, uh, … did you say yesterday?"

Kirth nodded affirmatively.

"The agency said they'd pick up the rental and leave another."

"Again, I hope you don't mind." Kirth smiled apologetically. "The car's been turned in. If you want another, we can rent one, but I don't think you'll be driving in the next couple of days. We can ask Doc Wade what he thinks."

"You're probably right," Sylvian replied. He certainly left little to chance. He'd taken care of her clothes, her room, and now her car. Did he also call her office? Something told her he hadn't. If not, why? "Did anyone notify my office?"

"No. I waited to see if you would wake up today. I hope that didn't cause you any problems. My office checked on your reservation. You'd already changed it, so we knew you weren't expected back right away. You weren't physically harmed. I felt you'd wake up soon, and as the hours passed, frankly, I forgot."

"There was no need to worry them." Sylvian smiled. She doubted that he forgot. He'd remembered everything else. She felt relief that the office hadn't been called. Someone might have come. Probably Ed, the protector. He'd be against her pursuing answers to the questions her brief stay in New Orleans had prompted. Worse yet, he'd insist she return home. She didn't want to do that. Not yet anyway.

18

*T*iffany lamps rested on rose-tone marble. The lobby's gilded, mahogany furniture blended with the oriental rugs covering a dark, wood floor. In places, the plaster showed the patina of time; benign cracks revealed the bricks lying underneath. The elegant but decadent ambiance of Hotel Tres Beau Danse made Sylvian feel as if she'd stepped into yesterday and a time more refined and cultured than existed in her world.

At first, she suspected the warmth shown by the staff toward Kirth and anyone with him related to his celebrity status. She soon realized differently. The proprietors' fondness for all of them had little to do with the band's current fame. They had a passion in common. All participated in a local youth home called Phoenix House.

The bellboys, desk clerks, and even the kitchen staff had lived at the home at some time or another. Kirth or any of the others could stay at this hotel, and as long as they weren't recognized on the street or in the hotel's common areas, no one would know they were in town, Sylvian reasoned.

Absolutely no one. The loyalty of the staff and proprietors bordered on devotion.

While she showered, Sylvian thought about the implications of such a hideaway. If any of them had been in town the night before the concert, they could have stayed here incognito.

Apparently, the band had long been acquainted with New Orleans. They'd spent time here, even before fame caught up with them. Especially Kirth. He might have made enemies he didn't know existed. From her own life, Sylvian knew all too well how some people were envious of the success others achieved.

A haven from a curious public and a prying press must be sacrosanct to celebrities, Sylvian mused. So, why would Kirth, who shunned publicity, take her, a reporter, into his inner circle?

She mulled the question over and over as she dried off and began dressing for dinner. She put on her black after-five dress, the one she'd bought on a whim, then debated about bringing because she felt almost certain she wouldn't need such flashy attire. Now, the short, fitted dress with its low-cut back and diagonally crossing straps seemed perfect for dinner.

She clamped the silver charm bracelet around her wrist. The gems in the horse charms, one black and the other white, sparkled in the light.

Moments later, when she heard the knock at the door, she still wondered why Kirth Naran had gone to so much trouble for her, a virtual stranger and a member of the press. The question had no answer. At least not one she could find outside her dreams.

As her hand reached for the doorknob, her Candied Apples polish taunted her, reminding her of the possibility that the answers she sought existed outside the world she'd accepted as reality. She pushed the bothersome thoughts aside. She must appear composed and professional. After all, she was a reporter. That was a fact. And reporters looked for factual answers, not those derived from dreams.

Kirth slipped into his sport coat and caught the phone on the second ring. "Can you be available if we decide to go?" He paused. "Veracruz. Great. Don't know. Yeah. All of us. Eight. Not much notice. Thanks."

Perfect, he thought. Now if he could only talk Sylvian into, first, getting married and then in doing so in Mexico. He sighed. He needed a miracle. A big one.

Closing the door behind him, Kirth wished he could dine

alone with Sylvian. His friends would understand. He slipped through the stairway exit and vaulted the stairs two at a time. She wouldn't fancy their dining alone. Too soon. She did seem pleased when Doc Wade thought the hotel a good place for her to convalesce. But she definitely had reservations about him.

He frowned as he stepped into the hallway on her floor. She may have agreed precisely because she didn't trust him or the others. She wrote for a newspaper. Nosey was their trade. He didn't care why. Not really. Having her here, in the hotel where he could protect her, that mattered. Not why. He knocked on her door, again wishing for a miracle.

"You look quite recovered," Kirth said when she opened the door. He wanted to take her in his arms, but knew he couldn't. She actually looked radiant, but he feared getting too expressive with her. If he came on too strong, she really wouldn't trust him. "Are you ready?"

Sylvian nodded, noticing everything about him. His hair, streaked even blonder than its natural color by the sun, was a lion's mane against his dark jacket. His eyebrows and lashes were a darker shade and served to heighten the intensity of his violet eyes. No doubt about it. Kirth Naran was almost too beautiful to be a man, yet he was all male. She'd really have to stay on guard not to fall under the influence of his charm.

"The others are already downstairs," Kirth said.

As the elevator opened on the first floor, Sylvian silently sought to still her nerves. She'd met the other members of the band when she'd interviewed them, so she didn't understand why she felt uncomfortable about meeting them all at once. She just did.

When they walked into the private dining room, she understood her jitters. The conversation stopped. Her view of the room seemed to expand and contract simultaneously. She saw a crystal chandelier, forest green drapes, a white linen tablecloth, sterling flatware, white candles, blood-red roses, and six pair of eyes focused on her with a startling intensity. Never had she felt such scrutiny.

Hale broke the silence first. "Good to see you again, Miss DuClair." Standing up, he shook her outstretched hand and smiled.

Sylvian hadn't missed his charms when she'd first met him. Smaller and more compact than Kirth, Hale emanated a devil-may-care manner that was both alluring and dangerous, especially when contrasted against his pretty-boy face and chameleon blue eyes. Certainly the women drawn to him had conflicting emotions. They wanted to tame and protect him in the same instant. During the interview, she hadn't been surprised to find he wasn't married and never had been. Only someone quite special would attract and hold him for long.

Kirth introduced Sylvian to the wives. While they ordered dinner, Sylvian briefly studied each couple.

Eric and Leigh looked as if they had Cherokee blood coursing through their veins. Both had high cheekbones, arresting dark eyes, and dark-brown hair. Gaylor and Jeanne spoke with the soft drawl of the deep South. Sylvian correctly guessed Alabama and discovered they were childhood sweethearts who had grown up down the road from each other in Marion.

"I hope we're not too much for you on your first evening out of the hospital." Rogert's green eyes studied her. "How are you feeling?"

"Actually, quite well," Sylvian replied, deciding Rogert's serious manner still reminded her of a priest. "I appreciate your thoughtfulness — all of you. I hope I haven't been too much of a bother."

"Oh, you haven't," Leigh said. "We're pleased to meet you. Any friend of Kirth's is a friend of ours."

Sylvian found Leigh's last comment odd, started to say something, then decided against voicing her question. Instead she simply smiled.

"Mike called," Eric told Kirth when the waiter left. "The deal's set." Eric laughed. "Except we have an extra week instead of one less."

"I bet they think it was their idea," Rogert suggested, chuckling as well.

"I'm sure of it," Kirth agreed.

"Mike Gallante?" Sylvian asked, certain she was the only one at the table who didn't know what they were discussing.

"Yes," Kirth replied. "The studio wanted us to move our recording date up. We didn't want to."

"We like to be real ready," Rogert interjected.

"And we're not," Hale added.

"I'm sure the studio wouldn't want to irritate Dragon," Sylvian suggested.

"In our dreams," Gaylor said.

"But the group is so successful," Sylvian protested, amazed when laughter filled the private dining room. She frowned. "Did I say something funny?"

"You just voiced a common misconception," Leigh said. "The studio doesn't necessarily want to irritate Dragon, but the money-is-the-bottom-line folks." She paused.

"Most of whom have never had a creative idea in their lives," Jeanne chimed in.

Leigh nodded her agreement. "Have little patience for artistic temperament."

"When they have the chance to get an additional group run through, they'll push," Jeanne said.

"So, Mike's a good negotiator?" Sylvian asked.

"The best in the business," said Kirth.

"The Viking motif — Mike's idea?" Sylvian asked, pleased with the chance to slip in the question she'd failed to ask during the interview despite its prominence on her list. The others she'd asked. Somehow she'd skipped this obvious question. The oversight had infuriated her. Now she'd get some kind of answer.

"Kirth's," Hale said. "But we all agreed. It's appropriate for what we're about."

"Warring and slavery and bounty. How does that fit the meaning of Dragon that we talked about after the concert?"

"Kirth feels the Vikings were misunderstood," Rogert explained. "That history has written them wrong. And rock musicians often fall into the same trap."

Sylvian looked at Kirth. "Written them wrong?"

Kirth shrugged. How much could he say without walking over a line, he wondered. Before he could speak, Hale answered her question.

"Hunger. The scarcity of food drove the Vikings from their homelands. Man's history — not necessarily in the books — runs wild with starvation and near starvation. When the Roman Empire in the West crashed, wheat trade hit a dead stop. Result? Shortages of bread." Hale pointed to Kirth. "You're on, Chief."

"I'm intrigued." Sylvian gazed at Kirth.

Kirth's eyes surveyed the plates the waiter had set down while they talked. "Steak. Fried chicken. Cream gravy. Paneed veal. Etouffee. Jambalaya. Mirliton. Gumbo. Soufflé potatoes. Fresh green beans. Black beans. Corn. Crisp salad. Several varieties of lettuce. Tomatoes. Croutons. Dressing. And —" Kirth picked up the French roll the waiter had left on his butter place, sniffed the bun and set it back down "— fresh rolls. We take these foods for granted, but nothing in front of us would have found its way onto a Viking table. Of course, the food was quite different during the Middle Ages as well. And people often went hungry."

"And this hunger drove the Vikings to pillage and plunder?" Sylvian asked, doubtful of the premise.

"When Rome fell in the West, the trade in wheat stopped," Kirth said. "Think of the battle over oil in our time. Oil means transportation, goods, and, for many people, the ability to work and provide food, necessities, and some luxuries. Before the Roman Empire, several nations fought for control of wheat for many of the same reasons. Remember —" Kirth waved his arm to encompass the dinner "— food sources weren't as varied as they are today. Cattle hadn't yet been bred for steaks; they were draft animals, vital to survival and often diseased —"

Interrupting Kirth, Hale quipped, "Twentieth century heaven," raised a piece of rare steak on his fork, kissed the meat, savored its flavor, and swallowed it. "Yummm."

"Ignore Hale," Leigh said. "At times, enthusiasm overrides what common sense he has."

Hale made a face at Leigh, smiled at Sylvian, and cut another bite of steak.

"Fortunately, Hale wasn't a Roman soldier," Kirth said. "The Roman army depended on wheat not beef. Ironically, Rome's distribution of wheat and Roman exotic tastes, which meant vast quantities of gold going to India for unusual foods, led to the fall of the Empire, but that isn't what you asked, is it?"

"No, but I'm interested," Sylvian said. "I've studied early civilizations. I know food supplies were a problem, but your perspective is slightly different from what I've read."

Only because I lived with hunger, Kirth thought. He smiled. "I know. Most Americans and West Europeans can't fathom a life-time of gut-wrenching hunger. Not now, anyway. But I fear our gut-wrenching time will come."

"The people of the North grew accustomed to wheat, then there was none," Eric said. "They couldn't raise wheat in large quantities, so they grew rye."

Rogert jumped into the conversation. "Next time you're at the grocery, check the ingredients of rye bread. Mostly wheat. Dark, leavened rye bread received its introduction into Scandinavia during the Middle Ages. Thin, crisp rye crackers didn't come along until the nineteenth century." He looked at Kirth. "Tell her about barley bread."

"Sure you're interested?" Kirth looked at Sylvian.

"I'm sure," Sylvian replied.

"The only bread the Northmen knew to make was barley bread. But they didn't know how to leaven it. The bread had to be eaten straight from the griddle pan while it was hot. Cooled barley bread was hard as a stone. Sometimes the bread was mixed with the ground-up inner-layer of pine bark."

Sylvian flinched.

Everyone laughed. Jeanne spoke first, insisting softly, "Each of us has been right where you are and had a similar strong reaction."

"Kirth makes whatever you're eating in the twentieth century sound like a feast," Gaylor added. "Even when we were first traveling on the road and didn't have enough money to do much more than split several hamburgers among us, we never complained. He has countless stories of the tasty morsels our ancestors ate. I guarantee you, they will make you grateful for almost any food today."

"True," Rogert said, nodding emphatically.

"The point is, Miss DuClair," Eric said, "most historians haven't written sufficiently about hunger and its effect on the course of human history. They talk about crusades, and just causes, real estate, money and power, but they often pay scant attention to hungry stomachs."

"Hunger is still with us," Gaylor said. "And we talk about it as a modern problem which must be solved, but in this decade we are no closer to doing so than we were ten, twenty years ago."

"Further away," Rogert said.

"Our Viking theme reminds us of the fallacy of thinking we are so different from our ancestors," Eric added. "It keeps us on the edge. Aware we need to do what we can to free people."

"A hardy lot — the Vikings," Gaylor said. "They overcame adversity. They reached out from the supposed safety of their surroundings and explored the world."

"Even today, safety's an illusion," Jeanne said. "On some level, we all know that even though we may want to deny it. We want to think we're secure. We insist on it."

"Securely nuts." Hale waved his mostly empty water glass like a conductor's baton, sprinkling Rogert, who sat next to him.

"Hey." Rogert leaned away from Hale. "Careful with that weapon."

"Thank me, Monk." Hale set the glass down. "You can skip your weekly bath."

"Pardon Hale," Rogert said, turning his attention to Sylvian. "His manners are mostly missing in mixed company."

"Don't mind Rogert, Miss DuClair," Hale said, smiling. "His manners are mostly missing." Before Rogert could respond, Hale continued, "The short of it is — our fans get the message.

On an intuitive level, they don't see a dichotomy between the Viking motif and the guardian dragon. They see the big picture. They learn to believe in themselves and not depend upon a group or a gang or any government that promises what it doesn't deliver. They are their own dragon, their own protector."

"For us, the Viking motif and the dragon keep our purpose clear, even for Hale," Rogert said, his determination to have the last word evident. "They guide us in deciding the songs we include on our albums and those we don't." He picked up his wine glass and took a sip.

Poker-faced, Hale said, "On that we agree."

Rogert gagged on his wine, then cracked up.

Eric shook his head. "Action, not talk, tells us who someone is. We try to live what we preach. We've — all of us — invested in farms in underdeveloped countries where people learn how to take care of themselves."

Amused by the antics, Sylvian smiled. "None of you mentioned the farms in the interview." Her first impression rang true, she decided. A tight-knit group and friends to boot.

"We never do," Gaylor said. "We don't want publicity for simply doing what needs to be done. We don't talk about the youth homes, either. We just do them."

"We're song and dance men, Ma'am." Hale bowed his head. "That's our gig; that's our story."

Leigh laughed and looked at Sylvian. "And so modest about it."

"Don't let them get on the subject of music," Jeanne confided. "You are a whole new audience for the guys. We'll be here all night. So, were you born in Houston?"

"No," Sylvian smiled. "San Antonio. I migrated south by way of Texas Tech in Lubbock."

"A Texan," Leigh said. "Hale, too."

"And proud of it," Hale said.

Rogert groaned. "Now you've done it, Leigh. Save us, Miss DuClair. Please."

"Please, call me Sylvian. All of you. Uh, what about movies?

Are they safe?"

"Definitely," Jeanne said. "Great idea."

For the rest of the evening, the conversation revolved around movies and current events. Sylvian still sensed the others evaluating her. She thought of Kirth's aversion to the press. Perhaps they felt as surprised as she did when he invited a member of the enemy camp to stay at a place where they so obviously felt safe from scrutiny.

But then, many things about Kirth Naran confused her. He hadn't asked her to keep her stay at the hotel off the record as far as her publication was concerned. In fact, he hadn't mentioned she was a reporter once. Neither had anyone else. She called that strange.

Despite all her misgivings about Kirth, when he escorted her back to her room after dinner, she asked him to come in and felt pleased when he accepted.

Sitting on the second-floor gallery outside her room, she watched without seeing the activity on the street below. They'd covered different subjects at dinner, but the youth home had been mentioned and passed over. "Is there a Mr. Phoenix?"

"No," Kirth replied. "The name comes from some of the first young people staying there."

"They picked phoenix?" Sylvian asked, surprised. "Why?"

"One of the boys loved legends. He'd read that when the phoenix senses death near, it makes a sweet-smelling nest, exposes itself to the sun's rays, and burns to ashes. Another phoenix rises from the bone marrow of the first. He said they were like the phoenix. The idea took hold."

"So where do they come from, the youth?"

"Troubled homes. Some are orphans. Doc Wade and the owners of this hotel are on the board of directors. They could tell you more about the backgrounds. And how they're selected."

"Selected?"

"There's only room for seventy-two and the collie, not surprisingly named Phoenix. Phoenix showed up one day and hasn't left yet. That was about two years ago this spring."

They talked for the better part of an hour, mostly about the home and its mascot. Sylvian studied Kirth's every move and listened to his voice's inflection. She couldn't find anything that even bordered on insincerity.

When he left, no more of the puzzle pieces fit into place than before, but Sylvian felt certain of one thing. Whatever she'd seen her first night had not been Kirth Naran slaughtering anyone. He didn't have a brutal nature.

What did he want, she wondered, as she crawled into bed and turned out the light. He hadn't made even a subtle pass at her, had, in fact, been careful not to touch her at all. She refused to lay awake contemplating what that might mean. She wanted the kind of answers that made sense in her well-ordered world. And yet, she fell asleep thinking of how her lips would feel being kissed by his.

In her dreams, she walked in a mist that floated around her like gossamer. Muted vignettes of her life flashed around her. She saw a succession of orphanages and foster homes, the university campus, and her office. The faces of those people she held dear became clearly focused, except one. Harold Lann. His blurred image floated around her, but she couldn't distinguish his features. Suddenly, she was being sucked through a swirling black void. "No!" she exclaimed in her sleep, the word falling into the silence of her room.

She awoke abruptly. Turning on the light, she picked up the phone and dialed. Then she saw the clock. Midnight. Surely, Harold had left for the day, but Ed might still be there.

Doom

19

*S*tanding concealed in the shadows of the hotel's second-story gallery, Kirth prepared for a long night. Everyone slept except for him. Since midnight, he'd felt the growing beat of disaster, like a storm, being channeled in his direction. Now the sensation was palatable. He could taste doom all around him.

Kirth watched as a van drove too slowly for his comfort past the hotel and stopped just beyond the entrance to the hotel's guest parking. He focused his thoughts on Sylvian while not moving his eyes from the van.

He felt no presence in her room. She seemed to be sleeping. The van presented a potential problem. He felt the malice from where he stood. His mind surveyed the surrounding streets until he found what he sought: a police car cruising two blocks away. Using telepathy, he influenced the driver to come toward the hotel and past the van.

Three men stepped from the back of the van and turned into the parking area. They waved at the night guard as if they were guests returning. Raymond was young in years but not in street smarts. He nodded in return as if accepting they were guests and secretly pressed the alarm.

At the same moment, the police car turned down the street. *Perfect. Just a little farther. Come on. That's the spot.* The car passed the driveway to the parking lot and stopped. The policeman radioed for back-up before he and his partner got out of the car.

Kirth turned his head ever so slightly. With his acute hearing, he could distinguish everything that was said, but he had to shut out all other sounds. He refused to do that; he'd have to close Sylvian off as well.

When a second police car rounded the corner, the driver of the van honked. Without waiting, he took off. Instead of pursuing the van, the police car stopped to assist the officers. Shortly, they returned, their three captives in tow.

Kirth smiled. New Orleans had an astronomical crime rate. This time, they didn't get away.

The men had the touch of The Beast — members of Drakus's brigade of blimey bastards. That's what the caustic Nyx sentry had dubbed Drakus's minions when Kirth faced them in Great Britain more than four hundred years ago. The name stuck.

Surely, The Beast monitored the calls to Sylvian's office. After all, the deceiver found her first. Those men served as merely a reconnaissance team. Now, Drakus would be forced to send out another. He'd be ready.

His thoughts turned to Sylvian. Earlier, the pain of being in her room, desiring her yet afraid to touch her, had become unbearable. He'd run out of willpower and left. Had he stayed another five minutes, he would have taken her in his arms and kissed her. That could have led to disaster. Once they touched, they would be out of control; the physical desire between them blazed so strongly.

Being in her presence was agony. Even standing outside her room, he could hear her soft breathing and smell the fragrance of her skin. So near, yet worlds apart. *Would they ever be free?*

Before Kirth had time to think further, Sylvian's breathing become labored. Moaning, she moved restlessly in bed. He scanned her room. She was alone.

And awake. Kirth wondered what had awakened her at this hour. More bad dreams? Perhaps. He prepared himself to flee quickly if she made a move for the gallery.

Sylvian sat up in bed, turned on the light, and stared at the telephone. What she needed to do wouldn't wait. She knew that.

If she was wrong, she'd feel humiliated. If she was right? She shivered at the thought and, picking up the receiver, dialed the operator. "Would you ring Kirth Naran's room, please?"

Kirth moved down the gallery to the hallway door and up the stairs with lightning speed. He had no clue why she'd be calling him at this hour, but he certainly wanted to find out. The door to his room opened on his command, the receiver lifting slowly off the hook as he walked toward the phone. "Hello."

"I'm sorry to wake you," Sylvian began.

"I wasn't asleep," Kirth replied. "What's going on? Are you OK?"

"Yes. We need to talk." Sylvian paused. Be honest. You called him. He didn't call you. "Actually, I'm not OK. I need to talk. The hour's horribly late, but may I come over? Now?"

"Of course." Kirth's heart pounded.

"Thanks. I'll be there in about ten minutes." Hanging up the receiver, she threw back the covers and almost leapt from the bed. *Don't think about it. Just do it.*

Rummaging through her clothes, she settled on white cotton shorts and a short-sleeved, red pullover shirt. Hurriedly, she brushed her teeth and then her hair. She pinched her cheeks as she glanced in the mirror. The green-eyed, white Persian cat her artist friend had painted on the shirt gazed knowingly at her. She made a face at the feline.

Not until she stepped into the elevator did Sylvian realize her error. She didn't know his room number. Shaking her head, she punched the button for the first floor. If she couldn't get the number out of the clerk, she could use the lobby's courtesy phone. Kirth would think her light on brains.

When the elevator doors opened, she was surprised to see him standing there. Waiting.

They both started to speak, then stopped.

"I'm on the third floor." Kirth smiled as he got in the elevator. "Room 311."

"Thanks. Sylvian sighed. "I forgot I didn't know until I got on the elevator and had no idea which button to punch."

"I forgot, too, until after we hung up," Kirth replied.

"How did you know I'd come downstairs to find out?"

"ESP."

"I didn't know that was one of your talents," Sylvian joked. "Is that how you've made so many successful investments in the stock market?"

"Absolutely," Kirth said when the elevator stopped on his floor. "This way." He pointed down the hall to the right. "Actually, I figured you'd try to talk the desk clerk out of the number, so you didn't have to call back. I thought I'd save you the trouble and the clerk his job since he most likely would have succumbed to your charms. Here we are." Kirth opened the door and stepped aside.

Sylvian gave Kirth a brief smile that said she'd heard his obvious compliment. She wished she had a ready response. She didn't. Too often the art of small talk failed her, and this was one of those times, she thought, as she took in the surroundings at a glance. A little larger than hers, the room contained a cozy sitting area. Her eyes were drawn to the bed's canopy. Covered in shimmering silks of silver and gold, which stretched to the floor and were tied with purple cording at each post, the double bed seemed to invite the weary to rest under its cover. Embarrassed and suddenly shy, she looked away.

Now that she was here, Sylvian felt almost foolish. "I'm sure you're wondering why I called at this hour in the morning," she said, her tone tentative. Was he always this confident?

"I'm curious, certainly," Kirth replied, again the master of understatement. She had such poise; she couldn't be as nervous as he was, he decided silently. "I have some soft drinks. Would you like one?"

"Yes." He didn't drink anything stronger than coffee at dinner, she thought. "Anything with caffeine." She sat down and watched him open two Cokes.

Handing her one, he plopped down across from her, easing back in his chair as if he had forever, his long legs filling the space between them. A not-uncomfortable silence ensued.

Finally, Sylvian spoke. "Before I begin I want a promise from you. Don't protect me. If what I say has anything to do with the unconscious state I was in for more than a day, tell me even if Dr. Tremain has insisted you don't." She waited for his response.

"Agreed." *Had she remembered?*

"I can't escape the feeling that we've known each other before. Yet, I have a pretty clear picture of my life, and I don't remember our having met. Did Dr. Tremain indicate that my memory might be faulty?"

"No. He didn't say anything to that effect." Thrilled, Kirth cautioned himself not to get overeager. He'd done that before, and the results had been disastrous.

"Have we met before?"

Kirth studied her for a moment. "If you're questioning whether you're suffering from some kind of selective amnesia, the answer is no. We have plenty of time, Sylvian. Why don't you just tell me what's on your mind?"

Sylvian debated over the long version of what she had to say or the short one. She opted for the latter. Either he'd think she was nuts, or he'd know she wasn't. "I believe we're both in danger, that some powerful force is out to destroy us. And I don't know what to do."

Kirth's slouched pose didn't flinch. Instead, he fixed her with a steady look. "Will you marry me?"

"Is that a proposal?"

"Yes."

"You're serious."

"Absolutely."

Since she'd awakened in the hospital, Sylvian had worked hard at convincing herself that her dreams were the workings of an overtired mind. She'd tried to sell herself on the idea that she was with Kirth because she wanted answers to the murderous scene she'd witnessed her first night in New Orleans. "You weren't in New Orleans the night before your concert." Sylvian spoke the words more as a statement to herself than a question she expected Kirth to answer.

"No. I wasn't." Kirth didn't have to know the particulars to understand Drakus had drawn Sylvian to the bayou near Laplace and tricked her with a nasty illusion. "We arrived mid-afternoon the day of the show. In time for the sound check. No earlier."

"I'm strongly attracted to you," Sylvian said.

"And I to you."

Sylvian had been acutely aware of the draw between them and his controlled efforts to not touch her even in the most casual ways. She'd fought accepting what that meant. In fact, she wanted to run from everything that had happened to her since she arrived in New Orleans. "It takes three days in Texas to get married," Sylvian muttered, almost to herself. Her birthday — three days. Too late. "I don't know about Louisiana. Do you?"

"It doesn't matter." Kirth barely concealed his excitement. "We can marry today. In Mexico."

Mexico was a hard drive away, Sylvian thought, immediately realizing that distances didn't mean the same to someone with the financial resources that Kirth had. "I called the office late last night. Left the number where I could be reached." She paused. Less than a week ago, her mind had been preoccupied with work and school. Everything that had happened to her in the past days had ripped apart her precisely organized world. Nothing was as it appeared to be. "I think that was a mistake."

"I suspect you're right." Kirth's words hung portentously in the room.

Sylvian shivered. "How soon can we leave?"

"As soon as we can be ready." Kirth struggled to control himself. Drakus had found them at the hospital because he'd used his powers to bring her home. Whatever Sylvian decided, he couldn't afford a strong emotional reaction. "The pilot's waiting for my call."

"What about your friends? Do they stay, or do they go?"

"They need to come with us."

Her telephone call to the office had somehow placed them all in jeopardy, she feared. Had the call inspired her last dream as well? The lonely shore, Kith's arms around her, his kiss, his home, the woods, falling, deathly fear, flames, and the darkness. Perhaps so. Kirth understood more than what he'd said about how things must be.

More than a thousand years ago, she'd been in that position courtesy of Aasta. The young woman had been a fierce warrior who faced life valiantly and died too young. Sylvian trembled at thoughts she hesitated to accept. She had lived before. Another time. Another place. Another life. If only she had escaped with Aasta's courage, the present might be less intimidating.

The underlying message in her dreams seemed to warn: There is no escape. She had little choice but to trust her instincts and follow his lead as he'd done with Aasta centuries before. "Let's wake them up," she said softly.

Less than two hours later, the silver jet cleared the airport. None of Kirth's friends complained about being awakened in the early morning hours. Not even Hale, whom she'd been told was impossible to rouse. Sylvian could see how years on the road would train someone to move at a moment's notice, but even Jeanne and Leigh had been ready in twenty minutes. And, they hadn't grumbled once.

Closing her eyes, Sylvian felt she could rest safely. The thought pulled her up short. She trusted those she barely knew and had little faith in those she'd had confidence in when she boarded the flight to New Orleans. She was getting married. Had she lost her mind? In a sane world, she knew the answer. Yes. Yes. Yes. But, her life had been turned upside down in less than a week. No longer did two and two equal four.

Sylvian ventured a glance at Kirth from underneath half-closed eyes. Although he went by a different name, he looked as he did in her dreams.

His sun-drenched hair. His penetrating eyes. Whether he was standing at the prow of a Viking ship, clad in mail and a golden helmet, or sitting, as he was now, in a high-backed seat in an airplane, wearing a long-sleeved turquoise cotton shirt and white slacks, he had an inexplicable charm that captured people. Charisma. Hard to explain; equally hard to define. But, she'd watched his friends defer to him now just as his brothers and his men had done then.

His father had been the exception. She couldn't believe those two had been related by blood. Kith had been kind; his father, cruel. Sylvian's pulse quickened as an overwhelming sense of impending doom filled her.

Images flashed in her mind: Kith standing in the doorway, Njall not Kith moving toward her, Aasta stepping into the fire, the heat of the flames encompassing her, darkness descending. Sylvian had felt the heat, then nothing. Somehow, she'd floated away from the deadly scene and awakened in the hospital. She'd escaped the horror, but Aasta had surely died in those flames. Fear gripped her. *Stop it.* Her thoughts returned to Kirth.

Did he remember those days? Had they been real? Or did they exist solely in her dreams? She could be suffering from a psychotic break with reality brought on by the accident. And Kirth's actions, his proposal, could be proof of the bizarre behavior of rock musicians who had too much fame, money and time. She'd said yes to his whim of a proposal and here they were. Against all logic and everything she'd been taught in school, she did not believe that was true.

Whatever he knew, he wasn't telling. She wanted to ask, but her instincts told her his actions had spoken louder than words. He'd never flinched when she'd said they were in danger. Instead, he'd asked her to marry him. At that moment, the dream had been tangible in the hotel room, and she'd been enveloped in its presence to the exclusion of everything else.

She felt trapped in a fog which grew denser with each step. Kirth's voice cut through the gray mist like a beacon. There and gone. There and gone. There and gone. Each step she took rested on faith and nothing more. She had to do what she'd been unable to do her entire life. Trust.

Kirth's voice broke into her thoughts. "Sylvian, is anything wrong?"

She opened her eyes and looked into his direct gaze. "I was thinking of all the things that remain unsaid between us."

"Ah," he replied. "Some words are best left unvoiced. Everything doesn't have to be spoken to be known, especially between those sharing a common bond. The language of the heart speaks in actions — not words."

She studied him quietly for a moment. "Did I receive any medications in the hospital which would cause me to have hallucinations or otherwise alter my reality?"

"No," he said. "They didn't give you anything. It wasn't necessary. They didn't find any signs of physical damage. No pain pills. Nothing. Not even an aspirin."

He told the truth. She could feel it. "I long to touch you."

His steady gaze held her. "And I you." An eternity of desire lay behind his words.

Neither moved toward the other. Finally Sylvian spoke. "Years ago, following a nightmare, which I can't recall, I wrote a poem. The words made little sense to me then. Part of the verse comes to me now. I'll tell you what I remember, if you promise not to laugh."

"Why would I laugh?"

"All of you write lyrics," Sylvian said, waving her arm to include the others, whose attention was focused elsewhere. "This isn't actually a poem. I just didn't know what else to call it."

"I'd like to hear it," Kirth said, his interest piqued.

"You won't laugh?"

"I won't laugh."

"Promise?"

"Promise."

"In the abyss of silent, screaming thoughts, my soul walks. The beauty, the sorrow, the hope, the fear, wait here. Like a clawing rake, they rip the net of time. The pain. The pain. No light remains. Chaos reigns. Out of the void of never, the moonlight calls to me. The dream beckons me forward, over the endless sea. The guardian of the Nightstar plays the song again. From the shadows steps the dark one to claim the victory's end. To extinguish the fire burning brightly and scatter it to the wind."

Before Kirth had an opportunity to speak, Hale jumped into the conversation. "I like that. Monk, what do you think? We could do something with those words, couldn't we?"

Rogert's serious eyes came to rest on Sylvian. "Would you mind?"

"You're kidding. Right?" Sylvian asked.

Kirth began laughing.

Sylvian pointed accusingly at Kirth. "You promised."

"Don't jump the track, Ma'am." Kirth's eyes twinkled. "The guys are serious. Monk never jokes about songs. They're his children."

Sylvian looked at Hale and Rogert. They didn't appear to be kidding. "Sure, go ahead. Do whatever you want."

"Would you mind repeating them?" Hale asked, passing a pen to Rogert.

When Sylvian had finished, Rogert asked, "Are there any more lines?"

Sylvian frowned. "That's all I remember," she said tentatively.

"Nothing else? Are you sure," Rogert said coaxingly.

"Well, that same night I wrote several other short lines, but they aren't related to the others. At least, I don't think they are."

"What are they?" Rogert asked.

Sylvian sighed. "Circles on the wall. Patterns as they fall. Weaving in and out. And nowhere at all."

"Ah." Rogert scribbled them down.

"What does that mean?" Sylvian asked Rogert, who was already lost in thought.

In a hushed voice, Hale said, "They probably gave him an idea for a riff. You know what that is?"

"Not really," she replied.

"It's a short rhythmic phrase repeated again and again in a song. Often, it's a bridge."

"Now I understand," Sylvian said. "Thanks."

"Thank you," Hale said. "They're your words."

"Such as they are." She smiled at him. "But you're welcome.

Enjoy yourselves."

"Without a doubt." Hale leaned over Rogert's shoulder. "Try that here." Soon, they were lost in their own world.

Sylvian looked at Kirth.

He whispered, "I can't save you in this. Rogert and Hale are brilliant song writers. Your words have inspired them. There's no telling what they'll come up with, but the result will be good."

"What do you think of the words? Kinda crazy, aren't they?"

Kirth studied her for long, silent moments. "They're prophetic."

"I have so many questions, but I suspect I have to guess the answers," Sylvian said.

"Charades is similar to other games where the ability to think quickly is vital to success," Kirth observed. "The game also requires a lot of movement. I know the pilot. He likes for passengers to keep their seat belts fastened. Just in case. A storm could turn this smooth flight into quite a roller-coaster ride."

"I love rides, but I'm not avid about roller coasters. They've been known to crash." Sylvian smiled. "My favorite rides are the Runaway Train at Six Flags and Peter Pan's trip to Never Neverland at Disneyland. But the parachute jump held no appeal for me. Once was more than enough."

Pleased, Kirth smiled. She'd picked up his lead immediately. "I know both rides and how you feel about the parachute jump. I've been on rides I didn't want to go on again. Sometimes I've had no choice. That's infuriating."

"I don't appreciate being forced either," Sylvian said. "It's frustrating when you're in a situation that limits your choices."

"Someone shows up who won't take no for an answer," Kirth suggested. "Or you're waiting for a ride you really want to take, and there's someone in line who's determined to get his way no matter the cost."

"Exactly," Sylvian agreed. "It can really spoil the day."

"Some situations can ruin more than a day," Kirth said. "I saw a fight once between two strangers. It was out of hand. Someone I knew, who cared for one of the participants, intervened. The fight broke up. That wasn't the end of the disagreement. They're still at war."

"What's going to happen to them?" A familiarity stirred in Sylvian's mind. "Are they going to spend their lives fighting?"

"It's hard to say. I guess they will until they resolve their differences. Their game's quite deadly. Actually."

Silence overcame them, as Sylvian thought of what had been said. They had a common enemy, of that she felt certain. Although she'd only known Kirth for a few days, she trusted him. Marrying him was vital. She didn't understand why. Not completely. It just was.

"Have you been to Veracruz?"

Kirth's question brought Sylvian back to the present. "No." Curious as to what his reaction would be to her next statement, she said, tentatively, "At least, not in this lifetime. How about you?"

"I've been within miles of Veracruz, but as for the city itself, I was there countless years ago. I'm sure everything's changed. But, Eric's been there before. He had some days off and came to fish. He caught more than he bargained for. He met Leigh."

Sylvian tilted her head where she could see them. Both slept. "They appear to be happy."

"Ecstatically so," Kirth replied. "They were married in Veracruz. Their anniversary is in four days. That's why we had the house rented."

Sylvian's eyes widened. "No wonder they were all receptive to coming. You already had plans."

"Yesterday, we were supposed to be there. But we're a tight group. They wouldn't leave New Orleans without me."

"Hold up," came Jeanne's voice. Sitting a couple of rows behind them, she released her seat belt, moved closer, and sat down. She brushed her close-cropped blonde hair behind her ears with her fingertips and said teasingly, "I woke up just in time to keep you honest, Kirth Naran."

She smiled at Sylvian. "Kirth has never left any of us in the lurch, so to speak. We weren't about to leave him in New Orleans, especially when he'd finally showed some interest in a girl."

"Jeanne," Kirth coaxed. "Sylvian's not interested in hearing this."

"Oh yes she is." Jeanne's blue eyes sparkled.

"Yes I am," Sylvian said. "Please go on."

"This guy's had women chase him to the car, invade his hotel rooms, attack him in public," Jeanne confided. "He's never showed the slightest interest in anyone. Why, my priest, who is not young and attractive, has spent more time in the company of single women than Kirth has."

Kirth groaned. He could stop her but didn't. He wouldn't use his skill on his friends just to save himself embarrassment no matter how badly he wanted to. Besides, the effort might alert their enemy, who by now was spreading its search for them in an ever-widening perimeter.

"Don't get me wrong," Jeanne explained. "He's not interested in guys either. He's just not interested. Until now. So, needless to say, when we — Leigh and I — hear he is keeping a vigil over you. Well. We know something serious is up. Did he tell you he missed the picnic with the kids? The one the concert and our plans to be in Veracruz for Eric and Leigh's wedding anniversary had been scheduled around?"

Sylvian acknowledged he hadn't.

"We figured not. Leigh and I. Anyway, we're coming to New Orleans. Posthaste. Wild horses couldn't keep us away. Leigh wasn't even upset that the trip to Veracruz was off. She made that decision. And this morning, when you called —" she looked at Kirth "— why we're all just delighted. It's about time you have a life. You've been wonderful to all of us and to the kids around the country, but you've had no life of your own."

Looking back at Sylvian, she gushed, "We watched you two at dinner last night. You were made for each other. I don't know how you talked him into marriage. He's so shy. I mean, we saw the way he keeps his distance."

Sylvian opened her mouth to speak, but Jeanne rushed on: "We don't care. It's obvious to us that he's happy. That's what counts. I'm speaking for us all. This is the only thing we've talked about since the day after the concert. This morning? It didn't matter what time you called. None of us would miss your wedding. No way. Not for anything."

"Thanks," Sylvian said. "Actually Kirth asked me to marry him, and I said yes. Not the other way around. But, if he hadn't, I'm sure I would have asked him. He's special."

"Absolutely," Jeanne agreed. "Are we shopping for a dress before the wedding, or do you want to take the time?"

"I don't think so." Sylvian looked at Kirth. "I'd rather get married immediately, especially now that I know how slippery you are. You might get away if we wait."

"There's no chance of that, Ma'am," Kirth replied.

"I'll say there's not," Jeanne interjected. "We'll not let him. Then, we're leaving you two alone. So you can have some privacy. We can celebrate later, on Eric and Leigh's anniversary. A kind of combined wedding and anniversary party. How does that sound?"

"Great," Kirth said. "That's four days away. But Sylvian and I won't be staying at the house. Not tonight. I've found a perfect spot for us."

20

Sylvian assumed the hideaway Kirth proposed for their wedding night lay in Veracruz. It didn't. Instead, they drove miles away from there. The winding road stayed close to the Gulf of Mexico and its aquamarine waters sparkling under an azure sky. Tropical flowers in primary colors of red, yellow, and blue deepened the densely wooded, forest-green countryside. In places, wild roses, and lilies grew in profusion. The breathtaking drive reminded her of a Van Gogh; the colors, not the forms, determined the expressive content.

They'd spent the last hour digging deeper into the jungle as Kirth drove up a steep, deeply rutted road. When they had arrived at the airport, a four-wheel-drive recreational vehicle awaited them. Now she understood why. This path was best suited for a mountain goat.

The road abruptly vanished. A living wall of vines and trees and shrubs filled her view.

"Are we lost?" Sylvian forced her voice to remain calm.

"No. The house is up ahead."

"It is?" Sylvian's tone was incredulous.

"The owner is a privacy enthusiast." Kirth laughed. "The road's going to get real bumpy. Brace yourself."

He poured on the gas. They lunged up the rough terrain.

Sylvian began questioning her sanity again. She'd married someone she'd never even touched. The quiet civil ceremony had not ended in a kiss. Then she'd climbed into this vehicle without asking the destination. "Have you been here before?"

"We're not lost, Sylvian, if that's what you're worrying about," Kirth said. "Keep watching ahead. We're almost there."

"It doesn't look as if this area of Mexico — we are still in Mexico, aren't we?" Sylvian said jokingly, "— has been inhabited for decades, maybe centuries. We haven't seen a sign of human life since we left the main highway. I don't know how you knew to turn off. I didn't see the road until we were on it."

"All of that is by design," Kirth said. "Look."

Stucco walls rose ahead of them. Sylvian gasped; she was so surprised. Still, the place looked abandoned as if there had been life here once, human life, but the jungle had reclaimed its property. Vines covered the walls. Frogs hopped across the deteriorating driveway. They passed through the main gates, which hung askew by the entrance.

"Who lives here?" she asked Kirth, as he drove inside the garage and electronically closed the door behind them.

"No one." Kirth smiled at Sylvian. "We're alone." At least for now. Opening his door, he quickly stepped out and around to her door. He held himself in check and made no move toward her as she got out.

"Thanks." Sylvian shivered. They'd never touched one another physically, and now they were alone. She avoided brushing up against the Land Rover. The vehicle's white paint was covered in dirt; its black tires, in mud.

"Cold?" Kirth asked, reaching into the back for their bags.

"No. Nervous."

"Me, too." He opened the door into the house and, after they stepped inside, bolted the lock behind them. "The house has a somewhat unusual design. The rooms are patterned after a maze. Just follow me."

They walked down a long, wide, glassed-in porch which had a dramatic view of a sapphirine ocean undulating under a sunkissed sky in the distance. The vines, so prevalent over the gates and entrance, had not overtaken the glass. They merely bordered the edges.

Sylvian found the floor plan fascinating. One room seemed

to spring out of another. Alone, she'd have difficulty finding her way. Even now, she'd have to search for the garage, and they'd just come from there.

Kirth opened a door which didn't appear to be a door at all. He moved aside so she could step in, then followed her.

"Wow," she murmured, walking into a spacious bedroom-sitting area. "The colors are incredible. Forest clean. Intense, yet soft somehow." She turned all the way around. "Silver. The paint has a silver sheen, making the colors appear captured by starlight."

"You like it?"

"Oh, yes." Sylvian turned around. "Lovely. The silver sheen reminds me of the wing tips of your dragon. Does the color mean something?"

"Time," Kirth replied. "Time is usually symbolized by a sheen as of shot silk."

"And the three dragons?"

"When a dragon is used in emblems, as on the sail, the symbolism comes from its form. For instance, the dragon biting its tail is symbolic of cyclic processes in general and time in particular." He stepped around her and over to the bar. "I'll fix us a drink. I'm afraid there's no alcohol, but we have everything else."

"You don't drink, do you?"

"I used to. A lot. But, in answer to your question. No, I don't. Not any more." He had to keep his senses on the edge. He'd learned by failure centuries ago that alcohol numbed even an immortal body.

"A Coke's fine." Sylvian idly ran her fingers down the arm of the Louisiana Federal chair with the lyre back. She pivoted as she sat, her eyes again scanning the walls. The room had no windows.

He handed her the drink. "I'm going to shower. Join me or stay here. The choice is yours."

He was gone. Sylvian sat alone in the room, holding her drink, wondering what in the hell to do. Kirth had been virtually non-communicative since the ceremony, taking even greater pains not to touch her. And now … he'd invited her into the shower. Obviously, he expected her to make the first move.

Incensed, she wondered, Who does he think he is?

What ego.

If I had any sense, I'd walk out of here right now.

She set the drink down hard on the round, glass-topped coffee table, stood, picked up her bags, and turned toward the door. *I'll show you, Mister Know It All.*

The opening had vanished.

The door couldn't just disappear. She cased the wall. Running her fingers across the smooth texture, she looked for a hidden button.

Nothing.

Damn.

The only door out of the room entered the shower area. She did *not* have a choice. If she wanted to leave, she'd have to go that way to look for another way out.

Sylvian paced the room until her anger was spent. She set the bags down. Now that she felt calmer, she realized something was amiss about her thinking. She did have a choice. Kirth had given her that.

He'd let her choose. She could join him or not.

That's what really angered her. She had to decide. The responsibility — hers.

Until this moment, she'd been reacting. Yes, she agreed to stay at the hotel. He'd made the plans. She'd said yes to marrying him. Again, he'd made the plans. And she'd climbed in the Land Rover without asking a single question. His plans. Again.

Now, she had to take action or remain inert. Her choice was that simple.

Her mind recalled an earlier time when this man's hands had touched her body. The episode may have been a dream, but the sensations felt so real. Regardless of the name she called him, the man was the same. His touch had fired her passion.

Sylvian heard the water come on in the shower. What had he said on the flight? *The language of the heart lies in actions, not words.* She wanted him. So what if they'd known each other mere days.

She could no longer see her life without him.

She began undressing, dropping, where she stood, the white lace blouse as well as the cypress green skirt and jacket she'd changed into on the charter flight. Next came her panties and brassiere. Not even in her wildest fantasies had she imagined her first time with a man would be this way — that she'd be making the moves.

Confrontation

21

*K*irth leaned against the shower wall, letting the Mexican tile cool his heated skin. He prayed she'd come. To succeed, he had to let her choose. She had to come to him. Willingly.

For the first time since he'd been engaged in this war, he felt encouraged. They had three nights before the shrine would appear. Three nights before Drakus could open the world, find them wherever they were, and instantly appear.

Not that The Beast wouldn't send messengers ahead. The fiend would. Especially now that they were wed. Surely Drakus knew.

Despite his attempt to govern his ecstasy, to curb his enthusiasm, the powerful emotional release he felt when they had wed had been impossible to control. Joy had filled him to the point of tears. Drakus must have felt the rush.

Kirth had feared his response would be too great to contain. Completely. That's why he brought Sylvian to this secluded spot. The house was well armored against attack, as were the others he had scattered around the world.

Each home contained enough weapons to take on a thousand angry demonic wolves or whatever else Drakus chose to hurl at him. But they'd have to penetrate his defenses first. He hoped his plans bought them enough time to finish what they'd begun centuries ago on that windswept beach.

Then, he'd been mortal. She'd been caught between mortality and immortality and knew things others didn't. But she'd lived too many times since, her awareness decreasing with each birth. He'd watched the process. In each lifetime, reaching this moment had been more difficult until last time, in desperation, he spoke to her of their past. His transgression caused her a painful death.

This time he'd played by all the rules, refusing to court disaster. Now, it was her call. She had to come to him.

Once they touched, he must be quick. He shook his head. He feared Sylvian wouldn't find their love-making romantic. He hoped she'd want him as much as he desired her. That way at least she'd be ready for the speedy release he gave her.

Relief washed his doubts away when she stepped into the room. Passion heightened inside him. She was naked. He'd only seen her that way in the lake when they'd bathed together. Then, they'd been unable to touch one another. Now, he vowed, no force would keep them apart.

"You are more beautiful than words can describe," Kirth said, reaching his hand out for her. "I love you."

Sylvian hesitated. Suddenly, she felt shy, awkward as if she were on a blind date. She'd never been alone with a naked man, much less alone naked with a naked man. Kirth was a strapping specimen. Golden skin. Rippling, sinewy muscles.

She gasped.

Scars. Scars covered his flesh as if he'd been through countless battles. Once she saw them and identified what they were, they didn't offend her. Instead, they reminded her of medals of honor. Odd. She didn't know why they struck her that way. They just did.

She reached out, and following his lead, as she'd done so often in the past days, she said: "You take my breath away. I love you." She took his hand. The jolt of energy that hit her almost knocked her off balance. He swiftly pulled her to him, enveloping her in his arms as he lifted her off the ground. His mouth closed over hers.

She drank from his lips as if she'd been drained of all sustenance, and his mouth held the elixir of life. Her fingers entwined themselves in his hair, and she pressed his face even closer to hers. She moaned when his tongue plunged deep inside her mouth.

Steam rose off the cool water pounding their bodies. Kirth heard the wails. Banshees. Drakus's legions drew near. He had to move quickly.

Guiding her legs around his, he grabbed her buttocks and lifted her into him. In one smooth movement, he pressed inside her. The velvet muscles gave way. He broke through the fragile barrier and began rocking.

Enthralled by his embrace, a fiery passion inflamed Sylvian. His love and her desire were consuming her; she could not let go of any part of him — his lips, his mouth, his tongue. She had to have all of him, his whole being.

Each thrust he made sent spasms of lightning coursing through her body. Every plunge he took deep inside her heightened her ecstasy. She wouldn't, she couldn't, release him. Finally, the only word her mind screamed was — *More*.

He exploded inside her, triggering her own climax. Fleetingly, she felt as if they were one, united forever in each other's arms. The questions and self-doubts that she had held as close as any lover slipped away. She had come home at last. In this single act of uniting her body with his, she had reached her journey's end. An unfamiliar sense of calm spread through her muscles, easing the tension she had harbored close to her throughout her life.

Instantaneously, she was bathed in moonlight and transported outside her mortal body. Blinding light engulfed her as she embraced the Nightstar. A bitter cold chilled her bones; the light gave way to darkness. Sylvian felt herself being pulled down, down, down. Back into her body.

Her eyes opened. Kirth held her body and his directly under the shower's cooling water. The floor outside the shower had been scorched. She felt too weak to move.

Kirth's eyes searched hers. "You know?"

She smiled, wanly. "Yes. I know. Everything." She put her

hand on his cheek, "My brave warrior. How I love you."

"And I love you." Kirth stroked her cheek. "I wish we had time, but we don't. We can't stay here. Did you not hear the banshees? Soon, Drakus's creatures will be at the door."

"I can't seem to move." Sylvian's breathing was labored.

"I'll carry you." Kirth lifted her in his arms. He stepped from the shower, laid a couple of towels over Sylvian, and moved quickly toward the far wall. He pressed a lever and a door appeared. He walked through, closed the door behind him, then headed down a long hallway lit by an emergency generator.

The elevator lay at the edge of a cliff which overlooked an inlet of water leading to the ocean. He had the lift installed with human labor so no hint of his powers touched the mechanism. He took the same precaution with the house.

He hit the down button, then opened a panel in the wall. He grabbed the clothes from their hangers, roughly dried himself off, and dressed. Gently, he dried Sylvian, who was unconscious by this time. Even though he'd not met her when he'd stocked his places, he had no difficulty selecting the correct size. Her outward appearance had remained the same in each life. The jeans and red cotton shirt fit.

Behind another panel hung the mountain-climbing gear and weapons. Harnessing Sylvian to himself, he prepared to scale the rest of the distance. Manual labor offered the safest use of his energy.

By now, The Beast had located the house and had sent its minions scurrying inside searching the rooms. The energy burst required to fly himself and Sylvian out would pinpoint their location. He wouldn't do that unless he had no choice.

The elevator stopped. Kirth listened. He didn't hear or sense anything lurking outside. Still, he stood ready. He released the safety on the light-weight machine-gun he held, turned out the light, and pushed the button to open the door. The cave felt secure. He strode through the cavern quickly, then pressed another button to open the door to the entrance.

He soon rappelled the sheer face of the cliff and hung closely to the waters below. He systematically tapped along the cliff wall until he found the hollow sound. His hand moved along the vibration to the upper-right corner, where he applied pressure.

An opening, large enough for a man to walk through, appeared. Once inside, he closed the door behind him and Sylvian before he turned on the generator. Light illuminated the cave, which housed a sailboat docked in the water below.

Taking the steps two at a time, Kirth pulled anchor and stepped aboard. He released the harness that held Sylvian and laid her gently in the bottom of the boat. The almost-silent running motor turned over immediately.

Kirth opened the lower entrance to the cave. When the boat slipped into the cove, he closed the entrance. Moments later, he made open water and headed away from the shore.

Fifteen minutes later, he cut the motor and allowed the vessel to drift. He removed Sylvian's gear and felt her chest to make sure she still breathed. She did.

Rana's mystical barge materialized beside him while his attention was on Sylvian.

"Well done, friend," Rana said.

"Thank you, but your congratulations may be too soon." He took the line she handed him, and tied the silver rope securely to his boat. "She's barely breathing."

"Move her quickly," Rana replied. "We knew this could happen."

"I feel as if I've harmed her in some way." He lifted Sylvian gently in his arms and turned toward Rana. "Maybe I acted too hastily. I heard the banshees and knew what would be next."

"You did well," Rana said. "You heeded our warning. You have saved the both of you so far. Let us have our sister now. There is much to do and little time." Raising her arm, she commanded, "Come."

Sylvian floated across the space between them and came to rest in her sister's ship.

"Be careful." Kirth threw the rope back to Rana.

"You and your friends are the ones in danger now," Rana

said. "Our sister will sleep more than a day. When she returns to you, the interloper will be close. Remember that and that the eye of the storm holds you in Nyx time. The first breath of the day of her birth lies in the second past midnight. Drakus can and will attack her then. The creature will strike your companions before then. Listen to the wind. Stay by the shore. Keep your friends close, but be aware that your energy is balancing itself anew. Using your cloaking net to protect them may drain you and draw The Beast. Be watchful."

"I will," Kirth replied. "When she's ready, you know where to find me."

He turned back to the land. To retrace his steps and walk a path he'd left his mark upon was foolhardy. After he moored the boat inside the cove, Kirth climbed the cliffs separating his house from the sea. He felt a tremor pass through the rocks and soil, and immediately let go, taking flight with the ease of an eagle.

The stucco home exploded, lighting the night sky. A second explosion brought the rocky cliff plunging into the sea. Instantly, Kirth gauged the angle of attack, discharged a bolt of his own lightning toward the assailant, and began taking evasive action. He dodged a quick succession of fireballs, then struck again.

The lightning flared when the strike hit its mark. Kirth smiled. *Drakus could smart over that blow.*

Snarling wolves formed in the air around him. Kirth's eyebrow arched. *The Beast had fine-tuned its talents since their last battle. Now the viper could fly its creations.* With the rapidity of a machine-gun, Kirth burst each wolf as he zigzagged across the sky, careful to keep the sea beneath him.

He narrowed his hearing to one sound in the night, the heartbeat of The Beast. He found what he sought northwest of the house. His lightning bolt struck the spot.

The creature howled. A dark, gray cloud rose out of the jungle. Kirth struck again. The Beast hurled fireballs in Kirth's direction and withdrew.

Kirth fought the temptation to pursue Drakus, his instincts warning him an easy chase meant one thing — a trap. He'd caught The Beast in a rage and managed to wound his foe. Not severely. But enough to inconvenience the bewitcher. No matter how much he wanted to, he'd not follow. Timing meant everything. Overconfidence could lead to a mistake he'd regret.

Kirth turned and flew southeast, charting a course along the Bay of Mexico. He'd catch up with his friends later when the way felt safe.

**What's past is
prologue.**

*The Tempest, Act II, Scene I
William Shakespeare*

22

*A*straea. *Nightstar of the Nyx.* The shadows whispered to her, filling her world with the sound of her name and soothingly coaxing her to stay. To rest. To be at peace. No need to hurry. No cause for alarm. She was safe. Protected. Loved. The battle fought and won. She felt herself being drawn in the direction of the compelling, soft voices. So gentle. So restful. So reassuring … .

A single blot of lightning cracked the darkness, leaving blood-red traces in its path. Astraea opened her eyes.

She lay bathed in moonlight, her skin damp with dew. Pearly sand shimmered around her. Sitting up, she ran her hands through the granules, watching them sparkle as they fell through her fingers. She knew this place. She was between worlds.

Did the voices speak truth? Had she succeeded after all? A sharp pain stabbed the base of her neck, then spread throughout her body. Her thoughts fell over themselves, creating fleeting images of the lives she had lived and lost. The white shrine. Silver and golden in the moonlight. Lilies. Roses. Crumbling to dust. Hot lava flowing inside her. Blood and tears. Decomposing flesh. Her beloved's body broken on the stones. Flames then darkness. And the cold.

Children. Smiling. Laughing. Dancing. Blood. So much blood and swords and axes. The river ran red with blood. Moonlight. His lips on hers. Ecstasy. Fire. Darkness. And the cold.

Scrubbing the floor, the water so hot it scalded her hands.

226

Robes rustling. Death. Decay. Screams. Darkness. And the cold.

Hunger. Castle walls cold and stark. Her keeper. So kind, so compassionate, so evil. Danger. Violet eyes to save her. Too late. Darkness. And the cold.

White horses bathed in blood. Sand and fire. Darkness. And the cold. Forever the cold.

A face in the water beneath her. Her father's. Coffins side-by-side. Hiding. Hiding. Always hiding. The belt strap. Pop. Pop. Pop. Stacks and stacks of paper. Tiny letters. *Family Life Through the Ages Molds Today's Youth.* Bolder letters. *Embrace the Boogeyman.* The white shrine. Always the white shrine.

"Enough." Astraea stood and shook herself off, determined to dispel the horrid doom surrounding her.

Forcing the dark images from her mind, she looked away from the sea toward the land. Sunrise caressed the horizon. A bright fire burned as it had the last time she'd been here.

Incredible joy overcame her. The years of tears and terrifying evil washed away as if they'd been but a fleeting shadow and not real at all. This was reality. She walked toward the flames. Soon, she'd be home.

Not until she drew nearer the fire did she see them. Her sisters. She began running, yelling to them. They stood. The tallest one held out her arms.

Laughing, Astraea took the outstretched hands. "I've waited for this moment. Now that I'm here, I don't know what to say."

Her sister squeezed her hands, then released them. They embraced. "Little one, at last you are here."

"Thank the Heavens." Astraea hugged each sister. *Little one.* Now she understood her fondness for the pet name. "We're here as we were the last time."

"Nay. 'Tis not as before." Arva pointed to the ground in front of her. "Sit there. Across from us. We must talk."

"Can we not visit later, at home?" Astraea asked, disappointed. "I've waited so long to embrace my friends and walk in the lushness of my land. I yearn for our home's soothing music. My body aches to breathe its fragrant air and bathe in its golden light."

"Our world remains sealed against you."

"No!" Astraea was horrified. She'd come this far to be turned away? "Why?"

"Sit down. Now."

The words were an order, and Astraea sat even though she'd not intended to do so. She tried to get up, but found she was pinned to the ground.

"This is not a social visit. We must talk. You must listen. When we last stood on this ground, you did not hear what was said. Now, you must."

Arva's tone frightened Astraea. Her sisters sat down in front of her. Their eyes held sorrow mixed with joy.

"Have I not paid enough for one mistake?" Astraea asked angrily.

"You are not being punished," said Rana, the green in her eyes deepened and turned smoky gray. "You were an innocent. Your heart pure, unblemished, your energy great."

"I loved him," Astraea declared, tears springing to her eyes.

"Love is not a crime," insisted Nata, her red hair glowed in the fire's light. "He was worthy of you and you of him. The Seers were adamant that you were to be allowed to offer him the choice. They saw your destinies entwined. The Council agreed. We came here to call you, to inform you of the decision, but we were too late."

"You must have made him immortal for he has been in every life I've lived," Astraea said wistfully. "Even now you keep us apart. Is he not waiting for me in our world?"

"Nay, Sister." Arva shook her head. "He is with his friends, the ones you met whose lives are now at risk. He is a loyal friend and a fearsome foe. Our enemy knows that well."

At the mention of her enemy, Astraea trembled. She fought to steady herself. Her sister continued, each word cut her like the blade of a knife.

"Are not the greatest heroes unsung, unspoken? Among our people, he will always remain legend. Even his name has acquired magical power. So much so that the words are no longer spoken aloud by our people outside our realm. But in the world he came from, the one you live in now, the time and place of his birth have been erased."

"And his people?" Astraea asked, her voice a whisper.

"We were here training him." Nata glanced at Arva.

"The Beast Drakus destroyed most of the Arnfinn," Arva said. "Those who escaped over the mountains were lost in history."

"They were a spiritual people as their leader's name implies —" Niniane's word were cut short.

"Njall?" Astraea asked, interrupting.

"Nay," Niniane replied. "Although he was not an evil man. Few have the power to withstand The Beast. You know that better than most."

Astraea winced. She did.

"The white eagle, Arnfinn the Rune Master, marked the beginning of their tribe. They were peace loving unless attacked first, then they were fearsome fighters. You witnessed that when they sacked the village where you were enslaved."

"Aye," Astraea agreed.

"They were adventurous and clever," Nata interjected.

"Rune masters with a written language that vanished with them." Niniane stared at Nata. "Their extinction was a loss their world suffered without knowing."

"Arnfinnland?" Astraea asked, fearing she knew the answer."No trace of Arnfinnland remains," Rana said. "The sea claimed the land as her own centuries ago."

Silence descended among them. One word throbbed in Astraea's mind. Losses. A sense of overwhelming sorrow filled her. Her eyes moved from one sister to the next. Her love had taken his name from the sisters — Nata, Arva, Rana, Astraea and Niniane. N.A.R.A.N. Clever. "When was he here?"

"When I found him near death in the forest bordering Eimund," Rana replied. "We offered him the choice."

"First, he wanted to return to his world to kill the one who had possessed and destroyed his father and you," Nata interjected. "We told him he did not have the power. He knew our words were true."

"All contributed to his transformation." Astraea's words were more a statement of fact than a question.

"To give him the greatest variety of gifts he could receive," Rana said.

"What must I do?" The question chilled Astraea even as she spoke the words. The title typed neatly across Sylvian's thesis flashed like a garish neon sign in her mind — *Embrace the Boogeyman*. She shuddered.

"Reclaim what has been stolen," Arva advised. "Only then may you go home. You are not alone. Our friend can help. But the actual task can be accomplished only by you."

"Who says this is so?" Astraea's voice held unspoken accusations.

Arva shook her head. "The Seers have no doubts."

"So, I am being punished." Astraea was enraged.

"Nay," Arva remarked. "This is your responsibility. What you have lost, you alone can retrieve."

Furious, Astraea spit out, "I did not lose my innate abilities or misplace the power bestowed upon me as the Nightstar. They were stolen — violently!"

"Your abilities and power are your responsibility," Arva insisted. "No one else's. Regardless of how they were taken, you must be the one to wrest them from the thief who has them now. Others may help, but you must be the one who acts."

"Make me immortal, and I will," Astraea challenged.

"We have done what we can," Niniane said softly. "We brought you here where you received the maximum benefits of our healing power, but we are forbidden to do more."

"You made him immortal!"

"He was mortal."

"So am I."

"Nay," Nata consoled. "The thief did not gain all your power. Our enemy's actions tell us this is so. When the creature comes for you, and it will, you must be ready. If you lose, The Beast will have the power to walk in to our world, use its knowledge in both. Had our enemy had this power, it would have already used it. Now that your mortal body has consummated your vows of love, you have been reunited with the Nightstar."

"Dear Sister, you cannot have forgotten the Nightstar has always been and will always be until the end of time when all worlds are reconciled or forgotten," Niniane chided. "If The Beast drains you completely, the fiend will gain the Nightstar."

"Why have you not destroyed this abomination yourselves?" Astraea snapped.

"We tried," Rana explained. "The universe operates on its own code — as you well know. We failed, for the task is not ours, but yours."

"We are here because our enemy overstepped the boundaries," Niniane added. "In so doing, Drakus laid open the door to your memory. Otherwise, would you have wed when you did?"

Astraea sighed and shook her head. "No."

"This foolishness allowed us an opening, a path into our enemy's world," Rana said. "But, we must move cautiously lest we alert the creature."

Arva raised her hand to silence them. "Our enemy delights in destroying those any of us love and has many followers who are willing to do its bidding. The actions of the followers do drain our friend's energy and test his patience, leaving him more vulnerable to making a poor choice when the real battle comes. Your place is with your husband." Arva stood and the others followed. "When you recapture your energy, then you may walk safely through the fire to home if that is what you want."

Alarmed, Astraea said, "I can't stop The Beast."

"You must," Arva said. "You must find your way. The Seers have prophesied that this is your last birth. There will not be another."

"What have they seen that makes them say so?"

"The numbers," Arva said. "After the initial attack, we waited twenty-one hundred years for your return. In the thirteen hundred years since, your spirit has made four attempts. Three plus four equals seven. Seven plus five equals twelve — the closed circle. Your births number six — the sum and the product of its parts as well as the product of the first male and the first female numbers. This time is the last, they say."

"No! I can't," Astraea insisted. "I don't have the power. I don't know the way."

"Your limitations are yours only when you believe in them," Arva said. "You —"

Interrupting her, Astraea insisted, "Listen to me! I can not. I don't know how. This fiend still has part of me. If I knew the way to stop this evil, I would. But I don't. I can't —"

Nata's blue eyes narrowed and hardened. "Fear holds you back," she accused. "Do not let it also make you a coward."

"How dare you!" Astraea raged. "Have you had the defiler's foul juice coursing inside you, inflaming you with disease? Felt the ghoul's jagged nails puncture your breasts while its sinuous tongue buries in your neck and sucks your blood? Nay, sister of mine. Nay. But I have. Did you know while The Beast held me pinned in a grip I couldn't break, the creature projected its thoughts into my mind? And that the abominable mutation read my thoughts as easily as if I spoke them aloud?"

Astraea's eyes flashed as she studied the shocked expressions on her sisters' faces. "I didn't think so. Am I scared? Terrified? I'd be a fool not to be. The creature's form is not only flesh and blood from the humans the fiend has consumed. Nor is the entity fueled solely by the powers stolen from the wizard. The Beast is more. Some unnatural source lies at the heart of the mutant's invulnerability. Something I've never experienced before. I don't know how to beat that force."

"You must," Nata said.

"I am no coward," Astraea said defiantly.

"Prove it," Nata snapped. "Face The Beast."

Niniane stepped between them. "Stop pushing, Nata. You can be so insufferable."

"Someone must inflame our sister," Nata replied. "No one else seems willing to do so."

Astraea patted Niniane's shoulder. "Let it pass. I understand what Nata is trying to do. And you're right." Her eyes glowed mischievously. "Both of you."

"Try to be helpful and you get slapped," Nata said wryly.

"Some pain is deserved," Niniane retorted.

"Enough," Rana said. "Petty squabbles are draining and solve nothing."

Visions of her sisters' lives since their last meeting crowded Astraea's mind. Stunned, her anger erased by overwhelming sorrow, she involuntarily stepped away from the others. The Beast's insidious touch had scarred their lives. Arva had been forced to live apart from her husband. Her other sisters remained single. They hadn't been allowed to wed because they shared the same blood, the same basic energy which fueled one, fueled them all. Their lives had been filled with waiting, planning for her return, plotting their next moves against the enemy. "Nay. Nay," she pleaded. "Say it isn't so."

"What you see holds truth." Rana's voice was caressing, forgiving, loving. She sighed. "Thirty-four centuries is long even for us."

Astraea turned to Arva. "Why this punishment?"

"A precaution only. The Seers feel we are vulnerable and will be easily wounded and absorbed if you fail." Arva shrugged. "Children are forbidden to us until you are victorious."

"Seers!" Incensed, Astraea spit out the words. "Hearts of stone and loins of dust."

"Aye," Rana replied. "But the Council agrees."

"And our parents?" Even as she asked, Astraea knew the answer. They were lost to her. Their tasks completed, they had evolved and moved on.

"Forced to evolve," Rana said. "When their time came, neither was allowed to join the Council."

"Membership was theirs by right," Astraea whispered.

"No longer," Nata said. "We have been moved outside the inner circle. Arva alone may gain access. And only when they allow."

"The flame, Nata?"

"Nay." Nata saw Astraea's shocked expression. "The loss is fitting. I gave that charge willingly to the one who holds your heart."

Astraea turned to Niniane. Had she given up her birthright as well?

"Aye." Niniane squeezed Astraea's arm. "He is also the guardian of the forest. My choice. I have that right. And the gift was necessary. We had an uncertain number of decades for training."

Anguished, Astraea pleaded, "Forgive my lack of vigilance, my disregard of your warnings, my inability to love without obsession, my thoughts which so colored my mind that I lost touch with now and was vulnerable to attack."

"We love you." Niniane stroked Astraea's hair before embracing her. "Grieve and turn the page on what might have been." Releasing her sister, she said, "Our vigil and our prayers have been answered. We have the opportunity to correct our transgressions." She looked at the others.

Nata took Astraea's hand. "We, too, did not fully understand the peril, or you would not have been alone at the shrine. If there are any who need to be forgiven, it is us. Your sisters."

"Nay, I hold no enmity toward my sisters." Astraea squeezed Nata's hand. "The Beast is the culprit. The creature is a thief, a disease, a transgressor who acts without shame. Without guilt. An evil that consumes all it touches."

Arva cradled Astraea's face in her hands. "We have spoken too long and said too much." She brushed Astraea's cheek with a kiss. "You did what must be done then; you must do the same now. Past sight and sound and touch, the solution awaits your breath to bring forth its life. Your answers lie within you. You must find them quickly. The darkness draws near." Releasing her sister, Arva ordered, "Go. Now."

The words were a command, and Astraea found herself sprinting down the hillside behind Rana. They boarded the ship anchored in the natural harbor and set sail. When she looked back, the landscape was gloomy, the flame had been extinguished. Moments later, the land vanished in the mists.

"They've gone home." Astraea's voice was sad. How she wanted to be with them, yet, she also wanted to be with her husband. How strange those two simple words sounded to her ears — her husband. Yet, they were finally true.

"Only Arva has returned home," Rana said. "She has gone to our favorite place. From there, she can project her thoughts into our friend's mind. Afterward, she will report to the Council. Then she will join the others who are already on duty in this world. None of us will contact the two of you directly unless there is no other choice. Usually, there is another way."

"Why can we not see you, speak with you?"

"I am not allowed to answer that question," Rana said, exasperated. "We all have already said too much. Think and you will know."

Astraea sat down, closed her eyes, and tried to clear her mind. At first, the effort seemed hopeless. Jumbled thoughts popped up. She opened her eyes and focused on the sail's mast. When her mind wandered, she refocused on the mast.

Not until her mind silenced did she sense the subtle pull. At first, she felt as if she were a small boat, anchored yet still floating freely in the water. She became live bait tethered to a line, bobbing here and there where she wanted, oblivious of being controlled by a devilish fisherman. The sensation gave way to an even more unsettling one. She was a spider weaving her web inside the web of another.

She shuddered. She was not independent. An insidious bond, formed when The Beast began draining her energy, existed. The Seers were right. She had to reclaim what was hers. Break that bond. As long as the tie existed, The Beast could use her powers to read her thoughts. She had to guard them well.

Now that she knew her plight, she realized how perilous it was for the others to be anywhere nearby. She must build a barrier around the thread that stretched between the creature's thoughts and her own.

Her eyes narrowed. She saw herself gathering the tools to build a wall. Cement. White bricks. Layer after layer began forming in her mind. Finally, she was satisfied.

She looked away from the ship. Only then did she realize they had sailed out of the mists. *Almost there.* She was eager to see her love. His life was in as much danger as hers. Yet, The Beast couldn't destroy him until after it had engaged her in battle. She had used her love's body to seal her portal between the worlds.

"Swim toward the shore." Rana pointed Astraea in the right direction. "The sea will wash away our presence."

Astraea kicked off her shoes, unzipped her jeans and removed them.

"Clothes won't slow you down," Rana said, throwing her knife to Astraea.

"I'm used to swimming in less," Astraea replied, using the blade to cut off the jeans' legs.

Rana let down the sail. "This is the spot. Caution is your banner."

Astraea ripped the sleeves out of her shirt and put on the cut-offs. "I'm ready. Tell the others I've seen the invisible bond which ties me in this destiny and know their wisdom is correct. My thoughts as we part are of my love for my sisters, my friends, my world, and the man who has protected me."

"And ours are of you," Rana advised. "Remember, the sea is your friend."

"I will." She dived into the water.

Destruction

23

*W*hen Astraea's head cleared the waves, the mists and the ship had vanished. She tread water until she spied the beach. *Good.* She was close enough to see the hacienda sprawled across the hillside beyond the sand dunes. She swam toward the house, taking long, steady strokes.

Shortly, she heard the hum of an outboard motor. Treading water again, she stopped, shaded her eyes, and looked toward the sound. Not until then did she see the yacht floating at a ninety-degree angle to the shore. The smaller boat bearing down on her must have come from there. Someone saw her. Is the person friend or foe? She strained to see the boatman.

Her love.

She started to wave, then decided to wait. If the boat and driver were a trap, she was a good underwater swimmer and ready to dive. The honey-colored craft pulled alongside her. "Caution is your banner." Kirth spoke as a sentry would to a comrade behind enemy lines. He killed the motor. He didn't make a move toward her. "The sea is our friend. Our enemy fears salt water." He paused. "Satisfied? That it's me?"

"Yes."

He lifted her aboard and into his arms. "It's good to have you back. I've moved us to the yacht. We're safer on water than land."

The feel of his body next to hers sent ripples of pleasure through her. Before he could set her down, she pulled his head toward hers until their lips embraced.

The ensuing long, lingering kiss whispered of lifetimes of

desire. Kirth trembled as he set her down.

"I want you." The gentle touch of her fingers tickled the curve of his cheek, the firm muscles in his neck.

"Dangerous," he warned.

"Impossible?" Her hands moved down his chest, then slid under the waistband of his gold swimming trunks.

Kirth's eyes closed, and he groaned from the sheer pleasure of her touch. "Nay."

She slid the trunks off his hips, closed one of her hands around his tender, hardened flesh, and began stroking him, while the other popped the snap on her cutoffs.

She released him and stepped back.

Kirth's eyes opened. He watched her in several smooth, quick movements, pull her blouse over her head and push her pants down her legs. The shorts fell at her feet. She knelt in front of him, the tip of her tongue tickled his hard, firm shaft, before her mouth closed over him.

His voice caught in his throat. *Steady.* His body flinched inwardly. Involuntarily, his fingers entwined themselves in her hair, and he pressed her head toward him.

Her lips and tongue caressed him, stoking his passion into an intoxicated furor of want and desire. When he could stand the exquisite torture no longer, and the hunger to fill her with his seed almost overwhelmed him, he gasped and let go of her hair. His hands grasped her shoulders, and he drew her upright, brushing her body against his until she stood in front of him.

His index finger tilted her head upward. Their eyes met. Neither spoke. There was no need for words. His lips closed over hers as he lifted her in his arms.

She was barely aware that he'd laid her on the deck. Straddling her body, his mouth released hers to burn a path across her bosom, where his lips enclosed and suckled one tender nipple then the other. His fingers caressed the mound of soft hair which lay at the entrance of her womanhood. His index finger slipped inside where it stroked her into a frenzy of desire. She moaned. "Now." Her loins ached with want.

"Nay." His tongue circled first one then the other hardened nipple, his teeth gently nipping each, before his lips kissed their way across her skin, leaving a trail of sensations in their wake.

Positioning himself between her welcoming thighs, his tongue plunged inside her as his hands began gently stroking her breasts. Wave after wave of agonizing pleasure enveloped Sylvian. Just when she thought she could stand no more, he stopped.

Her eyes opened to find him staring intently at her. He smiled. "Now."

"Aye." She groaned. Closing her eyes, she released herself totally to the sensations of the moment.

He entered her hard, slow and deep, then he quickened the pace. She could hardly breathe. The world began spinning out of focus. Still he thrust harder, deeper, faster. Pleasure washed in waves over her, as the pounding of their lovemaking peaked, then ebbed.

When she felt his gentle kisses falling first on her neck, then on her face, she opened her eyes.

"How do you feel?" His eyes were concerned. He was *almost* sure this time wouldn't leave her drained as their last lovemaking had.

"Marvelous!" She smiled. "I didn't blast through this world and mine and see my life as I did before. Thank the Heavens. Once is more than enough for that experience. This time, it was just you and me. Two people in love. The feeling was wonderful past description. And you?"

"As if the weight of many lifetimes has been removed. I, too, find the feelings … uh … marvelous. Yet, the action is danger-ous, perhaps foolhardy. The Beast can't stand our pleasure. Drakus is sure to know. Our foe may be afraid of the sea, but its servants are not. We've just given the enemy a good reading on our precise location."

"I know." She sighed. "But loving you is the only thing I can do today that I will never regret. For, if this is my last day of life, I would die angry that we hadn't made love. If we survive, I will always have the memory of those moments."

"And I as well." He leaned over and kissed her again. Then he stood and offered her his hand.

Before she took his outstretched hand, she ran her fingers down his arm. "Where do your friends think you got these scars and the others which cover your body?"

"They don't see them." He took her hand in his and pulled her to her feet.

"I do."

"Do they disgust you?" Kirth's matter-of-fact tone hid the fear he felt that they might.

"Nay. They are beautiful. But, why do I see them and the others don't?"

"Anyone from your world can see them as you do. It's humans who can't." He pulled on his trunks.

"I suspected as much."

Kirth looked at her questioningly. His eyebrow arched. "And what exactly does that mean?"

"I've seen your act. Remember?" She laughed. "Half naked. Dancing on stage." She sighed. "But I was sitting too far back to see you clearly."

"I'm glad you caught the show."

"I'm glad I caught you."

"I think it's the other way around," Kirth countered. "I caught you."

"Oh, really. I walked into the shower. Alone. Remember?"

"Perhaps, we caught each other." Kirth started the motor.

"Aye. Now that we've solved that, shall we settle our names? I've had so many, and you've had your share."

"Kirth is easiest for me. For my friends."

"I've grown used to the name, too. Actually, I like it. As for me, Astraea belongs to someone else — an immortal whose naivete was nearly fatal." She frowned. "May still be... ."

"Nay." Kirth's tone was gentle.

"We hope not." She picked up her clothes. "The other names I've had mean nothing except the one you gave me. It's lovely, but it is as Sylvian that I've found out who I am. Perhaps

Aasta could be my middle name. I don't have one."

"Sylvian it is," Kirth said. "Besides, those are the names on the wedding certificate. Easier all the way around."

"Good." She began dressing. "Where do the others think I've been?"

"They don't know you've been anywhere." Kirth steered the pleasure boat toward the yacht. "They think we arrived at the house yesterday when they were out. You're suffering from Montezuma's revenge and have remained in our room. Close to the toilet. The girls imagine they've checked on you. When I left, everyone still slept. On the yacht. But they will awaken soon."

"It must be around ten o'clock." Sylvian's eyes scanned the sky. "Right?"

"Aye. The night was long. We boarded the ship around four this morning."

Sylvian's eyes widened. "What happened?"

"We were spotted. In a club, downtown. I feel the shadow passing into my world when Drakus draws close, but I don't always immediately recognize those who have Drakus's mark on them. Hale was accosted by a gang when he stepped outside."

Sylvian gasped. How could that have happened? "Is he all right?"

"He's alive. His size is deceptive. He's tougher than he looks."

"Was he alone?"

Kirth, clearly upset, shook his head. "No. A girl." He paused. "They'd spent the better part of the evening together with us. The last place we went she realized she'd left her purse in the car. They went to get it."

The boat pulled alongside the yacht. Kirth tied the two together, then turned back to Sylvian. "The girl was young. Beautiful. They caught them by surprise. Hale was a madman." His expression was pained. "They cut her throat. She'd bled to death by the time I arrived. I was too late to do anything for her."

"It's not your fault." Sylvian placed her hand over his. "You can't protect everyone all the time."

Kirth shook his head, remembering. "She might be alive if

I'd spread my cloaking net over the area. But I didn't. I conserved energy." Kirth frowned as Rana's warning against using the protection came back to him. He'd followed her advice and an innocent girl had died. "I'd hoped since we were down the coast a good distance the other night that our enemy would have a hard time locating me here. In Veracruz. A horrible miscalculation. I've had my cloaking net out since. The yacht had already been leased for our trip tonight. So, I moved everyone on board."

"A coincidence perhaps." Sylvian wanted to soothe him but sensed his resistance.

"Nay. They'd been touched by The Beast. I know. Once I stood close to them, I felt its shadow."

"Did they run when they saw you?"

"They tried, but they didn't succeed," Kirth said. "I knew our foe would know as quickly if they reported in as it would if I used my power against them. I chose the latter. It was the least I could do for the young lady. The authorities were actually quite solicitous. Apparently, they suspected them of having committed other, similar crimes."

"And Hale? How is he?"

"Traumatized by the experience. Angry at himself because he wasn't quick enough to save her. He wouldn't listen when we tried to reason with him. Outnumbered. Surprised. He's lucky to be alive."

"He wouldn't be if you hadn't been quick," Sylvian insisted.

"He was in danger because of me," Kirth replied.

"You said the authorities recognized these men, this gang, as possibly responsible for other violent crimes. Don't be so hard on yourself. You've done them and their potential future victims a favor. Besides, you don't know that anything you did led them to Hale. You're speculating that it's so."

"I think they located me accidentally through my friends. Their faces are too well known to remain anonymous long, especially if someone is looking for them."

His last words replayed in Sylvian's mind. *Especially if someone is looking for them.* Her eyes searched his. "You can't live in a vacuum, without friends."

"I have before," Kirth answered. "It would have been better if I had chosen the lonely road this time as well."

"Dragon has done a lot of good. Don't discount that."

"They would have been better off without me," Kirth raged, his voice tormented.

"In this you're wrong," Sylvian admonished. "Not a one of them would agree."

"They might if they knew the price," Kirth said, morosely.

"The music wouldn't have the healing touch without you," Sylvian argued.

"It also wouldn't have the power to destroy." Kirth's voice sounded as plaintive as that of a spoiled child who hadn't gotten his way.

"Quit it!" Sylvian stood and walked toward the gangplank, determined to leave him to thrash around in his misery. He wasn't listening anyway. When she put her foot on the first step, she changed her mind, turned around and in several quick steps was standing in front of him. "This mood is of no help to anyone. Self-pity does not become you. Stop it! Now!"

Kirth yanked her back down beside him. "You have a lot of nerve saying that to me."

"That's right. I do." Sylvian snatched her hand out of his. "Someone has to. Yours obviously falters."

"There's nothing wrong with my nerve," Kirth spewed.

"Thank the Heavens," Sylvian said cuttingly. "For a moment you sounded like a child who'd lost his last toy. We must focus on destroying our enemy. We can't do that paralyzed by the creature's scare tactics. We know what The Beast is like. Small. Petty. Mean. Of course, the fiend will try to kill those you love. You have what The Beast wants."

Kirth glared at her, then his eyes softened. He sighed. "You're right," he agreed. "You've had a rough time, too. I understand how disappointed you are about not being able to go home."

Sylvian knew that of all the people she'd known, Kirth did understand. He'd been violently wrenched from his world just as she had from hers. At least, hers was still there. His was gone. Forever. "I was angry. Hostile, actually. But, my sisters were right."

"Aye," Kirth said.

A disturbing thought hit her. *He's never been to your home because he has the same bond.* "I know about the bond, the way our three destinies are tied to one another. That's why you're so careful about using your power."

Kirth nodded. "I've built a wall against The Beast, but the interloper still feels the surges, just as I do when the creature uses its abilities."

"Is your wall of white brick and mortar?"

"How did you know?"

"Mine, too." Sylvian reached out and ran her fingers across his cheek. "This life with its forced exile and unending quest has been awful for you, hasn't it?"

"I've had periods of rest." He captured her fingers in his hand and kissed them. "They've been necessary when the conflict has been too draining. The important thing was to be ready, recharged when I felt your presence stir again. That's all behind us now. We're together. And we have a chance to end this for all time."

His arms enveloped her, and he pulled her to him. Softly, his gentle kisses caressed her face. She pressed her mouth to his, her fingers played across his back. He felt himself harden again and released her.

"Perhaps we need more privacy?" Sylvian whispered.

"Aye," Kirth replied, huskily.

"Hey! Kirth!"

They looked up. Rogert stood at the railing.

"I've looked everywhere for you. We need help." Rogert's voice cracked. "Hale's crazy. Delirious."

Kirth cleared the steps two at a time with Sylvian right behind him. "Where are the others?"

"They're with him, trying to subdue him, but he's a wild man," Rogert replied. "He won't listen."

Kirth cursed himself, as the three of them made their way quickly to Hale's cabin. Drakus was aboard. He could now feel the presence of The Beast, but he had not sensed the nearness of his enemy until he stepped on board. Why? Was that what Rana meant? His cloaking net would act as a beacon rather than a deterrent?

Even after all these centuries, he still found the sisters' words obtuse at times. They all knew that using his energies alerted his foe but his cloaking abilities had always sufficed to warn him of his opponent's presence within his net. Be watchful, Rana had said. Kirth frowned. This time he had been caught unaware. His desire for Sylvian had colored his judgment and affected his abilities. Their lovemaking tightened the perimeter of the triangle making him and those he hoped to protect easier targets for The Beast than they'd been in the past. Perhaps he could not have saved the girl without sacrificing his friends.

Destiny

24

*T*he brightness and warmth of the morning vanished when Sylvian stepped into Hale's room. A sense of doom spread over her, chilling her, immobilizing her. She felt as helpless as if she had walked into a fog and become lost.

She blinked several times to focus her vision. The air lay dense in the room. Misty somehow. Her nostrils flared. The vapor reeked of decay. Her eyes strained to see the details.

Eric and Gaylor had Hale pinned to the floor. They were breathing hard. Jeanne and Leigh were on their knees next to the other three.

"It's not your fault," Jeanne pleaded. "You didn't kill her. They did. The gang that attacked you."

Leigh stood and walked over to them. "His head's screwed up," she whispered, frightened. "Somehow he thinks he killed that girl last night. We can't reason with him. Jeanne's been saying those words over and over. He seems to be listening. He calms down. The minute the guys let him go, he's out of control again. Thrashing wildly at anything around him. I've never seen Hale act this way. Or anyone else."

"He'll be OK." Kirth's words soothed her immediately. "He's having a reaction to the shot that doctor gave him. When the drug wears off, he'll be Hale again."

Kirth projected his thoughts toward Sylvian, forcing her to hear what the others could not. *Stay with me regardless of what happens. Our enemy's feeding on their fear. Don't let it feed on yours. Soon, you'll see the room. Do not be alarmed. The others won't remember the*

248

damage that's been done. Stay away from the door.

Sylvian heard the lock on the door click into place. A refreshing breeze wrapped around Kirth, then spread through the room. As the air cleared, she glimpsed the destruction. Clothes, shredded, had been tossed here and there. The mattress had been ripped; its bedding poured out. Deep claw marks ran down the walls. Chairs not battened down lay in pieces.

Hale's body jerked on the floor. The others were frozen in place, their faces caught in macabre expressions of terror. The vaporous gray mist began reforming, its density deepening and lengthening over the drummer's twisting form.

"Release him. Now!" Kirth demanded. His arm shot forth and flames began licking the smoky mist. "Reveal yourself!"

Shrieks filled the room. Drakus materialized.

Even as The Beast's form took on substance, Kirth flipped his head, and the creature rammed into the wall by the door, then rolled toward its hard wooden planking. Kirth covered his opponent in flames and blew the entity through the locked door.

"You'll regret this!" Screeched the injured Drakus.

"Show me." Kirth stepped toward the opening. "Stay and fight."

"We'll have you both before dawn." Drakus fled.

Light radiated outward from Kirth. In a flash, the devastation vanished. The room lay in order, except for a few clothes strewn around and a chair that had been knocked over.

Hale groaned, then opened his eyes. "What's going on?"

"You had a nightmare," Eric replied, releasing his hold on Hale's arms. "Probably caused by the shot the doctor gave you." He rolled off his chest and stood. Gaylor, who had been sitting on Hale's legs, also rose.

"Don't get up too fast," Jeanne advised. "You may get dizzy."

Sitting up, Hale grumbled, "A truck ran over my head."

"That was Eric." Gaylor laughed. "When he tackled you, your head hit the floor. Pow."

Hale put his elbows on his knees and rubbed his head. "Yeah. Thanks. I think."

"Probably knocked some sense into you," Rogert interjected. "It couldn't do any damage. Your head's too hard."

"That does it." Hale started to stand, then sat back down. "I'll get you for that, just not right now."

"In your dreams," Rogert replied.

"Don't count on it," Hale grumbled.

"Now that things are back to normal, I'm hungry," Eric said. "Anybody else for breakfast?"

Leigh spoke first. "Great idea," she told her husband. She looked inquiringly at Kirth.

"Go ahead," he said. "Sylvian and I will stay with Hale."

"We'll bring you something back," Jeanne offered. "What do you want?"

"Thanks, but I'm really not hungry," Sylvian said. "Not yet anyway. Do we have to eat at a certain time?"

"Of course not," Leigh replied, sympathetically. "The cook's at our disposal. Not the other way around." She looked at Hale. "How about you?"

"Later for me, too," Hale said.

Satisfied, they piled out of the room, leaving Kirth and Hale and Sylvian behind.

"Ready to get up?"

"Yeah. Thanks." Hale replied, taking Kirth's outstretched hand. He stood up, then sat in the closest chair and silently studied his friend.

"Dizzy?" Sylvian asked, when the silence among them had become uncomfortable.

"No. Just getting the world into its proper focus." Hale looked intently at Sylvian, then turned his attention to Kirth. "I didn't have a nightmare this morning. There was something in this room with me. An entity that appears to be human but isn't. We three know that."

Kirth sighed. Hale was, despite his joking and light-hearted manner, perceptive, insightful, and almost psychic at times.

"That's right," Hale said. "All my life I've had premonitions. They started in childhood. My father's illness was in some way connected to their development. I would know when he was worse and when he was better. And I knew when he died before anyone told me."

Nothing Hale could have said would have shocked Kirth more. *Had he read his thoughts?*

"Yes," Hale replied, quietly. "I didn't actually read your thoughts or hear them. I just know what they are. It hasn't always been that way for me between us. Just since last night when something happened that changed everything."

Sylvian wondered if Kirth had healed any of Hale's wounds last night. He hadn't mentioned that he had. He said he arrived too late to help the girl. Perhaps he'd assumed she understood that to save his friend he'd had to act swiftly. If so, could that have enhanced Hale's latent abilities somehow?

"I believe that's exactly what happened," Hale said, turning his attention toward Sylvian. "Kirth's healing powers acted as a catharsis."

She gasped. "Oh, my." It was most disconcerting to have someone tell you what you were thinking.

Kirth turned pallid. He'd never had this happen before with people he'd used his healing tears on. Even Sylvian couldn't read his thoughts.

"Perhaps no one else was as close as we are," Hale suggested. "Except Sylvian. She has the ability, but it's blocked. You can't heal that. She must."

"Damn." Kirth sat down on the bed. Only those from Fayre and Drakus had been able to project themselves into his mind. And they could do that now only when he let them or his guard faltered.

"This thing wants me. My body." Hale shuddered. "We're all in danger."

"Can you read The Beast's thoughts as well?" Kirth asked.

"Damn straight!" Hale exclaimed. "In technicolor. The suck fiend, scum gut, vomit vermin —" Hale spit the words "— puker, puke brain. Yeah. That's it. P.B. Puke Brain. Puke Brain's looking for a way on board. Not for its servants. For itself. You threw a protective veil around us last night that drew P.B. close and waiting for an opportunity to strike your friends. The puker believes your grief will weaken you. Slow your reflexes. That's what I sensed during the attack."

"The Beast didn't try to kill you?" Sylvian asked.

"Oh, yeah," Hale replied. "P.B. wanted me as a vehicle to get the others."

"But I would recognize The Beast," Kirth said. "I always do. I see through the current host to the bodies it's trapped inside."

"You weren't here," Hale observed. "But with Sylvian. By the time you returned, we would have been dead or worse. P.B. didn't expect any resistance." Hale smiled. "In that, it was surprised. But, why did it run?"

"The Beast couldn't win," Kirth replied. "I jolted it, but the creature wasn't really damaged. Pursuing would have been a mistake. One I've made before and won't make again. Now, our enemy's saving strength for the confrontation with Sylvian." Frowning, Kirth added, "I never meant to drag you and the others into this."

"You haven't," Hale declared. "Puke Brain has."

"The others may disagree," Kirth said.

"They wouldn't," Hale said. "You know that."

"No, apparently he doesn't," Sylvian interjected. "I've tried to tell him, but he has a hard time hearing this truth."

"Ask them," Hale said. "They'll tell you."

"I won't do that unless it's necessary," Kirth replied.

Hale stretched the upper part of his body and shrugged. "You know how they feel about you. How we all feel about one another. Your doubt has been planted by your enemy. Erase your misgivings. They won't be helpful in what is to come."

Kirth leaned forward. "Can you read The Beast's thoughts now? At this moment? Without it knowing?"

"Maybe, but I won't. The creature's mind is a morass of evil. A real puke brain." He looked at Sylvian. "The experience lent new meaning to your poetry. On the plane? *In the abyss of silent, screaming thoughts, my soul walks.* Remember?"

252

"Yes," Sylvian whispered.

"You've been there, too. In that swamp. There's no light. Just terror. And the awful fear feeding on everyone and everything around it."

Hale shook his head. "Not for anything will I go back there voluntarily. That damn hunting beast killed my friend. I felt her death clinging to the destroyer, whose mind thrives on cruelty and injustice."

"The hunting beast?" Kirth asked.

"One of its pet names for itself," Hale replied. "Humans are just fuel, energy, the creature's to harvest. The hunting beast."

"What other impressions did you get?" Kirth asked.

Hale grimaced. "The entity is filled with horrors — visions of assassins and serial killers stalking and destroying their prey, drug dealers hooking the young, politicians growing fat on bribes, lawyers selling out their clients, sadistic prison guards, child-slayers and wife-beaters. The list is endless. As I said, a regular puke brain with an omnipresent mind that contains this storehouse of pictures — a rogues' gallery. P.B. draws energy from them somehow as if —" Hale frowned "— it feeds on their energy, their spirits. And random acts of violence? Have I mentioned those?" Hale looked questioningly at Kirth and Sylvian.

"No," Kirth said.

"Oh, Puke Brain delights in those. Such acts are its pastime, its main sport when bored. I can't explain how exactly, but it actually feeds on that negative energy." Hale shuddered. "Damn! I've battened down my hatches against the puker."

"Keep them down. I've seen the destruction and know better than to suggest you eavesdrop. I — we —" Kirth looked at Sylvian "— can't. The Beast knows if we try to scan its mind."

"Actually, I might be tempted, but I suspect Puke Brain wants me to do just that. Read its diseased mind. Its cesspool. The old puker's a hunter setting a trap. Wham. I'm caught." Hale shook his head. "It's taking a new host. P.B. plans to walk in the body of someone close to you, Sylvian. Someone you knew and trusted before we met. That much I know for sure." He grimaced. "Old buds — pain and joy."

"What else do you know?" Sylvian asked, surprised and dismayed by Hale's words.

"Enough to understand this battle's been going on for centuries, which makes ya'll not, uh … your standard model nine-to-five human beings. Past that, don't tell me anything else. I'll try not to read your thoughts. Please keep them selective when we're together. I know what hunts you has insidious powers. I don't want unknowingly to give P.B. any info."

"Agreed," Sylvian said. "I'll try to think of other things. But I have a question that I can't leave alone. You may know the answer. Can we save this person — my friend — the creature plans to absorb?"

"I don't think so." Hale hesitated. "The process has started. Part of the person is formed and part isn't. Does that make sense?"

"It does," Kirth said. "Unfortunately."

"Which means —" Hale paused, waiting for a reply.

"Sometimes the creature prolongs a human's agony," Kirth said, thinking of Ingrid. "When The Beast has been injured and requires rest to regenerate, the creature takes someone to lie with it. Draining the body very slowly, The Beast eventually awakes in the human's form."

"Who's Ingrid?" Hale asked Kirth.

"Someone I once knew," Kirth said sadly. "Beautiful. Young. One of the few women The Beast has selected for its own form. Centuries after I knew her, I fought the creature wearing her form. She begged for death while The Beast boasted of the decades spent draining her body. I could not help her. She sought a release that even death can't grant her as long as the bewitcher holds her Breath."

"Chill!" Hale shuddered. "I've heard enough. Too much." He stood and stretched. "We need to eat. It's important to keep our strength up. And I want to stay close to the others. None of us needs to be alone."

"You think The Beast will try to influence one of the others?" Sylvian asked.

"Maybe. Maybe not. Kirth saved my life. I'm linked to the three of you through the bond you share. I don't know about the others." Hale looked at Kirth, "Coming?"

Kirth nodded, stood, and opened the door.

"By the way, thanks, ol' buddy," Hale said. "I'm really grateful to be alive."

Kirth insisted the three of them walk the ship together. He shook hands with every crew member on board and sent two of them ashore. They didn't want to go, but he paid them for the day and insisted they leave. Then, he walked the ship again.

Finally satisfied that no hint of his enemy remained, he ordered the captain to sail northeast.

Sylvian and Kirth spent every moment they could alone together. When she began dressing, he handed her black shorts with a gold waistband and matching golden shirt. A white-and-red rose formed the only ornamentation.

Sylvian smiled as she put on the clothes. "Have you taken up alchemy as a hobby?"

"Nay. I wanted you to carry a sign of my love for you." Kirth's finger outlined the rose. "And a reminder of the union of water and fire."

"I shall remember." Sylvian's fingers closed around his shoulders. "I like the yellow shorts and shirt you're wearing. That touch of purple sets off your eyes." She smiled up at him. "Much cooler. The guys must have wondered if you were wilting in the New Orleans heat in those long pants and long-sleeved shirts."

"I did what I must," Kirth answered pragmatically. "I felt the time approaching for us to meet, and I had to be careful. You would have seen the scars. You might have asked the others about them. Or worse, been repelled. I couldn't chance it."

"You could never repel me. *Never* forget that." Sylvian pulled his head toward hers. They kissed long and tenderly.

As evening approached, they stood on the upper deck and watched the rays of the setting sun burst red and gold on the horizon. Neither spoke until long after the sky filled with stars.

"With any luck, the sunrise will be beautiful," Sylvian whispered.

"Aye," Kirth agreed, then vanished, leaving her standing alone at the rail.

Sylvian's heartbeat picked up. She felt nervous. Scared. She'd be lying to tell herself otherwise. Centuries had passed since she'd faced her foe directly. Then, she lost. This time, she had to succeed. There wouldn't be another.

"Everyone's asleep, except Hale," Kirth said, reappearing at her side. "He's not susceptible to the suggestion as the others are. He insists we're safer if he's awake. I suspect he's right."

"I'm sure he is," Sylvian agreed. "Are they together in the lounge?"

"Yes."

"Good. He can watch the others. If we don't return, he'll know what to do. He's got a strong will."

"I agree," Kirth replied. "We are in the eye of a storm. No other ships will be able to break through. I have corrected our course to the right parallels, which will transport us to the spot. The shrine will appear then. For now, we wait. And remain alert."

"We have been propelled so hard and long toward this destiny that many things remain unsaid between us," Sylvian said.

"When a larger fate hangs in the balance, it can be no other way," Kirth reasoned. "Never forget I have loved you since I first saw you standing in the meadow bathed in moonlight. I don't regret following you to the shrine nor the commitment we made to one another. I would take the same path again to have the moments we have shared in this lifetime."

"I feel the same," Sylvian said. "But I've never told you that I saw you across that meadow. I was drawn to you and did nothing to stop you following me. In the ensuing days, I encouraged your attention. I had been warned that forces were moving against our kind. I didn't hear. I didn't know what the warning meant. My mind filled so completely with thoughts of you that nothing seemed to touch me. I awoke too late to thwart The

Beast's attack."

"You're not at fault," Kirth insisted. "Warning or not. No one knew the power of the Evil One or when the creature would strike. None suspected the entity would assault you at the mountain shrine. If I could have crossed the barriers faster, things might have been different, too. But I couldn't. None of us could. Not my father, nor my brothers."

"I don't know how you made it into the shrine at all," Sylvian said. "All the hounds were upon you."

"Love carried me there then as it has brought us here now," Kirth said. "It is the eternal force which keeps calling us together."

Sylvian's voice quavered. "My sisters told me I must destroy this festering boil of evil."

"Aye, 'tis true," Kirth concurred. "When the time comes, you will."

"If only I had your faith." Sylvian sighed. "But I don't. I'm scared. Frightened that I will fail."

"Use my faith in you until you find your own," Kirth suggested. "We do what we know to do, what our nature drives us to do. We've come too far to fail. Ultimately, our foe will be destroyed. If not now, then some other time, some other place."

"Nay," Sylvian said. "My sisters told me. The Seers have read the future. This is the final confrontation."

Kirth shrugged. "They've been wrong before. For centuries of human time, they didn't know whether you'd return or not. When you did, they almost missed finding you even though they'd been watching the monster the entire time. Your sisters' love for you saved me from a second death. Not the Seers."

"The Seers have read the numbers. They say now or never."

"Numbers can be interpreted many ways or not at all," Kirth countered. "Love and faith count for more than some fate the Seers imagine they see in the current battle."

"But my sisters told me this was it," Sylvian argued.

"I once believed as they do. Even days ago. But no more. The experience with Hale convinced me that there are powers at work here we don't understand. Besides, I've had centuries to think on the riddle. Fortune is with us this time. We've not come this far before." Kirth smiled coaxingly and caressed her forehead. "You've not married me before."

"I've always been ignorant," Sylvian replied.

"Well, yes, to run from such a charming fellow," Kirth began.

Sylvian punched him on the arm. "You know what I meant. Quit joking. My sisters say this war must be over. Now."

"The war won't be over even if we win," Kirth countered. "The Beast has ensnared others. They don't have its power or immortality because the creature isn't interested in equals, just servants. But they do exist. They will not cease to exert a negative force because Drakus is destroyed. If we don't succeed this time, you must seal the entrance again. Love will find a way to bring us back together."

"Why would my sisters not tell me this is so?" Sylvian asked, doubtfully.

"They believe the Seers as I did," Kirth offered. "Don't let fear cloud your time with them. Think on everything they said and what you know from the experience of being with them. Your answer lies there."

Irritated, certain Kirth was wrong in this, she allowed her mind to rummage back over her conversation with her sisters, picturing each one in her mind. She recalled Arva's words — Your limitations are yours only when you believe in them.

What did she mean? Sylvian sighed. She didn't know. Her situation was all still so confusing.

Days ago, she'd been Sylvian DuClair. An orphan. A writer. A soon-to-be psychologist, she'd hoped. Those dreams had been washed away in the flood of remembering. She had been a person with financial woes and problems she considered major. Then.

Now, she had multiple lives merging as one. The shrinks would have a heyday with that. An overactive imagination. Split multiple personalities. Feelings of inferiority. A deep-seated need for punishment. Blah. Blah. Blah. Ad nauseam.

In reality, all her human lives had been lived for this moment, this confrontation, this battle. She trembled at the thought of facing The Beast Drakus.

Was she worthy of the faith her sisters and Kirth had in her? Did she have more power than she claimed? She prayed so. It had to be true, didn't it? Otherwise, they were lost, cut adrift, facing horrors they'd not dreamed of even in their worst nightmares.

"The yacht's secure." Kirth's words broke into her thoughts. He pointed toward a mist taking shape above the ocean. "It's time."

Sylvian watched as the island's highest mountain peak rose within the vapors. The wavering landscape stilled as the air cleared. The shrine lay in rubble. The stones blackened. The land, once beautiful beyond words, now lay in waste. Moonlight washed the desolation with a silvery glow.

"Ready?" Kirth offered her his hands.

"Have I a choice?"

"Nay."

"Then, I'm ready." She slipped her hands in his and closed her eyes.

25

Sylvian stood alone near the center of the desecrated shrine. Instead of Kirth's hands, she held a sword. A flame burned in the broken pit. Before she had time to savor the warmth, the air cooled noticeably. She smelled The Beast before she saw the corruptor. The stench nauseated her, reminding her of the battle she'd lost so long ago.

"So we meet again, our pretty pet," Drakus hissed, materializing behind her. "We hated leaving without speaking earlier, but the Norseman is such a cretin. The insufferable Kith the Bold. So understandable that you've run from him these many centuries. He can make the best times the worst times with little effort."

She turned toward Drakus. "Your foulness precedes you."

Malicious laughter filled the air. "Only you and your lackey husband complain. Others find us most attractive. Irresistible, in fact."

"Others see the glory of your appearance. They don't see you as you are. A thief trapped in the bodies it's stolen. A decaying, glutted mass of avarice and self-interest. You're disgusting." Sylvian fought the urge to vomit. She must not underestimate her foe. No matter how nauseating the creature looked, the incubus had the power to destroy.

"Soon, we won't be." Drakus smiled. "We shall have your beauty. Your light. Your power. All of you for all time."

With lightning speed, Drakus reached for her, but she had expected the maneuver and stepped aside. She brought the sword down on The Beast's right arm, severing the decaying branch from the body. Maggots poured out of the stump. Sylvian gasped.

"Once we possess all of you, we may let you live," Drakus whispered, malevolently. "We'll give you this body you so admire. You can discover how being eaten alive feels. Forever."

Sylvian stepped closer to the flame.

"Retreating so soon?" Drakus asked. "Go ahead." The creature moved closer. "Whatever you do, we shall have our way. Our hands will possess your body, our mouth your breath, our power, yours. We shall absorb you, and there's nothing you can do to stop us."

Before she moved, The Beast's remaining hand brushed past her cheek, over her neck, and squeezed her right breast before withdrawing. Pain as intense as if a dagger had impaled her followed the loathsome touch. Her skin burned. Enraged, she struck savagely at her foe with the sword. Drakus reacted quickly and easily stepped aside.

"Ah, our pet beauty, how we have looked forward to this moment," Drakus purred. "Shame on you. Keeping us waiting these many centuries. Then again, time has so little meaning when eternity lies within our grasp. Don't fret your pretty head. You're worth the wait. If your boy hadn't bedded you, we could have had that pleasure again." Drakus waved the stump in dismissal. "But it's not important for we've drained that fountain before. Still, it is such a delectable treat filling your body with our seeds."

Sylvian cautiously stepped backward, careful not to trip over the rubble.

A malicious smirk teased The Beast's lips. Its furtive eyes fell on the severed limb. The bewitcher nodded, and the appendage rose off the ground and reattached to the arm. "Never you mind, when we're through having our fun, you will be screaming for death, eager to embrace the boogeyman to have it over."

"Talk is cheap," Sylvian challenged. Embrace the boogeyman? Never. "From you, it's tripe."

Drakus's black eyes glowed red at their centers. "So it's action you want?" A bolt of fire singed her arm.

Her seared skin ached with pain, but Sylvian forced herself not to react. Drakus played with her. She must somehow turn the game around.

"Don't you know it's unwise to say always or never. To even think such thoughts has a price." Drakus roared with delight. "You will embrace us before we're through."

"Never!"

"Look at us, our pet. Try to move. You'll find you can't."

Sylvian tried to step back and couldn't. Horrified, she knew she'd stood too close. The bewitcher trapped her in a spell.

Drakus's eyes wandered the length of her body, stripping her with their intensity. "We're sure he wasn't disappointed when he had his way with you. After all, we're the first who sampled your goods. We even told him what to expect."

The ravager licked its lips. Her lips were wet.

"See what we can do? All the way from here, we can do whatever we want. Bring you pain."

A thousand needles pierced Sylvian's skin. She bit her tongue to keep from screaming. The pain ceased.

"Or exquisite pleasure."

Sylvian felt Kirth's hands caress her body, sending wave after wave of desire through her until all she could think of was possessing him. She fought to control herself.

Drakus howled. "See how we can seduce you, our pretty pet. Whatever we imagine, we can make you feel. Or see. You're powerless to stop us. And we do so admire your outfit, but did you not know —" The Beast lowered its voice to a whisper "— alchemy is only a residual whimper from a time long gone. When we're through, we shall be golden with your power, while you ferment in the blackened depths of putrefaction. We shall become the Nightstar. You will be our slave."

Something warm began sliding around her ankles and up the calves of her legs. Sylvian tried desperately to break the spell, to look down and see what climbed on her, but her efforts met defeat.

"Oh, do you want to see? How rude of us. Of course, you

do. And, the time is ripe to call your handsome prince. The boy's tried so hard for so long, we must in all kindness put him out of his misery once and for all. Don't you think?"

"You don't have the power," Sylvian growled. "You're no match for Kirth."

"Did your loving sisters not tell you what happens to your lover when he steps foot on this shrine?" Drakus gloated. "They didn't, did they?" The Beast cackled. "They don't know. The Nyx and their Seers aren't so smart after all. As he was before so will he be again. He loses his immortality. Here, he's mortal flesh and blood. Easy to digest. Then, the contest's between you and us and whatever we want to do. Look down. Go ahead. Be our guest."

Sylvian fought the pressure she felt at the back of her neck. Her enemy was forcing her head down. If The Beast wanted her to see, she didn't want to. Her screams would call Kirth. If Drakus were correct, Kirth would die. She closed her eyes. Immediately, her chest felt as if her ribs were being crushed. She couldn't breathe. She gasped for air.

"Open your eyes," Drakus commanded. "Now."

Using all her strength, she pressed against the pressure on her neck and straightened up. Then, she opened her eyes. "You're slipping."

"We took the liberty of eavesdropping on your parting conversation with your champion," The Beast confided, its tone conspiratorial. "He's wrong, you know. This is the last time. And you are as doomed as he is. Shall we tell you what's crawling around your ankles, waiting for our command to explore you further? They are our special gift to you. As you've told us — we're such a good boss, always thinking of those under us. Your trip to New Orleans: Wasn't that fun, our sweet treat?"

Sorrow assailed Sylvian. She'd been so caught up in the horror that she hadn't looked closely at Drakus. She was sickened. Harold's veil-like form draped The Beast.

Drakus chuckled. "Harold's been a follower of ours since his youth. Eighteen or so. But we have to admit he wasn't particularly pleased to have us under his skin." Drakus guffawed. "If he could speak, we're sure he'd admire the gift we're giving you. Women are so fond of snakes. We just couldn't resist."

Sylvian tried unsuccessfully to keep fear from registering on her face.

"We knew you'd be pleased. These are our prized snakes. Some are small enough they can slip anywhere. In your mouth. In your ears. Up your nose. We're sure you can imagine where their favorite point of entry lies. When they start crawling inside you, then you'll scream. And scream. We've waited centuries. We can wait these short moments we have to share together before you begin begging for mercy. We have all the time in the world. You don't."

Terror filled Sylvian.

"We might add, these are our special snakes, our little treasure hunters. They find their spot and dig in. Oh, pretty one, we don't have to drain your immortality this time, or drink your tears, or eat your brain. Our little friends will do the deed for us, and we will taste every delicious morsel."

Sylvian fought the urge to struggle. Resisting would do her no good. She knew that instinctively. She had to overcome her fear and revulsion; the more she thought of her tormentor's creations crawling on her and digging inside her the worse they became. Before any of them settled into her, she must refocus her energy. Quit giving The Beast's magic any power.

"You were so right with your sisters," Drakus snorted. "You don't have the power to stop us. But we did so enjoy the family squabble. That Nata's a real firebrand, isn't she? Once we are you, we'll look her up. And of course, Niniane's sweet meat. She'll be no match for us."

Closing her eyes, she blocked out The Beast's threats and focused on Kirth's words — carry my love for you — when he outlined the red of the rose with his finger. But he'd said something else as well. What was it?

"And don't you fret, pet, we won't forget Hale Knight." Drakus edged closer. "He's got a real touch on those drums we do so admire. All that power, that primal sound. Delicious. We're eager to make his talent ours. And he's clever. Puke Brain. What a tasteful name, don't you think?"

Sylvian felt the creature's subtle movement toward her. Panic blocked her ability to reason. *Let go. Surrender. Be calm.* Kirth said? What? Ah. *A reminder of the union of water and fire.*

Even Rana reminded her of the sea's friendship. She called the waves to her as she dreamed of the sea, its beauty, its rolling waves, its healing power. She imagined she bathed in sea water. Then she felt moisture showering her skin.

Drakus shrieked.

Sylvian opened her eyes. The sea's salt water pelted the shrine. She could move again. Raising both her arms toward Drakus, she commanded, "I claim my power. And the power to destroy you. Release what you've stolen. Return to the void."

Pale streaks of blue-white lightning formed in the space between them. Sylvian pulled them toward her. The Beast tugged them in its direction. Back and forth the lightning crackled in the air, as the two adversaries vied for control. The ground shook, then roared. The ruptured stone floor began crumbling under their feet; the cracked pillars that had once supported the domed roof started splintering asunder. Still, neither would release the other. In a blinding flash of light, the energy split apart.

26

Drakus screeched. "This is not over." The Beast's body shape shifted uncontrollably and vanished.

In the instant the creature disappeared, Sylvian fleetingly spied a partially haloed, handless gray figure standing in its place. She'd seen the apparition before, but where?

Exhausted, frustrated that she'd only reclaimed part of her power, Sylvian forced herself to stumble away from the shrine, pondering the question until she remembered. In the dream. Of course. Drakus — the silent form reaching for her, calling her, drawing her toward its incomplete body. She'd felt compelled to reach out and touch the halo. Now, she knew why. The answer was so simple. She saw herself.

Collapsing on the scorched earth some twenty feet away from the temple, she lost consciousness. Before she fell through a fissure erupting in the ground, Kirth swept her up in his arms.

Instantly, they were back on the ship. Nothing had changed. Everyone still slept.

Kirth sat on the deck, cradling Sylvian in his arms. He mentally checked the yacht's current course. Satisfied they were back in the waters outside Veracruz, he dissipated the storm and began humming until his tears rained on his love.

Easy. Caution is your banner.

She moaned.

Satisfied, he stopped. Rocking her back and forth gently, he began singing, softly.

Kirth didn't know how much time had lapsed, only that he'd

fought the hardest battle he'd been through. And the fight had been with himself.

He watched the encounter frozen just outside the shrine where millennia ago he first heard her scream. This time, an invisible barrier separated him from Sylvian and Drakus. Beating against the obstruction, trying to break through an obstacle he could not see, his mind replayed the scene that had transpired more than three thousand years ago.

His brothers and father came with him to meet the woman he loved. When they heard her screams, they rushed to help. The Beast unleashed its monstrous wolves on them. His last view of his family had been their bodies bleeding on the ground outside the shrine. He fought his way to the sacred flames before the hounds brought him down as well.

Then, the bewitcher's wolf pack had been the deterrent to his success. Tonight, the invisible shield foiled his effort to attack early. He quit fighting the barrier, deciding the obstacle would vanish only when she screamed.

Instead, the wall dissipated without a sound from Sylvian. No wolves raced to destroy him. Even as he started to move toward the shrine, he spied scorpions hiding in the crevices formed in the cracked and broken temple steps. He stopped. The ground trembled in front of him. The air above him buzzed. He didn't have to look up to know the source of the sound, but he did, finding the urge to do so irresistible. Thousands of bees swarmed in the sky overhead. Rather than racing ahead, he waited, certain he needed to remain where he stood. Perhaps together they could have destroyed their enemy totally.

Sylvian stirred in his arms. "You were right to wait," she whispered, patting his cheek. "Our enemy released the barrier, wanting you to cross. If you'd stepped on the shrine, you would have become mortal, easy to destroy."

Her words reminded Kirth of the scorpions stinging him outside New Orleans. Such vanity. He totally missed the message of vulnerability. Thank the Heavens his instinct screamed at him to stay away from the temple.

"Even if that weren't true, I have to do this," Sylvian continued. "Alone. I know that now. I'm not afraid anymore."

Relief filled Kirth, who'd feared she wouldn't understand. That she would think him insensitive or, worse, a coward.

"Nay," Sylvian said. "I would never think that."

"You're reading my thoughts!" Mockingly, he added, "Is there no one left I can trust?"

"Certainly not Hale or me," Sylvian replied.

"Which would you never think I was?"

"A coward."

"You're saying I'm insensitive?"

"You're putting words in my mouth," Sylvian said. "That's not what I said."

"I'm sometimes insensitive or most of the time insensitive?"

"Is this a multiple-choice quiz? If so, what happened to the other choices?"

"Either I'm sensitive or I'm not. Now, quickly, which is it?"

Sylvian burst into laughter. "Look at you. You're getting puffed up, you toad."

"Oh, so now I'm no longer your handsome prince, but a toad."

"Who said you were my handsome prince? I thought you were my husband."

"Ah. Husbands can't be handsome princes, huh?"

"Not when they act this way," Sylvian chided. "Let me up, Sir, so we can fight on equal ground."

Kirth released Sylvian, and she rolled out of his arms and sat next to him.

His eyes narrowed, as he looked at her. "And just how am I acting?"

"Prickly and puffy."

"Ah, just because I want an answer to a simple question, one you brought up by reading my thoughts, which we both know is a most invasive action — I'm a toad, prickly and puffy."

Shrugging nonchalantly, she replied, "That's about it."

Kirth sighed. "Give a woman a little power, and she wants it all."

"Deserves it all," Sylvian retorted.

"Fail to die for her, and you cease to be her prince. She wants to throw you away as if you were no more than an old shoe."

"An old shoe may still serve a purpose," Sylvian countered.

"And an old lover doesn't?"

"Debatable. Depends on their performance record."

"How about mine?"

"Pretty slim, considering how long we've known each other. Two hits? Not much to write home about."

"The first one sent you into orbit."

"The second didn't pack the same punch," Sylvian quipped.

They heard steps, then Hale walked into view. "Hey! Are you two fighting or just flexing your mental muscles?"

"Flexing," Kirth replied. "But it's a good thing you came along. The debate could have grown serious any moment."

"What do you mean, 'could have'?" Sylvian said, antagonistically.

Kirth's eyes widened. "I wasn't serious. You weren't, were you?"

"Ah, now you don't know for sure. Is she? Is she not?"

"Nay. I know. You're not."

"Oh, well, can't fault a girl for trying, can you?" she looked at Hale and patted the deck beside them. "Join us. Please. Kirth's right. We were just letting off steam. The release seemed necessary after an encounter such as ours tonight."

"And we were celebrating," Kirth said. "Sylvian read my thoughts."

"So what? I can do that." Hale looked at Sylvian and added, "There isn't much to read is there?"

"Pretty sparse." Sylvian agreed. "Sort of an insensitive lump."

"Truce!" Kirth smiled. "I'll not take on the two of you."

"Doing so would be such good practice, but if you insist, truce it is," Sylvian said.

"Do join us," Kirth said to Hale. "We have some questions you may have the answers to."

Hale sat down across from them. "It's not over, is it?"

269

"No," Kirth replied. "But old Puke Brain has been weakened and is on the run."

Hale smiled at Kirth's words. "I suspected as much. I felt its presence shadow the ship twice. The first time, the sensation pulsed with energy. The later sensation did not. At first I feared P.B. would try something here, but I don't think it even gave us a thought. The puker was so determined to get away."

"Do you have any idea where The Beast went?" Sylvian asked, cloaking her thoughts. She didn't know Hale well enough to be sure of his reaction if he knew how easily their enemy eavesdropped.

"No." Hale added, "It's someone you know, isn't it?"

"Yes," she replied, softly. "And you're right. Pain and joy too often go together. I saw Harold Lann's shade on the creature. The editor. My boss."

"Damn!" Hale exclaimed. "Does that mean you're unemployed?"

Sylvian frowned. "I hadn't thought about it, but, yes, I think it does. Even if we succeed, I can't go back to work there. Not now. Although Harold had just recently been absorbed, he had long been controlled by our foe. He was never my friend as I thought he was. The loss still hurts regardless of the deception and lies. I hope The Beast doesn't get to anyone else I know before we fight again."

"Me, too, but you know the puker will try," Hale replied.

Sylvian sighed. As long as The Beast hadn't absorbed its victim, hope existed. The person might break free. Sylvian recalled The Beast's threats. Her sisters. Hale. Never. Not if she could help it. The idea that she might lose someone else she cared about before this ended saddened her. Would the losses never cease? But, she didn't speak of her sorrow. Instead she asked, "Do you know the time?"

Kirth chuckled. "Hale's the wrong person to ask. His pocket watch always has the same time. Six twenty-three. And we don't know whether that's morning or evening."

"Why?" Sylvian looked at Hale curiously.

Hale shrugged. "Call me cautious. I found the watch in a pawn shop — of all places — the same day we got together and jammed. The guys. All of us. As we are now. The session was the start of something big. Then, I didn't have two dimes to rub together for extras. The watch is an antique. There aren't many who can fix the time piece properly. By the time I had the money to get it repaired, I didn't want to let it go."

"He's superstitious," Kirth confided.

"Damn straight. I am. I carry the watch as a good-luck piece. I always have it on stage. On a chain around my neck."

"May I see it?"

"Sure." Hale pulled it out of his shirt.

"He won't take it off his neck." Kirth smiled. "He even sleeps with it."

"It looks like a woman's watch," Sylvian said.

"That's what I thought, too," Hale said. "But a jeweler told me the watch could have been carried by a man."

"It's lovely," Sylvian said. "May I touch it?"

"Sure." Hale leaned closer.

A flood of emotion hit Sylvian when she held the watch. "Oh, my. It contains deep sorrow and unbounded joy." And something more, some type of power, she thought, trying to place the sensation. "Some of that emotion is yours. Some is not. I suspect the person who owned it lived passionately. But you know that, don't you?"

"Yes," Hale concurred. "I'd like to have known her. Maybe I will someday."

"Hale is a hopeless romantic," Kirth said. "Doc Wade's diagnosis. And I agree."

"Look who's talking," Hale countered. "You waited for one special woman. Who says I can't do the same?"

"No one." Sylvian spoke softly. "I'd recommend you have the watch repaired. Even if you have to stay with the watchmaker while he does the work."

Surprised at her seriousness, Kirth asked, "What makes you say that?"

"I don't know. Just a feeling I got when I held it. There's something about it I can't quite place. But I suspect the watch may have helped protect Hale from our enemy. Somehow."

"What!" Hale exclaimed. "I thought Kirth's healing touch had done that."

"That, too," Sylvian said. "But I felt some kind of protective power when I held the watch. I don't know the source."

Kirth eyed the watch with new respect. "I too thought that healing Hale had kept him from being consumed. I had no idea the watch could have been involved."

"I'm not saying it was for certain," Sylvian said. "But the watch is different from any I've ever touched. I think it needs to be repaired to find out what makes it unique. Keep the cracked crystal, but let the watchmaker put on a new one."

"That's a great idea," Hale said. "I can stay while the watch is repaired. Why didn't I think of that?" He tucked the watch inside his shirt. "Thanks for the suggestion. But I know you've got more important things on your mind than my good-luck charm."

"Actually, it was refreshing to think about someone else's dreams for a while." Sylvian smiled. "And your good-luck charm reminded me how fortunate Kirth and I are to be together. Our lives have been so unusual, so spectacular, we'd be the last to tell you that anything is impossible."

"She's right," Kirth agreed. "I don't think there's a cure for what ails us. We're romantics, too. Even when faced with impossible odds, we still believe in love."

Sylvian stood up. "This distraction's been helpful. I know what I must do. Hale, do you mind looking after the others a little longer?"

"I'll check on them now." He rose. "See ya."

She watched Hale leave, then turned to Kirth and said, "I don't have enough power to get where I need to go on my own."

"I wouldn't let you go alone if you did," Kirth said. He held out his hands.

She brushed his cheek with her fingertips. "I know." When she placed her hands in his, they vanished into the starry sky.

27

A steady, pounding rain had been beating the shore for hours when Kirth and Sylvian touched down upon Galveston sands. Although morning nudged the night to move on, the fog rolled so thick visibility was zero. Ordinarily, someone would be around at this hour, but even the sea gulls had sought shelter from the driving, cold wind.

"The Beast is here all right," Kirth said. "Look at the slimy, green tracings in the fog. The creature's clouding the area on purpose. Why stop here? Why not farther inland? Our enemy so hates and fears the ocean. Whatever is The Beast doing this close?"

"Ed has a home here, and one he inherited from his family," Sylvian replied. "I think they sit side by side. Near the beach. Harold's leased the larger of the two."

"The closest haven the creature could find to recharge its energy," Kirth mused. "The sooner we find The Beast, the weaker the savage will be."

"Time is against us," Sylvian said. "When I held Hale's watch, I knew we must act quickly."

Sylvian's words evoked a similar revelation for Kirth. "The fiend's not going to bury itself to heal. The Beast's preparing to feed. Even now, the ghoul calls its servants. Dragon can't perform again until the creature is contained."

"Yes," she concurred. "I feel our foe's thoughts tightening around its lackeys as it prepares for a feeding frenzy to increase its power. Then The Beast plans to attack you — us — when you are the most vulnerable. At a concert. We must squelch the evil plan. Now."

From listening to Ed's stories about his childhood here, Sylvian knew that Galveston, under its beauty and charm, had a seamier side, one whose foundations stretched back to the beginnings of its history and grew out of its port location on the Gulf of Mexico. Ed said the tourists came to enjoy the island atmosphere and thrilled at the tales of the wide-open gambling in decades past and the hurricane which nearly destroyed the town.

Sylvian couldn't believe her co-worker was capable of the kind of deceit required to play a dual role, but Galveston was his hometown. He understood more about its underbelly than anyone else she knew personally. Was he Harold's pointman here?

No. He couldn't be. Well, maybe. Maybe without knowing he was being used. She hadn't known. She had confidence in Harold. He seemed the perfect boss. His behavior had been a sham. A facade. The kindness masked a black soul, one mesmerized by its own desires and schemes. She winced at the painful truth. Was Ed a willing participant or a pawn caught as she'd been in the illusion of Harold's friendship?

Sylvian shivered. What other fallacies held her prisoner? Running and stumbling and running again. Always running. Never escaping. Caught in the web. Again and again. Over and over.

Kirth's nostrils flared. "This way. If we're quick, we may find The Beast before the creature's regrouped forces."

"Our foe has great power here," Sylvian said, holding back. "I can feel it."

"There's no other way," Kirth said. "From now on The Beast will not be unprotected. We both know that."

"But are we ready to strike?" Sylvian vacillated between charging ahead or holding back. She'd had one direct confrontation. Could she withstand another? So soon? Suddenly, she knew she couldn't.

Kirth stopped and turned toward her. Taking her face in his hands, he said, softly, "The Beast knows we're here and is working its fear in your mind. Do you not know that?"

"You feel the uneasiness, the stifling calm, too?" Sylvian's voice shook.

"Of course," Kirth said.

Panic filled Sylvian. The muscles in her throat constricted. In choked breaths she gasped, "I'm behaving cowardly. Please forgive me." She fought the desire to wrench herself away from Kirth's tender touch and run willy-nilly down the beach in the opposite direction.

"Don't be hard on yourself." Kirth's arms closed around her. "I've had centuries of practice walking into the creature's web. This fear isn't yours. Drakus is projecting darkness into you. Fight back. Don't let the creature intimidate you. "

"How?" Sylvian whispered.

"Breathe deeply and draw nature's power to you," Kirth said. "Like you did earlier."

Long minutes later when Kirth released Sylvian, her breathing had returned to normal. Before she could speak, the cries of banshees tore through the mists surrounding them.

"We must go now. There's no time." Kirth's arm closed around her, and they rose into the air. "Our foe's creatures are on the run."

"How can we bridge its defenses?" Sylvian asked as they hovered above the fog-covered land.

"Picture our enemy in your mind, then extend the view and see the surroundings," Kirth replied.

"You can do this?"

"Yes," Kirth said. "But not until we're closer. We don't have to see where the creature is to follow the malodorous scent. For both of us, the emanation's strong. Humans don't smell the stench at all."

"Hale did."

"Hale's different. He knows reality is often a veil cloaking reality. The average person doesn't. When we are closer, I will read our enemy's surroundings. Not before. But our adversary can feel us approaching. Once I open my mind to visualize The

Beast, the fiend will know we're on top of its hideout. We won't have long to strike."

As they approached a long house sitting back from the beach, both felt the darkness intensify.

"There." Kirth pointed to the structure. "In a large room. The chamber feels as if it's below ground level, but it's not. Not here. Ah. The room's sealed, with computers and screens. Large screens. On the wall."

Amazed and encouraged by Kirth's expertise, Sylvian focused her mind on seeing through the wood-shingled roof to what lay within. Nothing. She could see nothing. She tried again. Still, she was unsuccessful.

Exasperated, she complained, "I can't see anything. Nothing except the blurry outline of the house."

"Make the fog separate for you," Kirth said, calmly. "Pick out a point and focus your intent on the spot, then through the site to what lies inside."

Sylvian hesitated. "Must I?"

"Aye, unless you want to announce your approach by walking in the door or climbing in a window. I'll put you on the porch —" Kirth pointed into the fog "— there. If that's your desire."

Kirth's hand parted the mist, and Sylvian saw the long, low veranda that ran the distance of the house.

"Thanks, but no thanks," she snipped. He teased her. Now. Of all times. "Our lives hang in the balance. And all you can do is joke. I can't project myself inside. I have to go through a door or window."

"Through, perhaps, but not in," Kirth replied.

"I don't have the power to project myself inside."

"Don't waste our time arguing for what you can't do. Claim what's yours. Now."

"Kirth! I can't!"

"Have your way. I'll meet you inside. Don't stand on the porch too long or the snarling pack will be nipping at your sweet ankles." Kirth released her and disappeared.

"Don't leave me," Sylvian pleaded to the empty air. Her sister's words came back to her again. *Your limitations are yours only when you believe in them.*

Sylvian looked down. She was floating without Kirth's help. An encouraging sign. Refocusing her energy, she imagined the fog separating in front of her. The dank, grayish-green haze swirled and separated. Just as Kirth instructed, she picked a spot then moved her sight inside. The room he described came into view.

She felt more than saw The Beast. The savage wasn't alone. Its companion came into view. Ed. Chained to a chair. Was her vision real or an illusion?

"'Tis real," Kirth whispered, reappearing at her side.

Startled, Sylvian replied, "I thought you'd left me. Gone on inside."

"Nay. I would never leave you. I merely wanted you to exercise your abilities." He added, his tone wistful, "Soon, you won't need me at all."

"You're fretting again," Sylvian said. "For nothing. What's The Beast up to?"

"Our enemy knows we're here. Your friend is the reason we can't announce our arrival in the room. We must simply appear. In front of Ed. Otherwise, when we confront the creature, the incubus will drain Ed's life force to fuel its own energy. The death will give the predator a burst of power."

An overwhelming sense of loss assailed Sylvian. Soon, everything would change. The thought was debilitating.

"This is no time for regrets," said Kirth, understanding her hesitancy, for he'd felt the same sensation. "We must act. Quickly. Follow my energy inside." He offered her his hand. "Our enemy doesn't realize you've regained this ability. The creature expects me to materialize. Alone. Then, help you gain access. That's why The Beast is surrounded with monitors. Surprise gives us an advantage." He looked at her quizzically. "Ready?"

"If I fail … ?" Sylvian faltered. They'd be unable to materialize separately anywhere if she couldn't carry her own presence.

"You won't. We won't. Don't even contemplate failing."

Sylvian took her hand out of Kirth's. "'Tis safer if I follow you alone, rather than risking mixing our energies. If I fail, you'll be able to continue without me."

"I don't want to go on without you." Kirth reached for her hand.

She withheld it from him. "Nor I without you. But we must."

"I've had enough of going on alone."

"Without effort I smelled the stench and saw The Beast as it is. I can do this as well. You go first, my love. Then I'll follow." She ran her fingertips down his cheek, then withdrew. "Now. I'm ready."

"Alone? You're sure?"

"I'm sure."

He signaled the go-ahead. His intense eyes glowed a radiant violet. Instantaneously, he was gone.

Sylvian followed his lead, focusing her energy on standing in front of the chair. Whoosh. The shock of suddenly doing what she'd thought she couldn't do moments before made her landing slightly off balance. Yet, the sight of The Beast's startled look from its vantage point not ten feet from her helped plant her firmly in the room.

Before her adversary had a chance to speak, she raised her arms against the thief. "Release your hold on that which was never yours," she commanded. White hot streaks of lightning discharged from her fingertips, striking The Beast and forcing the creature against the wall.

Remains of the mortals The Beast had seduced through the centuries since their first meeting began falling away. The entity hissed at her like a serpent as the fiend began reverting into the form of the handsome, gray-eyed hunter who'd attacked her millennia before.

"I am Astraea, Nightstar of the Nyx, I claim what's mine, what you have stolen."

The thief's appearance altered into the androgynous being that had instigated the attack on her. An insolent smile shadowed its lips.

Sylvian stepped toward the creature. "I command you, The Beast Drakus, to return to the void, to the nothing you were, and the nothing you will be again."

"Be cautious," Kirth warned from behind her. "The creature's not as weak as it appears. Don't step too close."

Sylvian stopped, yet continued to pound The Beast with her electrical charge, pulling energy out of its writhing mass as she did so. She knew, if she let up, the creature would flee or strike back.

"Our pretty pet," Drakus whined, slithering against the wall. "So, it's to be this way. No greeting. Not even so much as a how-do-you-do. And after we've meant so much to each other."

The incubus burst into flames, howling, "You impudent Nyx! You think you can take us, but you can't. We've grown much too strong for your paltry power to claim, our pretty pet, pity you."

The roof blew off; the walls fell away. The wolves pounded the ground with the intensity of a stampede of wild horses as they raced toward Sylvian.

Striking the flames with her lightning bolts, Sylvian levitated fifteen feet into the air, aware of Kirth next to her, holding the unconscious Ed under his left arm. A dozen of The Beast's creations materialized around them. "Pay them no mind," Kirth commanded, disintegrating the wolves. He watched for more.

Never taking her eyes off the fire or slowing her attack, Sylvian began calling the sea. She imagined a whirlpool of waves rising out of the Gulf of Mexico, bridging the land and pouring over her before falling on the fire. Soon she was covered in a steady deluge of salt water. As moisture fell on the fire burning below her, smoke billowed toward her.

"Careful," Kirth ordered. "Drakus is not dead. Merely waiting for a chance to escape."

Sylvian narrowed her focus until she could see Drakus swirling in the smoke. Quickly and without warning, she dropped and grabbed the creature. Instantaneously she rose and projected her energy toward the Gulf, then dived into its healing waters.

Drakus fought to escape, but Sylvian held the squirming figure tightly to her. The Beast didn't speak, yet Sylvian heard its threats form clearly in her mind: *We will win in the end. We will have you and all you are. That boy of yours will be dust under our feet. The Enchanters will be stones we skip across the lake of our desires. Your world will be ours.*

Nothing her enemy could say would slow her attack. Nothing. Still, she ignored the words, remembering how dangerous listening to Drakus had been for her before. The Beast's voice alone carried its own power. No one in her world knew that better than she. Now that she had the creature captured in her grasp, she would never let go until she had destroyed the abomination.

The force of the dive carried them to the ocean floor. The two hit the sand struggling and buried waist deep in the gritty soil. The diseased form began disintegrating in her hands. She pressed the body into the sand deeper and deeper. When Drakus became still and silent, she felt the bond between them sever.

She pushed herself out of the sand. Kneeling on the sea floor, she placed her hands against the sand under which the creature lay. She opened her thoughts to the life around her.

Sea and sand and all who dwell within hear me. Herein is buried the scourge of Earth. The destroyer of dreams and maker of nightmares is captured within your watch. Guard the demon well.

She stood and rose out of the water. Kirth burst from the waves close by, holding Ed. Exhilarated, Sylvian exclaimed, "We're free! Thank the Heavens and the Sea! Free!"

His smile as gentle as the dawning light of the sun, Kirth agreed. "You did it. You've reclaimed all that is yours."

Looking at the sleeping form in Kirth's arms, Sylvian said, "He's been a good friend. I fear that got him in trouble. The Beast always delighted in destroying anyone close to me. This time Drakus failed, right? Ed will be OK."

"Aye. I had to ensure he had no mark of The Beast left on him. He's clear. We all are. Shall we leave him at the office or his home?"

Sylvian turned toward the Texas shoreline. "At his place."

Grandstanding

28

*T*he fog had lifted when Sylvian and Kirth stepped on the beach outside Ed's small, frame cottage. They cloaked their presence from the early morning risers who were now assembling outside the remains of the house next door.

Kirth smiled wryly. "I'm not sure what they'll make of the destruction, but I'm certain Ed has a busy day ahead of him."

"What do you think he'll remember?"

"Not much, if anything. The events will be hazy to him."

Fretful, Sylvian asked, "Why is joy so often mixed with sorrow? Ed won't know how lucky he is. How close he came to dying. I can't tell him. He'll have to deal with the loss. His family home. His boss." She sighed. "Poor Harold. What's left of him is buried at sea."

"I couldn't save my father," Kirth said. "You couldn't save Harold. He'd been consumed."

"How painful for you to fight your father's shade," Sylvian said, sympathetically. "And Ingrid's."

"Aye, but it's over now," Kirth replied. "They're at rest. As are our people. At last."

As they entered the house from the back someone pounded on the front door. Sylvian looked at Kirth. "Ed's public calls him, and duty calls me."

Kirth laid Ed in his bed.

"I have an accounting to make, a question to ask that won't wait," Sylvian said, her tone tentative.

"Aye," Kirth said.

"Are you coming?" Noticing his dismal look, Sylvian added, "I'd like for you to be with me."

Kirth smiled in relief. "I feared you wouldn't ask."

"You need no invitation. You are the bearer of the sacred flame, the guardian of the forest."

"I wanted an invitation."

"And my husband," Sylvian said softly. My husband. The words still sounded foreign, odd, as if they belonged to someone other than herself.

"That will change soon, I hope," Kirth said.

Sylvian pressed her fingers to his lips and smiled. She would have to remember to block her thoughts if she wanted to have any that were private and hers alone.

They left the area as unnoticed as they came, walked into the breakers, and took flight east toward the rising sun.

When they were miles out over the Atlantic, Sylvian stopped. "It's been a long time. Nata's better at this than I am, but —" she frowned "— actually I was never good at storms."

"What do you want? Clouds? Rain? Thunder? Lightning? Hail? Hurricane? What?"

Rubbing her index finger back and forth across her lips, Sylvian studied Kirth.

"Madame, your wish is my command." Kirth snapped a salute.

Sylvian turned away from him. "Oh, bother," she muttered mostly to herself. How frustrating. She couldn't remember creating a diversionary storm. Not successfully. Not one. Not ever.

"Does that mean yes?" Kirth struggled to keep from laughing.

Exasperated at herself, Sylvian nodded that it did. "Clouds will do nicely."

Before she had time to fret about what lay ahead when she faced the Nightstar, cumulonimbus formed underneath them and began multiplying outward. She half-twisted around, her vision focused on the expanding cloud cover, then looked at Kirth over her shoulder. "Grandstanding."

"Just aiming to please," Kirth replied, straight-faced.

The clouds continued massing and spreading toward the

horizons, reminding Sylvian of the Great Cloud Disaster she'd caused as a child. The memory closed in on her. She had been playing alone. Quietly, she'd slipped away from the house and called the clouds. Her creations had been small at first and delicate. Then bigger. More grand. She so enjoyed the elaborate patterns and sculptures she could make that she became careless. They'd gotten away from her and began growing on their own. No matter how hard she tried to dissipate them, they wouldn't vanish. They covered the whole village and were still expanding when her mother intervened. These suddenly reminded her of those. Alarmed, Sylvian exclaimed, "Please stop. Now!"

"As you wish." With a simple flick of his wrist, the activity ceased.

"Disgusting." Sylvian looked at the clouds Kirth had created and controlled with the barest of effort.

"You're welcome."

Kirth's polite tone grated on Sylvian, who knew he struggled to keep from laughing. "You know of my childhood misfortune," she said matter-of-factly.

"The Great Cloud Disaster? The story's still told."

"Let me guess. Nata?"

"Aye."

"Nata's a royal pain —" Sylvian suppressed a smile. The incident was amusing. More in memory than in reality. "The accident did create quite a stir."

"So I've been told. The Michelangelo of clouds."

"You're impossible."

"Aye, 'tis true."

"I love you anyway."

"And I you."

She took his hands in hers. "I can call the shrine to me from this spot. But, again, I need your help. Picture the temple as the structure existed when you first saw it, unmarred by the touch of The Beast. I also will see the shrine in its glory."

As they closed their eyes, their forms began spinning, slowly at first, then faster and faster. Sylvian saw the wild roses growing abundantly around the perimeter of the temple, the path opening into the inner chamber wherein burned the sacred flames, the white lilies standing in the seven golden vases perched on the pedestals surrounding the fire, and the rainbow-hued lyre resting on its silver stand.

She smelled the mountain air and felt the warm breeze that often moved through the temple. Her feet touched the hard firmness of stone. She opened her eyes. "It's done," she whispered, reverently. "Wait here."

Kirth squeezed her hands and released them. He crossed his arms and stood, his feet apart, under the archway between two of the stone columns which held aloft the shrine's domed roof. Directly beneath the star-shaped opening in the center of the ceiling burned the sacred flames.

Stepping between the lilies and the fire, Sylvian stopped three feet away from the blaze and raised her arms. Blue white bolts of lightning poured from her fingertips up through the roof and into the Heavens.

"Nightstar, I am Astraea, your protector, returned from the long night of darkness. No longer am I an innocent. I have felt the web of The Beast hold me tightly in its embrace, while the chill of death and enslavement covered me like a shroud. I know the depths of evil after being held captive in its morass. I am intimate with the pain of sorrow since being locked in the emptiness of loss. I stand here no longer lost. My faith in the eventual reckoning of all things is greater than before. My love for all life is deepened and strengthened through the fire of remembering."

Lowering her arms, she fell to her knees, her fingers touching the stone floor. "Do I still bear your mantle, Nightstar, or is there another to take my place?"

A blue-white strip of energy burst from the flames and covered Sylvian. She vanished from the shrine.

Kirth willed himself to remain still. He could not help her now. This decision belonged to the Nightstar.

Instantly, as her body disappeared from the shrine, Sylvian was bathed in moonlight. She stood. A dark forest surrounded her. A single moonbeam lit a path through the shadowy trees. She followed the light until the outline of a trefoil formed in front of her. She stepped through the clover onto the high peak of a mountain. Ahead lay a lake; its gentle waves glittered like diamonds in the moonlight.

A lamb lay sleeping peacefully under the branches of a laurel tree growing on her right. Gently, she ran her fingers over the lamb's head and down its back, but the animal did not awaken.

She closed her hands together in a loose ball then opened them. A dove rested briefly in her palms before flying away. She watched its flight until the mirrored reflection off the lake obscured the bird from sight.

On her left appeared a staff with two serpents facing each other, their lithe bodies twined around the wand. The caduceus gleamed golden in the light when she touched the small wings atop the serpents' heads. A windstorm blew across the sky. The bluster drew close, revealing the form of a winged dragon shimmering golden white and silver in the tempest.

The dragon's breath burned a circle in the ground ten feet in front of her. A chalice floated in the center of the circle, buoyed by the waters streaming up from a natural fountain growing out of the ground.

Slowly, she stepped to the goblet. When she moved inside the circle, a singed sceptre materialized on her right and a dingy sword took form on her left. She steeled herself then, crossing her arms, closed her right hand around the sword and her left around the sceptre. The hilt slipped through her fingers. The sharp blade cut her as the sword fell to the ground and disappeared. The sceptre burned her skin before fading from sight.

Kneeling, she rinsed her hands in the fountain. Its gurgling waters ran red with her blood. The fount shrank into the ground, leaving the cup floating in air. She drank the misty brew it contained, then stood and, raising her arms toward the moon, held the chalice in her upturned palms.

The vessel vanished and with it, the moon. A silent, still darkness enveloped Sylvian, freezing her like stone. Locked in blackness so deep she could not see where she ended and the dark began, she felt the power of the Nightstar flood her veins, filling her to overflowing.

Again, as had happened those centuries before when she'd claimed her birthright, her breath stopped while her heart pumped faster and faster. A single bolt of lightning formed out of the nothingness surrounding her.

Striking her chest, the lightning raced through her body then burst forth around her, erupting into thousands of tiny lights twinkling like fireflies in the dark texture of space. Soft notes plucked on the Nightstar's lyre replaced the silence.

The melody belonged to her. She'd not recognized the musical phrasing by the lake outside New Orleans nor on the following night at the concert, but now she did. The Beast had tried to steal her soul by despoiling the cadence of her song. She breathed deep to assimilate the unique rhythm that encompassed her essence, and the feeling of being shattered like glass vanished. The lives she had lived flowed together as one. She was restored. Healed.

Cold steel touched her raised hands. Her fingers closed around the sleek, silver sword and the golden sceptre, now cool against her skin. Both sparkled briefly, then disappeared. Her fingers curved upward; she held her hands together side by side. The dove flew back to her, nestling in the center of her palms. Then the bird also vanished.

Flames rose around Sylvian, who lowered her arms as she stepped from the fire into the shrine. Her sisters had joined Kirth. She ran to greet them, hugging each one. To Arva, she said, "Go home to your husband." She watched their curious looks, knowing the question they held in their hearts before they spoke. "Tell the Council of our triumph."

Walking back to the flames, she reached into the fire, raised her arms in a victory salute, and spun around. In one hand she held the sword; in the other, the sceptre. "Tell the Council you have seen the proof that Astraea, Nightstar of the Nyx, has returned from the long night of darkness. She has asked the question and watched the answer unfold. The lamb sleeps peacefully; the dove set free returns."

She pivoted toward the fire and released the sceptre and sword into its depths. "The Nightstar's mantle is in place. The shrine is intact."

Her arm extended toward the blaze and she began circling the flames. "I have unveiled the shrine and in so doing called the sanctum sanctorum back into the world of life and death. We of the Nyx know the human drama now unfolding around us leaves no site safe for this sanctuary. I do what must be done to protect the shrine."

A silvery mist formed between Astraea and the sacred flames. She twisted her wrist and the mist began whirling. Slowly the gossamer haze moved over the flames, absorbing them into a golden glow which shone through the whirlwind.

"We must go," Arva whispered. "This way." She stepped past the marble basin and between the fifteen-foot-tall columns supporting the arch above the front entrance, then paused. "Each of the steps — the five outside and the two under this archway — has a code, a universal cycle. Step firmly on each one as you leave."

"If we don't?" Nata challenged.

Kirth smiled. Nata balked at orders. Always.

"You will find yourself transported into the dimension of the shrine every time the cycle you skipped unfolds."

"How inconvenient," Nata said. "Not for me. Lead on."

"Alarming," Niniane added.

"Sounds wretched," Rana chimed in.

Arva glanced at Kirth. "Comments? Complaints?"

"Nay, I know the price," Kirth said. "I'm with the others. Lead the way."

Quickly, but cautiously, they followed Arva down the steps. Soon, they hovered above the cloud bank lying between them and the Atlantic.

The whirlwind moved through the shrine, absorbing all it touched until nothing remained except itself and the one who had called it into being. At its creator's command, the whirlwind became smaller and smaller until it also vanished from sight, leaving Sylvian behind.

"Well done," Arva said, taking her sister's hands. "And wise. Although this world certainly needs the peace the shrine contains."

"Needs but doesn't want," Sylvian replied, regretfully.

"Hale would disagree," Kirth said.

"The majority would desecrate the shrine," Sylvian said. "And those of Hale's character carry their own peace."

"True," Kirth agreed.

"Are you coming with us?" Nata looked at Kirth.

"Nay, my job here is not done," Kirth replied, his eyes on his love. He wanted to plead with her, beg her to remain with him. Instead, he asked, "Do you stay or do you go?"

"For now, I stay." Sylvian ran her fingers across his cheek. Looking at her sisters, she continued, "Until the next full moon calls us together, be well and happy. We must go. It's past time to check on Kirth's friends."

Minutes later when they landed on the yacht, Hale jumped up from the deck chair he'd been resting in and quick-stepped toward them. "Got a bone to pick." He wagged his finger at them. "You didn't tell me this deal included a pre-dawn dip."

Startled, Sylvian replied, "What are you talking about?"

"I had an urge to swim. Drakus hates the sea, so I figured I'd better take a dip. While I was in the water, I felt the bond with the creature vanish. Poof. It wasn't a fluke. My wanting to swim. Was it?"

"No," Kirth said, amazed.

"If I'd been eaten by sharks, no one would have been the wiser." Hale motioned for them to follow him into the lounge, where he pointed to his dozing friends. "The crew and the captain haven't budged either." He shook his head. "You pop a powerful tranquilizer."

"It was necessary," Kirth said.

"Without a doubt," Hale replied. "I'd hated explaining. They'd lock me up. Especially if you two hadn't returned. Before you wake the others, I'd like the story. The truth. From the beginning to now."

Sylvian looked at Kirth, "You first?"

"Let's get comfortable," Kirth said. "This is going to take a while."

They followed Kirth out of the lounge to the deck, where they pulled three deck chairs together. An hour later, Sylvian and Kirth fell silent.

"That's quite a tale," Hale said. "You needn't fear discovery."

Kirth's eyebrow arched. "Why not?" His friend's ability to sense what others felt was remarkable.

"Even *The National Enquirer* would scoff," Hale explained. "Your lives sound like a fertile, hallucinogenic imagination in overdrive. The story might see print in fiction. Nowhere else. This is the twentieth century, almost the twenty-first. People don't believe, not really, in magic. Or sorcery. Or see illusions as a potential reality."

Incensed, Sylvian blurted out, "Our abilities don't come from those things."

"Met many people who'd believe you were from an alternate reality — another world occupying Earth? That one even existed?"

"Worlds. Not just two." Sylvian countered. "No, I haven't."

"Exactly! They wouldn't believe where your abilities originated any more than they believe in magic or sorcery. Your Drakus, a.k.a. Puke Brain, was born, as far as we know, into this world. Much of the creature's juice comes from sorcery."

Sylvian's eyes widened. "You think Drakus is still alive — that I've not destroyed the interloper!"

Kirth reached for Sylvian's hand. Taking it between his, he said, "Easy. You've reclaimed what's yours. We're free." Perplexed, he asked Hale, "What are you sensing about our enemy?"

"Puke Brain sleeps. For how long, I don't know. Forever? Maybe. Its power is contained, not dissipated. Lessened, not destroyed." Hale grinned at Sylvian. "You nabbed the old puker. Did what was yours to do. Gave P.B. the old choke hold."

"Embrace the boogeyman," Sylvian mused.

"What?" Hale and Kirth asked simultaneously.

"Oh, it's a long story." Sylvian fell silent.

"We're not going anywhere," Kirth said.

"It's probably nothing. Just a detail."

"Detail us, Ma'am," Hale coaxed. "I'm curious." He looked at Kirth. "You're curious, right, Chief?"

"Absolutely."

"We're curious," Hale continued. "You've got an audience. Speak."

Sylvian shrugged. "Days ago... ." She laughed. "It seems a lifetime now, but it was the day of the concert. In the hotel. My thesis was tampered with. I'd just hung up with Harold, and dropped the thing on the floor. When I picked up the pages, the title read: *Embrace the Boogeyman*. I'd never written that. I crumbled the page, threw the wad in the trash, then retrieved it, and flattened the sheet of paper. The words were gone! The correct title was there. I was angry. Frightened. But I didn't think of the episode again until I saw my sisters. Those same words flashed in my mind when I asked them what I must do. Later, Drakus used them during our first confrontation. Somehow the creature must have toyed with my thesis."

Kirth leaned forward in his chair. "Was this before or after the concert?"

"Before. Hours before."

"It wasn't The Beast," Kirth said. "It couldn't have been."

Surprised, Sylvian asked, "Are you sure?"

"Positive. I was there hours after the show. I would have felt the creature's meddling, even if it had exerted its power from afar. Even as Harold. If your boss had manipulated anything in your room when you were speaking with him, I would have sensed the residue when I was in the hotel locating your room. No trace of Drakus existed then. None. The Beast worked a spell by the bayou the night before. Not until hours after the show, when you were asleep, did Drakus make an appearance at your hotel."

"Then who?" Sylvian asked, tersely.

"I haven't a clue," Kirth said.

"Neither do I." Sylvian sighed.

Silence fell between them. Kirth snapped his fingers. "The Nightstar guided you."

"Maybe." Sylvian frowned. "Strange. In the end, I did that which I feared the most. I embraced the boogeyman. I had to in order to bury The Beast."

"The deed's done," Hale interjected. "Chill." His eyebrow arched. "Now's the time to embrace the boogie-woogie man."

"Kirth?" Sylvian looked from Hale to her husband.

"He plays a mean guitar, a hot keyboard and some good licks on drums. Especially for one so old. He's a song-and-dance man. As we all are, Ma'am. 'Course right now none of this matters." Hale stood and gave a mock bow. "Not to Kirth. His mind's cruising private waters."

Kirth groaned. "Nothing's sacred around you."

"If you don't want me to know it, don't think it," Hale quipped. "Wake the sleeping beauties. I'll field their questions, if there are any."

Hale ambled toward the lounge. He turned back toward Kirth and Sylvian. "Hey! Lighten up." He leapt into the air, somersaulted, landed on his feet, and danced a few steps. "We're alive!" He thrust his arm upward in triumph.

Kirth stood and raised his arms in a victory salute. Hale was the eternal optimist.

"I've heard great deeds go unnoticed." Hale's eyes glistened with tears. "They don't. Not really. Someone, somewhere, is watching. If the others knew what you'd done, they'd say thanks." He saluted. "You've saved our lives. Even if we never speak of those events again, I won't forget."

He was gone before they could reply.

"He's a good friend." Sylvian slipped her hand in Kirth's.

"Aye," Kirth replied, his voice charged with emotion. He

cleared his mind and released the hold he had on the yacht. They walked to the deck's railing. Arms entwined, they stood silently studying the waters. Kirth spoke first.

"Neither the waters, the stars, the Earth or the Heavens can contain the love I have for you."

"Nor my love for you." Sylvian brushed her fingers across his lips.

Kirth ran his fingers gently through Sylvian's hair. "What's Madam's pleasure on her birthday?"

"I don't know," Sylvian said, slowly. "Surviving was everything. I never thought about afterwards."

"While you decide, shall we go below and see if I can improve on my slim track record?" Kirth asked, his tone amused.

"By all means," Sylvian replied. "I'm always pleased to help you fine-tune your skills. And you know what they say. Practice makes perfect."

"Absolutely." Kirth chuckled. "We've had so little practice. We can certainly use more." His lips closed over hers.

They drank deeply from one another, until the passion that flowed between them left them breathless, and they broke the embrace. Only then did they realize they were no longer standing on the deck but floating some ten feet away.

"Oh, my." Sylvian looked down at the sea beneath them. "We'll have to work on that."

Pulling her tightly against him again, Kirth whispered, "Fortunately, we have all the time in the world."

The  *End*

Author's Note on Glossary

Elusive forms danced in the shadowy, sleeping world, made visible by the silver glow of moonlight cast against the dark terrain. The name Kithnaran slipped into consciousness, awakening this scribe. Whispered words spoke of a journey born in blood and sacrifice.

I arose, knowing that I would sleep no more that night until I had captured the scene in words. My eyes read the lighted dial on the alarm: three o'clock. Thus began my nightly task of transcribing the tale told by the voices that would not let me sleep.

Born in a distant time unknown to me, the story came through me, not from me. The idea for the following glossary also was not my own but rather one suggested by others who felt such an addition would amplify the work. To those approaching the story for the first time, know that *Embrace the Boogeyman* has been understood and enjoyed by numerous readers without any explanation at all. If the glossary proves to be a distraction that breaks the flow of the real work, ignore it altogether.

For the reader seeking the glossary's guidance, the following caution is offered: The characters told their own story little changed by this writer's mortal hand.

Any attempt to alter even a word before the work was finished met with resistance and a total drying up of the well of words. If there was to be a book at all, this writer learned to allow the characters to speak. Only when they were finished could the story be arranged in the order that it appears. Thus, the glossary's interpretation of the symbolic elements may represent the characters' understanding totally, partially or not at all.

Fortunately, a reliable source does exist for Astraea and the Shrine of the Nightstar, one written in her own hand only days before the disaster that befell her. The account, apparently all that remains of her diary and certainly all that has been provided at this time by the tellers of the tale, offers insight into the world of Fayre and has been incorporated into *Embrace the Boogeyman*.

All else is suspect.

The Author

Glossary

Color

Black: signifies darkness as the beginning of light, unconscious wisdom stemming from a hidden source as the origin of illumination.

Black and White: represents the opposition of the two worlds, the divine and the mortal, which has been expressed in Indo-Aryan mythology through one white and one black horse. In ancient times, white was used to symbolize timelessness and ecstasy while black characterized time.

Blue: signifies devotion, and for the ancient Egyptians, truth. When juxtaposed with red or yellow, blue suggests a sacred marriage. Blue and white express a detachment from the things of this world and the flight of the liberated Breath towards the Heavens.

Brown: is the color of earth and relates to yellow and to red.

Gold: indicates all that is superior. The pure metal is the essential ingredient in the symbolism of the hidden or elusive treasure. In alchemy, gold represents the state of glory.

Gray: is the color of ashes and of mist and can signal neutralization, egoism, and depression.

Green: suggests the awakening of life; relates to Nature; represents the function of sensation; and stands for water. This

Green: transitional color spans warm, advancing colors and
(continued) cold, retreating ones, thus creating a complex character: the green of the bud and the green of decay.

Orange: lies between gold and red, suggesting the point of balance between the spirit and the libido, a symmetry that
is difficult to maintain. Orange has been associated
with fire and flames.

Pink: stands for sensuality and emotions. In some belief systems,
it was the color of resurrection.

Purple: represents power, spirituality, and transformation.

Red: represents fire, purification, passion, and sentiment and is
associated with blood and wounds.

Silver: relates to the moon and hence to the feminine principle
of fertility. A shot of spun silver indicates time.

Violet: represents nostalgia and memories and has been used to
symbolize water.

White: can signify either the absence of color or the sum of all
colors. Its function is sometimes derived from that of the
mystic illumination attributed to the sun, which appears
out of the darkness that also follows it.

Yellow: represents magnanimity, intuition and intellect and has
been used to symbolize air.

Forms, Objects, and Systems

Alchemy: was an ancient art of transmutation which endeavored to turn base metals into gold. On a spiritual level, the process offered a mystical art for the transformation of consciousness. Twentieth century Western interest in alchemy has been fueled by the works of psychiatrist Carl G. Jung, who saw the art of alchemy as a spiritual process of redemption.

Boogeyman: is a terrifying specter.

Correspondences: refer to the symbolism of relatedness of different aspects of the cosmos: life, nature, color, direction, numbers. Some experts in the field of symbolism believe that music is the key to all systems of correspondences. A system of correspondences seems to exist in the realm of Fayre as demonstrated by the colors of the garments, the hidden designs, and the numbers attributed to each group. Only a portion of how the system works is revealed in Astraea's diary entry and in the work itself.

Fame: is, in the United States today, connected with celebrity status. As such, the power of fame/celebrity status is impossible to overestimate. With mass media has come the proliferation of massive doses of infotainment and celebrity fluff that viewers and listeners and readers digest daily. Although credence is given in the spoken word to the fact that money, power and fame won't buy happi-

Fame: ness, the heart of man thinks they just might. One of the
(continued) most powerful icons of popular culture is the rock star.

Hunger: represents, in modern times, barbarism and greed. A symbol of hunger brought into all homes equipped with a television is the image of small children with enlarged stomachs in a world where food is discarded nightly in garbage cans.

Midnight: is a time some ancient tales claim when animals and spirits can talk. Midnight and midday are starting points for ascending movement of opposing principles. The spiritual Sun is at its zenith at midnight, in converse analogy with the material Sun. Initiation into the ancient mysteries was connected with the midnight Sun.

Music: indicates the hidden framework girding the universe. Some scholars believe that all symbolic meanings have a musical or sound root. Musical instruments often demonstrate the marriage of masculine and feminine. For example, the drum, which is feminine in shape, is masculine in its deep tones. Singing (and by association the singer) signifies that the harmony of the successive, melodic elements creates an image of the natural connectedness of all things.

Night-Sea Crossing: is an expression whose origin lies in the ancient belief that the sun, when it is unseen above the horizon, travels a nightly course through the lower abyss, where it suffers death followed by resurrection.

Shrine/Temple: is identified with the symbol of the mountain top as the focal point of the intersection of the Heavens and Earth. For the Nyx of Fayre, the

Shrine/Temple: shrine of the Nightstar is the spiritual center
(continued) connecting many universes. When Astraea is
attacked and the shrine ripped from its earthly
soil, this center and its protection are lost to
them.

Silver Cord: signifies the inner path binding the intellect with
the spiritual essence. Thread characterizes the connection between different planes of existence.

 **Names**

Arnfinn: Norse, white eagle.

Arva: feminine of the Danish Arve, the eagle.

Aster: Greek, a star.

Astraea/Aasta: from the Greek, Asta, the starry or the star. In mythology, Astraea was the goddess of justice, of innocence and purity. In the north countries, the name began as Aasta, which is also the loved.

Ansgar: Teutonic, of divine guard.

Baldur: Old Norse, bold prince. In Norse mythology, Baldur was the god of peace and wisdom.

Banshees: female spirits in Gaelic folklore believed to presage a death in the family by wailing. A warning system.

Boden: Old Norse, the ready.

Chantre: French, cantor, bard.

Dag: Old Norse, day. In Norse mythology, Delling, the very shining one, was a god and the father of Dag, the day. The Dag of Fayre daily guard the portals between worlds, the implication being they bear a close association with the sun and daylight.

Drakus: origin unknown. Called, among other names, the Accursed Hunter, a name that symbolizes action for its own sake, repetition and the unrestrained pursuit of desire.

Ed Todd: Ed is from the Teutonic, wealth. Todd: Old English, a thicket.

Eimund: Old Norse, ever guarding.

Einar: Old Norse, warrior chief. In Norse mythology, the Einherjar, or warrior kings, were the heroes of Valhalla.

Eldred: Norse, old counsel.

Eric York/Leigh: Eric is derived from Scandinavian, the kingly. York: Celtic, the yew (wood). Leigh: from Lea, Anglo-Saxon, the lea or grassland; Latin, to shine or a clearing.

Fayre: Old English, fair one.

Gaylor Witt/Jeanne: Gaylor is derived from old High German, beautiful and good and, dropping the "d" from lord, Middle English, a bread-keeper, thus, the guardian of the household or manor. Witt: Anglo-Saxon, action of mind, thus, the wise or witty. Jeanne: from Jane, feminine of the Hebrew John, meaning God is gracious.

Geb, Ra, Enlil, Ishtar, Marduk: all come from ancient civilizations that predate the Christian era. The first two gods mentioned by Astraea are Egyptian: the earth-god, Geb, and the

Geb, Ra, Enlil, Ishtar, Marduk: sun god, Ra (Re). The other
(continued) three are from the Assyro-
Babylonian pantheon. In
Sumer, Enlil symbolized the
forces of nature. Ishtar was the
self-described "goddess of the
morn and goddess of the
evening." Marduk, the god of
Babylon, was originally an
agricultural god of Sumer. The
point in mentioning these gods
seems to be to indicate that
none are as old as Fayre.

Hale Knight: Hale is from Old French, from the hall, and from
Old English, the hearty or hale. Knight: Middle
English, a military follower. Knight has been considered to mean the master that prevails over matter after a lengthy period of apprenticeship.

Harold Lann: Harold is from Anglo-Saxon and Danish, army,
to rule, thus, one in command of an army. Lann:
Celtic, a sword.

Hotel Tres Beau Danse: French, beautiful dance.

Kith: Old Norse, a young roe or kid. In usage, a child.

Kirth Naran: Kirth is Kith plus "r" and was designed to conceal
Kith. Although he doesn't say so, possibly the
choice of "r" also is a private joke with the "r"
standing for resurrection. Naran is derived by taking the first letters of the sisters' names — Nata,
Astraea, Rana, Arva, Niniane.

Nata: Sanskrit, a dancer.

Niniane: Celtic variant of Vivian with two possible sources. From the Latin vivere, life, actually, the vital or animated; or the Latin, Perpetua, meaning the ever-lasting.

Njall: Old Norse, thought to mean champion.

Nyx: Greek, of the night. In Greek mythology, Nyx was the goddess of the night, the female personification of night and a great cosmological figure, feared even by Zeus, the king of the gods. Astraea implies that her race predates mortal recorded history. The Fayre Nyx may have been mistaken as manifestations of a goddess; thus, the name came to signify the goddess of the night. The Nyx of Fayre nightly guard the portals between worlds, the implication being they have a close association with the moon and stars and possess certain characteristics that enable them to move freely in what mortals would consider limited light.

Ragnar: origin unknown.

Rana: in Norse mythology, the goddess of the sea.

Rogert Greene: Rogert is from Old High German, Robert, a spearman, bright of fame. Greene: English, the green or verdant.

Seers: the prognosticators in Fayre.

Selene: Greek, the moon. In Greek mythology, the moon goddess.

Sylvian DuClair: Sylvian is from the root Silvia: feminine of the Latin Silvester (Silvius); and a derivative of silva, wood. The root word bears a relation to

Sylvian DuClair: the forest and, thus, to trees and wood. Trees:
(continued) the word "trees" meant learning in all the
Celtic languages. Wood: a mother-symbol.
Burnt wood: wisdom and death. DuClair:
Latin, Clara, the bright or clear, from clarus
meaning famous.

Tyr: Old Norse, lord. In old Norse mythology, the chief god,
equivalent to the Greek Zeus.

Valhalla: the hall of the slain; the great hall of immortality in
which the souls of warriors slain heroically are
received by the Norse god Odin. The hall has 540
gates from which the warriors go out each morning to
fight. They return at night for another banquet on the
boar, Saehrimnir.

Wade Tremain: Wade is from the Teutonic, one who wades or
moves forward. Tremain: Celtic Tremayne,
from the town of the stone.

 Nature

Cat: has been associated with the moon and indirectly with marriage.

Cloud: symbolizes the fulfillment of a metamorphosis.

Cypress: was viewed, by many ancient peoples, as a sacred tree, its incorruptible resin and evergreen leaves suggesting immortality and resurrection.

Emerald: is a brilliant, transparent green beryl used as a gem stone. Jewels and gems often signify spiritual truths. Alchemists believed that the light of the emerald pierced the most closely guarded secrets.

Frogs: are amphibious in nature and as such relate to water and earth. Their alternating periods of appearance and disappearance associate them with the idea of creation and regeneration. Many are familiar with the legends and tales which turn a prince into a frog and back again. Carl Jung said, given its anatomy, the frog, more than any other cold-blooded creature, anticipates Man.

Halo: is a visual expression of supernatural force.

Hand: represents, when covering the eyes, clairvoyance at the moment of death. The left hand signifies the unconscious; the right hand, the conscious. Hands joined indicate a mystic marriage. Linked hands represent sol-

Hand: idarity in the face of danger. The hand has been called
(continued) the physical or outward expression of a person's inner
state.

Lake: signifies the mysterious.

Lightning/Thunderbolt: represents celestial fire as an active
force. The flash of lightning relates to
dawn and illumination.

Lily: stands for purity.

Moon: is associated with the imagination and the fancy as the
intermediary realm between the spiritual life and intuition. The lunar rhythms, utilized before the solar
rhythms as measures of time, seem to be a part of Fayre.
The Moon has its own mystic connection to the members of the Nyx in general and Astraea in particular.
The Moon is closely associated with the night; the pale
quality of its light only partially illuminates objects.
Most twentieth century mortals believe that clear sight
is only possible in broad daylight. Yet, too strong a light
blinds the eyes to subtleties as well as perhaps to
glimpses of the unseen world in which the Nyx travel
with ease.

Oak: represents strength and long life, and, like all trees, symbolizes a world-axis.

Rain: stands for the celestial influences the Earth receives.

Rose: means perfection when singular. The white-and-red rose
symbolizes the union of water with fire in alchemy. The
lily and the rose are essential symbols of white and red
implicit in all mystic thought. The eight-petaled rose

Rose: represents regeneration.
(continued)

Roses: relate, in symbolic terms, to the wheel (gothic rose-windows). Roses may represent any or all of the following: the chalice of life, the soul, the heart and love. Because of their association with blood, they have been viewed as symbols of mystical rebirth.

Sea: is a symbol, in dreams, of the collective unconscious, and represents emotions, archetypal energy, power, and food. In symbolism, the sea has been viewed as a mediator between air and Earth and, by analogy, between life and death. The waters of the ocean are viewed as the source and goal of life.

The Sexes: symbolize spiritual principles; consciousness and the unconscious, Heavens and Earth, fire and water. The union of Heaven and Earth in astrobiological religions is a symbol of conjunction, as is the marriage of the princess with the prince who rescues her. The sexual conjunction is the most graphic and impressive of all images expressing union.

Valley: symbolizes life and a spiritual passage.

Water: represents the essence of being and is vital to the healthy integration of personality as evidenced by the hero finding absolution through the salty waters of the font of the Nightstar. Salt is a necessary ingredient for life.

Wheel: symbolizes cycles, new beginnings, and renewals.

Wolf: stood for valor in some ancient civilizations and has been depicted as a guardian in many monuments. Both images apply to the creations of Drakus. They fiercely guard their creator, destroying any threat to the Accursed Hunter, who is reminiscent of the monstrous wolf, Fenrir, of Nordic mythology. The Fenrir myth is connected with other concepts of the destruction of the world whether by water or by fire.

 *Numbers*

One: indicates unity and symbolizes the divine without a second: the creator.

Two: relates to the Gemini twins or the opposition of worlds, the concept of timelessness and time, creators and destroyers.

Three: represents integration and the spiritual trinity.

Four: is connected with the first known order in the world. Coordinates for earthly life in the cosmologies of Asia, Europe and pre-Columbian America came from the four phases of the moon — crescent, waxing, full and waning, which then served as the organizer of time, the four cardinal points, the four directions, and the four winds. The world of Fayre seems to be ordered through one group, the Council, acting through three: Nyx, Dag and Seers. The indication from Astraea's diary is that the members of the Fayre Council come from Nyx or Dag with Seers serving as advisers. There may be a fourth group in Fayre, the elders.

Five: is associated with the Nyx (the design of five-petaled blossoms, stars and starfish interwoven in the uniform lining) and with Astraea and her sisters, a total of five siblings. Five, as the first number to be composed of an odd (masculine three) and even (feminine two) number, has been called the number of life and love. Five is often con-

Five: nected with the five senses. From ancient times, five has
(continued) been the number of, among others, the goddess Ishtar
— one of many names for The White Goddess — and
her Roman successor, Venus, as well as the Roman goddess of wisdom, Minerva. The willow and the apple,
signs of the White Goddess, have five as the number of
their letter-strokes in the Ogham finger-alphabet. The
number five (V) was sacred to the White Goddess, also
known as the Triple Goddess and the Triple Moon
Goddess. All three names bear numerous and often tri-
adic forms that stretch back into antiquity.

Six: may be associated with the Dag (the design of snowflakes
and beehives reputedly hidden within the lining of their
uniforms). Six was considered in ancient times as the
most perfect number because it is the sum and the product of its parts.

Seven: may be aligned with the Seers, whom Astraea calls the
wisdom-seven Seers. Among numerous other associa-
tions, seven corresponds to the pillars of wisdom, the
days of creation, and the days of the week as well as
being a combination of the spiritual three and the
material four.

Eight: is the number of cosmic balance.

Nine: announces, as the last of a series of figures, an end and a
beginning.

Ten: symbolizes a complete cycle and carries a sense of totality,
of fulfillment, and of a return to oneness.

Eleven: may be linked to the zodiac for one of the twelve signs
is always behind the sun and therefore invisible.

Eleven: Scholars have noticed that groups of eleven persons
(continued) are found in history without an obvious reason for
the grouping. Astraea calls the name, Enchanters(
which in some systems equals eleven), a misnomer
that is used about her people but not by her people.
She claims their power is not derived from the practice of magic. She also mentions that the number and
the vibration do not bode well for them. Perhaps
their hesitancy is based upon their desire to remain
hidden.

Twelve: is, as the product of three times four, a combination in
which the spiritual and the material are contained.

Eighteen: is an astral number. Eclipses of the sun and moon recur
in the same sequence after eighteen years.

Twenty-five: contains all the sacred numbers used in magic:
one, three, five, seven and nine.

Fifty: expresses repentance and forgiveness.

Seventy-two: relates to the number five (one-fifth of the circle's
circumference).

One hundred twenty: is connected with the lifespan.

Ten thousand: is referred to by Astraea, who calls her race
"ten thousand strong." She doesn't clarify if
she is referring to an actual population number
or a symbolic one. For instance, in China, ten
thousand years equals immortality and the ten
thousand things refers to everything that exists.
According to Lao-tzu: "Out of one come two,
out of two come three, and out of three the ten
thousand things."

∽∽∽ *Word Usage* ∽∽∽

Breath: means spirit. Centuries ago, air, breath and wind were world-wide synonyms for spirit, a universal entity that provided the Breath of Life. Spirit is currently defined as: the vital principle or animating force traditionally believed to be within living beings; the soul. The word is derived from Latin, spiritus, meaning breath. This ancient interpretation of the word is hardly found in English. (In Middle English, one meaning of breath was the faculty of breathing; hence, spirit, life. The term 'breath of spring' alludes to this meaning of spirit or life.)

Byrnie: is a hauberk, a piece of armor originally intended for the protection of the neck and shoulders but early developed into a long tunic of mail often reaching below the knees. A byrnie can be sleeved or sleeveless.

Frisson: is a French word that means a brief moment of emotional excitement; a shudder or a thrill.

Hudfats: were skin sacks used as sleeping bags.

Mail: is flexible armor composed of small overlapping metal rings, loops of chain or scales.

Norse Helmets: were conical in shape and made of iron, bronze or horn. The strips would have been of bronze or gilded copper. Those for the chiefs

313

Norse Helmets: and more valorous warriors were often made
(continued) of finer, costlier materials, and it was not
unusual for them to have underlying plates of
silver or gold. The helmet often had added
protection: a tail, cheek pieces, noseguard, or
a facemask. Few, if any, concealed the eyes.

On the Mark: is not a modern construct. The expression "I can
not be wide of the mark" was known as early as
1667; the meaning "attaining a desired end" dates
as far back as the thirteen hundreds and is
believed to be much older than that.

Quietener: was a sack used to muffle or silence slaves.

Sanctum Sanctorum: represents the holy of holies; an inviolably
private place.

Shape Shifting: is the ability to shift the shape of one's body
into an alternate form. In human history,
shamans are credited with the ability to shape-
shift, heal, divine and control the elements. A
thief, Drakus has stolen certain abilities from
others. The creature has a long memory and is
able to shift shape between its original form and
any form it has used as a host. The Beast does
this on purpose to horrify others; however,
there are times when strong emotion evokes the
change.

Son et Lumiere: is a dramatic spectacle using special light and
sound effects.

Acknowledgments

No words of thanks can adequately praise those who have read this manuscript and offered their insights. Edna "Babe" Keith, a teacher and mother with a vast experience of life, has been an avid reader for most of the decades of the 20th century. She was my rock, my inspiration when all else failed. Ed Todd, whose name appears by permission within this book as a fictitious character, is a writer in his own right and an editor par excellence. Wanda Streicher has an unwavering eye for details and a passion for science fiction and fantasy. Ann Tubbs read this book when she had no time to do so, offering her considerable talents to the final manuscript. Lyn Fishman paused in her hectic and demanding schedule to lend her reading and editing expertise to the final work.

Between the first draft and the last, other readers of all ages contributed to the work: Rick Gordon, Linda Singer (who read it twice and offered valuable suggestions both times), Gina Coldwell, poet Larry Griffin, Dave Singer, Vonelle Vanzant, Dorothy "Dottie" Powell, Rebecca Watson, artist Kermit Oliver (who first suggested a glossary), Gordon Hartman, Judith Cain, Sherry Belyeu, William Paul "Bill" Temple, Jr., author Tracy Daugherty, and artist Charlotte Seay, whose work so speaks to the story. Thank you all.

Also, *"Embrace the Boogeyman"* was enriched by the mortal knowledge found in the following books: *"A Dictionary of Symbols"* by J.E. Cirlot, translated from the Spanish *"Diccionario de Simbolos Traditionales"* by Jack Sage; *"The White Goddess, A historical grammar of poetic myth,"* by Robert

Graves; and *"The Mystery of Numbers"* by Annemarie Schimmel.

Additional valuable sources were: *"The Larousse Encyclopedia of Mythology,"* translated by Richard Aldrington and Delano Ames, introduction by Robert Graves; *"The Lost Language of Symbolism"* by Harold Bayley; *"The Penguin Dictionary of Symbols"* by Jean Chevalier and Alain Gheerbrant, translated by John Buchanan-Brown; *"The Vikings: Lord of the Seas"* by Yves Cohat; *"Harper's Encyclopedia of Mystical & Paranormal Experience"* by Rosemary Ellen Guiley, introduction by Marion Zimmer Bradley; *"Book of Names"* by J.N. Hook; *"Man and His Symbols"* by Carl G. Jung, M.L. von Franz, Joseph L. Henderson, Jolande Jacobi and Aniela Jaffe; *"Food in Civilization, How History Has Been Affected by Human Tastes"* by Carson I.A. Ritchie; *"The Great Thoughts"* compiled by George Seldes; *"The History of Magic and the Occult"* by Kurt Seligmann; *"The Little Encyclopedia of Dream Symbols"* by Klaus Vollmar; *"The Occult: A History"* by Colin Wilson; and four dictionaries: The American Heritage Dictionary, Funk & Wagnalls Standard Encyclopedic Dictionary, The Oxford Universal Dictionary, and Webster's Dictionary.

In the course of writing this novel and those that follow in The Scrolls of Dust series, there were others who helped clarify details: history professors, antique dealers, New Orleans guides, residents of New Orleans, the staff of Le Richelieu in the French Quarter, the staff of Hotel Galvez in Galveston, residents of Galveston and former residents of Veracruz. Thanks to all.

Footnotes

{1} armor. See word usage.

{2} the holy of holies. See word usage.

{3} spirit. See word usage.

{4} shudder or thrill. See word usage.

{5} flexible armor. See word usage.

{6} dramatic spectacle. See word usage.

{7} sack used to muffle or silence slaves.

{8} skin sacks used as sleeping bags.

{9} changing the appearance of the body. See word usage.

Coming Soon from
The Scrolls of Dust

"*Bittersweet*"
by Georgia Temple

A spiteful and malicious presence has invaded the land Annabella has known since childhood. Evil, tangible, real, unseen, yet felt, descends upon Darby Ranch in the waning months of 1897, taking first her brother and then her father. Now, it's her turn ...

Translation due in 2003

About the Author

Georgia Temple is the Entertainment Editor for a West Texas newspaper. She earned a Bachelor of Science Degree from Texas Tech University in the fields of English and Government, moved from Lubbock, Texas, to Dallas upon graduation and worked as a private investigator for Pinkerton's Inc., Dallas, before teaching seventh-grade English for three years. She studied journalism and photography at the University of Texas at Arlington where she worked on the school's newspaper, The Shorthorn. She was the Lifestyle Editor of the Grand Prairie Daily News before returning to West Texas. While in West Texas, this award-winning writer and photographer hosted a daily radio program, On My Mind with Georgia Temple. Although a lifelong Texan, Ms. Temple was born in San Francisco, California. She attended summer school in Monterrey, Mexico, and spent her junior year in high school at Saint Mary's Hall in San Antonio. She also spent one fall teaching Texas English to German businessmen in Hanover, Germany.